Grease Monkey

VARI SCOTT

PLAYLIST

Forget Me - Lewis Capaldi
Take Me Away - New Medicine
All For You - Cian Cucrot
Fire Up The Night - New Medicine
Ghost Of You - Mimi Webb
Figure You Out - Voila
We Belong - Pat Benatar
So Good - Halsey
Fireworks - You Me at Six
Kiss Me - Dermot Kennedy
Hurt - Nine Inch Nails
Drops of Jupiter - With Confidence
Shapeshifting - Taylor Acorn
I Think I'm In Love - Taylor Acorn
Drinking with Cupid - Voila
Exile - Loveless
Be Alright - Dean Lewis

Full playlist can be found on Spotify.

Can I dedicate a book to me? If so, this book is for me. These characters, as much as I love them, were the death of me while starting a new job and moving houses.

Trigger Warnings

While this story has a HEA, it does take Teddy and Morgana some time to get there. Like real life when you break up with your high school sweetheart, one or both move on with someone else. This happens to Morgana. When she reconnects with Teddy, she makes some questionable choices while being engaged to another man. This book has the main characters cheating *with* each other, not on each other and while I don't condone cheating, this is fiction and we love Teddy and want him and Morgana to be together.

Additionally, Morgana's parents and fiancé are gaslighting a-holes.

Other than that, there is angst, steam and sassy banter I hope you enjoy!

Vari x

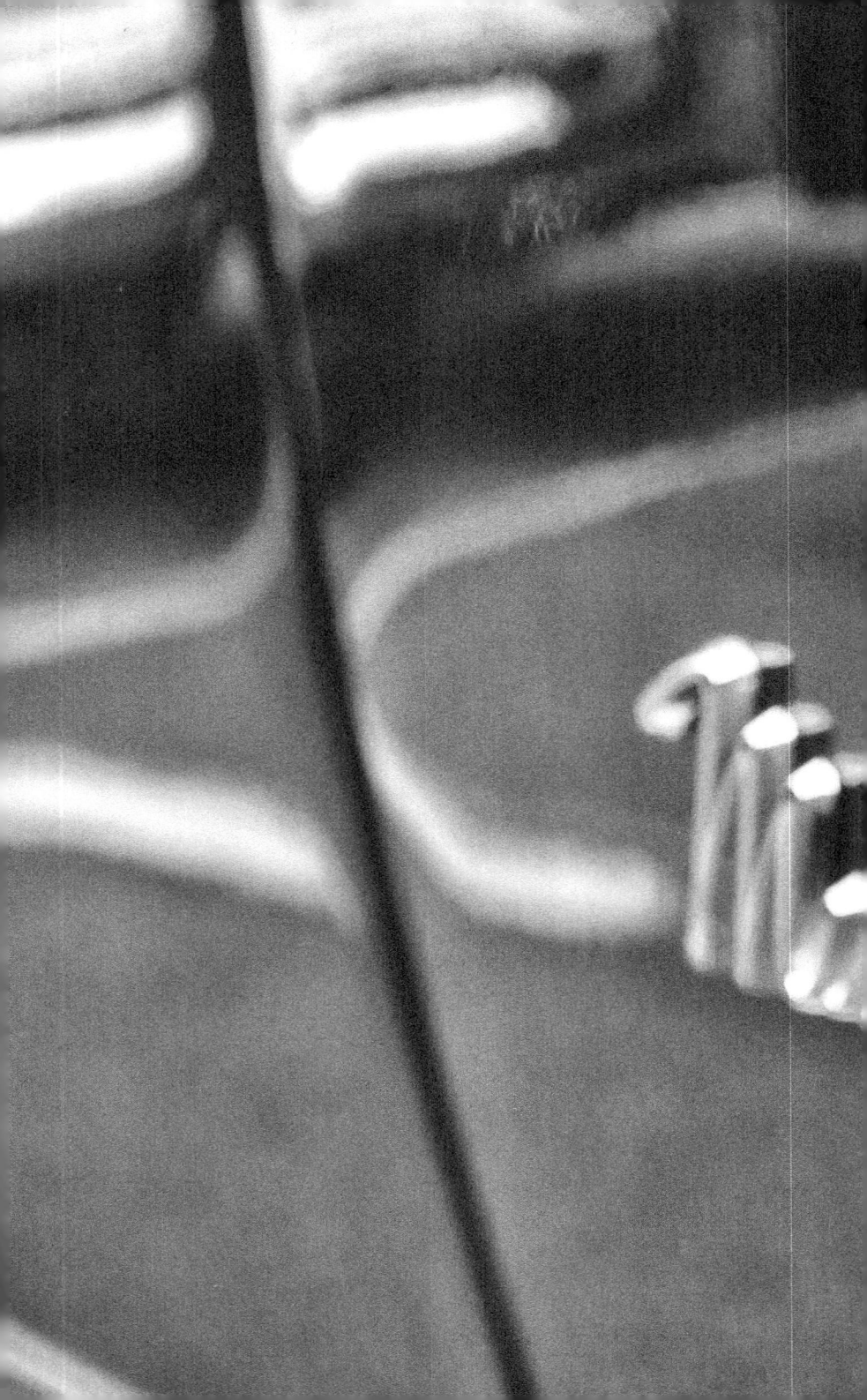

Author's Note

Vari Scott is a British author and as this book is set in the US, there *might* be some Scottish-isms that have managed to sneak their way through. But that's all part of the fun right?

Chapter One

Teddy

January

"C'mon, baby, that's it. You're doing so well. I promise you'll look so goddamn pretty when I'm done here." My fingers slide soothingly along the outside of her body, caressing every dip and curve while I slowly twist the smooth metallic ball in place. It glistens in the fluorescent overhead light as I straighten, smiling at the beauty beneath me. "Good girl, I knew you were only teasing."

Heat prickles my skin as laughter echoes around the front bay, and my head whips to watch Harry drag himself out from under a black Mercedes.

"Boss, there is something fundamentally wrong with your kid," he yells, his lopsided grin pulling his face into what I can only describe as real-life *Dopey* from *Snow White*.

"What?" I ask, grabbing a grease-soaked rag dangling over the edge of the cherry red 1971 Chevrolet C/K Action Line and wiping my hands.

"Do you whisper dirty things to all the cars you work on? Or just the ones that are a hunk of junk?"

My mouth drops in mock horror as I press the palms of my hands to either side of the bumper, just above the headlamps.

"Shh, asshole, she can hear you." Leaning down, I keep my eyes on Harry's as he shakes his head, biting back what I assume is more laughter. Narrowing my eyes at him, I whisper, "It's okay, Cherry, you're not junk."

Harry pushes up from his mechanic's creeper and swaggers over to the car, leaning his hip against it.

"Cherry? Couldn't you come up with something a little more original?" He tweaks the dome nut I just fastened, along with a few others running down the side of the rocker cover. I shove him away, and he stumbles backward, snickering while rubbing at his chest.

"Don't double-check my work, novice," I say, checking that the nuts are still tight. I wouldn't put it past Harry to loosen them off to fuck with me. He's a shit hot mechanic—an apprentice like me—and the biggest pain in my ass. Glancing at the gleaming components nestled beneath the hood, I drum my fingers on the engine. "Mr. Hall named her, not me. Besides, it suits her."

"He's an oddball." He scrunches his nose. "Actually, you're both oddballs. I swear you're one vintage car away from becoming one of those people who marries trees, or airplanes, or..."

"Whose marrying an airplane?" Dad asks, his tall frame eclipsing the doorway to the office. His huge, bearlike hand thunders down on Harry's shoulder, making him wince as Dad kneads his traps.

"No one, boss, just your boy here." He shrugs out of Dad's hold and gestures to me. "He's just got some weird obsession with cars."

"Oh, don't I know it. No idea where he gets that from," he says, a mixture of pride and smugness donning his face. Humming, he runs a hand over his beard. "Never thought my youngest son would be a car perv, though."

"I'm not a *car perv*," I grumble.

Only a few people understand my obsession with cars, and coming from a long line of mechanics, it was inevitable. Engines make sense in a way I imagine the brain does to neurologists, and I wake up every day, longing to get to the shop and work on what I love. How many people can say that about their careers?

"Do you need anything, or are you just here to annoy me?"

"Aw, Son, lighten up. I'm only teasing." I flip him the bird, and he winks. "If you're a car perv, then I'm one too. I'm just thankful one of my sons took after their old man."

And isn't that the truth. Three boys; one a pilot, one a photographer, and then me, who was our dad's shadow growing up, pretending to fix my toy car while he fixed real ones.

"Actually, I did need you, Teddy. You got a minute?" Dad tips his chin toward his office. I glance over my shoulder at the Chevrolet sitting pretty with her impeccable engine on show, begging for me to touch her, finely tune her up just right so she purrs for me.

Fucking hell, even in my head, I sound like a car perv.

Dad chuckles, sensing the struggle with leaving a car half-finished for even a second. Father like son. "Don't worry, it isn't going anywhere."

Harry sniggers as if I've just been caught cheating in class as I walk past. Tossing the oil-ridden rag I still have in my hand, it lands on his smug face, and I pointedly say, "You touch her, and I'll cut off your fingers."

The cloth hits the back of my head a moment later, dropping to the floor as I close the door. Dad leans back in his chair, the black leather creaking under his weight. He's not a fat guy, not by a long shot, but he's built like a fucking linebacker and as tall as one too. Running his hand through his salt-and-pepper beard, his eyes drop to the seat in front of his desk.

I trudge over, dropping my ass down and wait, glancing at the pictures lining the wall behind him. A dozen or so are of him working in Pop's old shop when he was about my age, some from before he met Mom when Wyatt was just a kid—my grumpy half-brother scowling at the camera as Dad tries to entice him with jumper cables. The majority, though, are of the five of us; him, Mom, Wyatt, Bowie, and I from various family vacations. But it's the candid ones of Dad and me, the ones we didn't know were being taken, where we look natural—at ease—doing what we do best, that always catch my eye.

"How are you settling in?"

I frown. "Really, Dad? We're going to have one of *those* talks?"

He might be the boss, but he's not one of those *one-on-one* bosses. Sure, he keeps an eye on us, but there are enough older guys who work for him to ensure we're doing what we are meant to. Dad lets us work on our shit without micromanaging.

He shrugs. "Yeah, you're right, but your mom wanted me to check in." He drops his chin slightly. "You weren't exactly thrilled to be moving to Connecticut."

Three months ago, my parents said three words, that when on their own are pretty meaningless, but when put at the start of a sentence can end up leading to the worst possible thing... "*Don't panic, but.*"

Okay, so in the grand scheme of worst-case scenarios, "*don't panic, but we're moving from Phoenix to Connecticut*" isn't exactly like "*don't panic, but your brother's plane hit a flock of birds and came crashing down into the Hudson, but he wasn't as fortunate as Chesley "Sully" Sullenberger.*" Or "*don't panic, but your other brother's been bitten by a radioactive spider while taking pictures in the Amazon, but he wasn't as lucky as Peter Parker.*"

My lips dip down at the sides, and I shake my head. "I was fine about moving."

Dad barks out a laugh. "Okay, so the whole, '*You're ruining my life. I can't believe you're making me move across the country to some rich-ass state, you selfish motherfuckers,*' was 'fine.'"

He air-quotes the word *fine,* the dramatic asshole.

"I didn't sound like that." Slouching down, I cross my arms. "And I didn't call you selfish motherfuckers."

"Might have made that bit up." He grins wide, his teeth peeking through his beard, before sobering and leaning forward, resting his elbows on the desk. "Your mom worries."

I itch the back of my head, avoiding his knowing stare. "I know. But she doesn't need to. This place has grown on me."

"Really?" he asks, his eyebrows flying upward.

"Yup," I say, with an obnoxious pop of the *P*.

He inspects my face and just sort of... looks at me. I roll my eyes. Goddamn him.

"Fine, I don't *love* it," I admit, my arms falling to either side of the chair. "But you and Mom do. And I'd be an idiot not to have come with you guys."

"I told her you're a big boy and could have stayed behind. But every time I remind her that the last of her three boys is no longer a kid, those big brown eyes fill with tears, and..." He trails off with a shake of his head. Inhaling, he raps his knuckles on his desk. "So, I agreed I'd check how you were doing."

Now it's my turn to lean forward, but instead of a desk, my elbows plant firmly on my thighs as I narrow my eyes. Out of the three of us, I'm the one who resembles our dad the least. I got his height and messy dark hair, and from the side, you can tell we are father and son, but the rest of me is all Mom. Brown eyes, an angular jaw, that thankfully doesn't look as feminine on me as it does her, and I inherited her ability to see through dad's bullshit.

"You want me to say it again, don't you?"

His eyes sparkle as they grow wide, trying to look all innocent. "I have no idea what you're talking about."

"Is your ego not big enough without me having to stroke it, old man?"

His lips twitch, fighting a grin, and he rubs his jaw. "Indulge me once more, Son. My memory isn't what it once was."

"You're relentless." He cups a hand behind an ear and waits. I wait, too, in a sort of stalemate until he wiggles his fingers behind his ear. Snorting, I concede to his demand. "You're the best mechanic Phoenix has ever seen. It would have been stupid not to have moved with you and learned from the best."

"You..." he prompts.

"You are the mechanic G.O.A.T, and soon Stamford will know it too," I finish, and Dad clears his throat. I drop my head with a groan. *Jesus.* Taking a deep breath, I amend, "And Stamford *already* knows it too."

He claps in delight like the man-child he is. "The mechanic *Greatest of All Time.* Man, oh man, do I love that title."

I push up from my chair, "Great chat, Dad." Thumbing toward the door, I step backward. "Now you've had your god complex restored, can I...?"

Dad stops gloating and waves for me to sit back down. "Nah, there is something I need you to do this afternoon." He digs around his desk, looking under mountains of paperwork until he finds a set of keys with a fluffy pink pompom keychain. He doesn't need to tell me who the keys belong to. There's a matching air freshener version dangling from the internal mirror, one I've stared at too many times to count from the back seat. He sets them on his desk and stares up at me. "I need you to take Brittany O'Malley's car to her."

"Take it?"

"Yeah," he says, drumming his fingers next to the keys, each thud against the wood, making the keys jingle. "As in, drop off. As in, the service we have never done, nor do we intend on starting."

I snort, removing my baseball hat to push back my overgrown hair, before setting the cap backward on my head. Reaching to take the keys, Dad's hand covers them, little strands of pink fuzz poking out between his fingers. He pulls on his desk drawer with his other hand and digs inside before putting something next to the keys.

My eyebrows dip, meeting in the middle, as I glance down at the long metallic object on his desk.

"You might want to speak to your girlfriend about how much she's costing her father. This is the third time this month I found something like this," he says, tapping the broken nail file with pink rhinestones on the thin handle.

What the actual fuck. That was in her tire? And third time?

And wait, what did he say?

My eyes flash up to his.

"She's not my girlfriend," I say vehemently. "She's just..." I trail off. I don't exactly want to say she's just a fuck buddy, a hook-up, a pretty twenty-one-year-old with a stick so far up her ass, she thinks she's doing me a favor by *letting* me fuck her.

"Yeah, well, as long as you're being careful. Ms. O'Malley is not someone you mess around with. That kitty's got claws." He picks up the nail file like he's trying to prove a point.

"It's not like that. She knows the score; it's just a bit of fun."

Dad hums thoughtfully. "You've been having *a lot of fun* since we moved here."

"Didn't realize you were keeping track," I mutter, and Dad raises an eyebrow suggestively.

Fuck my life.

"Hey! There's nothing wrong with that. You're twenty, you can do whatever you like. And you've certainly not lacked for anyone to *do* things with anyway," Dad jokes, and I cringe. I've never tried to hide my sexual activity from my dad—c'mon, I'm a horny as hell young man—but having the "sex talk" with your parents is like being tied up and tortured for information.

Adjusting the framed photo of my mom, his gaze flickers back to me. "Don't you want more? Something meaningful?"

I shake my head so forcefully I swear I can feel my brain move. "Fuck no. Not with anyone from here."

"Why not?"

I stare at him, incredulous. "Have you seen half the girls who live here? This place is full of trust-fund-Instagram-model wannabes who are practically lining up to get a piece of this..." I wave a hand downward, and Dad rolls his eyes and pinches the bridge of his nose.

Yeah, your son's a cocky bastard. Wonder who I got that from too.

I offer a small smile, then lift my shoulder dismissively. "I'm not ready for anything serious, plus, what's the point in starting something, when pretty soon, I'll be looking to move back to Phoenix?"

"That still the plan, then?" Dad asks, and I nod. He looks at me thoughtfully, bobbing his head like he's answering an internal question. "Morgana is a nice girl."

"What?" I ask, scrunching my face in confusion. How did we go from moving back to Phoenix to our neighbor's daughter? "Are you alright, old man?"

"Just sayin'." He itches at his beard, trying to look all coy like this is something that just popped into his head and not something he's clearly been mulling over for a while. *The sneaky fucker.* Bet Mom's in on it too.

I can't deny that Morgana Adler—the girl with the wild golden curls, burnt-out freckles, and a death glare that makes my cock stir when I call her by the little nickname I gave her—is a nice girl. A little *too* nice. But I'd rather agree to a life of celibacy in this town than let Dad know that, even against my better judgement, I've already noticed her.

A noise falls from my lips, and that I hope it sounds more like a lighthearted laugh than one of frustration. Being so close to someone I can't have—shouldn't *want* to have—is infuriating as hell. "Yeah, alright. The saying *the apple doesn't fall far from the tree* was invented for the offspring of the Wicked *Bitch* of the West."

Dad tuts. "Morgana is nothing like her parents. She's polite and sweet and your mom loves her."

Interesting.

"Good to know," I say drily.

"She's around your age too."

"There's no way. She looks about fifteen." I scoff, trying harder to deflect, but I know all too well that innocent baby face hides a sharp tongue and a voice I'd love to hear moaning my name.

"She's going to be eighteen in a few months. Set to be a lawyer, if you can believe that. The kid's smart."

"How do you know all this?" I ask, dumbfounded. I knew she was around my age, but the law thing?

"As I said, your mom loves her. Speaks to her all the time." He picks up some papers and taps them against his desk before stapling them together. Nodding to the pink keys, he says, "Take the rest of the day off when you're done dropping off the car."

Guess we're done here, then.

I nod, head spinning, and tug at the zipper of the gray overalls covering my jeans and black t-shirt, letting them pool at my feet and then kicking them up, catching them mid-air. Dad watches as I grab Brittany's keys, threading my finger through the metal hoop and twirling the pink pompom around.

Crossing the small office, I hang my overalls on my designated peg before opening the small locker to grab my phone and wallet, shoving them into my pocket. My hand is on the office door handle, just about to pull it open, when Dad calls my name.

"Teddy?" I turn just as the metallic nail file soars through the air. I catch it and roll it around in my palm. "Don't be that dickhead who leads girls on and fucks around on them."

I pocket the file and stare back at my dad. "You don't know what you're talking about. I'm not fu—"

"I might have had a three-year-old by the time I was your age, but that didn't stop me from getting out there, Son." I close my eyes and shudder. The thought of my old man with anyone who is not my mom is... in fact, picturing my dad with *anyone* is an image I never want in my brain. When I reopen my eyes, his have darkened as he continues. "But after what Cassandra did, I made sure I never treated anyone the same way. Your mom and I brought you up to be better than that."

I nod, and suddenly the file in my pocket feels like a lead brick. I tilt my chin and knock against the door, signaling I'm heading out. Dad nods and gets back to work as I pull my phone out and shoot a quick text to the girl I have been *fucking around* with for the past few weeks. I need to end it with her. Especially now that it seems like she's purposely damaging her car to see me. This was never part of the deal.

Me: Your car is ready for drop off. I will be at your place in fifteen, twenty minutes tops.

Brittany: My dad's home. I'll come to you. Text me your address so I can show my appreciation for all your hard work.

So maybe one more time won't hurt.

Chapter Two

Teddy

Thick curls shining in the winter sun capture my attention as soon as I drive onto the street. Bringing the car to a crawl, I roll the window down, shivering as a blast of cold air hits my bare arms, and I let out a long, obnoxious wolf whistle.

"Hey, Ana Banana," I call out with a laugh as she stumbles at the sound of my voice. She blinks, pushing back the mass of curls from her face.

"That's not my name, Teddy," she says, her words surrounded by plumes of white as she tugs her huge scarf tighter around her face. Between that and her hair, I'm surprised she can see where she's going.

"I know," I say, smiling when I'm rewarded with a scowl, and she tilts her chin to side-eye me while resuming walking. "But how can I resist when you blush so sweetly whenever I call you it?"

She stops abruptly, and I quickly stomp on the brakes. Putting her hands on her hips, she takes in the obscenely bright pink Evoke.

"Nice wheels," she deadpans, and I grin, letting my eyes drift over her puffer jacket, hating that it's winter, because Ana has a banging body hidden under all those layers. She shifts under my stare as I linger on the edges of her skirt that's poking out from under her coat.

"Nice ass," I tease.

She glares at me.

There it is.

One look, and my dick's awake. I move in my seat, her intense gaze heating my blood and filling my head with all sorts of weird teacher-student fantasies. Her bent over a desk, that short, plaited skirt bunched up around her hips, me diving into her tight...

Fucking fuck. What the hell was that? I've never thought about her like *that* before. So maybe I have had some less than PG-13 thoughts about her, but none where we're actually fucking.

She inhales, her nostrils flaring, jaw tight, then continues walking. I lightly step on the accelerator, keeping up with her pace as she tries to ignore me.

"How was school?" I ask, glancing at the road, then back at Ana.

"Fine," she replies, but it's more of a question than a statement. She peers over her shoulder skeptically, something she seems to do more frequently during our short conversations, like she's looking for the hidden meaning in everything I say. That, however, doesn't stop her eyes from wandering up the length of the arm I have hanging out the window, along my bicep that I purposely flex, and up to my shoulder before finally meeting my gaze.

"Aren't you cold?"

Fucking freezing. "Nah, babe. When I look at you, you're so hot I could get a tan."

She buries her chin into her scarf, hiding what I hope is a smile.

When she picks her head back up, she narrows her eyes playfully. "Do those lines actually work?"

"You tell me." I wink. "You were the one still blushing for me."

She quickly looks away, and I know that under her thick curly hair, the tips of her ears will be pink. We've danced this dance too many times before.

"Hey, Ana?" Slowly dragging her gaze back to mine, her brilliant sea-green eyes bore holes into my soul in a way no one has ever done before. She chews on her bottom lip, her hand wrapping tightly around her tote bag strap as she slows her steps. Lowering my voice, I inject as much seduction into it that it could toe the line with creepy. "What's a guy to do before you finally admit you want to go out with me?"

I swear she gasps, those large eyes turning into disks, and I am almost unsure if the red seeping out from her collar is from lust or embarrassment. Although with the smoke coming off her shoes as she takes off down the sidewalk, I'm going to go with lust.

I laugh, hitting the gas pedal, and the car lurches to catch up with her.

"Ana?" I sing, unable to help myself. "Ana Banana. Don't leave a guy hanging."

She exhales, her warm breath puffing around her in annoyance, but I'm not deterred. If anything, it spurs me on.

"C'mon, Ana. Tell me. I promise it would be the best date you ever go on. You just have to tell me what to say to convince you."

She nibbles on that lower lip again, pulling back her shoulders, and my blood hums with excitement as I wait for her sparring tongue to whip me with something sassy. Instead, the fire dies as quickly as it was ignited, and she answers in a small voice. "I'd say you're an idiot, Teddy."

It's laced with something I can't put my finger on. Sadness? Anger, maybe? Shit, I might have gone too far. Watching her squirm as I use the worst pick-up lines known to the internet is fast becoming my favorite thing to do whenever I see her. Every bashful flare of amusement, quickly hidden smiles, and sharp comebacks are always worth the late-night google search for the cheesiest ones I can find for our next chat. But the usual buzz that follows our interactions has somehow dimmed and the unfamiliar voice that suspiciously sounded like my dad in the back of my head, the one that urged me to kick it up a notch, has immediately silenced. Now I feel awkward and unsure of how to navigate through this unknown territory.

For fuck's sake. Grow a pair, Teddy. Clearly, Dad's got in your head and making you think. *We both know that's something you don't do too much of, so don't start now.*

Swallowing roughly, I ignore whatever emotion is pushing its way into my chest. This is our dynamic, and I'm not changing that after a few off-handed words from my dad.

Pushing the car forward again, I pass her, but only to slow down and wait for her to catch up, watching her through the sideview mirror as she looks everywhere else except at me.

"It's okay, you don't need to admit that I'm your dream guy," I drawl, as she appears by the window.

"I'm surprised you're able to get out of bed in the morning with how big your head is," she quips, and I instantly relax, letting her stroll away, and watching her whip her long curls over her shoulder. My fingers twitch with the urge to feel them tangle between each digit, pulling sharply to tug her head back, as I push my tongue inside her mouth. I choke, blinking out of the vivid picture of us together, and continue on after her. Honestly, with the amount of starting and stopping I've done along this street, people are going to think I don't know how to drive.

Ana's smirking knowingly as I slow down again, resting my wrist against the top of the steering wheel. I force a lightness into my tone and hold my hand to my chest. "You're breaking my heart, Ana Banana."

"I'm sure you'll get over it," she replies. "A good-looking guy like you? I bet you have a long line of girls waiting for you to ask them out."

"You think I'm good-looking?" I preen, puffing my chest out at her words.

I drag my teeth across my lower lip, fighting the need to run my thumb across hers as she sucks it into her mouth, her cheeks darkening to a deep shade of red. When her wet lip slowly reappears, my dick twitches in my pants. So it's not just her glare that makes my cock hard, but also the thought of those plush pink lips too.

"You know you're good-looking," she says quietly, almost whispering.

"Yeah, but I didn't know you did, too." I smile, pumping my eyebrows up a few times. "And I'm going to drive away now, so you can't take it back." She huffs, her mouth gaping like she wants to suck the words back out of existence. I press harder on the pedal, the car speeding up as I yell, "Ana Banana thinks I'm sexy."

"I didn't say that!" she calls after me, and I laugh at the reflection in the rearview mirror, her eyes wide, her mouth still open, and her tote bag resting on the sidewalk. It quickly dies, though, as I turn into my driveway and notice Brittany sitting on the porch steps. She's dressed in a tight baby pink ski suit that looks more appropriate for the Alps, and she's unzipped it so ridiculously low that she runs the risk of slipping a nip.

Fuck, I forgot about her.

She hops up as I pull to a stop, twisting her long bottle-dyed blonde hair around her finger. Shrugging on my sweatshirt, I hop out of her car, closing the door and leaning against it. Folding my arms across my chest, I watch her slowly walk across the finely trimmed grass, the frost crunching under her snow boots.

"Didn't realize there were ski slopes nearby," I tease.

Her hips sway with every step until she stops in front of me, her hands sliding along my arms, so much longing shining from her blue eyes; it's bordering on desperate.

"You're so funny, Teddy." She giggles, her fingers walking across my biceps, each of her sharp nails biting into the cotton sleeves like an annoying scratch that comes with getting a vaccine. She runs her tongue along her bottom lip, practically salivating as her hungry gaze rakes down to my jeans hanging precariously low on my hips.

"Brittany," I say, and she melts against me, pressing her too-big-to-be-real tits to my chest. "You need to be more careful, doll. Someone's been wasting daddy's precious money to get my attention."

Her perfectly manicured brows dip, her fingers hesitating in their walk up and down my arm. I reach into my back pocket, hips thrusting out to brush against her, and she smiles wide, right until I pull out the shiny piece of metal Dad had removed from her tire. Holding it between us, Brittany giggles again and doesn't even try to look embarrassed.

"I can assure you, Teddy, that back wheel was close to falling off," she says, grabbing the nail file and slotting it inside her bra. I watch with morbid fascination as the tip slips easily between her tits, her silicone cleavage holding it nice and snug.

Not exactly the safest way to store that.

Dropping my arms to my sides, I lace my thumbs through her belt loops. Brittany toys with the edge of my sweatshirt, dipping her fingers under and brushing against my stomach as she tries to edge closer to the button on my jeans.

Fuck, her fingers feel like ice.

"Daddy was getting suspicious, so I needed to improvise. Can't blame a girl for trying. I missed you."

I tense, her words confirming this has gone way past two people just fucking for fun. There is never meant to be any *missing* involved when you just use each other for getting off.

Raising my hand, I trace Brittany's jaw just as gold fills my peripheral. Ana's curls halo Brittany's head, the girl having enough hair to rival a jungle cat, and I follow her climbing the three wooden stairs to her front door. The swish of her plaited private school skirt kisses the backs of her creamy thighs until she steps through the threshold and into her house. She turns, her sight landing directly on me and moving to the girl pressed against me, her fingers still tickling my flesh, unaware I'm eye-fucking my neighbor. Ana's face darkens, and the door closes, leaving Brittany and me in my front yard.

"Maybe I'll need to be more creative next time," Brittany whispers, tugging my attention back to her. She looks up at me from under mascara-thick eyelashes, and drops her hand, her palm covering over my jeans and pressing against my dick. Between the pressure of Brittany's hand and the image of Ana's disapproving stare, I'm rock hard in seconds. With one expert flick of her fingers, Brittany unbuttons my jeans and slips her hand inside. Looking down, I watch as the slim fingers belonging to the girl I wish was someone else cup my stirring cock.

Beautiful, untouchable, Ana.

"Brittany," I warn, gripping her wrist and pressing my ass into the car. If she manages to get those icicles around my dick without the material of my boxers separating us, she might just freeze the poor guy off.

"Come on, baby, let me make you feel good, like I normally do." She pouts, squeezing my erection through the fabric of my boxers, her thumb teasing the head of my cock. A shiver of pleasured chills racks my body, and she leans up on her tiptoes, lips brushing my ear as she whispers, "Take me to your room and fuck me."

A car drives past the house, and I let go of Brittany's wrist, wrapping my arms around her, trapping her arm between us. Not that I particularly care if people can see what we're up to. She giggles, flexing against me, loving that we are out in the open. There's a reason we usually do this in the back of her car—Brittany *wants* to be caught, whereas I just want to come. But not in my room. *Never* in my room. That might make me an asshole, but I don't want to hook up in a place girls can make themselves comfortable. It's much harder to toss someone out on their ass without sounding like a jackass after they've made you come, and they want to snuggle.

Unless...

I release my hold and drag her toward the double garage. Pulling my keys from my pocket, I unlock the door and shove her inside, latching the lock behind me as she circles the room with a wrinkled nose.

"Really, Teddy? Here? Can't we go to your room? It's freezing in here." She makes a show of rubbing her hands up and down her arms.

"The sooner you suck my cock, the quicker you'll warm up, doll," I reply with a cocky grin.

Her lip curls. "Such a gentleman."

I stalk toward her and grip her chin between my thumb and forefinger. "You and I both know you're not after gentle when you're with me. If you want that, find a rich little boyfriend your daddy would approve of." She glowers, but it doesn't have the same visceral reaction Ana's death glare does. I cock my head to the side and smirk when she doesn't say anything. "Thought so. Now, get on your knees and thank me for fixing your car."

Her eyes flare, and she shoves me back until my ass hits the side of my baby with an oomph. When Brittany wants to go, she wants to go. I grip her shoulders and drop my mouth to hers, demanding entry with my tongue, and as she moans, too distracted to notice, I push us away from my 1973 Mustang currently tucked under a dust sheet. Saying I have a thing for vintage cars is an understatement. The beauty currently tucked away is my pride and joy and no one will be pressed up against her while she's sleeping.

We stumble over to the tool-covered workbench, and I break our kiss to grab a foam kneepad, dropping it by her feet. It flutters to the ground, and she looks at it, confused.

I wink. "What? Don't want you getting sore when you're kneeling for me." *Not always a dick now, am I?*

I give her a gentle but firm push on the top of her shoulders, and she lowers to her knees, dragging her hands up my thighs and curling her fingers around the waistband of my jeans. She licks her lips and slowly peels them down my legs, leaving me in my boxers, and palms the outline of my hard cock. I grit my teeth, biting back my annoyance at her trying to tease me. Seeing the bleach blonde girl with the giant tits eagerly wanting to please me would be any of the local preppy assholes' wet dream. But for me, this is just transactional. All I want is to blow my load down her throat and send her on her way. Which won't be long, if I'm being honest, because my earlier sparring with Ana was like foreplay.

I tug my boxers down, my erection springing free and hitting my stomach as I tuck my shirt under my chin. Brittany squirms below me, and I fist my dick to bring it to her mouth, brushing my free hand along her jaw. "Open."

She does, and I run the tip along her bottom lip, smearing it with the bead of precum before sliding into her hot, wet, and ready mouth. Her lips close around me, taking me as far back as she can, and she moans, the sound vibrating up to my balls.

Fuck, I love head.

Her tongue swirls around the crown as her hand reaches up to wrap around the base, and she starts to pump in time to meet her lips. She sucks like she's going for gold, slurping and choking herself, and I can see stars. I jolt as her teeth brush the underside of my dick, and for a brief second, I'm worried she might try to bite me. I thrust my hips forward, pushing farther down her throat, and the hand I have balancing behind me slips, knocking a trowel onto the floor with a clatter. Brittany gasps and tries to stop, but I lace my hands into her hair and push her back down onto my cock.

"Don't stop," I rasp. "Just no teeth."

The need to come is barreling down my spine as she hollows out her cheeks and lets her hand take over the work. My head tilts back between my shoulders when her tongue does another sweep of the head of my cock. That almost has me second-guessing calling off our arrangement, but not enough that I like the idea of making this permanent.

"Fuck, that feels good," I groan, the fist in her hair tightening just as a shadow dances across the ceiling, catching my attention.

Shit, shit, shit, no one should be home yet.

I look at the tiny windows that line the garage doors, surprised when a mass of curls bobs past them one at a time. The girl I cannot seem to get out of my head today. The daughter of the next State Attorney General—if the vote is in his favor—and queen of all the stuck-up moms of suburbia. The one who seems like an imposter in her own family.

The tingling in my balls comes hard and fast as I glance down, and instead of the straight bottle-dyed blonde, it's natural with loose, wild coils. Brittany pops off my dick, licking and kissing and playing with the tip, breaking the illusion of it being someone I have no business fantasizing about.

"Swallow me down," I say, using the hand still in her hair to lead her forward before I fuck up hard into her mouth, my hips thrusting roughly with every pump.

"That's it. All the way. Take all. Of. Me," I grit out, my eyes darting to the back door as the sounds of Brittany slurping and choking are lost to the thundering of blood rushing around my ears at the thought of Ana...

I come with a guttural roar, spilling rope after rope of cum as I remain locked with the wide sea-green eyes of my neighbor through the backdoor window.

Brittany nips my thigh and pushes hard, making me drop my hold on her head. My eyes dart back to the door and disappointment seeps into my chest when I find it empty. She's gone. No longer watching me.

"What the fuck, asshole?" Brittany seethes. "You know I don't like to swallow."

Oops.

I turn and grab her some tissues. "Sorry. I got caught up with how perfect your mouth was."

That and the thought that she was someone else.

"Really?" she almost squeals, loving the lie, and I shrug noncommittally. She wipes the edges of her mouth and drops the used tissue on the workbench. "Well, it's okay then, I guess. Just don't do it again."

Chapter Three

Morgana

"It's okay, you don't need to admit that I'm your dream guy."

Teddy's words are on a loop in my mind for the rest of my short walk home. If only he knew that my smiles are becoming harder to fight. My eyerolls less dramatic. Because even though I know he's only playing, only winding me up when he says the things he does, I really wish he wasn't. He treats me the way my brother did when we were younger. But unlike Skip—*because eww, he's my brother*—Teddy's teasing brings waves of nerves and excitement and butterflies that crash and roil and mix in my stomach to nauseating levels, that at the end of each encounter, I'm an overthinking, blundering mess, replaying every sentence spoken from his lips. Especially when he calls me by that juvenile nickname.

No one calls me anything but Morgana. Nobody would dare risk the reprimanding scorn of my mother. Except for Shay. She calls me Morgs, and I think she only does it because my mother hates it. Or maybe it's because my mother hates my best friend. I should really demand Teddy stop calling me something so childish. I'm almost eighteen, damn it, all set to attend one of the world's most prestigious universities, but I melt every time that smooth-as-country music voice sings that name.

My forehead leans against the cool panels of the front door, the three-inch piece of wood the only thing separating me and Teddy and his *girlfriend.*

"Morgana, you're home!" Mom calls, coming from the kitchen. "I missed you, baby. What do you think?"

Her hands encase my upper arms, and she rotates her face from left to right. Her new teeth are so white they are almost blinding, and they don't look natural at all, regardless of what the brochure said.

"They are lovely, Mom." I smile, hoping it looks more convincing than it feels.

She turns to the mirror hanging on the wall and examines her beaming reflection. "They are, aren't they? I could pay to get your teeth done for your birthday. Fix that overbite you have?"

I face the mirror and gnash my teeth together, barely noticing the slight misalignment of my front teeth.

"It's okay, Mom," I say, grabbing my tote bag and heading for my bedroom. "You'll need that money for Dad's campaign."

"Oh, you're right. Well, how about whitening, then?" she calls after me.

I sigh. Just what every girl wants for her eighteenth birthday, chemicals to whiten her already white teeth.

With a tight-lipped smile, I glance over my shoulder. "Sure."

"Great! I'm going to book in with Dr. Christian now. His waiting list is long, but that's alright. I'm sure he can bump us to the top. Nothing but the best for my daughter."

Woopie. Can't wait.

Closing my bedroom door, I toss my bag to the corner, the books inside clunking against the wall and sliding to the floor. Stripping out of my uniform, I tug on yoga pants and a sports bra, covering it with an oversized zip-up sweatshirt that once belonged to Skip, the worn logo of his favorite baseball team long faded from overwear. Standing in the middle of my room, I chew on my lip, staring at my bedroom window. I want to go over, look out, and see if Teddy is still with *her*. Check if she's still got her perfectly shaped body pressed against his and if his hands are holding on to her like she was him.

"Morgana?" I jump at the sound of Mom's voice muffled through the door. My hand flies to my chest, covering my erratically beating heart as she speaks again. "Morgana? Can I come in?"

Without waiting for a reply, she opens the door and walks over to my discarded school clothes, bundling them into her arms. She is still smiling— although I'm not sure if it's from her joy at having her teeth done or if it's a side effect of her treatment. Either way, it doesn't look right on her face.

"I need you to go next door and ask for my casserole dish. It's *Le Creuset* and cost nearly two hundred dollars." I stare at the woman who has never cooked a day in her life like she's grown an extra head. "Three months they've had it, Morgana. Can you believe that?"

I can't, but only because I don't care. My mom might style her looks and phony personality on Bree Van de Camp from *Desperate Housewives*, pretending to be the put-together homemaker, doting wife, and loving mother with amazing culinary skills. But she can't cook to save herself, has never picked up a needle and thread in her life, and her overbearing tendencies have only worsened since my brother up and left.

I part my lips, but any protest of going next door and interrupting the happy couple dies when Mom's hand cups my cheek. Her soft thumb brushes lightly across my skin before moving to smooth down the long blonde strands of hair I inherited from her in a fruitless attempt to calm the mess of curls I got from my dad.

"Why don't you wear your hair off your face, sweetheart?" she asks, setting my dirty clothes on the end of my bed, then walks over to my desk and grabs a clip. Coming behind me, she gathers the top of my curls and pins them back, circling to stand in front of me again. She pulls a long strand over my shoulder, watching with pursed lips as it pings back into place. I look into her brilliant green eyes and want to argue that looking like I've got the top of a pineapple on my head is not a fashion statement.

"There, that's a bit better. You've got too much of a pretty face to hide behind these curls." She toys with the strand again, pulling it down and letting it go several times. "My hair stylist could have these chemically straightened for you."

I shake my head and step out of her hold, reaching up to touch the pin. "Mom, I'm just going to ask for a dish back. I don't need to look good doing that." I tug at the clip, letting the ringlets loose to frame my face again. "Besides, I like my curls. I don't want them gone."

Mom throws her hands in the air. "Fine. What do I know?"

"Mom—"

Her arms suddenly engulf me, pulling me into a hug and holding my head close to her chest.

"Now your brother's gone; you're all I have left, Morgana. I'm sorry that I care so much."

Guilt floods me whenever she mentions Skip like he's no longer alive. I wish she would reach out to him.

"You could call him?" I don't know why I bother asking. I know she'd never swallow her pride, not even for her son. I pat her back stiffly and hold the clip out in my hand. Keeping Mom happy is easier for everyone, so I turn and let her make my hair look ten times bigger than it actually is.

"My gorgeous girl," she whispers, squeezing my arm gently before collecting my clothes again and making her way to the door. She pauses on the threshold and says, "Please get my dish back, Morgana."

I really don't want to do this.

Sighing, I follow her, taking each step slowly to the ground floor, trying to delay the inevitable. Sliding on my shoes, I edge my head forward, watching Mom pull out a bottle of cheap chardonnay from the wine fridge and fill her expensive Baccarat wineglass straight to the top.

Silently, I slip outside, shivering as I dart across the lawn that separates our house from theirs, and quickly run up the wooden steps to the front door. Their house is almost identical to ours; two stories, with large windows overlooking the front yard, and white shuttered frames lining them. But unlike ours, theirs looks warm, inviting, and happy. There's a double swing over in the corner of the porch, bright mismatching-colored pillows scattered across it, making it look the perfect spot to cuddle up with a book or in the arms of a loved one and just get lost in the day. I wonder if Mrs. Grant was sitting out here earlier or if she leaves the pillows out even in winter. Either way, Mom would never have something so out in the open for anyone to walk past and see her acting human for once.

Stop stalling and knock on the door, Morgana.

Squaring my shoulders, I raise my hand, knock quickly, and wait. Seconds turn to minutes, and I squirm on the spot, shifting from foot to foot and shoving my cold hands into my sweatshirt pockets. *Come on, Teddy.* Why isn't he answering? Oh, right, because he and his gorgeous girlfriend are probably in his room, in his bed, doing what every couple their age does. Not that Teddy is massively older than me, but one look at him, and I can bet my trust fund he's massively more experienced than me.

I'm about to leave, make up some excuse that no one is home, when a clatter from the garage falters my steps. Of course, that's where he'd be. Every chance he gets, Teddy is out fixing up a red Mustang—his baby I've heard him call it—in his front yard, and like the creeper I am, I sometimes like to watch him from my window seat. The boy next door is everything I'm not, and that fascinates me. He's laid back, like he has no worries, expectations, or a predetermined future weighing him down. And how I wish I knew what that was like for even a second. Not to mention, he is insanely good-looking. Dark brown eyes, dark stubble lining his jaw, and thick dark hair... God, he looks like Stefan from the *Vampire Diaries*—eye color aside—and could be on the cover of romance novels. For someone only two years older than me, he doesn't look like a boy. He looks like a man, all rugged and impossibly sexy. And worse—if you could call it a bad thing—he doesn't appear to have the ego that surrounds many of the "popular" boys in my school.

My palms feel slick, curled into balls by my sides as I walk down the narrow pathway to the back of the garage. I hesitate at the corner, chewing on my bottom lip as I scuff my toe on the path and tug the zipper of my sweatshirt, pulling the clasp up and down the teeth, the high-pitched sawing noise doing nothing for my nerves.

For the love of God, stop acting like a child and pull up your big girl pants, Morgana. You're his neighbor, for crying out loud.

I swallow, closing the gap to the garage door, and peer through the window into the dim space. Suddenly, I've forgotten how to breathe, my tongue's grown ten sizes too big for my mouth, and my heart has developed an arrhythmia so severe I think I might be tachycardic. Holding up his shirt,

Teddy's standing, sculpted chest on show, trousers around his ankles and hand on the back of his girlfriend's head, locks of blonde hair tangled between his fingers as he guides her up and down his...

Oh.

Ooh.

I can't move. I'm hypnotized by the smooth muscles on his stomach flexing each time her head almost touches his hips, his large hand gripping her hair, his thighs contracting as he thrusts in time with her head. She pulls off, her chin tilted upward, holding him in her hand. Oh, sweet baby Jesus, he's huge, slick and shining with saliva on every hard inch. My hand flies to my neck, cupping it like it's my throat he's fucking. This is the first dick I've ever seen in real life, yet it's not enough. I want to be the one on my knees for him, the one he's not being gentle with if the fistful of hair is anything to go by, the primitive bare of his teeth as he whispers something I can't hear.

This is insane. Never have I done something so taboo as watching someone intimately like this. Sucking in as much air as my lungs allow, my body inches closer to the window, and I curl my fingertips around the bottom rail surrounding the glass. My eyes leave the back of the girl's head, traveling back up Teddy's defined chest to his nearly black eyes.

Oh crap.

My lips part at the same time his do. A mixture of serenity and anguish spreads across his flawless face, his unblinking eyes never moving from mine, and when his lips twitch, it zaps my brain with a powerful rush of something hot, unknown and unfamiliar, overriding everything—the need to move away from the door, to stop watching, to retreat to the safety of my mundane world where I don't know what Teddy looks like as he finds his release.

His shoulders sag, and that's when the spell is broken. I push away from the door, stumbling over my feet as I scramble back in the direction I came from. Dazed, I slip on black ice and crash over a plant pot, the ceramic bowl landing on its side with a definite crack.

"No. No, no, no, no," I hiss, ignoring the pain radiating up my butt cheeks as I back away from the soil scattered across the pathway. Shoving the broken bowl upright, I frantically shovel the dirt inside and push the ceramic shards against the earth, hoping they'll stick in place.

"Quite a mess you've made there."

I still, hands covered in mud, my blood turning to ice.

Please kill. Me. Now.

I look up at Teddy, amusement shining from every pore and an afterglow I can only assume is from his orgasm. An orgasm that felt like it was just for me.

"I... uh... I..."

The corner of his lips quirks as he crosses his arms and leans his shoulder against the beige stonework of his house, surveying my mess. Being this close is intoxicating, drugging my brain into an incoherent mess, that I'm only mildly aware I'm still sitting in mud and shards of broken pottery. Teddy's stare is unbearably heavy as his gaze drops to my chest. I look down and gasp, tugging my sweatshirt to pull on the sleeve that's slipped from my shoulder, revealing my sports bra and nipples so hard they could cut glass. *Goddamn you, winter.*

My face heats as he swipes his tongue along his bottom lip. What must he be thinking with me sitting here basically half naked, showing him my *bra* while his girlfriend is right there? The same girlfriend I *watched* suck his dick? And as if by thinking about it, my eyes take that as permission to drop to his crotch. I mean, it's right *there,* in my eye-line. The perfect bulge that leaves nothing to the imagination. Not that I'd need it.

Morgana, stop staring at his dick!

"Oh gosh," I breathe, my gaze returning to his face, which has only expanded into a full-on grin. He pulls off his baseball cap and drags a hand through his hair. I track that movement as he reaches up and pushes the strands from his face before putting the cap back on backwards. *Gah,* why is that ridiculously hot? And when he shoves his hand into his pocket, my eyes are immediately drawn back to his penis.

Oh, for the love of...

When people say their face is on fire, no one in the history of embarrassment has ever felt the scorching licks of mortification quite like I do now.

Teddy laughs and jingles his keys in his pocket. It's like my eyes and his dick are two magnets, pulled by their magnetic fields until they find their way back to each other. The only way to stop me from looking is to cover my eyes. If I can't see him, he can't see me, right?

Oh, Morgana, you poor little creepy perv. You couldn't be less smooth if you tried.

"I didn't see anything," I blurt.

Okay, I was wrong. Apparently, I can be. Didn't I pray for death?

"Didn't see what?" he teases.

"Erm... You know." With my free hand, I circle it in the air, hoping he will connect the dots without making me finish my sentence. Teddy's husky laugh rings louder, like he's closer to me somehow, but the fear of looking at something I can't stop myself from looking at prevents me from peering out from between my fingers. My hand falls when warm skin touches beneath my chin, lifting my head upward.

"Surprisingly, I didn't mind that," he admits, his voice low and gravelly. It's not hard to guess this is what he sounds like when he's turned on.

My breath gets caught in my lungs as our eyes meet. "But your girlfriend—"

"Is not my girlfriend," he says, his fingers pressing more firmly into my skin, his touch burning and soothing at the same time. I knew he could get any girl he wanted. He probably has a few of them on speed dial. And while my heart does this happy kick in my chest knowing he's not in a relationship, it's squashed when he calls me by his nickname. "Need a hand, Ana Banana?"

"Jesus, Teddy, you could have waited until I left before you called some different slut over to get your rocks off."

My eyes tear from Teddy's in horror, darting to the person who is not his girlfriend glaring down at us with smeared lipstick, hair disheveled, and shirt pulled so low it reveals her bra.

"Hate to break it to you, *honey*, but I've already sucked him dry." She sneers and props her arms on her hips. Teddy's jaw flexes, and he stands, leaving me sitting on the ground like a fool.

"Don't be a jealous bitch, Brittany. She's just my neighbor."

My stomach recoils like I've taken a punch to the gut.

Just my neighbor.

Suddenly, the warm winter sun is chilling, and the sweet intoxication from before turns to nausea. *Just his neighbor.* Teddy bends and wraps his hand around mine, pulling me to my feet, lingering longer than needed. Recognition dawns on Brittany's face, thanks to my father's highly public campaign for State Attorney General, and I snatch my hand from Teddy's.

"Oh, wow, Morgana Adler." She pauses and laughs, but it's not a pleasant sound. "I didn't realize you're slumming it with a mechanic. Didn't think the great *Adlers* would let their daughter stoop so low."

Ouch.

Teddy bristles as she looks between us, the corner of her lip turning up at the side. I shift uncomfortably as she stares at me, silently judging me like she had to everyone when she was still at my high school. I hadn't realized it was *her*, the old Queen B, when I had first seen them together, her back facing me, preventing me from seeing her face. How would Teddy be with someone like her? They are polar opposites.

"I—I better go," I whisper, glancing at Teddy from the corner of my eye. His shoulders are tense, his hands fisted by his sides, and I want to reach out, touch his arm and tell him... tell him what exactly? If I were ever given a chance to get to know him properly, it wouldn't take much to see that he's so much more than his job and monetary status. Which is stupid. This is my first non-mocking conversation—*conversation* used loosely—with him. But something in my stomach is telling me that I'd like Teddy on a deeper level, trousers around ankles and fucking into some hook-up's mouth aside.

Just my neighbor.

I spin and dart toward the end of the path when I hear him call after me. "Ana, wait."

I pause. *Ana*, the shortened version of my name has never sounded so good in this new gravel-infused tone I hadn't heard until now. I look back, and his coy smirk before *Brittany* interrupted is back. He taps his fingers to the side of his nose. I blink, confused. He stalks closer, his long legs eating up the distance until his scent, a blend of mint and coconut—an odd combination for a guy—washes over me, and I want to press into his shirt and breathe in deep. His fingers brush along my nose, and I try so damn hard to suppress the shudder that wants to course through my body at his touch. God, how I want him to keep touching me.

"You have dirt... right here."

Brittany laughs, and my hand flies to my nose. I need to move. Turning sharply, I almost reach the end of the house when I hear his voice again. "See you around, Ana Banana."

I glance over my shoulder, and he winks, his eyebrow quirking ever-so slightly as his mouth twitches. I frown and shake our interaction and his disgustingly handsome face from my head as I run back to my house, throwing open the front door and barreling up the stairs.

"Morgana? Did you get it?" Mom calls from the kitchen.

Oh, shoot—the casserole dish.

"No one was home," I lie and bang my bedroom door closed. Leaning against the wood, I squeeze my eyes shut, pressing the heels of my hands into them. I'm flooded with the look of Teddy's blissed-out face, the strong hold he had on Brittany, and for the second time today, I wished it was me.

Chapter Four

Morgana

My window seat is calling out to me, beckoning like a siren, but with what happened this afternoon, the past three months of quietly enjoying my vantage point feels like crossing a line. My feet don't agree, though, as they carry me across the room, passing my bed where I grab my phone and tucking themselves under my butt on autopilot. I clutch my phone to my chest and tentatively peek down toward his yard, a gust of air escaping my lips at seeing the pink SUV now gone. I'd heard voices raised and arguing when my back was pressed against my door, but the double-glazed window muffled any defining words. I *should* feel bad that their argument was most likely because I'd been there. After all, Teddy had defended me when Brittany said those things—the slice of pain the word *"neighbor"* evoked ignored—but I can't summon the guilt or regret.

Brittany O'Malley is an entitled, over-privileged, mean girl who hasn't changed much since leaving school a couple of years ago. She still thinks she can get what she wants with the click of her fingers, just like everyone else in our small slice of Old Greenwich. Nature versus nurture screwed with Skip and me; we never bought into the elitist rubbish, and now he's free to follow his dreams, leaving me behind to keep pretending to be someone I'm not, just to fit in with everyone around me.

That is why I'm fascinated with Teddy. He doesn't seem the type to care about what others think or expect from him. Though, I can't help thinking that may be an act. The way he tensed when Brittany said "*slumming it*" wasn't a reaction of someone who doesn't care.

Pressing my forehead to the window, I let the cold glass chill my overheated skin and watch Teddy bring his Mustang out to his driveway. His long arms are extended, hands hidden slightly by the edges of the white covering, and his back is flat as he slowly pushes his car to the middle of the driveway. A laugh boils as he dashes to the driver's side, throwing open the door before diving inside to pull up the hand brake. The car jolts to a stop, and he reappears, dusting his hands and panting.

I must be an idiot, a glutton for punishment, and I wish I could get over this infatuation. This stupid spell he's had me under for the last three months. My schoolgirl crush has been soaring daily, going way past the stratospheric level and into the mesosphere—thick and breathless—where all the meteors that threaten the survival of Earth roam around. And the meteor that threatens my existence burning hot around me, ready to cause devastation in an instant, has dimples whenever he smiles.

You just caught him with his dick in someone else's mouth. He thinks of you as just a neighbor. All those times he's asked you out... a joke, a game, a wind-up because he enjoys making you squirm.

But I can't stop thinking about it. I need to speak to someone; the only person I know who can talk me down and make me see sense. Steeling myself for what's to come, I pull up my text thread and start typing out the events from earlier to the one person, since my brother, who I can tell most of my secrets to.

Morgana: I saw his dick.
Shay: Dick? Whose dick?

I huff a laugh. I knew I wouldn't be waiting long for a reply. My fingers hover above the keypad for a beat.

Morgana: If I tell you, you promise not to make fun of me?
Shay: When do I ever do that?
Morgana: ...
Shay: Okay, fine, I promise. Spill. Whose dick did you see? And can I see it too?

This is why I love Shay.

Shay Sylvester, the only child of *the Sylvesters*—socialites with more money and connections than an A-list celeb—is my best friend. Displaying all the stereotypical traits of being an only child, she is needy, hates sharing, and is one hundred percent a brat, but she is also the annoying non-bio sister I never knew I needed. More importantly, my mom despises her. She claims she's a bad influence—true—gets us both into trouble—also true—but that doesn't stop her from sucking up to Shay's extremely well-off and well-connected parents whenever she can.

Morgana: I sort of, maybe, watched Teddy getting a BJ.
Shay: OMFG. You climbed up the trellis by his room and spied on him

like a creepy-stalking-motherfucking pervert? I'm so proud.

I can practically see her devious grin and hand pressed to her heart.

Morgana: No, you idiot! Why do I tell you things?

Shay: Because you love me.

Morgana: Well, I'm done. I'm not telling you anything else.

Shay: Okay, okay, I'm sorry. Continue, please.

Morgana: Mom wanted me to get a dish back, he was in the garage, I walked around and saw THROUGH THE WINDOW, Brittany O'Malley sucking his dick.

Shay: Urgh, I hate that bitch.

I sigh and close my eyes, taking a second before replying.

Morgana: Not the point, Shay.

Shay: You're right. Okay, so you watched him get sucked off by that skank. Then what happened? Was he big? Tell me he was hung like a horse?

Morgana: He saw me.

Shay: OMFG, this is brilliant.

Shay: What did he do? What did SHE do?

Shay: What did he say?

Shay: Are you purposely ignoring the size question?

Shay: What's his surname again? I want to IG stalk.

My throat feels thick as I read her messages, firing in one after the other. Shay knows all about my insanely good-looking neighbor, but until now, I've managed to dodge any questions about him because I felt like he was mine. I love Shay to the ends of the world but know without any doubt that if she saw Teddy, she'd want him too. Bitterness and jealousy swirl in my veins at the thought of her being anywhere near him, and I'm not entirely sure why.

Yes, you do. It's because you have a crush, you silly, naïve girl. Albeit a superficial one, but it has definitely amplified after today.

My phone buzzes in my hand.

Shay: Found him. **Link to Instagram account**
Shay: He is hot as hell, Morgs! Go for it. If you don't, I will **winky emoji**
Morgana: He sees me as his neighbor, Shay.
Shay: Well, maybe you should make yourself seem more than a "neighbor"...

Easy for her to say, Miss Always-Gets-What-She-Wants. I click on his Instagram account instead of replying. I've never checked his social media accounts before. Facebook, Twitter, IG... nothing. Apparently, my perving has levels and searching out his socials is a step too far.

But a little voyeurism is okay?

Teddy's profile illuminates my screen. My heart thuds heavily, feeling like it somehow moved from beneath my ribcage to my throat when my finger clicked the link. Carefully, I scroll, ensuring I don't do any accidental 'liking' on photos posted months ago. There are endless photos of Teddy with family members—due to the minor similarities between them all—several more standing with cars, some at baseball games or the beach, all different images depicting his life before he moved here. Several pictures of a shirtless Teddy ignite the small amount of lust still coursing through my body. My fingers pause over one where he's playfully looking up at the camera, lying on a towel, his body half-propped on his elbow as he grins at the photographer.

His biceps bulge, his skin shines from sunscreen, and aviator sunglasses cover his gorgeous brown eyes. I swipe upward, the feed stopping on one of him and another guy, surfboards slung under their arms as they jog along the sand, running toward the photographer. It's a fantastic shot. Looks almost professional, like it's been taken as part of a photoshoot for beachwear or something.

"*Sand, sea, surf. Twenty is not too bad. HBD to me. July 25*," the caption reads.

My leg begins to tingle with the telltale signs it's about to go numb—an unfortunate side effect caused by the distraction that is Teddy, as notifications fill the top of my screen. My heart lurches again like I've been caught looking at something I shouldn't. Oh, wait...

Shay: You know I was joking, right?

Shay: I'd never go after him knowing you like him.

Shay: I might be a bitch but never to you.

Morgana: It's not like that.

Shay: What is it like then? He's hot, you're hot, ergo, you bang.

Morgana: Ergo? Really?

Shay: Oh, c'mon, you big prude! You don't want to be the only eighteen-year-old still holding their V-card.

Me: I'm not eighteen yet.

Shay: Oh good, there's still time for you to get rid of it. I vote for the hottie next door.

Me: It's not a game show where the winner gets my virginity, Shay. Besides, why would he be interested in me? The creep who watched him get a BJ?

Shay: HAHAHAHA. Oh, my sweet, innocent Morgs. Maybe he was into you watching. Were you into watching him?

Yes.

But that is one thing I can't tell her.

I wait to reply, needing to carefully think of a response that doesn't open up to ridicule, choosing to watch Teddy instead as he bends in half under the hood of his car, giving me an unobstructed view of his butt. Only when I hear muffled voices, do my eyes unglue themselves to watch Miles join his son, handing him a bottle and clapping Teddy's shoulder so hard you can see him buckle from the weight. Miles laughs, so loud and animated, that it can be heard clearly through the closed window, and a pang of longing threatens a sob that wants to choke me. If Skip chose to stay, would he and our dad have ever been like them?

Miles grabs Teddy in a headlock, the colorful tattoos decorating his long arms shining in the winter sun, his salt and pepper hair flopping about as they wrestle. Face red and laughing, Teddy frees himself, snatches his fallen cap from the ground, and shoves it on his head. The pair of them sip their drinks and set them to the side before returning their attention to the car.

Teddy stretches his arms above his head, and I'm spellbound. My lips part, and a gust of air fogs up the glass just as he grips the back of his sweat-soaked hoodie, tugging it over his head, the tee pulling up along with it to reveal his muscled back. They ripple as he works to untangle himself, then tosses the hoodie to the ground. I want to run my fingertips across his shoulder blades and down his spine, feel each contoured ridge of muscle against my skin. I didn't think I had a thing for backs, but I definitely have something for Teddy's back. I have something for many things about Teddy, it seems.

I bite down hard on my thumbnail, wanting him to face me while he's still not fixed his tee. I want to see the front without Brittany's stupid head in the way.

Please turn round.
Please turn round.
Please turn round.
Holy...

His front is even better than his back and much more defined in the sunlight, even when his muscles are relaxed. He wipes at his forehead with the bottom of his Henley, before pulling it down and covering himself back up. No longer is the tingling in my legs from loss of circulation. Pressure builds, and my body begs for some release. Today has awoken something dormant inside me, something I've never felt before. Teddy isn't doing anything sexual, and I don't understand how guys never seem to feel the cold in short-sleeved shirts, but as my mind drifts, so does my hand, lower and lower to the hem of my sweatshirt, dipping under so I can run my fingertips along the waistband of my yoga pants. My skin pebbles with goosebumps as my fingers tickle along my sensitive skin, slipping beneath to feel the lace of my panties. I know what I'm about to do is wrong, but I'm too far gone to care. I need this. I need to feel a fraction of the pleasure he had when our eyes met and I witnessed his release. Just as my fingers press lower, his stormy orbs look up straight at me like, somehow, he knew *again* that I was watching.

Losing my balance, I squeal, hand catching in my pants, as my free arm and legs flail and I crash to the floor. My phone smacks the side of my face, and the clip in my hair digs painfully into the back of my head. Mortification and shame crush me as I lie still, rubbing my smarting cheek and panting like I've just run a marathon. Muted laughter from outside hits my ears again, and I groan.

Of course, they must be laughing at me.

I dig around my hair, tug the broken clip from my curls, throw the mangled plastic across the room, and pull my hair over my face. Embarrassed and foolish, I lie on my plush pink carpet, quietly wishing I'd never need to see Teddy again. My phone buzzes from beside me, and I blindly smack along the floor, trying to find it.

Shay: YOU WERE SO INTO IT TOO, WEREN'T YOU?

I whine and put the device face down on my chest, wanting the world to swallow me. But worlds don't open up, and instead, fate decides I've not suffered enough as my phone buzzes again. I don't want to read Shay's ribbing messages, but the fear of missing something important quickly turns into full-blown anxiety as I stare at the screen.

"GreaseMonkey69 started following you."

Sitting up fast, I swivel until my back slams against the window seat. What the hell?

I quickly pull up Instagram, and my body turns numb instantly. So, this is what having a stroke feels like. Shining bright, mocking me like it has a pulse, is the little heart filled in red. I liked a photo on his feed from a year ago, and I have no idea how. Stupid-*stupid* touch screen. And now he's following me. How can I go back in time to stop completely embarrassing myself...

@GreaseMonkey69: Why'd you stop staring, babe? You've already seen the main attraction. Don't get shy with me now.

Chapter Five

Teddy

I am many things. A flirt, a fuckboy, a bastard—the last one courtesy of Brittany after I told her our little arrangement was no more. But one thing I am not is someone who laughs at other people's expense. And God help me, I'm trying not to, but between Dad's witch cackle and the constant loop of Ana's beautifully panicked face as she dropped from her window quicker than someone on fire is downright comical.

Although, when that deer-caught-in-headlights expression is replaced with wide eyes, hitched breathing, and an adorable blush that constantly coats her cheekbones, suddenly, my laughter dies. Each of her reactions is raw, refreshing, and utterly different from any other girl I've been with. I need to know more about her. She's a little mystery I'd like to solve. Innocence I'd like to corrupt. And I swear, the whole time she stood watching as I shot my load down Brittany's throat, there's a hidden dirty side to her too. A side I want to explore and coax out of her.

And now it's like we're connected through one of the most intense and powerful orgasms in the history of all my orgasms, giving me this sort of sixth sense when it comes to her. I could feel her gaze on me the whole time I was working, enjoying those unusual sea-green eyes on me again. So, when my Henley got caught while removing my hoodie, who was I to deny her another glimpse of my abs? It would have been rude to not turn around and let her see everything once more.

Fuck.

I tug at the neck of my Henley, the collar feeling tighter around my throat as my heart pounds under my rib cage. What am I doing? This taunting and teasing from afar is not like me. I usually like to do my teasing up close and personal with her, but today has messed with my head. Dad's words in his office, the thrill of imagining it was her bringing me to ruin and not some fake princess, have created this psychological pull I shouldn't—*don't*—want. Ana is trouble. She's not the girl you fuck in the back of a car. She is the girl you bring home to your parents, take out for fancy dinners, make *your girlfriend.* These new thoughts about her are unwelcome and unwanted and need to stop. I'm leaving... eventually. Going back to my hometown to live out my dream, and a relationship will only fuck that up. Long distance doesn't work. Connecticut doesn't work. And I'm sure as fuck not dragging someone across the country at twenty years old when high school romances never last.

Even if Ana was down for casual sex, the irrational unease of hypothetically thinking she could be someone I could call on for a booty call, or worse, be non-exclusive friends with benefits with, leaving her free to be with anyone else, doesn't sit right. It would have to be all or nothing.

Woah, calm the fuck down. That went from zero to one hundred fast, you idiot. Nothing's happening, nothing's going to happen, so push those fucking thoughts away. Ana is off limits.

I scrub a hand down my face, turning from her window, and Dad nudges my shoulder with his, a Cheshire smile beaming from under his dark beard as he smugly catches me looking for her. She might not have reappeared, but something tells me she's still there, hidden out of sight, maybe even a little embarrassed.

"Morgana's a nice girl," he says casually as he passes my beer. I might not be able to drink legally, but when Dad and I work on my car together, this has become a thing—bonding and being manly and shit.

"So you've said."

"You could pursue something with her. Maybe?" He cocks his head. "Now you and that O'Malley girl are no more."

That makes me choke on my beer and Dad chuckles.

"I'm not an idiot, Son. I saw her face when I drove into the neighborhood. She was mad, and there is only one place she could have been coming from, considering you were supposed to be doing a drop *off.*" I keep my mouth shut. Deniability is key, but only when I'm not sure how much he thinks he knows. Dad laughs into his bottle, taking a swig, then says, "When a car as bright as a highlighter drives past at the speed she was going, along with the thunderous glare she had on her face, it doesn't take a genius to figure out you took my advice."

I throw back half my beer in one gulp. The conversation about my love life is not something I want to talk about again.

"When someone starts sabotaging their cars, that says a lot about them as a person," I tell him, lifting my head to the late afternoon sun.

"Couldn't agree more, Son."

We're quiet for a beat, listening to the light hum from the seventies rock playing from Dad's phone he'd left on the driver's seat when he came out to help me.

"If we're done gossiping, can we finish working on her?" I ask, angling the bottleneck toward the car. Dad plucks the bottle from my hand just as my phone buzzes from my back pocket. Swiping my thumb over the screen, I read the notification, not needing to click on the banner to know *Addy2000 liked your photo* isn't some random who happened across my Instagram page. The page pops up with a post, a little more than a year old, from a car show with Bowie and me grinning like idiots. My brother's arm is casually slung around my shoulders as we stand on the sidewalk in Virginia Beach while the cars on show drive by. I smile. Ana's been stalking my social media page, that *like* a dead giveaway, and I would bet my 'stang that she did not mean to click that.

I flick off the photo and pull up her profile. It doesn't have much, a couple of pics of her and some brown-haired girl, a skyline or two, but nothing that hugely says, *this is the real Morgana Adler*. Then again, with the high-profile highly publicized campaigning her father is doing to be voted next Attorney General, that doesn't surprise me. News outlets, opponents, and anyone who doesn't want her dad winning would use her account to twist an innocent picture into something sinister.

I press *Follow*, and then, because apparently trying to forget 'all or nothing' doesn't exist with her, I send her a message.

@GreaseMonkey69: Why'd you stop staring, babe? You've already seen the main attraction. Don't get shy with me now.

It goes from unseen to *Read* in seconds, and I begin typing another.

@GreaseMonkey69: You know I don't mind.

A little thrill runs through me as *Typing...* appears at the bottom of the screen.

@Addy2000: Can we pretend today didn't happen?
@GreaseMonkey69: And why would we do that?
@Addy2000: It was inappropriate.
@Addy2000: And rude.
@GreaseMonkey69: And hot.

I tap my cell to my bottom lip before adding...

@GreaseMonkey69: Now you've seen my come face, when do I get to see yours?

"And that look screams you're up to no good, Son."

My eyes flick off my phone and up to my dad. "Huh?"

He raises one of his brows in that annoying way only some people can, just like the Rock in his WWE days. But unlike the Rock, Dad's not asking if I can smell what he's cooking. He's looking at me like he's saying, *I'm not fucking dumb,* and he doles that out not nearly enough to my brothers as he does to me. I slip my phone back into my pocket and take my hat off, wiping the sweat gathering at the band.

"Don't look at me like that," I say, sounding like a petulant child as I bend down and rummage in the toolbox, anything to avoid eye contact. Dad's big hand slaps mine out of the way as he reaches for a torque wrench, hitting it into my palm with a crack as he smiles smugly. The way he can say a thousand words with one look alone is infuriating as hell.

"Shut up," I say, rolling my eyes and turning to my car to tighten the pully. Eventually, Dad nudges me out of the way, checking over the work I'd done before he came out, grunting words of approval as he barely has to redo a thing. Lifting a cloth I had draped over the hood, I wipe my hands and watch my dad at work. This right here is why I moved with my folks. Dad might like his ego inflated, but he's earned it.

"All I'm saying is..." he begins, his voice muffled as he speaks into the car. *Seriously? He's like a puppy with a bone.*

"You haven't said a damn thing. You keep *looking* at me," I say through clenched teeth. "There is nothing you could possibly say anyway. Haven't you realized that we're from different worlds? Her mom would never think I'm good enough for her daughter, so why bother?"

Dad swings the wrench around and points it at me. "She'd be fucking lucky to have you, Teddy. Don't let something as fucking stupid as *class* stop you from going after what you want. Her folks don't like you, fuck 'em. It's her you're with, not her mom."

"Easy there, big guy," I say with a humorless laugh as tension seeps from his jaw. I snatch the wrench out of his hand before he damages my baby, holding it by my side. "Thanks for defending my honor or whatever, but you're getting ahead of yourself. Can we drop it, please? Ana and I won't be happening. No girlfriends, remember?"

Dad grunts just as Mom appears from the house, sidling up to his side and making him forget about his agitation.

"How are my boys getting on?" she asks, running her hand up his back. Growling, he playfully grabs her, swatting her ass and pulling her into his chest. They are the most open PDA couple I've ever seen, kissing like a pair of goddamn teenagers every chance they get. I swear I'll need therapy by the time I'm in my thirties. Noisily, I drop the wrench into the toolbox, trying to make it painfully clear that their son is still here and doesn't want to witness their nauseating show of how much they love each other.

Mom whacks Dad's chest, trying to wriggle out of his hold as she laughs. "You're getting oil on my jeans."

Dad grins and plants his huge hands on her ass, hauling her closer, nuzzling at her neck.

"Gross. I'm standing right here."

Dad pouts like an overgrown baby when Mom swats him again. She turns in his loosened hold, sinking into his chest as he possessively grips her hip. Arching a brow, she asks, "What's this I heard about no girlfriends?"

I frown, not realizing she heard me say that.

"Your mom's got the hearing of a hawk," Dad says, leaning down to kiss her shoulder.

"Jesus, Dad, can you just not?" I groan, flicking a rusted bolt from the ground at him.

He bats it away and shrugs. "Can't help it, Teddy. When you get a knockout like your mom here, you'll barely be able to keep your hands off her too."

Mom elbows his stomach in mock chastisement, pulling a face, then smiles softly. "Tell me, honey, why the sudden change of heart about girls... wait?" She inhales sharply, her eyes the same shade as mine, growing wide with excitement. "Is this...? Are you... coming out?"

My hands fly to my face, and I rub up and down, exasperated. "Fucking hell, Mom."

"What? You know we will love you no matter what, Teddy," she says warmly, and I know she's thinking back to when Bowie came out. He'd kept his sexuality a secret for four years after discovering he was attracted to guys, too scared to tell our parents in case they disapproved. Mom cried because he had lived in fear for so long, but was thrilled that he could finally be the person he was always meant to be.

"I'm not gay, Mom. I like pu—girls, but not enough for a relationship." Getting my own shop is my first love. Ana's face pops back into my subconscious and at this rate, I'm thinking she will never leave it.

Mom hums skeptically, then throws her head back against Dad's chest. "I'm never going to be a nana."

Why are my parents so damn dramatic all the time?

Ignoring her, I nudge the lid of the toolbox closed with my foot. "Well, one of your other sons will need to get to work on that."

She scoffs. "Yeah, right. Wyatt, 'the perpetual bachelor,' living his best life in the skies and Bowie off in the wilderness with his camera for company?"

"Ah, baby, don't worry," Dad coddles, spinning her around and lightly tipping her chin up. "We can always have fun pretending to make more kids while we wait for one of our boys to give us grandbabies." He shoots me a wicked grin as he loops his hands under my mom's thighs, lifting her to wrap her legs around his waist and she giggles.

"You guys are disgusting," I say through choking noises as I grab the beer bottles and my discarded hoodie. "I'm going to wash up and try to scrub my brain of this entire conversation."

"Okay, okay, we'll stop," Mom says, wriggling out of Dad's hold. Beaming, she hands over a packet of spark plugs. "Here."

"Are you sure?" I ask, my voice sounding uncharacteristically unsteady as I look at the cardboard package that could ruin my day. Dad nods and I swallow thickly. I've put so much time, effort, and cash into restoring this car. She's the first step in knowing my dream is achievable: if I can fix this baby from a hunk of junk into something sexy and fully functioning, I can make it as a mechanic.

Tearing open the packaging, I carefully fit the spark plugs and drop the hood. Mom squeals with excitement as I round the car to the driver's seat and glance back at Dad with trepidation.

Here goes nothing.

Chapter Six

Teddy

February

My car is fully functioning. Every time I turn the key and hear the ignition tick over before that classic Mustang roar... chills, fucking chills rack my body, and a sense of pride and accomplishment surges through me. I did this. I made this piece of engineering growl, and it's like music to my ears. Long gone are the days of relying on Dad's truck for work. Now it's nothing but me and my baby on the open road. And with this, the plan to move back to Phoenix is in full motion now. While I might not know everything I need to make it on my own, this is no longer a pipe dream. It's real, and I can practically taste it.

The only thing that would make all of this better would be seeing Ana again. For two weeks, I've been ghosted. Left on read. I'm starting to think asking when I'd get to see her 'O' face *might* have been a mistake. What did I think the reply would be? *Sure, no problem. Your place or mine?* I wanted to apologize, but after I fitted the spark plugs and heard the engine's powerful roar, my last message to her was forgotten until the following day. By then, it felt weird to say anything. So instead, I'm hiding like a goddamn pussy, conflicted with leaving her alone and craving to speak to her, to touch her soft skin, to be around her again.

I turn up the volume of the radio, drowning out the hammering of the rain on the roof as I finally drive home after a long-ass boring day of inventory. Driving past a bus stop, I double take, looking up to the rearview mirror and spot Ana alone, like thinking about her makes her appear like magic. She's soaked through, her flimsy jacket doing nothing to protect her from the weather as she holds it over her head. Her curls are flat and sticking to her face and her navy shirt clings to her body like a second skin, plastering to the curves of her tits, her flat stomach, and disappearing into the short private school skirt hovering above her knees. I'm still staring at her through the window, waiting for a stoplight to turn green, my thumbs drumming a beatless tune against the wheel.

Leave it, Teddy. I'm sure she's fine.

...Fuck it.

Yanking the wheel hard, the car almost aquaplanes in the middle of the road as I do an illegal U-turn and pull up beside her. Thank fuck no one is around to see that.

"Ana?" I call loud enough to be heard over the rain. "Are you okay?"

Her arms tighten around her waist as she nods with a shiver. "I, uh... yeah, I just missed the bus."

"Your mom lets her precious princess take the bus like some commoner?"

I gasp jokingly, although, come to think of it, it actually is surprising. Mrs. Adler is so concerned about their public image, I'd have thought the idea of being caught dead setting foot on public transport would be a hard no.

"Of course, I'm allowed to take the bus. I'm not a child," she snaps, folding her arms across her chest and fighting a shiver.

I hold my hands up in surrender. "Okay, sorry, didn't mean to upset you."

Her shoulders drop from around her ears and her face loses some of the tension held there. "Mom doesn't know I take the bus. It was hard enough convincing her to let me walk to school. Usually when the weather is bad, she picks me up, but she's out running errands for another campaign meeting, or charity lunch, or whatever Dad has planned."

"So she expected you to walk home in the rain?" I ask, almost with a growl. How fucked up is that.

Ana glances up the street before shaking her head. "No. I told her Shay's mom was driving me home."

I laugh at the little white lie she told her mom, like it is some huge act of defiance against her strict rules set by her parents. She smiles, nervously itching the back of her neck.

"You won't tell her?"

I shake my head and draw a cross over my heart. As if I'd willingly speak to her mom, let alone tell her something that isn't a big deal like taking a bus. Oh, the horror.

"Do you want a ride?" I offer. She looks at my car, weighing up the pros and cons of getting in the vehicle with me. "C'mon, baby, get in. We live next door. I'm going that way anyway."

She bites her bottom lip, and fuck me if that little movement doesn't make my dick stir in my jeans.

She nods, hitching her bag farther onto her shoulder, and runs to my car. I stretch out over the console and open the passenger door. As she slides in, I study her placing her tote bag and balled-up jacket between her feet in the footwell and tugging at her skirt. The hairs on her arms, as much as they are soaked from the rain, are standing on end, tiny goosebumps prickling her skin, and she fidgets in the seat. Shivers rack her body, and my gaze drops to her chest, where her nipples visibly poke through her thin shirt. Two round peaks standing at attention, begging for my hands, my lips, or my tongue to touch them.

Seriously, dude. Get yourself under control.

I think I've been caught staring when she covers her chest with both arms, but then she rubs her hands up and down the length of them, trying to warm up. Turning the dials on the console, I crank the heating up full blast, angle all the air vents in her direction, and then grab a hoodie from the backseat.

"Here," I say, draping the zip-up sweatshirt backward over her cold, wet body and tucking the edges over her shoulders. Ana's slim fingers clutch at the hood, pulling it closer to her chin and she slowly stops shaking. Her lips return to their natural soft rosy shade of pink, and her skin dries as the car heats up.

"Thank you," she says in an almost whisper. "The forecast didn't mention rain when I left this morning, and it was unusually warm today."

I nod and pull the car back onto the road, driving toward home. I'm facing the wrong way, but the extra ten minutes it will add to the journey doesn't seem so bad with Ana sitting next to me, the smell of rain and something citrusy tickling my nose. Except as the silence between us becomes almost deafening, the sound of splashing from the road and the rain hitting the car roof the only noises to fill the car, I'm wondering why I stopped and offered her a lift. Remove the flirty banter and it's a little awkward.

"So, what kind of music do you listen to?" I ask and cringe.

Kill me now. I hate small talk.

Her head bows down, and her hand peeks out from the sweatshirt to tuck a lock of hair which has started to dry into a ringlet behind her ear. "The usual, I guess. Chart stuff."

"Chart stuff?" Oh my God, this is painful. I would have thought seeing my dick would have made her feel comfortable around me, but apparently not.

"Actually," she says, her voice taking on an oddly strong tone compared to the mousey squeak it was a second ago. "I prefer the music from before I was even born. You know, old-school Rock and Roll. Neil Peart makes playing the drums look like an art."

I feel my eyebrows disappear into my hairline, and my hand slips from the wheel, making the car jolt slightly. "You know Rush?"

She laughs. The sound light and warm, finding its way into my chest and settling there.

"Who doesn't know Rush?" she asks. "Neil Peart is arguably the greatest drummer of all time."

I'm stunned, unable to form words, as the girl dressed in a private school uniform, with a mother who is more judgmental than the town gossip, has me shocked into silence.

"Jeff Porcaro, John Bonham, and Keith Moon are pretty good too."

"Toto, Led Zeppelin, and The Who. Fuck, Ana, you know your seventies rock bands."

She smiles, sucking that bottom lip between her teeth, and I wish she would stop doing that. It drives me fucking crazy for something I only noticed recently.

Tucking her hair behind her ear again, she says, "It's my little secret. Mom hates anything from that era. She'd much rather I spend my time listening to classical composers."

"Sneakily listening to forbidden music, taking the bus when you're not allowed. You're a little rebel, aren't you?"

She chuckles lightly, and I lean over to tug the auxiliary cable stuck under her bag and shift to grab my phone. Plugging it into the jack, I click *Play*, and David Gilmour's voice comes from the speakers.

"Pink Floyd," she whispers.

I groan, slapping my hand over my heart. "Marry me, Ana, just fucking marry me right now." She giggles, not the high-pitched, whiny giggle girls usually do, but soft and sweet, and I like it. "My family lives for seventies rock. My brother, Bowie, was actually named after..."

"David Bowie," she interrupts, a blush creeping onto her cheekbones. I glance at her from the corner of my eye, utterly amazed at the conversation we are having right now. She's also somehow managed to rearrange my sweatshirt, so her arms are in the sleeves, and the zipper is facing the right way and pulled up to the top. From what I can see, she looks pretty damn good in my clothes, and when she thinks she's being subtle, I see her pull the material to her nose and breathe in.

I must groan because she drops the sweatshirt and wrings her hands in her lap, keeping her eyes on the road like she's scared of my driving or something. No, not that, like she's nervous being around me.

"Sorry," she murmurs, then nibbles at her lower lip again. Her perfectly plump lip in the shape of a bow, desperate for...

Fuck, she's trouble.

"Do you only have one brother?" she asks, tugging the sleeves up and over her hands, and I'm grateful for the subject change. These intrusive dirty thoughts of Ana are getting worse.

I drum in time with the music, moving into the easy topic of my family, and shake my head. "Nah, got two. Bowie is two years older than me, and I miss him like crazy. He's been in the Amazon for the past eighteen months, but we speak every week on Skype or FaceTime or whatever. And then there's Wyatt. He lives near New York, but he's a high-flying pilot and eleven years older than me, so he doesn't exactly hang around with his kid brother much." I smile, thinking about my brothers. It's been too long since the whole family was in the same room. "What about you?"

Ana sighs. "An older brother, but I haven't seen him in years. He's also in New York, working in a restaurant the last time I checked."

"You guys not close?" I couldn't imagine not speaking to my brothers regularly.

"We were. Until..." She lets the sentence die, and we listen to the song transition to the bridge until she adds, "He calls me on my birthdays, but that's about it."

I hate how sadness lines her voice as she speaks of her brother, and I want to know more, but I'm learning my lesson about pushing too hard, too fast with her. Turning onto our street, I purposely slow down the car. Now I've got her speaking, I want to keep going. Learn more about my little mystery and I'm not sure if once she leaves my car, I will hear from her again.

"You got any graduation plans? I mean, you're eighteen, right? So it must be soon?" I might also have done a little googling of Mr. Adler's campaign to learn more about his daughter at some point in the last two weeks.

I told you, I'm conflicted when it comes to Ana.

"I turn eighteen on the day of graduation."

"Ah, sweet. You doing anything nice for it? Double celebrations and all?"

She's quiet, even more so than before, which I would have thought impossible.

"I would have liked to have gone to New York for a night, maybe see Skip," she admits. So, Skip must be the brother. I'm quiet as I wait for her to continue. "But Dad's got a fundraiser for his campaign that day, so we won't be celebrating."

"Birthday or graduation?"

"Both. Campaigning comes first."

"That's shit," I say, my tone harsher than I mean it to be. Ana turns her head to look at me, her eyes dropping to where I'm strangling the steering wheel. My blood simmers. Every part of that sentence is all sorts of fucked up. Her parents aren't celebrating her graduation, her goddamn birthday, because of some fucking campaign?

I swing into my driveway and turn off the car. Ana glances toward her house, where her yard sits empty, and lifts her bag onto her lap. She rummages for several seconds, pulling out her purse, phone, and other crap girls carry in oversized bags, before hanging her head in defeat.

"Shoot," she sighs and repacks her bag.

"Everything okay?" I ask, watching intently as her small fingers curl around a cylinder pencil case. She is definitely trying to kill me. Not only has the fantasy of her being the one getting me off in the garage been the image I've replayed in my head when in the shower or lying in bed, or pretty much any time it's me and my hand, but now—as she runs her thumb over the end of the pencil case—it's painfully obvious how oblivious she is to the little movement that's far too erotic for a fucking pencil case. My dick unhelpfully agrees and wants to volunteer as tribute to swap places.

"I forgot my keys." She clasps her hands over her closed bag, pencil case safely stowed away inside. I smile broadly and thumb up to my house.

"C'mon, you can wait inside until your folks get back."

She hesitates. "Are you sure? Your parents won't mind?"

"Nah, they won't. Anyway, they aren't here." Her eyes widen, and she shivers as the cool air from the storm slowly floods the car now that the warm air has stopped since I cut the engine. I shift in my seat, my face serious as I run my gaze over her. "Ana, you're freezing and wet. Come inside, and you can use my shower while you wait for your mom or dad to come home."

Chapter Seven

Teddy

Why did I ask her to come inside? Not only that, why did I *insist* on it when she was clearly hesitant? This is a clusterfuck. It's not my fault she wasn't prepared for rain, and now I'm playing knight in shining armor by inviting her into my house—the first girl to ever come into my space. I'm waiting for the usual feeling of unease to creep its way across my skin, but as I remind myself she's not here for us to hook up, I find it doesn't come. If anything, I'm almost disappointed that's not why she's quietly following me up the stairs.

I briefly check over my shoulder and catch Ana observing the photographs my brother has taken throughout the years as we walk through the hall. The whole house is like a shrine to Bowie. Not that anyone minds. He is talented as fuck, and it makes everyone happy whenever they pass a candid photo they didn't know he'd taken.

"These are beautiful," Ana says as we climb the stairs to my room. Pausing at a cupboard, I turn to pass her a towel to find her staring at a photo hung right at the top of the stairs. Coming behind her, I stand close to her back. With her damp hair flattening her curls, she's a couple of feet shorter than me, and if I wanted, I could easily rest my chin on the top of her head. Instead, I reach forward, my arm brushing against her shoulder as I point out everyone in the photo.

"Every picture in this place was taken by Bowie. Mom begged him to take this one—" I brush the tips of my fingers along the mirrored frame, "with his tripod so he could be in it too."

"I did notice he wasn't in very many," she said, pointing to Bowie in the picture.

"Yeah, he's a diva when it comes to his art." I chuckle and gently guide her toward my room. "Hates staged photographs, always says he wants his art to flow, be organic, authentic, to really capture the subject's spirit." I put on this phony English *professor* accent as I mock my brother.

"He's very talented," she muses as I push my room door open, allowing her to go inside.

"He's alright," I tease.

Ana smiles and slowly walks across the room, eyeing everything as she reaches the center. The space isn't much, a king-sized bed taking up most of the room, a desk and chair over in the corner, and a heap of old car parts decked out on a bookshelf. The walls are still the same color of blue the old occupant had.

I watch from the doorjamb, noticing things I wish I wouldn't about my pretty neighbor. Like how her eyes sparkle with interest as she scans over my assortment of brake pads, carburetors, and an air cleaner on my shelves. Or the tiny smile on her parted lips when she notices a picture of my dad and me standing outside our old house, his arm around my shoulder, the pair of us covered in grease and motor oil, noses red from the sun after standing out too long working on my car when I first got her—a picture taken on my mom's iPhone rather than Bowie's supped-up Canon. Or how my room feels warmer just because she's in it.

She clears her throat and I snap my eyes to hers, unaware I'd zoned out for a second as she clutches the towel tight to her chest, and nervously looks around, unsure what to do now. I push from the jamb and point toward a closed door.

"Bathroom's in there. Use whatever you like," I say. The citrus smell of her skin is stronger now that she's slowly drying, and I step farther, closer than is polite, drawn in by the fascination to know if her skin tastes like it too. Ana's breath catches as she stares up, short curly strands of hair falling into her eyes. I swallow hard and push my hands into my jeans pockets, stopping myself from reaching up and brushing them away. "If you throw out your clothes, I can put them in the dryer while you wait for your mom to come home."

The gentle smile she wore before falls, and it doesn't take a genius to figure out that if she gives me the clothes, she'll have nothing to put on. The image of Ana in nothing but a towel is almost too good to pass up. But I'm a gentleman... or at least I'm trying to be, so reluctantly, I drag myself over to my dresser, pull out a t-shirt and a pair of cotton sweatpants, and offer them out. She tucks them alongside the towel and my eyes drop down to where all three items are pressed against her chest. Her tits push up to sit under the open V of her shirt and directly into my eyeline. Fuck, she has great tits. Even obstructed beneath a bundle of clothes, they look like they were made to fit in my hands and my hands alone.

Get over yourself, Teddy. Rich girls like Morgana don't go for grease monkeys like you.

"Thank you, Teddy," Ana says, and my eyes jerk to hers. Her cheeks pinken, and she ducks into the bathroom, quickly locking the door behind her. I listen as she turns on the shower, and I'm stuck, unable to move, still thinking about her tits and liking how she said my name in a breathy whisper.

The door opens just a crack, and her slender bare arm snakes around the wood. Holding out her clothes, I stare as steam billows from the gap. I move closer, arm outstretched to take her soaking clothes, and then it's my turn to watch. In the mirror above the toilet and sink is Ana's reflection. Coils of steam, like some Greek goddess, are slowly enveloping her naked body. One of her long legs is bent, her toes and the ball of her foot resting on the tiles while the other supports her weight. Her ass is fucking delectable, and all I want to do is sink my teeth into each round globe of her cheeks. My hands twitch to trail down her hips and tapered waist, and I want to paint her delicate skin with the shape of my fingerprints. Her arms are covering her chest, obstructing my view from this angle except for a sliver of side boob.

My cock is achingly hard in my pants, and I want to shove the door open, push her against the wall, and sink to my knees and worship her pussy I know will be every bit as perfect as the rest of her. Either that or sink inside and fuck her until she's panting and coming around my dick.

"Um, Teddy?" her question calls from behind the door, "are you sure you don't mind?"

I snap out of my stupor and take the balled-up material.

"Uh, yeah, sorry, not at all. Take your time."

The door locks again, and I hear the shower door sliding back and forth. I'm a masochist. That must be it. That's why I've made her off-limits, and then invited her up to my room—something I've never done before—to taunt myself with the knowledge that she's naked in my shower, and there's fuck all I can do about it.

Groaning, I drag myself away from aimlessly staring at the bathroom door and leave to shove her wet clothes into the dryer. I pause, bringing my zip-up sweatshirt to my nose to see if it smells like her. She might not have worn it for long, but a faint scent of citrus is strong enough to fill my lungs, and I almost don't want to wash it. Shoving it into the laundry basket, I open the dryer and drop Ana's clothes inside. A ball of black misses the drum, fluttering to the ground, and I bend, scooping up the material in one hand as I choose the settings for the machine with the other. I'm just about to throw it inside when I glance at what I'm holding.

One hundred percent a masochist, for I am holding Ana's bra and panties.

I stare, open-mouthed, and hard as fucking granite, at the flimsy cut of material Ana calls underwear. The thong is all kinds of sexy; black silk with intricate flowers detailed on the waistband, and the bra makes them a matching set. Something I'd have never thought hid beneath her private school uniform. Forcing my hand to release them from my death grip, I slam the lid shut, hiding the cock-teasing set of underwear from view, and turn on the machine. I brace my hands against the edge, urging the erection straining against my zipper to die down. The machine shakes beneath my hands, the whirring of the drum echoing around my ears as my imagination continues to torture me with scenarios of stripping her from her underwear and taking her hard. In my room, in the shower, fuck, even in the back seat of my car. Filthier and filthier, the images become, flooding my head and doing nothing to help my dick. I need to get laid or maybe rub one out. Either way, both should not involve Ana either physically or mentally.

I take a deep breath, resigned to the fact I'm not going down any time soon, and do some tactical rearranging before leaving the laundry room. I come to an abrupt stop as Ana stands in the kitchen, squeezing her long hair with a towel, fully dressed in my clothes. I take one step, then another, running my gaze from her bare toes, painted a light shade of yellow, and up to her head. She watches as I peruse her, following the blush that travels up her neck.

"Thanks for letting me use your shower. The water pressure is amazing." She scrunches her nose a little, looking around the kitchen as if trying to find something. "Uh, where should I put this?"

"I'll take it," I say, grabbing the towel from her and tossing it behind me without taking my eyes off the petite girl in front of me. She might have mere months until she's eighteen, but Ana is all woman. Even wearing my tee and sweats, which drown her entirely, I can still see her curvaceous waist, her round tits and her sweet tight little ass underneath it all.

Her breathing labors as I reach out and lightly graze my thumb under one of her eyes, wiping a faint dark smudge from her mascara. Whatever she sees in my face has her cheeks darkening further, and her eyes drop to my mouth as she licks her lips. I'm crowding her again, unable to stop myself from being in her personal space. It calls me forward, pulling me in like it wants me, *needs* me there. I can smell my coconut body wash, a fragrance I had not been happy that Mom bought for me while at the store, but on her skin, it smells incredible, a scent I'll be regularly buying from now on. I like that she smells of me, that she's dressed in my clothes, and standing in my house. I feel almost possessive—a subconscious claiming that neither of us is even aware exists.

I place a hand on her hip and run my thumb along the waistline of the gray sweats. A sharp breath escapes her, and her head drops to look at where I am holding her. It's not nearly as tight as I want to grip her. I want to see red and purple bruises created by my hand so badly that the strain in my muscles practically aches. Her head snaps back up as I swipe my thumb on her heated flesh again, her eyes flashing with nerves and a slight hint of panic as she stares unblinkingly into mine. I reach up with my free hand and tuck a strand of damp hair behind her ear.

Without thought, I lean my head down and whisper, "You have no idea how badly I want to kiss you, Ana. Would you let me if I tried?"

She's quiet for a moment, thrown by either my question or my mouth still lingering by her ear, ghosting the outer edge. I'm just as surprised as she is at those words spilling out before I had the chance to process them. But now they're out there, I don't regret it because I really want to kiss her.

Her body trembles under my grasp. I watch her pulse quicken in the corner of my eye, the rapid drumming at the side of her neck beating a crazy tune as adrenaline floods her. Unspoken excitement escapes with a small gasp from her pink lips. To know that she's affected by me, responds to me like this with a simple touch, ignites something deep inside me.

She places her hand and pushes me back, breathily asking, "What about Brittany?"

"Don't worry about her," I say, wrapping my free hand around the base of her head, threading my fingers into her hair, and smile. "She's not important. Never was."

Her eyes close before I even bring my lips to hers, and I watch her face as my mouth descends. She whimpers at the first brush of our lips, a sound unlike anything I've ever heard before, going straight to my already aching cock. Her lips part and I take the chance to slip my tongue inside, circling it with hers. She wraps a hand around my forearm and sucks gently on my tongue. I almost stop, my languid strokes taken off guard by the bold move, but when her other hand comes to my waist, I tighten my grip on her hair and pull her into my chest. Soft moans have me deepening the kiss, moving her body backward to lean against the counter. She squeaks in fright as her back hits the side, and I chuckle into her mouth.

Panting, she breaks our kiss, and I can't lie and say my lips don't chase after hers.

"Teddy," she whispers, looking up at me. The little fragments of blue in her eyes are completely missing as dark green overpowers them. It might not be her 'O' face, but knowing this happens when she's aroused makes me want to see what else her body does. I should slow down, take my time and savor everything about her, but I can't. My body and mind are fighting against each other, one telling me she isn't some bimbo who'd drop her panties if I winked at her. That this girl deserves to be treated like a queen, not to mention that she's my neighbor and her family, for some reason, hates mine, and things can get complicated. But the other part wants me to push the boundaries with every tremble that rolls through her body.

Her chest presses hard into me with every breath, and her pink tongue licks her bottom lip.

Yup. It's a fucking losing battle.

Our lips meet again, and my hand drops from her hair to dip under her shirt. Smooth, warm skin greets my fingertips, and she shudders. I drag my knuckles up the side of her hips, waist, and ribcage, her body squirming as I map lines on her with my hand. I skim the side of her boob, the same one teasing me from the bathroom mirror, feeling every goosebump as it forms under my touch like tiny pinpricks. She sighs, melting into my hold, and I hesitate, wanting so badly to flick my thumb across her nipple and feel the hard little peak I know is waiting for me. Instead, I move and wrap my arm around her back, completely banding up her spine to grip the base of her neck, my fingers edging out of the t-shirt collar and tangling with her damp hair.

I pull her tighter, her back and ass moving off the counter and closing any gap between us. She grips my shoulders as I move the hand on her hip to slide easily into the waistband of the sweats. When she shifts onto her tiptoes, I palm one of her ass cheeks, the skin just as soft as the rest of her, and groan into her mouth. I kiss along her jaw to her ear and down her throat, sucking lightly but with enough pressure that she will wear my faint mark. Her hold on my shoulders tightens as my fingers knead the muscles in her ass, teasing the crease and following the line down and under, so close to where I really want to touch, and without any underwear preventing access, nothing is stopping me.

"Oh God." Ana's whispered moan is like a drug, and I want more.

"I know," I murmur against her skin, my lips never leaving the velvet of her flesh.

She groans, the sound different from before—unsure, hesitant—making me freeze.

"Teddy, I've never..." She tenses in my arms, and although not spoken, her admission is like a kick to my ridiculously blue balls. I can't do this. It isn't right. Ana doesn't deserve a quick finger-fuck in my kitchen. She's never done this before, and I'd go as far as to say she's barely even been kissed. She deserves care and somewhere comfortable to be worshipped.

My hands slide out from beneath her clothing, and I force a step back. Her eyes widen, bouncing back and forth between mine in horror and confusion.

"Did I do something wrong?" Her voice is meek, and I'm shocked at how much regret flows into my chest. It's present and aching as I stare at her swollen lips.

I trace them with my finger and shake my head. "No, Ana. You are perfect. And that's why I can't do this."

Her face falls, and she drops her chin to her chest. "Oh."

I tuck my fingers under it, forcing her head up until she's looking into my eyes. "I want to, Ana, so fucking much. But not like this." I kiss her forehead, her temple, the side of her nose and finish on her lips.

A clearing throat makes her jump, and she pushes me away, turning her back and burying her bright red face in her hands. Dad stands in the doorway with a shit-eating grin plastered on his oil-stained face, wiping his hands on a dirty old rag.

"Morgana, what a surprise," he sing-songs like a jackass, dropping the cloth into his open workbag on the floor by his feet. I shoot him a look as I wipe the corner of my mouth with my thumb.

"I thought you were working late today?" I question through gritted teeth.

"Nah, the part didn't fit, so I needed to order a new one." He looks between Ana and me, still fucking smiling. "Your mom's home now, Morgana sweetheart, in case you didn't already know."

Ana tugs at her shirt and quickly skirts around me toward the hall. Her head is still down as I quickly follow her as she scurries to the front door, and I race ahead to grab the bag and jacket she'd left when she first came inside.

Holding out the strap, I say, "Sorry about him."

I thought it would have been impossible, but her face darkens even more as she glances back at him, leaning against the doorjamb, eating an apple as he happily watches us. Her hand darts out, going for the doorknob, when I spread mine wide on the paneling before she can pull it open, boxing her against it and hiding her from view. I cup her face and place a gentle kiss on her lips.

"Go out with me, Ana," I murmur. Everything I'd been telling myself over the last few weeks, now long gone after that kiss. She tilts her head to the side, her hand pushing against my chest.

"Please don't start that again," she whispers, her eyes downcast after looking so alight before. "Don't play games after kissing me like that."

I frown. "I'm not. There are so many reasons why I should leave you alone. I'm leaving in a few months. You're going to college soon. You can do so much better than me, but I can't stop thinking about you." Her eyes widen, scanning my face for a hint of a lie as she listens. "I'm being serious, Ana. Go out with me."

I brush a chunk of her unruly curls behind her ear. The girl's hair is wild when it dries naturally. She blinks, no doubt dissecting my question while trying to glance over my shoulder toward our audience. Finally, her smile may be small, but she nods. "Okay."

I hold out my hand. "Give me your cell. I know you've got my Instagram account, but I want your number. If that's okay?"

She fumbles in her bag and pulls out her phone, keys in the passcode, and holds it out. I type in my number and click *Call*. My phone vibrates in my pocket, and I end it, leaving her number as a missed call.

"Bye, Morgana," Dad manages to call out through a mouthful of fruit, and pushes away from the door, retreating into the kitchen. Ana has the door open before I even get a chance to fully step away from her, taking off down the porch steps, across the grass, and up to her house. I wait as she reaches her door to see if she will look back. It's tiny, barely even a glance over her shoulder, but she did.

I fight my grin as I kick the door closed and then round on the man who thinks he's a goddamn comedian. Dad's eyes gleam as he watches me storm into the kitchen, leaning on the counter in the exact spot Ana and I were making out moments ago. He quirks an eyebrow and smirks as I glare at him, dragging a hand down my face.

"Not one word," I say, jabbing my finger in the air.

He shakes his head and pretends to look confused.

"Wasn't going to say a word, Son," he says, but the mirth behind his steely eyes speaks a thousand. "I was only going to ask if you wanted to work on your car now that I'm home, or if you needed a cold shower first."

Chapter Eight

Morgana

"Hi, Morgana." Sadie waves from the porch, her smile beaming as her husband slinks behind her, wrapping his arm around her waist and hauling her to his chest.

"Good morning, Mr. and Mrs. Grant," I say, darting down the stairs without making eye contact with Mr. Grant. After avoiding that family for the past week, you'd have thought the embarrassment of being caught in a compromising position with their son would have ebbed. Apparently not. Especially when Mr. Grant leans down and whispers something in Sadie's ear, and she tries to stifle a giggle.

Great.

"Sweetheart, how many times do I need to tell you it's Sadie and Miles? Mrs. Grant makes me feel like his mother"—she thumbs up to her husband—"and she's a miserable old bat."

"Hey, that's my mom."

"And? You call her much worse," she says, looking up at him pointedly.

"That woman gave me life..."

I scurry down the pathway, leaving them to bicker playfully, and my stomach squeezes when their laughter carries on the wind. They love so freely, out in the open for everyone to see, compared to my parents. God forbid my father holds my mother the way Miles had Sadie for even a second. It could be snapped by paparazzi, plastered all over the internet and manipulated in a smear campaign by his opposition. Or at least that's the excuse my parents give whenever I'm being lectured about etiquette in public.

Morgana, don't smile too wide; it looks like you're overcompensating.

Morgana, don't speak too loudly; no one likes an attention seeker.

Morgana. Morgana. Morgana.

"Hey, Morgs," Shay sings as she thunders down from her house, joining me on the sidewalk and linking her arm in mine. "Have I told you that you're my best friend in the whole world?"

I narrow my eyes. "What do you want?"

"Always so suspicious." I purse my lips and wait. "*Urgh,* fine. Think I could convince you to skip school today? Madame Baudelaire is going to hand me my ass. I didn't study for this test at all."

"Maybe you shouldn't have taken AP French, then," I say, tugging her along. "Just because your parents take you to Paris every spring does not make you an expert on the language."

She gasps and knocks her hip into mine, making me stumble as we laugh. "You take that back! When I am a big blogger writing about French cuisine, I'm going to post a picture of me eating snails, giving you the middle finger with the caption, *Va te faire voir, Morgs.*"

"Why do I get the feeling you only know dirty words in French?" I pull her arm closer to my side. "I cannot wait to see it."

"See it? You'll be taking the photo. There's no way you're not coming to Paris with me."

My smile dips. If only I could.

Shay sighs. "Honestly, Morgana, when will you start standing up to your parents and start doing the things you want to do?" I stay silent. It's an argument that never goes well, so I've stopped trying. It's what's best. She tugs out of my hold and twists me around, stopping us mid-step, her eyes filled with a fierce determination that makes me squirm.

"You *have* told them you want to go to business school, right?" I bite my lip, my chin dropping. "Morgana, why the hell not? You've already applied to five different schools and received acceptance letters from them all. What's stopping you?"

I shrug. "It's never come up."

"Bullshit," she snaps, and my mouth drops. She's never this abrupt with me. "As soon as graduation is done, your dad is going to send you to Harvard. *Harvard.* As in Boston. As in nearly one-hundred and eighty miles away from here."

"I know."

"To get a degree in something you hate. Not that business is any better." She grimaces.

"I might not even get in. I still need to take the LSATs," I tell her, hoping that might placate her and get her off my back, even if she is right. I should have sat them months ago, especially with graduation looming, but I was hoping that the longer I left it, maybe—just maybe—I wouldn't be accepted and wouldn't need to tell my parents anything.

"We both know that's just a formality. Your dad will click his fingers, and the Dean of Admissions will personally show you to your dorm room." My shoulders sag because she's right. Dad is like a rock star there. "You need to talk to them, Morgs. You can't be miserable for the rest of your life when it's barely begun. You'll be stuck being their puppet forever, babe."

I look down at the sidewalk and kick at a single stone, watching it bounce off and down the storm drain. "I can't disappoint them, Shay."

She pulls my arms, crashing our bodies together as she wraps herself around me in a back-breaking hug.

"I hate them for making you miserable."

"It's not that bad. They are just doing what they think is best," I say, pushing out of her hold, and Shay rolls her eyes, thankfully dropping it. "C'mon, we better get to school."

She groans, throwing her head back to the sky. "Why couldn't my best friend break the rules just this once?"

She stomps behind me, her satchel scraping along the ground like a child mid-tantrum when the roar of a car rumbles down the road before pulling up alongside us. My stomach flutters as Teddy grins, leaning across the center console. His fingers curl around the open window, his corded forearms flexing as he peers up at me, reminding me that my hand was wrapped around those strong arms not that long ago while he kissed me.

"Hey, Ana Banana," he says, his tongue swiping along his lower lip after raking his gaze up the length of my body. "Want a ride to school?"

"We'd love one," Shay interjects, leaping forward and thrusting her hand into the car. "I'm Shay, bestie of this one."

Teddy shakes her hand, looking over her shoulder with an amused look flitting over his face. "I'm Teddy, Ana's neighbor."

"Oh, I know all about you," she drawls, her tone suggestive and mocking. I want to kill her, but then she rushes forward, opens the door, and plops herself inside, grinning widely as I scowl.

"You going to join your friend?" Teddy asks, and Shay jolts forward, pulling the chair back so I can't join her in the back.

"You called shotgun," she says, squeezing her head between the empty passenger chair and the door frame.

"I don't think I did," I say through gritted teeth.

"Huh. Weird. I could have sworn I heard you call it." She grins wide like she's just won the biggest prize at the county fair. "Oh well. Get your bony ass in the car, Morgs. We're gonna be late."

Mouthing, "*I hate you,*" I drop into the seat, and we make our way to school in what must be the longest drive of short rides. The whole time, Shay does not stop talking. Her incessant need to fill a silence with her constant chatter is bordering obnoxious. No topic is off-limits as she asks Teddy any question that pops into her head; childhood, siblings, last sexual encounter—which I know was mainly for me when she pokes my shoulder from behind and winks when I turn to glare at her.

"Don't feel like you have to answer that," I say, my cheeks flaming. "Shay doesn't know the meaning of boundaries."

Teddy chuckles, flicking on his signal before turning.

"Last sexual encounter was... torture," he says easily, and my heart drops into my stomach. I fight to not bring up my breakfast. Puking in front of him would almost be as mortifying as knowing he didn't feel what I did back in his kitchen. Why did I think what I found to be the most exhilarating experience of my life would have been different for him? Wringing my hands together on my lap, I silently wish we hadn't accepted his offer to drive us to school.

"Oh, really?" Shay enquires, her head popping through the gap between the front seats. Her arms dangle loosely over the back of them as she looks between Teddy and me. "That's a shame. Shit sex is the worst."

I am so embarrassed I could cry. The backs of my eyes prickle as I swallow hard against the lump rising in my throat. I know she didn't bring up this topic to hurt me—she doesn't know about last week, so the last encounter she thinks she's asking about would be with Brittany—but right now, every laugh between the pair slashes my poor, naive heart.

"We're here," I croak as the school comes into view. Teddy pulls through the gates and parks in a visitor's space, shutting off the engine. As he watches me with a weird intensity, I quickly jump out of the car and slide the chair forward to let Shay out. Just as I lean back inside to grab my bag, Teddy wraps his hand around my wrist, tugging me down, and I unceremoniously tumble back into the seat.

"Teddy, what the—?"

He reaches across me and grabs the door, slamming it shut, trapping me inside, and my breath catches when his dark orbs pin me in place.

"To make it clear, Ana. You are the best kind of torture." His eyes drop to my lips, and I swallow thickly.

"It wasn't terrible?" I mean, we just kissed, but it was more than I'd ever imagined.

He smirks. "I haven't been able to stop thinking about the little moans you made when you were pressed against me."

"Teddy." It's a breathy whisper.

"Or that... the way you breathe my name." His hand reaches up like he is going to run his fingers against my heated flesh, when he catches himself and clears his throat. Leaning back, he scratches along the stubble on his jaw. "What are you doing Saturday?"

I blink, my brain screaming, *you, you, you.* "Nothing."

"You promised me a date." This time when he reaches up, his hand threads into my hair. "Let me take you out on Saturday."

What? In five days? That's not enough time to prepare.

"She'd love that," Shay coos, leaning against the car, head through Teddy's window, watching us closely. Teddy's hand drops from my hair as he turns to face her, and my eyes widen with menace. She stands, holding her hands up placatingly, with a shit-eating grin on her face that says she's not even sorry she was eavesdropping on our conversation. "What? You two are too cute not to watch. And maybe if you didn't keep your windows down, you'd have had privacy."

"Or you could just turn around and give us a sec?" he growls. Shay huffs, turning her back to the car and tapping her foot on the path leading up to the entrance of the school. Teddy spins back around, his fingers curling around my nape and crashing his mouth to mine. It's fast and hot and I practically melt against him, whimpering a little when it doesn't last nearly as long as I want.

"Have a good day, Ana Banana," he says, licking his lips as I flounder for my bag and slide from the car.

Shay chuckles, waving as Teddy speeds out of the parking lot.

"I hate you, Shay," I snarl, gripping her arm hard and tugging her through the school doors and down the hall toward our lockers.

She laughs, pinching my side. "He is so hot, *Ana Banana...*"

"Don't call me that."

"Right, sorry. That's *Teddy's* adorable pet name for you."

"Did you hear me when I said I hate you?"

"Yeah, yeah, you hate me." She waves her hand in the air dismissively. "I am so bummed you got to him first, Morgs. Like uber jealous."

Ignoring her, I put the combination into my locker and open the door. Shay's eyes appear through the little air vents. "You really like him, huh?"

I pull out my chem textbook and close the door. "I don't know. This is all new and weird, and I don't like it."

"Why?" she asks, cramming her huge bag into her locker and slamming it shut, containing the avalanche of textbooks, snacks, and other rubbish threatening to drop inside.

"I'm constantly nervous. I'm a big blubbering mess, can barely think of anything interesting to say, and all I do is stand and smile like a fool when I'm around him."

Shay grins. "This is what dating is all about, babe. The excitement, the anticipation, the thrill of what's going on. It's such an amazing feeling."

I groan, banging my forehead with the hardback of the textbook. "That doesn't sound amazing. It sounds awful. I'm going to cancel."

"What? No!" she practically shrieks. "Give me one good reason why."

"He's twenty..."

"Oh Jesus, the horror," she says sarcastically. "You're eighteen in two months. That's not a big deal."

I roll my eyes. "Okay, well, my mom *hates* him."

"She doesn't *know* him. Plus, she hates everyone."

"True."

"Besides, she doesn't need to know you've got a date this weekend. You can always say you're coming to my house?"

The bell rings before I can give her idea much thought, and the corridor fills with students making their way to first period. We walk toward the science building, my head spinning with every step down the white-painted brick corridor. When Teddy asked me out, I thought it was another joke or something he'd soon realize was a mistake and not follow up on. It's not like he messaged me the week after our *encounter*, so I assumed he'd forgotten.

I stop dead.

"Shay, I have nothing to wear. Everything I own looks like I'm about to teach at Bible Camp."

A new rush of butterflies joins my nervous ones. But these ones have little spikes that make me feel sick.

"Don't worry, I've got you covered."

"Thank you," I sigh, sinking into her side.

"Okay, now tell me you love me."

I laugh. "I love you."

"Miss Sylvester, don't you have calculus first period?"

"Yes, Mr. Grover," she says with a tight-lipped smile.

"And isn't that up on the second floor?" My science teacher asks with a chastising arch to his bushy eyebrow.

"Yes, sir," she says brightly before muttering, "You ask this every morning."

"Well, I suggest you and Miss. Adler resume your conversation about pedicures and the latest boy band after class."

"We were actually talking about boys, Mr. Grover. I was just about to give Morgana here some sex ti—"

"Keep talking, and you'll get detention, Miss. Sylvester," he growls. "Get to class. Now."

She holds her hand in the air, gives a dramatic backward wave, and walks toward the stairs leading to the school's other floors. "See ya, Morgs, don't miss me too much. Bye, Mr. Grover. See you tomorrow."

Chapter Nine

Morgana

Two big suitcases sit by the door on Friday night. One white, the other black, both monogrammed in silver with my parents' initials.

"Where are you going?" I ask as Dad walks out of the living room. Holding a finger to his ear, he continues speaking on the Bluetooth device I didn't even see him wear.

Didn't realize people still used those things.

Mom quickly walks into the hall, setting her designer handbag on the sideboard and checking out her reflection. Flawless, as always.

"We are going away for the weekend, Morgana. There's money on the counter for dinner for the next few nights." She rummages through her bag and brings out a lipstick. Pouting, she slides the tube across her lips before rubbing them together. "We will be back late Sunday night."

Mom presses her cheek against mine as Dad opens the door, taking their suitcases in either hand, and strutting outside without uttering a goodbye. It's been this way for the past couple of years, ever since his campaigning ramped up, and he only ever needs me to look pretty for press photos. Otherwise, I doubt he remembers he has a daughter.

"Have a nice time," I call after him.

"You didn't want to come, did you?" Mom asks, cocking her head like it just occurred to her that maybe they should have invited their child to go with them. I shake my head. "I didn't think so, sweetheart. It will be boring meetings and mingling and whatnot. I'll miss you, though."

Sure you will, the daughter you forgot to invite.

"Miss you too."

She blows a kiss, and then they're gone. I rest my palm on the door and shut my eyes, a stillness washing over me as the calm quiet of the empty house fills my ears. There's no pretending to be a version my parents approve of when I'm alone. No one to ask what I'm doing, or who I'm with, or what I'm wearing. I'm free to be *Ana*.

And *Ana* has a date with Teddy tomorrow.

I run to my room as nerves resurface—not that they ever really stopped. Every day this week, Teddy has given Shay and me a ride to school, and sometimes, if he's finished at the garage, he's driven me home too. I swear my mom knows something's going on since she keeps commenting on how much I've been smiling recently. It's not like we're *sneaking* around, but once I could have sworn I saw the twitch of the living room curtain as I scrambled out of Teddy's car. I'm simply trying to avoid the inevitable *he's not good enough* talk for as long as I can.

Throwing open my closet door, I swipe through my clothes, vetoing everything my fingers touch. This is hopeless.

Morgana: Why didn't you tell me my wardrobe was *this* bad?

Shay: Oh, babe, I tell you all the damn time. You just didn't care before.

Morgana: You're so helpful.

Shay: Don't worry, I told you, I've got your back. It's not your fault your fashionably impaired mother styled her only daughter like a nun.

Morgana: It's not like she makes me wear a habit.

Shay: She might as well. At least you could accessorize that.

I throw myself onto my bed and groan.

Morgana: Can you please help me?

Shay: Girl's night at my house? Sleepover, movies, and we can look at what I've got that could work for a first date.

Morgana: Can you come here? My parents are away for the weekend.

Shay: Even better!

"Morgana Tallulah Adler, stop blinking. You're making me mess up." Shay smacks the eyeliner tube on my head, making me wince, before continuing to poke the wand in my eye. I flinch, and she grips the top of my head, the tips of her fingers digging into my scalp as she growls, "Hold still!"

When Shay insisted on helping me get ready for my date with Teddy, I was thankful. Now... not so much.

"I am!" I whine, not used to this amount of primping. "And that's not my middle name."

She gently blows across my eye, drying the black liquid. "Well, if you had one, I'd use that, but instead, I have to make up my own."

"Last time, it was Louise," I say, peering through slitted lids, too scared to open them fully and smudge her work. My best friend's wrath isn't something I can endure, especially when I'm already on edge tonight. Shay rummages around in her makeup box, one of those fancy things professionals own to store and cart around their collection. She opens the lid to a lipstick before shaking her head and pulling out a different tube. Gripping my chin, she pouts her lips, and I copy the action.

"Whatever. You need a middle name when you're being a pain in my ass and won't sit still." She lightly lines my lower lip with the pigment, mimicking my pout like it helps her put it on and then tilts her head. "Rub your lips together... gently."

I do as I'm told and take the handheld mirror she passes. Her eyes soften, and a smile morphs across her face. I turn the mirror over and look at the girl in the reflection.

"Not that you don't normally, but holy shit... you look absolutely stunning."

I glance up at Shay, then back to mirror me. I look... different. My eyes are more defined, my cheeks have a rosy glow, and my lips look fuller than usual. It's not caked on either; it's elegant and natural, and nothing like how the professionals Mom hires to do our hair and makeup for campaign functions make me look.

"Okay..." Shay claps her hands together, spinning on her heel and marching toward the bed where three outfit choices are laid out. "We have..."

She holds out outfit number one; a red bodycon minidress that would show more of my ass than cover it. I scrunch my nose, and she tosses it over her shoulder to the floor. Number two isn't much better; a violet low-cut top with the V so far down you'd be able to see my belly button. She sighs when I shake my head, the top meeting the same fate as the dress.

When she holds up choice number three, I huff, "Really?"

She grins, shaking the spider web out in her hand. Because that's what it is—a contraption made to snare and trap and looks painful to be caught in, and it only has enough lace to cover nipples and what I hope is also the crotch area. Holding the strips of fabric against herself, she wiggles her eyebrows.

"Don't you want to be prepared if he, ya know..." She gyrates her hips and hums something that sounds a lot like Tom Jones "Sex Bomb."

"I'm not putting out on the first date, Shay." I scoff, pushing from my chair to grab the *underwear* and add it to the *over-my-dead-body-am-I-wearing-that* pile. I push her onto my bed, and she groans theatrically, telling me I'm a lost cause.

I bend down and drag over the extra-large suitcase she brought over last night, filled with what—if I didn't already know better—could be her entire wardrobe. Riffling through the clothes, I try to find something that won't make me look like a stripper.

"Do you know where he's taking you?" Shay asks, swinging her legs around to lie down on her stomach, chin resting in her hands as she watches me go through the suitcase.

I shake my head. "Nope, he just said to be comfy."

"Comfy? What the hell does *comfy* mean? Oh—oh—" She stretches her hand out and waves it at the side of my head at a yellow top in my hands. "That would be perfect. It would go with your eyes and hair. Sunshine personified." I hand her the top and continue looking for bottoms to go with it. "What about those dark jeans?" she asks, pointing to a pair of jeans that had fallen out of the case. "And you could pair them with your Chucks? The ones with the platform sole?"

"That could work," I say, finally happy with something that isn't too revealing or just isn't me.

Shay hops off my bed and whirls my chair around, tapping the backrest for me to sit. Brushing a wide-toothed comb along the length of my hair, she creates the beach wave I love so much but can never quite manage myself. My hair isn't one thing or another, more like a cascade of curls that have a life of their own and don't like to be told what to do. But when Shay gets her hands on it, it could be used in an advert for shampoo or something. The girl is seriously talented.

Once she finishes, I duck into the bathroom, quickly pulling on the clothes and brushing my teeth. Shay wolf whistles when I open the door and walk over to the full-length mirror, admiring her hard work.

"Damn, Morgs, you look so fucking hot. Where were you hiding this body?" she asks and slaps my butt. I blush, taking in my reflection one last time before grabbing my coat and handbag and walking downstairs with five minutes to spare.

The sound from Teddy's Mustang outside is almost as loud as Shay's squeal as she runs to the front door and waits for the bell to ring. I want to puke. My heart is hammering so hard I wouldn't be surprised if it punched a hole through my chest and it squelched on the floor. Shay, however, looks like she's about to wet herself with excitement as she flings the door open before the first chime of the bell finishes.

"Well, aren't you punctual?" she coos, leaning against the doorjamb and shamelessly checking him out. "And you scrub up well, Teddy Bear."

"Teddy Bear? Really, Shay? You know I'm twenty, not a kid?"

"I do, but I like it," she says, standing at her full height, which is pretty tall for a girl. Setting her hands on her hips, she puts on her best authoritative voice as she warns, "Now, ground rules, pretty boy. I expect you to bring my girl home no later than eleven... actually, twelve. But that's the latest."

Teddy steps forward, the corners of his lips turning up as he towers over her. "Is Ana ready?"

"I'm here," I say, joining the pair in the doorway. Shay spins, grinning ear-to-ear as her eyes bounce between Teddy and me.

"Fuck, Ana, you look..." Teddy's eyes dance down my body, staring at the tight-fitted top peeking through my unbuttoned jacket. He takes another step closer, bypassing Shay, and slips his hand under the coat where he rests it on my waist. Dropping his head, he kisses my cheek and whispers, "Un-fucking-believable."

I feel hot and tingly all over. Surely, this isn't how dates are meant to start. I thought they were meant to be awkward and unsure and stealing glances at each other. At least that's how I'm feeling, but Teddy appears to be his usual confident self, as he's completely unaware of how his large hand is currently burning through my clothes and straight to my skin.

"Bye, you two. See you when you get home," Shay says, almost pushing me out of my own home.

"You'll still be here?" I ask, glancing over my shoulder. I assumed she'd be leaving now too.

"Uh-huh, got to make sure he doesn't take advantage of the fact your parents aren't home."

"Your folks aren't here?" Teddy asks, eyeing Shay from the porch. He turns to me and smirks. "You sure she needs to stay?"

Maybe not. Maybe you could instead of her.

Shay widens her stance, planting her feet firmly in the doorway.

"Looks like she's not going anywhere." I laugh, relief as well as disappointment dripping into my stomach.

Teddy chuckles and leads me toward his car, his hand on my lower back. Opening the passenger door, he calls out to Shay as he helps me inside,

"Have a good night, cockblocker."

Chapter Ten

Morgana

When I ask Teddy where he's taking me, he mimes locking his lips and throwing away a key.

"Just tell me!" I laugh. "I hate surprises."

"Really? I love them." He turns on a playlist of old rock bands and joins the freeway. "Good thing we don't have that far to go then, huh?"

What's within driving distance that won't take a while to get to? The beach isn't miles away, nor is the arcade—although I suck at all those games, so I hope it's not there. We've not been in the car for long when we pull off the freeway and eventually into a parking lot. Looking up at the building, it's the last place I'd have thought he would plan a first date.

"The planetarium?" I ask, craning my neck to take in the dome-shaped building lit up in blues and greens. "I didn't know it was open so late."

Not that eight p.m. is late or anything.

"Tonight they are," Teddy says, finding a space and shutting off the engine. He grabs two glossy tickets from the cupholder and fans them in my direction. I scan the information printed in black ink and look up with eyes so wide I swear they could fall out of my head.

Roger Waters presents The Wall.

"You got these for me?" I ask, fingering the corner of a ticket. Then I frown because— "What is it?"

Teddy chuckles. "A laser show—I've been to a few back home and they are epic. It's a light show in time to an album. Creating the story to the lyrics, but with lasers and sometimes holograms like they're doing tonight." He taps on the small *hologram* in italic text. "After you said you loved seventies rock, I thought you'd enjoy this."

I can only stare at Teddy. This is the sweetest thing anyone has ever done for me.

"It's pretty cool, too, because in multiple states around the U.S., planetariums are playing this show at the same time." He unlocks his phone and pulls up the Twitter app, typing in a hashtag and searching. He shifts, leaning over the center console and scrolling through his feed. "See? Right now, some dude in Arizona is getting ready to watch it, and it's six p.m. This guy"—he points to another post—"he's in Anchorage right now, and that's what? Four hours behind us? So, when this starts, we're all going to be watching the same thing together. It's insane."

I surprise myself by pressing my lips to his. It's short and light, but I still feel it all the way to my toes.

"Thank you," I whisper as I pull back, but his hand curls through my hair and brings us close. His mouth is back on mine, his tongue swiping along the crease, wanting access. I open, and he delves in, one flick, then another against my tongue before breaking the kiss.

"You ready?"

We walk to the ticket stand, our hands by our sides, yet so close that if I stretched out my fingers, I could touch him. I want to feel my hand in his, but it's too soon, right? Teddy smiles at the woman, handing over our tickets, then guides me to the concession stand.

"Burger or hotdog?" he asks, looking at the menu board hanging on the back wall. "I'm not sure about the food quality here, but if it's shit, we can find somewhere to eat after?"

"Oh, no, it's fine. I'll have a hotdog, please."

He nods and orders our food and a couple of sodas from the guy behind the counter. I offer to pay, but he bats my hand away, tossing some dollar bills on the desk and ushering me to find our seats.

The planetarium's main room—a domed amphitheater with a pitch-black roof used for their standard daytime showing of stars and planets—is filled with excited Pink Floyd fans slowly filling the rows circling a massive platform in the center that has a thin layer of smoke misting across it.

"This is us here," Teddy says, gesturing toward our seats with this soda cup. I shimmy through the row, smiling at an older couple wearing matching retro t-shirts with the band's logo.

"I love your shirt."

"Thank you, sweetheart. My John here bought it on our first date." She smiles fondly at the man sitting beside her. "His excellent taste in music made him a keeper."

Her husband picks up her hand and brings it to his lips. "Best ten bucks I ever spent."

I grin and sink into the oversized recliner. "If I forget to tell you, I had a really great time tonight."

Teddy's smile falls as I take a big gulp of my soda, slowly sucking on the straw as his eyes heat. I let the thin plastic linger between my lips and he groans, pushing his tongue into his cheek.

"Ana," Teddy growls, his fists clenching against the armrest like he's trying to stop himself from reaching out, but before he can say another word, he's knocked forward as some guy behind bangs against his seat.

"Sorry, dude," he slurs, and I face the front, hiding my smile as Teddy mutters not to worry about it. It might have been small, but being the one to tease Teddy is exhilarating.

When the hall fills, the lights dim, and smoke machines flare up, spurting fog into the crowd as the gentle melody of the introduction to "In the Flesh?" quietly fills the room, followed by the thudding interruption of distorted guitars and organ notes. Goosebumps scatter across my arms, the hairs rising as I am swept up in the music, just like everyone else here. Beams of lights scatter all around us, the blues, greens, and yellows illuminating the faces in the audience, all filled with the same awestruck expression.

The rock opera might be an acquired taste, the music and lyrics often dark at times, but it's a piece of rock history, and nothing like it exists.

In my opinion.

As the intro fades and the lyrics begin, an old-school rocker's hologram appears on the platform, holding onto a mic and singing the haunting words as the story plays out before us. My hands are wrapped tightly around the handrails of my seat, my food and drink forgotten, and I steal a glance at Teddy from the corner of my eye, double taking when I notice he's watching... me.

"What?" I mouth, my voice drowned out by the song.

He smiles and leans closer, his lips brushing against the shell of my ear. "You're singing."

I recoil and vehemently shake my head. "I was not."

I totally was.

I can tell he's laughing, although I can't hear it. He licks his lips, and my eyes follow. Moving to my ear again, he loudly says, "You have no idea how beautiful you look right now. I can't stop staring at you. You're more mesmerizing than the show." The vibrations from his words tickle my ear, and the goosebumps on my skin are there for a whole other reason.

The needle slides from the vinyl when side two has finished playing. Skip's breathing shallowed long ago, and I stare at my brother, fast asleep on his stomach on my bedroom floor, while I sit, legs stretched in front of me, against the foot of my bed. We'd listen to old vinyl records whenever our mom and dad were away on "business trips" on a player Skip bought at a yard sale. The thing looked like an old suitcase and was kept under his bed for safekeeping.

"Enjoying it so far?" Teddy asks, and I open my eyes, the memory of another life disappearing.

"I just... I can't... I have no words," I beam, my cheeks hurting from the non-stop smiling.

"Do you want anything? I'm going to run to the bathroom."

I shake my head, and he pauses like he wants to say something, glancing between my eyes and lips, but instead nods once and politely squeezes out of the row. My shoulders sag as I watch him climb the stairs and out of the auditorium.

"What do you think of the show, honey?" the woman with the vintage shirt asks.

"Oh, I love it. I can't stop singing along with them. I'm just glad the music's loud enough that you can't hear me."

She laughs. "I wish that were the case for my John here. He keeps thinking his knees are a drum kit and won't stop tapping along." She elbows her husband in the ribs lightly.

"I've always told you, Maureen, I was meant to be in a band."

"Yeah, a rubber band, maybe."

He laughs and pulls her in for a kiss. Is this what all relationships are meant to be like? Teddy's mom and dad have no problem showing each other they care in public, and this couple, sitting next to a stranger, have no trouble either. I think... I want that too.

"How long have you been married?" I ask.

Maureen taps her lip thoughtfully. "Oh, it will be forty-two years this December."

"Oh wow, congratulations."

"What about you? How long have you and your boyfriend been together?"

I flush pink, my eyes darting to the ground. "Erm, this is our first date."

"Oh, sweetheart, did you hear that?" Maureen says, turning to elbow her husband again. "He took her to the same show we saw live in concert for their first date."

"Sorry, ma'am, can I get in?" Teddy asks, appearing behind the couple, his arms tucked behind his back. They stand, and he shuffles in, grinning wide, as he towers above me. "Gotcha something."

From behind his back, he holds up a vintage Pink Floyd band tee, and my heart takes off, galloping uncontrollably as I look up into the dark eyes of the man who's quickly making me fall for him. Harder and faster than I thought possible.

"Oh, sweetheart, look." Maureen coos at her husband from behind

Teddy. "He took a leaf out of your book."

Teddy turns to the older couple and smiles. "That I did, ma'am. But I don't think my girl will look half as good as you."

He glances back at me and winks.

Maureen laughs. "Oh, you cheeky charmer. So much like my John when he was your age."

Teddy sits back down as I quickly tug the shirt over my head, pulling the material taut in front of me and looking down at the image.

"I love it. Thank you so much."

"You're welcome," he replies.

I run my hand over the shirt and glance back to find Teddy watching me again. It feels like the air is being sucked out of my lungs as our gazes lock, and I bite on the corner of my lip. Teddy's eyes dart to my mouth, his nostrils flaring a little as he swallows roughly. I release my lip as the house lights flicker, people quickly taking to their seats as part two is about to start. Just as the lights dim, Teddy's hand slips into mine. We may now be shrouded in darkness, but I feel like a spotlight is directly shining where our hands are joined. I'm that transfixed on something so simple that I don't notice when he leans over the armrest separating our seats and presses his lips to my ear.

"Ana?"

"Yes?" I croak, but I'm not sure any sound comes out at all.

"You're missing the show." He laughs, his warm breath ghosting down my neck as he moves his head slightly, and I shiver when his lips make contact with a spot I had no idea felt so good behind my ear.

What did he say?

I was missing what?

Oh.

Right.

The *show*.

I snap back in my seat as Teddy's mouth twitches with humor, his hand never letting go of mine. I glance down again, loving how it feels, and when I look back to the platform where lights are fighting, dancing, and strobing, I can't make out what they are meant to be. All I can think about—all I can feel—is Teddy's fingers playing with mine. The scorch of heat where we're connected. I don't want it to ever end. If tonight is the only chance I get to be with Teddy Grant, I don't think my teenage heart could handle it. One night and a few kisses is all it's taken for me to become utterly obsessed with the boy next door, and now I've had a taste, I don't want to give it up.

Chapter Eleven

Teddy

March

The auto shop has been the busiest it's ever been, not that I can complain. I've learned more from Dad than I would have if I stayed in Phoenix and got an apprenticeship with some run-of-the-mill mechanic. Ana's studying has ramped up too, so between car rides to and from school, hot and heavy secret make-out sessions around the corner from our houses on the weekends, and late-night texting, we haven't managed a second date. A few times, though, I've snuck over and climbed up to her bedroom window, all Romeo and Juliet style, holding her in my arms as we watch a movie while her bitch of a mom sleeps. I didn't think that would bother me as much as it does. I mean, sure, I'm enjoying the fuck out of our over-the-clothes action in my car, but my balls are the bluest they've ever been, and that has to be some medical issue, right?

But it's more than that. I've never wanted to spend as much of my free time as possible with a girl quite like the way I do with Ana. I know she feels the same way too; I feel it with every kiss. I can also see the guilt eating her up as we try to hide what we mean to each other from her parents. Her desire to keep her mom happy while taking something for herself is causing her added stress. So while we are still testing out whatever this is between us, I'll keep being her secret. I know Ana isn't doing it because she's embarrassed about us.

The promise to treat her like a queen still rings in my head too. Every time my hand slips to the waistband of her skirt or her leggings or jeans, it's like the hem is laced with electric fencing. Not that Ana's noticed my turmoil as I snap my hand away and thrust it into my pocket, keeping the damn thing away from temptation. I know she wants more. The whimpers that used to escape her every time our lips touch have morphed into little moans. Her body now migrates effortlessly to mine, either from across the center console—so it wouldn't take much to pull her over and onto my lap—or damn near lying on top of me when we're on her bed. But I'm trying to be good, damn it.

"You want to go into town tonight? Try to bag some college girls?" Harry asks, finishing the decal for some skater dude who wanted flames running along the side of his car. Fucking ugly, but whatever.

"Nah, man. Busy," I say, winding jumper cables around my arm before taking them to a wall filled with hooks.

"What's her name?"

I pause, my hand mid-air. "What makes you assume there's someone?"

"You never come out anymore, and you've stopped telling me all about your dirty antics."

"I never told you things to begin with."

He huffs. "You didn't have to. It's like a sixth sense. Plus, your mood changes the day after you've railed a girl to within an inch of her life." He winks. "I'm the same way, dude."

"You're an idiot," I say, and because I want him to drop it, I add, "She's just someone from my neighborhood."

"I knew it," he exclaims, far too interested in my sex life. Honestly, why do people care so much? Him, my parents? It's weird. "You fucked her yet?"

I miss the hook, the cables clattering to the ground. "What is wrong with you?"

"That's a no, then." Harry laughs, running a clean cloth along the wheel arch. "She not putting out?"

"Fuck you, man."

Harry whistles low. "You are a cranky boy when you're not getting your dick wet. That's a shame. You know those "girl next door" types are always secretly filthy sluts. Wonder why she's not—"

I round on him, forgetting all about the messed-up jump leads and pushing him against the white Camaro with the ugly flames. "Say that again. I dare you."

A loud beeping has me stepping back. Customers don't need to see this shit. A cute little lime green Bug pulls into the forecourt, coming to a screeching halt, and then Shay pops her head out of the driver's window.

"Teddy Bear!" she sings, and I groan.

"Shay." I nod in greeting as she flings her door wide. Gently, the passenger side opens, and then my girl steps out, a shy blush dotting her cheeks as she offers a small wave.

I stalk toward her, my face splitting in two as I grip her hips and look down at her. She drags her gaze up the length of my overalls, heat blazing in her green eyes.

"Hey, baby," I say, pressing my lips to hers. "This is a nice surprise."

"Shay's car needs servicing," she says. Her eyes widen as she hears the innuendo. "I mean..."

I laugh, kissing her again because I can't help it. "I know what you mean."

"And who else would be better to do that than my BFF's boyfriend?" Shay says, throwing her arms around both our shoulders.

Boyfriend.

I tense.

"Oh shit, I messed up, didn't I?" Shay says, wincing at Ana, who pales. "Well, this is awkward. I'm just going to..." Dropping her arms, she turns to Harry, who has been watching the whole time. "Hi, I'm Shay..."

"I'm sorry about her." Ana grimaces. "I don't know why she would say that."

"It's fine," I say, dropping her hips and creating space between us. It doesn't feel fine, though. That word is like a chain tied tightly around my lungs. But wasn't I just complaining that I didn't get to see her as much as I wanted? It's just, the word *boyfriend* means relationship and... and... fuck. I need air. I take another step away from Ana, hurt flashing in her eyes as I thumb over to Shay. "I better get her signed in. If I knew she was going to come earlier, I'd have had her paperwork all ready for her. You guys gonna be okay to get home? I'm going to have to stay late now to get her into the system so I can't drive you back."

Fuck, I'm a dick when I'm freaking out.

Ana's face falls, and I hate that I'm the cause of it. But I can't be around her right now.

"Oh, right. Yeah, erm, okay. Don't worry about it," she says with more bite than I'm used to. "Shay, I'll be outside."

I want to stop her from leaving, but she's out and around the corner before my mouth has time to catch up to my brain. I sigh and drag myself over to where Harry is flirting his ass off with Shay, and grab a clipboard and pen, holding them out.

"Put your details here; number, address, service history, and Harry will start on it tomorrow," I say, thrusting the board into her hands. "Harry, I'm going to call Ms. Smith and let her know she can collect her car. You good here?"

Harry grins and nods enthusiastically as I head to my dad's office to make the call. I really should check on Ana, apologize to her for being a jackass, but I'm not in the mood to talk. At least not until I get my head straight.

Tossing the baseball upward, I contemplate letting the damn thing smack me in the face. It's the least I deserve too. Even Harry—the King of Sluts—said he understood why I was so hung up over Ana, saying if he had met her first, he'd have fucked her so hard she'd have trouble walking. That made me want to crash my fist into his face and knock him out cold. The thought of my Ana fucking him, or anyone else really, makes my blood boil... Yeah, I'm so far gone for this girl I hadn't realized it until today. No point in even trying to deny it. So why did "boyfriend" make me want to run with my tail between my legs and hide?

The ball thuds into my hand, and I spin it in the air again. I never catch feelings. I mean, I always duck out when a girl gets too close—hence the whole Brittany bullshit—and being on this end sucks ass. Catching the ball, I set it on my comforter and grab my phone.

Teddy: Can we talk?

Ana: If Shay freaked you out earlier and you want to stop seeing me, you can say that over text.

Shit.

Teddy: I'm sorry, okay? Yeah, I freaked, and I shouldn't have. Please come over. I want to see you.

I stare at the message, and then a few others, the words bold and black, and how was it not obvious before?

She doesn't reply, and I get the sinking feeling I've fucked everything up before it's really even begun. Lying back down, I resume tossing the baseball until a soft knock sounds at my closed bedroom door.

"Come in," I yell, not taking my eyes off the red stitching.

"Hey." Ana's beautiful face pops around the door, and I turn, narrowly missing my head as I forget all about the ball above me. "Your mom let me in. That wasn't awkward at all trying to explain why I was here to see her son."

Scrambling off the bed, I make the two steps needed to open the door fully and slide my hands into her thick blonde hair.

"I'm glad you're here," I say, my relief palpable as we lock eyes. I press my lips to hers, then link our hands together, kicking the door closed and tugging her to my bed. The concept is still foreign. And even though I always sneak into her place, I guess I've been subconsciously trying to avoid her being here. But as she sits, legs tightly pressed together, nothing has ever felt more right. I join her on the bed, shifting back against the headrest, and pat the space beside me. She eyes the gap, but remains still. I wrap my arm around her waist and haul her around as she squeaks until she's nestled between my legs.

I can tell she's nibbling her lip, and I reach forward and pull it out with my thumb.

"I'm sorry I was an ass earlier," I say, burying my nose in the crook of her neck. "I—"

"Freaked out?"

I exhale a laugh, her hair fluttering against my breath. "Yeah."

"I never told Shay that you were my boyfriend," she says, shifting out of my hold and avoiding my gaze.

"I know." Her eyes snap up, and I brush my fingers along her jaw. "Well, I didn't *know*, but I thought that would be a conversation we'd have before you said it. You know?"

I drop my hold on her face and cringe. How many times can I use the word "know" in one sentence?

"Would it really be so bad?" she asks. "To be my boyfriend?"

"Nah, it's not that." I sag back against the pillows and pick up her hand, playing with her fingers. "It's just that I've never been someone's *boyfriend* before, and I don't think I'd be very good at it."

She chuckles. "I've never been someone's girlfriend before."

"I'm not good enough for you, Ana." The words oddly feel like a weight has been lifted. "I don't want to stay in Connecticut. I—"

She puts the tips of her fingers over my mouth. "I'm not exactly expecting a lifelong commitment from you, Teddy. I'm not asking for you to fall in love with me." She sucks her bottom lip between her teeth, trying to hide the mirth behind a small smile. "I'm only seventeen, for crying out loud. And I know that high school romances rarely work out. I'm not naïve. But it would be nice to be with you... officially... for however long this"—she waves a hand between us—"lasts."

I swallow, mulling over her words as she reaches up and brushes back my shaggy hair, my cap long discarded somewhere on the bed.

"But if that's too much, I understand."

I don't have to think about it to know it's not too much. This girl has managed to dig her way into my head and change my thoughts on pretty much everything—exclusivity, dating, girlfriends. Everything I might want to try with *her*.

"So I'd be like your senior fling or something?"

She shrugs, biting the smile growing at the corner of her mouth. "If that's less scary for you."

That kind of sounds perfect. I never want to hurt Ana, and knowing I'll leave in the near future would inevitably hurt us both. With this "expiration date" over our heads, both of us understanding this will run its course, it makes it easy to say yes.

I push off the bed and drop to the floor, taking her hand in mine. "Ana, will you be my girlfriend?"

She laughs and tries to pull out of my hold. "You're an idiot. Get up."

"You didn't answer me."

"Okay, fine. Yes, yes, I will."

I launch myself at her, pushing her onto the mattress and blanketing her body with mine. Our lips meet in a clash of teeth and tongues and moaning, and my hand trails down her side. She wraps her arms around my shoulders, squirming beneath me and pressing my hard cock against her hip. I rub against her, the feel of her under me incredible, and I could blow from this alone. It's been me and my hand for far too long.

She pulls back, giving my shoulders a gentle push, and I stop rotating my hips. "Is everything..."

"I want you to touch me," she whispers, and my eyes blow wide.

"What?"

"Please," she says, the blue in her eyes replaced with green. "Will you touch me?"

"Are you sure?"

She nods. I fall onto my side and slowly roll her shirt up, exposing her stomach littered with goosebumps. My fingers trace her skin, her muscles jumping under my touch. So damn responsive.

"Tell me to stop if it's too much, okay?"

Again, she nods.

I kiss her stomach, brushing lightly against her skin, before moving up to her lips again while flicking the button on her jeans, trying to remain hyperaware of any changes that could be a sign that she's uncomfortable. There's nothing but unadulterated lust spilling from her as her tongue matches mine for dominance, and fighting myself to slow down is nearly impossible.

I break the kiss, moving to my knees to tug her jeans down gently, leaving her panties on—the design similar to the ones I've seen before—and pull them over her feet, tossing them to my floor. I sit back and take in her long, lean legs right up to her panties. Pushing to her elbows, she extends her arm and hesitantly goes for my jeans.

"Can I... touch you too?"

I grin and undo the button. "Whenever you want, baby."

Leaning up, she kisses me as she pushes the denim over my ass to my knees and I wriggle the rest down my legs. She giggles against my lips as I struggle, finally relenting and detaching my face from hers to kick my pants away. Lying down, her legs part slightly, and I slot in between them, my painfully aching cock lining up with her core that I so badly want to be inside. One day. If she'll let me.

I roll to my side again, hooking one of her legs over my hip, opening her wide. I run my hand up the inside of her thigh, getting closer and closer to her hot pussy. Her hand covers mine when I get to the waistband.

"Can we keep them on?" I raise my brows questioningly. "Just for right now? I've not, erm, *landscaped*."

Her face turns a brilliant shade of scarlet, and she tries to look away. I push back the curls from her forehead and press my fingers under her chin, urging her to kiss me.

"Of course, baby." Moving to her jaw, I kiss along the sharp line toward her ear. "But you never need to be embarrassed around me." I give her pussy a light tap over her panties. "And just so you know... I'd want you any way you'd let me. Now, let me take care of you."

She makes this noise between a moan and a whimper as I shift her panties to the side and run my finger along her slit. She's soaked, absolutely fucking soaked, and I love it. Never has a girl been *this* aroused for me, and if I do say so myself, I'm so fucking proud right now. She shudders, fingers digging into my forearm as I do it again, lingering for a beat on her clit, and applying a little pressure.

"Teddy," she pants, her hips bucking in search of more. I shift against the leg flung over my hip, my dick pressing into it, relieving the ache. She's not moved to touch me since asking, and I won't push it, as much as I'd love to direct her hand to my cock. She will get to it when she's ready. But it doesn't take her long, especially when I circle her clit again more firmly. Her delicate fingers dip into my boxer shorts, gazing my treasure trail, and my cock twitches in anticipation.

"Tell me what to do," she whispers, reaching farther in.

I tug my boxers down with my free hand to sit under my ass and turn her hand face up. With my fingers slicked in her arousal, I brush them over my shaft before running them along her palm, then guide her to circle my cock. I groan as her warm fingers envelop me, and I thrust upward, loving the feeling of it being her hand touching me rather than my own.

"Just pump your hand," I breathe, and she drags it tentatively up and down my cock, making my eyes roll back. "*Yeeess.* Like that. A little harder. That's it."

She's a quick study, giving me what she might think is a shit first handjob, but for me, it's maybe the best one I've had in a while. I want to savor it. Lie back and enjoy the feel of her hand around my dick that's coated in her. I move my hand back to her, rubbing around her swollen clit and down before pressing one finger inside her. She's so fucking tight. I cannot wait to fuck her. Because I will fuck her. I will take all of her firsts because, the very moment I touched her, they became mine.

Her hand speeds up, and her thigh over my leg begins to shake.

"Oh God," she breathes.

"That's it, baby."

Now, let's see if I can get her to gasp. I curl my finger deep inside her, and I'm rewarded with the most beautiful sound. I want more, I *need* more. Her breathy little moans are fucking addictive.

"Oh no," she pants, and I dig my face into her shoulder, smiling as I pump a finger fast in and out of her. "Teddy, fuck."

Her walls contract tightly around me as she says my name over and over, burying her head in my shoulder as she shudders, muffling her cries. Her hand moves faster and hurls me past the finish line, my cock shooting over her fist and making her gasp. I want to roar through my release, the feeling of my orgasm making my whole body shudder with ecstasy, but with my mom in the house, I groan into her skin, and pant through my orgasm instead. Ana's fingernails dig crescents into my arm, but I don't care. She could make me bleed, and I still wouldn't care.

Because Morgana Adler already has her claws so deep inside me, there is nothing I can do about it.

Chapter Twelve

Morgana

April

Shay's acting weird. I swear she's giving me the silent treatment—even though she says she's fine and we're good—but considering she *loves* to talk, she's lying through her teeth. It's unnerving, walking to school, arm in arm with someone who feels stiffer than a body with rigor mortis. The little huffs she releases when she thinks I'm not paying attention are a dead giveaway too.

"Teddy couldn't take us today?" she asks, and I don't miss the slight hiss in her words.

"No, he had a customer dropping their car off early, so he needed to be in before seven."

She *harrumphs*. "I'm surprised he can get through the day without his morning dose of his girlfriend."

"Hey, it's thanks to you that we even decided to label us," I say, lightly nudging her in the ribs playfully.

"Shoulda kept my big mouth shut."

I halt, yanking my arm from hers. "Okay, what is wrong with you? You're acting like a bitch. Do you not like Teddy or something?"

"It's not that," she replies.

"Then what?" Her jaw hardens as she stares at the ground. Snapping, I say, "Shay?"

She groans, tilting her head back to look at the sky. "I feel like I'm losing my best friend, okay."

That wasn't what I expected.

I recoil, my eyebrows disappearing into my curls. "What?"

She sighs, sounding exasperated, and throws her hands up. "You know what? Forget it."

Turning her back, she storms down the sidewalk toward school. I jog to catch up with her, grabbing her shoulder and pulling her to a stop.

"Shay?" I plead, not sure what else to say. We've never had to deal with one of us having a boyfriend and changing our dynamic.

"Ever since you started dating Teddy, it's like you have no time for me." Her eyes widen as she realizes what she's just said, and she grabs my wrist, frantically shaking her head from side to side. "Not that I'm not happy for you and expect you to spend all your time with me, but..."

"I've hardly seen Teddy either, Shay. Most of my time after school is spent studying. We've got our exams soon."

"Doesn't stop you sneaking off to find time with him, though." She slaps her hand over her mouth like she can't control her snarky comments. "I don't mean to sound like an asshole, Morgs. Believe me, I've seen how happy he makes you. He seems really good for you, but..."

"But?" I prompt.

"But I never see you anymore. Like after school or whatever. I miss hanging out. Just us two."

Is that really what's happened? Have I been choosing Teddy over Shay any chance I could? Oh God, I have. Suddenly, I throw my arms over her shoulders, catching her off guard before she loops hers around my back, burying her head into my neck. I squeeze her tight, hating the sickly feeling that's made itself present deep in my stomach.

I've been in my own bubble where it's me and Teddy and no one else. When I'm not with him, we text or call. When I'm not with him, I miss him. He's the first thing I think about in the morning and the last thing at night. All the sneaking around is getting tiring, though, and the constant thrum of fear and adrenaline has my stomach tied in knots. We're going to get caught. I can sense it. She might not have come out and directly asked me if I'm dating Teddy, but Mom's hurtful comments about his family, or her over-the-top tutting whenever she sees Teddy's car drive past have been happening more often lately, too often for it to be a coincidence. It's like she hopes if she mentions her dislike enough, it may rub off on me. She even started monitoring what I do at night too, like she is a night warden at a prison, checking in my cell at different times between dinner and lights out. But when she's safely tucked up in her room for the rest of the night, Teddy climbs up and through my window. Things have... progressed. He can't stop touching me whenever we're together, and I'm just as bad. He's been a perfect gentleman, going at my pace—which I love—but I'm ready for more. Ready for something that's been circling my mind ever since I watched him.

"I'm so sorry, Shay," I say, giving her one last squeeze and letting go to see her face. "I never meant to put him before you."

"I know that. I'm just feeling neglected, that's all. It's stupid." She shrugs and manages to lift the corners of her lips, downplaying what an awful friend I've been.

"It's not stupid. It's just..." I pause, biting my lip.

"It's new and exciting, and you want to spend time with him, I get it," she says, filling in the gap I couldn't quite manage to myself. Trying not to laugh, she says, "Just remember that when I get a boyfriend, I'm gonna ditch you all the time."

My gut twists, a new knot adding to the numerous others. I'm torn in two. I want to spend time with my best friend, I do, but I want to be with Teddy more. And even though I love Shay to the ends of the earth, Teddy makes me feel free and elated and someone I never knew I could be.

"Oh God," I inhale, and Shay's eyes flash with concern.

"What?"

"I think I'm in love with him, Shay."

Her smile is genuine this time, lighting up her whole face, and while relief washes over me that she isn't mad anymore, I somehow feel worse.

"*Eeeck!* I can't believe my little girl is growing up."

"It's fast, though, right? Like I can't love him... it hasn't been long enough." I turn and pace a few steps before spinning and pacing back. Shaking my hands out by my sides, I suck in a breath. I am so close to a panic attack. "This is bad, this is bad, this is bad."

Shay's hands land hard on my shoulders. "Calm the fuck down, Morgana. What's going on?"

"He's leaving Shay."

"What? When?"

I rub at my temples. "I don't know."

"Okay, babe, you're making no sense."

I groan. "He's going back to Phoenix at some point. And I'm going to

Boston." Shay purses her lips in annoyance, but lets me continue without a word about that place. "I told him I didn't expect forever from him. He's dead set on moving back to Phoenix, and let's face it, I'm only seventeen, but..."

I stop talking as Shay bobs her head from side to side, wrinkling her nose. "Yup, that checks out."

"What does?" I ask.

"You're head over heels for the boy."

"Thanks. That helps a lot," I snap, harsher than I meant to. "This wasn't meant to happen, Shay. Mom's making it so hard. She is one step away from demanding to check my phone."

"Bet it's pretty hot, though? All the sneaking around?"

"It was." She lifts her brows and offers a knowing smirk. Rubbing my stomach, I say, "Okay, it still is, but I swear it's giving me an ulcer."

She laughs. "Okay, calm down. It's not a big deal." She releases her hold on my shoulders, and I notice how strong she's been gripping me, the bite from her fingers releasing a dull ache that I rub away, and stare at her incredulously. "Are you going to tell him you *looooove* him?"

"Nope," I say defiantly.

She frowns. "What? Why not? When are you seeing him next?"

"I was supposed to be seeing him tonight. Mom and Dad have a campaign thing, so I can finally be out of my cage for a few hours unsupervised," I murmur, but after how Shay's been feeling, I need to put her first. Even if it's shitty of me to use her as an excuse to avoid the boy I've accidentally fallen in love with and am too scared to tell him. "But I'm going to cancel. You were right; we need to spend more time together."

"Oh no, you are *not* using me as a cop-out to avoid your boyfriend just because you moved way past catching feelings and developed a full-blown case of being so in love with the guy, it's sick."

My chest tightens, and I turn my best puppy-dog eyes on my best friend.

She huffs. "Okay, because it's you and I love you, you can use me. Your whole wounded puppy look is making me sad," she says, waving her hand around my face before sternly pointing her finger at me. "But this does not count as us 'spending time together.' This is a favor because you're freaking the fuck out for some weird reason and need to chill." She inhales excitedly, a salacious grin pulling at her mouth. "Oh, I could maybe score us some weed to chill you out?"

The school bell rings just in time to stop Shay from coming up with other stupid ideas. I slip my arm into hers, the both of us stepping in sync through the school gates.

"Yeah, that would be great. I come home, stinking of pot, and my mom bans me from seeing you. Right after she's done locking me in my room and throwing away the key when she finds out about Teddy," I say sarcastically. "Sign me right up."

Chapter Thirteen

Morgana

I t's late when I get home, the lights are out, and Mom and Dad are in their respective bedrooms asleep. Thinking about it, their two rooms side by side, connected by a shared bathroom, didn't seem weird when I was a child, but seeing how couples *can* be around each other, I'm starting to wonder why they even bother to stay together. They clearly don't like each other enough to sleep in the same bed.

Quietly, I close my bedroom door with a soft click and peel my denim jacket off, letting it drop to the floor. I didn't realize how much I've been missing Shay until she pointed out that we've barely hung out lately. Manicures, boba tea, and aimlessly walking around the mall was definitely what I needed to relax and calm down about the whole *love* thing. I'm being an idiot, mistaking lust for love. Just because I like spending time with him—all my time—doesn't mean I love him. It's just really strong lust... really, really strong.

I rub my eyes as I walk to the bathroom, moonlight filtering through the gap in the curtains, guiding me toward the light switch. A shiver races down my back, and the hairs on my arms rise as another shadow joins mine on the carpet. Adrenaline surges, making my legs feel like lead and as I try to scream, the noise is muffled by a hand plastering across my mouth. Panting through my nose, my breathing shallows and quickens as fear digs its sharp claws into me. We've gone over this, a fabricated—and, in my opinion—ridiculous scenario, where someone trying to hurt my father during his campaign may potentially do so by targeting his family. Maybe I watch too many movies where that means kidnap, but as the hand tightens around my jaw, images of vans with blackened windows, rope biting into my wrists, and newspapers with today's date showcased on a ransom video flood my imagination.

It's real. It's happening, and I can't remember a single thing the secret service or military or whatever his job was instructed to do in this event. I'm getting lightheaded, not getting enough oxygen to my brain, blanking my mind as the seconds tick by, robbing me of valuable time I can't afford to lose to escape this.

Think, Morgana, think!

I can free my arms. My assailant's grip—clearly a novice—is loose enough to wriggle free, and with a strength I don't possess in normal circumstances, I pull my arm forward and throw my elbow backward into my attacker's crotch. The hand around my face drops with a breathy *oomph,* and a knee thuds to the carpet.

I spin, scrambling backward to press against the wall, gulping in air and trying to create as much space between me and the shadowed figure. Blindly, I slap the wall, searching for the light.

"Fuck, baby, you got me right in my balls."

Light spills from the bathroom door as my fingers collide with the switch, illuminating Teddy, bent over, hands clutching his crotch and looking a little green. Relief is just as strong as the initial fright. My nerves are frayed, and my brain is whirling so fast it's taking what I have left not to burst into tears.

"What the hell, Teddy?" I whisper-yell, my voice shaky as I glance at the closed door, scared the scuffle may have woken my parents. My heart hammers against my ribs as I rub furiously against it. "You scared me half to death!"

"I wanted to surprise you," he groans, his other knee falling to the floor as he leans forward, pressing his head into the carpet and releasing a painful groan.

"I thought you were an attacker."

He turns his head, looking up with his dark eyes scrunched at the sides. "Why the hell would I be *an attacker?*"

"My father's campaign," I say with indignation.

He looks at me like I've got three heads, then groans again. He doesn't think my reaction was called for. He thinks this is an overreaction. Well, good. I'm glad he's in pain. But when he groans again, I suddenly feel awful. I want to check that he's okay, but he really did scare me.

"Fuck, Ana, I can't feel my left ball."

Oh, that isn't good.

"Are you okay?" I step forward, my hand reaching out to rub his back, but instead, he grabs my wrist and gives it a sharp tug. I whirl around as he pulls me to his knee, then slowly guides me to the floor, rolling us over, so I'm lying on my back, blanketed by his warmth above me. His eyes soften as he brushes his fingers through my curls, and I practically purr.

No, Morgana. Stay strong.

"Hey." He presses his lips to mine, but mine remains straight and motionless, my teeth digging into the flesh of my lower one as I demand my body not to react. I will not react. I will not sink into his kisses like I desperately want to. This behavior cannot be condoned, and he needs to know that.

He chuckles to himself, dotting kisses across my jaw, my cheeks, my nose. "C'mon, Ana Banana, don't be pissed. I'm the one who should be pissed. You elbowed me in the dick."

"You deserved it," I say, moving my head as he tries to take advantage of my lips parting and instead meets my chin. "I texted you saying I'd see you tomorrow. I didn't think you'd break into my room and attack me like that."

He pulls back, his arms bracketing my head, his eyes darting between mine. "Shit, I really scared you, didn't I?"

I nod while a mixture of embarrassment and calmness slowly replace my shock. He frowns, opening and closing his mouth as he thinks.

"I'm sorry."

"I'm sorry I elbowed you." I swallow thickly and brush my thumb over the bulge in his sweats. I look up, meeting his dark eyes, and bite my lower lip. He covers my hand with his, pushing firmly over his growing erection, and smirks.

"I am in a lot of pain," he says, the light from the bathroom making his eye shine mischievously.

I cock a brow. "I bet."

"I know how you could make it feel better." My pulse ricochets in my ears as he stretches his hand out, and his finger plays with my bottom lip. "But only if you—"

"I want to," I say, the high-pitched words tumbling out in a rush.

"Are you sure? I was only joking," he asks, brushing my curls from my face. I nod, my voice disappearing. "We don't have to do anything you're not ready for. I'm more than happy with your hand, baby—"

I cut him off, wrapping my trembling hand around his neck and tug him down, kissing him long and deep. He pulls away, a wide grin crossing his face.

His finger runs across my lips again. "I've been dying to get inside this mouth."

I feel like I could wretch, and not because I'll be gagging on his dick pretty soon. But as soon as his mouth slants back over mine and his hands go under my thighs, I melt into him. No longer nervous. He guides my legs to wrap around his waist before he slowly gets to his feet and carries me over to the bed.

Every touch is gentle, the way he lays me down, removes my shirt, and pulls down my pants, leaving me in my underwear. He ghosts his pointer finger down the center of my chest, from the hollow dip at my throat, between my breasts and stopping at my belly button. Resting a knee on the mattress, he tugs his Henley over his head, the muscles in his chest jumping under my gaze as he drops it, and it falls to the ground. When he deftly unbuttons his jeans, I squirm, his slow movements like a striptease. I can't stand it. I need to touch him.

But first...

"The door," I whisper, my eyes darting behind him briefly.

He looks over his shoulder. "You kinky girl. I have been wondering if you had a voyeurism kink since that day in the garage."

"Please don't talk about another girl sucking your dick when I'm just about to," I say with narrowed eyes. He grins cheekily. "What I meant was, can you lock the door?"

"Oh, right." He hops off the bed and locks it, coming straight back, his knees resting against the bottom of the mattress as his searing hot gaze rakes down my body. He squeezes his cock through his boxers, rolling his bottom lip between his teeth. "Just for the record, I know you're going to be so much better than anyone else."

Oh God, the pressure. I can't do this. I can't do this.

He climbs onto the bed and shuffles toward me, his thighs brushing mine as he crawls up either side of my legs. He leans down so we're chest to chest and kisses me. I moan, my anxiety downgrading slightly when his tongue slips past my lips and strokes softly over mine. I want more of him. I *need* more of him. His fingers thread into the waistband of my panties, and I tilt my hips upward, letting them slide under my ass and down my legs.

"I've been dreaming about what it would be like to have you come apart on my tongue," he says.

Erm, what? He wants to go down on me too? Is he serious? Not once did that cross my mind. Okay, maybe it did; it's not as if Shay is reserved when it comes to her sex life, but I've been so focused on being the one to go down on him, it sort of slipped my mind that he might want to return the favor. Shit.

I firmly push at his chest. "Can we... um... can we...?"

Urgh, why is this so embarrassing?

"What?" he asks, dropping his head to kiss my neck.

I slide a hand into his hair, holding him to my skin and using the opportunity of not having his eyes on me to ask, "Can we do it together?"

He stills, his hot breath billowing against my throat. "As in *69?*"

I shiver as his lips tickle me with those three words. I nod, the embarrassment clogging other words from getting out.

This is the perfect scenario. While I want to feel the hot flesh of his dick against my tongue and taste his heady flavor as he comes undone by my mouth, I am so not on his level. Where I've *never* done this before, he's most likely had a whole cheerleading squad worth of blowjobs. So, if he's busy *doing* me while I'm doing him... he won't be able to tell if I suck. And not in the good way.

His lips crash onto mine, demanding, possessing, devouring. Like my question was the key to unlocking something carnal inside him. He nips at my lips, tugging my lower one into his and sucking. "Where did you come from?" he asks, panting as he breaks away to look down at me. "We can do whatever you like."

He rolls to his side, and I sit up, watching him slide up the bed until his head rests on my pillow. "C'mon baby, get that pretty ass up here so you can sit on my face."

I can't help the laugh that bubbles out of me. "You're vulgar."

"Nah, baby, if I were vulgar, I would have said to get that pretty ass up here so I can tongue-fuck your cunt and make you come in my mouth, drenching my chin in your juices."

Thank goodness the bathroom light is dim enough to hide my scarlet face because Teddy Grant's mouth is filthy.

He grins salaciously and then leans over, gripping my thighs hard and taking me with him as he lies back down, shifting lower before positioning my legs on either side of his head, and my feet touch the headboard.

"Fuck, this view is beautiful."

And with that, he wraps both arms around my thighs, lifts his head, and swipes his tongue in one long lick up the length of my pussy. My head falls between my shoulders, my hand smacking his chest as I let out a low groan. This feels unbelievable, the warmth of his mouth against my skin making my eyes flutter shut. He moans, swirling his tongue around my clit, and I almost forget that I'm meant to have my mouth on him too. Eyeing his huge cock, I bend at the waist, lifting it from where it rests on his stomach with one hand as the other steadies myself by his hip. Tentatively, I bring it to my lips and release a stuttering breath. His cock jumps in my palm, and I smile before copying Teddy's first move, licking a line up the length of his impossibly hard and silky-smooth shaft.

His fingers dig into the muscles in my legs as I circle his crown, then take him fully into my mouth as far as I can. Which isn't as far as I want, so I push down farther and instantly regret it. Coughing, I splutter off him and wipe at my mouth as spit trickles down my chin.

"It's okay, Ana," Teddy says soothingly, rubbing the palm of his hand up my spine. "Don't force yourself."

"But—"

"It feels amazing. Just keep doing what you're doing."

Inhaling deep, I try again, smiling around his hard cock when I manage to get farther than before. The muscles in his legs jump and tense as I continue to suck him and lick him and tease him, loving every moan and groan I cause, the little vibrations going straight to my clit, sending wave after wave of pleasure through my body. I feel like I'm on fire, my arms and legs tingling with a sensation I've never felt before. I can't keep up with what I'm doing as I let Teddy slip out of my mouth and press my forehead to his thigh, my orgasm coming hard and fast as I buck against his face. Teddy's hands grip my waist, tugging me harder against his mouth, and rolling my hips so I'm damn near riding him as I come, biting my lip so hard I can taste blood to stop my screams. As the shock waves ease, I push up on an elbow, my hand bringing his cock back to my mouth as I greedily suck him back down, triggering my gag reflex, and Teddy kisses the inside of my leg to my knee.

"Fuck, Ana, keep doing that. Yes, just like that," he groans against my skin, his hips thrusting upward in time with my mouth. His finger lazily strokes around my sensitive clit, sometimes dipping back inside me, and I moan. He lightly bites my thigh, breathing hard through his nose. "Baby, I'm gonna come. Move now if—"

But I don't move. I swallow down every last drop of his hot cum, the taste a mixture between sweet and sour, and lick the length of his dick until he's all cleaned up. My name is like a prayer as he praises me, his hands still biting into my hips as he comes down from his high. Swinging my legs from his shoulders, I turn and nervously face him. His eyes are closed, his lips parted and turned upward, and his chest rising and falling with each deep inhalation.

This right here is what I've wanted for so long. Teddy blissed out and sated because of me.

His arms wind around my back, pulling me to his chest.

"Fuck, Ana. That was..." He chuckles and drags a hand down his face. "You sure that was your first time?"

I laugh, beaming with the compliment, and nuzzle into him, closing my eyes with a massive smile.

Chapter Fourteen

Morgana

"**M**orning, baby."

I stretch and look up into the beautiful dark eyes and lazy smile belonging to Teddy. He looks so handsome when he's just woken up. I smile back, tracing my finger around his abs as the sunlight spills through the open blinds, and he runs his hand down my back. Then everything comes back in a rush of ice-cold water.

The "almost" kidnap.

The unbelievable joint oral.

Falling asleep.

"Shit, Teddy," I gasp, flying upward and looking around the room. Our clothes are still in their small discarded piles at the bottom of my bed, my door is still locked, and the alarm clock says 9:30 a.m. "We fell asleep."

"Yeah," he says groggily, wiping the sleep from his eyes. "I guess we did. Gotta say, I've never woken up next to a girl before." He runs his gaze down my practically naked body, my bra the only item of clothing he never removed. His cock bobs against his stomach, and he reaches out for me. "C'mere, Ana."

I push back and shake my head. "No, Teddy, it's morning. You need to leave."

"Shit. What's the time?"

"Nine-thirty."

"Fuck." He springs from the bed and grabs his boxers. "Shit, Ana, I'm sorry."

"It's okay. Just hurry." I say, searching for a clean pair of pajamas and pulling them on.

"Will your parents be awake?"

I nod, shrugging on my bathrobe and tightening the belt. "Mom and Dad are early risers. He'll be in his office on the other side of the house, so he'll be fine. It's my mom we have to worry about." I nibble on my thumbnail, watching him tug on his Henley, now fully dressed. "How did you get in here last night?"

He glances toward the window. "Climbed, but I don't think I can go back that way. I didn't realize those trellis plants were roses when I've climbed up here before. No idea how I missed the thorns all of the other times, but..." He rolls his sleeve. Raised, reddened welts run up the inside of his forearm. I hiss and lightly touch the edges.

"Oh gosh, are you okay?" I ask, angry at myself for not noticing he was hurt last night. Thumbing to the bathroom, I say, "I have Bacitracin. I can..."

He tugs me into his arms by the bathrobe belt.

"I'm fine." He kisses me before I have the chance to worry about morning breath. "Think we can sneak me out of here without getting caught?"

Silently, we reach the front door without a hitch. Teddy twists the lock and slowly slips outside, his shoes in his hand. Turning back, he catches the door in his hand before I can close it. I tense, quickly looking over my shoulder as I hear movement from the kitchen.

"It's your birthday soon."

"Yeah, so?" I ask, glancing back again.

"Do you have plans?"

I blink. "No. Nothing."

Teddy grins. "Good. Keep the weekend free, okay?"

"Whole weekend? Why?"

He winks. "It's a secret."

"Morgana? What are you doing?"

I jump and rudely close the door in his face. "Nothing."

Mom eyes me skeptically. "Who was that?"

"Shay," I say without thinking.

"At this time in the morning?"

"Uh--huh. She was giving me a textbook for my exam next week." She looks down at my empty hands. "I mean, *I* gave *her* a textbook for her exam. Brain's not fully switched on yet. Think I need some coffee."

Teddy: What are you wearing?

Ana: Yoga pants and Skip's hoodie. Why?

Teddy: We need to work on your sexting.

Teddy: We also need to get one of my hoodies for you.

Ana: You don't have to be jealous; it's my brothers. Not some random guy.

Teddy: No girlfriend of mine will wear another dude's clothes. I don't care if he is your bro.

Ana: Girlfriend *smiley emoji* I like that.

Teddy: Good. Now let's try this again. What are you wearing? *wink emoji*

"Morgana, what is this?"

I jump, the grin hurting my cheeks dropping as I place my phone face down on my desk and turn to look at Mom holding my vintage Pink Floyd t-shirt between two fingers like it personally offended her.

"Erm, a shirt?" I say, trying to act unaffected, as my heart jackhammers in my chest. Taking a breath, I twist back to the Econ textbook I'd been reading to cram in some final studying before school starts, something that completely slipped my mind while staying up past midnight texting Teddy. I wanted to ask him to sneak over, but almost being caught last week has me paranoid.

"Morgana," Mom snaps, storming across the room to stop at the side of my desk. "Don't play smart with me, young lady. I know what it is. What I want to know is, where did you get it?"

I side-eye her and try to see the edge of my bed. I'm sure I'd done a better job of hiding that, made sure it was hidden away under my mattress, along with some other things, where she'd never find them. But the bed is tucked in neatly, with no ruffled edges or anything, which means...

"Did you search my room?" I ask, my eyes narrowing. She pouts her lips, a muscle in her jaw ticking. "Mom? Why were you looking around my room?"

She takes a harsh breath. "My daughter has been acting strange for months. I had to check that that *girl* you call a best friend hadn't gotten you involved in drugs or something."

I scoff and shake my head in disbelief. The audacity of her to accuse Shay of something like that.

"But if my suspicions are correct, Shay might not be the one I have to worry about. Now, I'll ask you again. Where did you get the shirt?"

"At a concert."

"And who were you at this *concert* with?"

"Shay," I reply quickly. Mom grabs my biceps tight with her bony fingers, forcing me to face her.

"Never would I have imagined my daughter lying to me." Her Botox must be wearing off because I can see she is mad, practically spitting fire bolts from her emerald eyes. "Tell me the truth."

I want to lie again. Tell her she's delusional, completely lost the plot, but she knows. She just wants me to say it out loud.

"Teddy," I whisper.

"And I assume the other clothes I also found stashed away with this are Teddy's?" She glowers, shaking the shirt for emphasis. I nod and drop my gaze from hers. "And he's the one who has been running you to and from school? And the one who you let out of the house the other day too?"

I nod again.

She's silent, but I can feel her hot gaze on the top of my head, a scalding weight I can't bring myself to look at.

"Are you fucking that *boy?*" she asks, her voice cold and disconnected.

"Mom!" I gasp, my head flying upward so quickly I could get whiplash. "Wha—"

"I will not let you embarrass our family by dating beneath you."

"He's not beneath me," I say, my throat growing thick with a surge of tears that I need to keep in. I will not satisfy her with tears. *Women don't show their emotions, Morgana.* "What is your problem with him? With his whole family? I see the looks of disdain every time you have to leave the house and they're outside. Or what about how unbelievably rude you are whenever one of them tries to interact with you."

"He's not good enough for you, Morgana," she yells, and I rear back. She's never yelled at me... ever. She swallows hard. "What do you expect? To fall madly in love and for him to support you? To be able to give you this life?" She gestures around my large bedroom. "Wake up, Morgana. Women like us don't get a happily ever after. We get convenience, wealth, and, if you're lucky, a man who's not an adulterer." Her voice softens, and she reaches out to stroke my cheek, the sudden change making my head spin. "Sweetheart, that boy is not worth the air he breathes. And the day you wake up and realize it, it will be too late. I'm only trying to do what's best before you're trapped in a life you hate."

A rogue tear escapes and trickles down my cheek as pain fissures through my heart. She wipes it away with her thumb and steps back.

"Now, get your things together for school. We're leaving in five minutes."

"What?" I ask, my voice thick and croaky.

Mom laughs. "Do you really think I'd continue to let him chauffeur you around?" I part my lips to speak, to argue that I would get a ride with my *boyfriend* if I wanted, but she turns and marches toward the door. "Now get changed. You're not going to school dressed like that."

I ball my hands into fists, my nails digging into the palms of my hands as frustration bleeds from my pores. My muscles are tight, my throat is burning, and I want to kick and scream and tell her to... to... fuck off.

Slamming my textbook closed, I shove it in my satchel and quickly get changed into my uniform. Storming down the stairs, I stand in the hallway watching Mom in the kitchen as she pulls out a trash bag and shoves my shirt and the clothes Teddy gave me when I used his shower inside before disappearing out the backdoor. If she thinks I won't go in that trash straight after school, she's an idiot. And if she thinks her little chat has influenced me in any way to stop being with Teddy, then she clearly underestimates me.

Is this why Skip left? Did he fall in love with some girl Mom didn't find acceptable?

I'm chewing on my bottom lip when Mom comes back inside, her heels creating a dull echo in my brain as I wonder if this is how my brother felt. Hurt, betrayed, confused, angry. Parents are supposed to support their children, not issue ultimatums. She opens the front door and makes her way to her silver Mercedes as I lock up and follow. Teddy bounds down his porch steps at the same time as my mom clicks her keys, and her car lights up with a loud *beep*.

Teddy smiles wide and bright, but it drops the moment I give my head a sharp shake. A frown creases his brows as he raises his hand to wave instead.

"Mornin', Mrs. Adler," he calls, his voice strained as he looks over at me. "Hey, Ana."

Mom tosses her handbag inside the car with such force that it bounces across to the passenger seat and falls to the footwell, the contents scattering across the floor mat.

"Theodore, her name is Morgana, and I'd appreciate it if you were to call her by her proper name."

Teddy scrubs a hand across his stubbled jaw, curbing a smirk. "My apologies, Mrs. Adler." He turns to his Mustang and manually unlocks it. The door opens with an obnoxious creak, and he chucks in his jacket. He spins slightly with a foot on the ledge, staring directly at my mother. "The same then applies to you."

"Excuse me?" Mom sneers.

Please just leave it, Mom.

"Teddy. The name on my birth certificate is Teddy, not Theodore." He looks over the yard and shoots me a wink before getting into his car and starting it with a roar. Mom stands, dumbfounded, as he tears out of his driveway and down the street.

"Get in the car, Morgana."

Silently, I slide into the back and pull out my phone when it vibrates in my bag.

Teddy: What climbed up her ass?
Morgana: I'm so sorry about her.
Teddy: Are you okay?
Morgana: Can we not talk about it?
Teddy: Ana...
Morgana: I'm fine. I'll talk to you later.

I close the thread and open a new one with my brother.

Morgana: Can you call me? I really need to talk to you.

Later that night, when Mom goes to bed, I sneak downstairs and slip out the kitchen door. I jump as the automatic backlight flashes on, and I curse myself for being so damn forgetful. Stealth mode clearly isn't my forte. Cringing, I open the lid to the large trash can, gagging as one of the rubbish bags spills open, the rancid smell of whatever the chef cooked three days ago, turning my stomach. I turn my head over my shoulder and fill my lungs before holding my breath and digging deeper until I find the bag mom threw away earlier.

Thankfully, it's sealed and dirt free as I pull it out, quickly replacing it with a decoy bag filled with a couple of Skip's old clothes in its place, just in case Mom is psycho enough to check I hadn't done exactly as I am doing right now. Once back inside, I pause outside Skip's room. Biting my thumbnail, I glance toward Mom's bedroom door, darkness shadowing the gap at the bottom, and then I quickly twist the handle and step inside. Pressing my back to the door, I inhale, a sudden wave of sadness taking over me as Skip's scent fills my lungs. For someone who never speaks to her son, Mom refuses to touch this room. When Dad suggested it, they didn't speak for a week.

Thankful for this one thing she holds on to, I walk across the room to his chest of drawers, opening the bottom one and shifting some clothes from the top of the pile and tucking Teddy's hoodie, sweats, and my Pink Floyd t-shirt inside. I pause on Skip's old basketball jersey, my fingers circling the New York Knicks emblem before sliding the drawer shut and disappearing back into my room, feeling a mixture of heartache and relief as I drift to sleep.

Chapter Fifteen

Morgana

May

The smell of the evening sun filters through the Mustang's open window as we drive to Stamford. Teddy's arm rests casually against the doorframe, his free hand linked with mine, and propped up on the gear stick. We don't speak, enjoying the company in blissful silence after not being with each other for a while. I have one more exam, taking up most of my evenings with studying, and Mom has been the Devil. I swear she's enjoying making my life miserable, monitoring my every move with shrewd interest. We've barely spoken since our argument, only interacting when needed; her running me to school—without Shay—collecting me at the end of the day like some kindergartener. Then we drive home in silence, eat in silence, and I excuse myself to study for the final exam of my high school career.

Same routine, day after day.

"I'm glad you managed to sneak out tonight," Teddy says, bringing my knuckles to his lips. "I sorta missed you."

I pretend to gasp, all the while slowly melting on the inside into a gooey puddle on his seat. "You missed me?"

He flushes, and I want to reach out and poke his cheeks to see if it's real. He never blushes.

"Don't tell anyone. You'll ruin my street cred." Pushing the turn signal down, he clears his throat. "So, what're Mommy and Daddy doing tonight that you could sneak away?"

"Dad's got a city-wide town hall, and Mom obviously has to go and show support." I glance out the window and watch the city go by.

"You didn't want to go?"

I scoff an ugly and unladylike noise. Oh, how my mom would disapprove of me right now.

"I don't get to go to those things. I don't even think my dad really wants my mom there either." I shrug. "Besides, I'd skip every single one just to spend time with you." I cringe. "That was really mushy, wasn't it?"

Teddy kisses my knuckles again and smiles wordlessly, but I hear him. Or at least I hope I do. The undercurrent of words we want to say—I want to say—but know we shouldn't.

Pulling into his father's auto shop, Teddy kills the engine. "You can wait here if you like. I'll only be a sec."

"And miss out on seeing Teddy in his natural habitat? No way, I'm coming." I grin when his smile widens, taking over his entire face.

Unlocking the side door, he holds it open, arm spread wide. "Welcome to where the magic happens."

"I thought that was your bedroom?" I tease, and he groans.

"I knew a dirty girl was hidden underneath that good-girl-next-door vibe you give off."

Teddy has brought out this new side of me; relaxed, easy-going, and entirely insatiable for him. Whenever we are together, I can't keep my hands off him, always needing his lips or hands on me, and he's just as bad. But it's not just the sex stuff. He brings calm to the constant storm that is in my life. He makes me see the world in a different light, and I've experienced more with him in five short months than I have in my seventeen years on this planet.

"Come over here," he says, sliding his hand into mine and pulling me over to a huge flatbed truck. "This is what I've been working on this week."

Running my hand along the grill, I stare at him in awe. "This is huge."

"That's what all the girls say."

I cock a brow and laugh, before turning back to the truck. "You know how to fix one of these?"

"Yup." He nods and drags over something similar to a skateboard with his foot. "Want to see underneath?"

My eyes widen as he drops to the board and spreads his legs, patting the space in front of him.

"Are you sure we won't get stuck?" I ask, nibbling on my bottom lip.

Teddy lies back and slides under the vehicle. I drop down to my haunches and watch as he moves his hand between his chest and the underside of the truck.

"Think we'll be all good," he says and shuffles back out with his heels. "C'mon, Ana Banana, hop on."

I position myself between his legs and lie back against his chest. Slowly, he pushes us back under and starts pointing out components, excitement and passion dripping from every word. His whole body is animated as he describes everything in great detail, and all of it goes straight over my head. But listening to the way he talks, the way he clearly loves cars, only reiterates that what I feel for him isn't simply lust. I don't think it ever was. I love him. Full-blown and head over heels in love with him. I release a shuddering breath. I am so screwed. The unknown expiration date—like a huge clock, *tick, tick, ticking* in my head—is sounding louder, drowning out Teddy's words with white noise. But a small glimmer of hope that this could be something more, something permanent, comes in the form of a small white rectangle tucked away inside my bag.

He has to feel this too. That what we have could be real. We are stronger than two silly young people pretending to be in love.

Teddy's arm slips around my waist, and his hand splays against my stomach. "What do you think?" Teddy asks, kissing the top of my head, breaking me out of my thoughts.

"Huh? Oh, it's incredible."

His chest vibrates under my back as he chuckles. "You had no idea what I was talking about, did you?"

I'm glad I'm lying on him so he can't see my flushed cheeks. "Well, no, but I enjoyed listening to you talk. You really love this stuff, like you're passionate about it." I wave my hand in front of me as best I can without hitting anything on the truck. That would be my luck that I would break something by mistake.

"I really do. I've wanted to be a mechanic for as long as I can remember." His hand on my belly tenses. "That's why Phoenix was always the plan."

...was?

Before I can ask what that means, he moves us slowly forward and into the open. "You want to grab some food?"

I nod, moving to stand, and then hold my hand to help him. "There's an amazing food truck that should be parked up at Silver Sands beach now that the weather's warmer if you don't mind the drive. Skip used to take us, and believe me, nowhere makes better tacos than Something to Taco 'Bout."

He laughs. "You eat food from a truck?"

I nudge my hip into his side as he wraps his arm around my shoulders. "Hey, I'm not a food snob. My brother's a chef, remember? He'd take me to all kinds of places to try out new food. It's my mom you wouldn't catch dead standing in line waiting for something someone prepared in the back of a van."

He kisses the top of my head before turning the lights out and locking up. "You keep surprising me every day, Ana."

Chapter Sixteen

Teddy

"Fucking hell, these are amazing."

Ana nods her head, swallowing her bite of food. "Told you."

"This might be my new favorite place."

"It's mine too. Especially in the summer; good food, great weather, the sound of the waves lapping at the sand..." She places her half-eaten taco back in the cardboard dish and sets it on her knee. "It's peaceful."

I look out over the beach, the pair of us sitting on the hood of my car, the smell of salt and sand filling my lungs as I watch the girl I've fallen pretty damn hard for play with her food. I mean, that's what this is. She's goddamn special—I wouldn't let just *anyone* sit on my baby like we are now. Even though there is a blanket under us, it's the principle.

Scrunching a napkin in my hand, I drop it in the empty dish. "You done?"

She passes me her leftover taco, and I pop it into my mouth in one bite, chewing as I take the trash to the can and toss it inside. Hopping back up, I wrap my arms around Ana's waist and pull her closer. Her skirt flutters in the wind and she giggles, holding it down with her hand as my heart fucking patters in my chest at the sound.

So far gone for this chick, it's embarrassing.

"What time do we need to get you home for studying?" I ask through a tight throat.

She nuzzles her head against my shoulder. "I'm not studying tonight. I've done enough, I think. I'll never remember it all if I keep cramming."

"When's the exam?"

"Friday."

"So you've got a couple more days," I say, watching a couple walk hand in hand along the sand. Bowie would love this place. I'll remember to tell him about it during our next Skype call for when he comes home. "You thought any more about what you want to do when you graduate? I know you're unhappy about your parents wanting to send you to Harvard."

Ana tenses in my arms, moving out of my hold and sitting ramrod straight. "I want to go to business school."

My eyebrows shoot up my forehead. "Business school?"

She spins and looks at me with fierce determination. "Yes. I'm good at that sort of stuff, econ, calculus. Maybe after I graduate, I'll look into finance or something, but I know I don't want to be a lawyer."

She's breathing heavily like those words weighed a ton, and she's finally managed to release some of the tension she's kept inside by letting them be voiced. She slides from the hood of the car and paces.

"Have you told your parents that?" I ask, watching as she threads her hands into her hair and tugs a little.

"And be disowned for not wanting to follow their pre-destined path for me?" she scoffs, pausing to look at me like I'm insane, then resumes her pacing.

I recoil. "Baby? Why would they disown you?"

"They did it with my brother."

"I thought you didn't know if that was true?"

She sighs, some of the fight leaving her. "I don't, but I can only assume. Why else would he have left? Unless he fell for someone they disapproved of."

She's muttering to herself about different scenarios as to why her parents and Skip no longer speak, but it's the *someone they disapproved of* comment that has my blood turning to ice. That would be me if Ana was to ever come clean to her parents about us and actually wanted to be with me for the long haul. My chest aches as I cannot see the possibility of that ever happening. And could I really let her walk away from her family because she chose me?

I'm not asking for you to fall in love with me.

High school romances rarely work out.

For however long this lasts.

The problem is, I've fallen in love with her.

I rub my sternum, willing the stupid emotions holding my heart in a vice grip to let go.

"... I've applied to five schools and got into every one."

That snaps me out of my thoughts. Jumping off the car, I stand in front of her, stopping her pacing and run my hands down her arms.

"All five want you?" She nods, nibbling that bottom lip I want to bite. I press my lips to hers, and she sags into the kiss. "That's amazing. Damn, I knew my girl was smart."

She smiles, but it doesn't reach her eyes. The wind whips her hair around her face, and I brush a mass of curls behind her ear.

"What? What's wrong? Why aren't you happy? You have your pick of any school you want."

She steps back and disappears into the passenger side of the car. I turn and watch her through the front window as she rummages around her bag and pulls out... is that an envelope? She closes the door softly and stares at the crumpled envelope with the top torn off.

"I also applied to another school." She glances at me through her lashes, worry filling her eyes, making them look more blue than green in the dying sun. She shrugs, her face twisting like she's trying to make out that whatever's in that envelope is not a big deal. "I don't know why, but..."

She pulls out a letter and holds it out to me. I take it and unfold the paper as Ana practically runs away from me, pushing herself back onto the hood of the car and looking anywhere else as I read it. I frown and gaze at an acceptance letter, my pulse skittering to a stop when I see the University of Arizona header.

"Dear, Ms. Adler. Congratulations. It is with great pleasure that I offer you admission to..." I mutter, reading and re-reading the first lines over and over. University of Arizona. Less than a two-hour drive away from Phoenix. "You got into UA?"

She nods timidly.

"For this fall?"

She winces and there's that face again. But this is a big deal. Bigger than big—fucking huge.

"Yeah. I know it was stupid and foolish, especially when we agreed that we couldn't be more than this weird casual but not casual *thing*, but I was researching schools, it was right there, and I clicked apply before I knew it and..."

I silence her with a kiss, diving my tongue between her lips and stroking it over hers. She groans, the entire top half of her body sinking into me as I wrap my arms around her waist, plastering the best piece of paper to her back.

"You're coming to Phoenix?"

Her lips are swollen, and her pupils blown as her eyes meet mine. "Well, Arizona. But I don't have to go. I can decline. I don't want you thinking I'm rushing you or forcing you to..."

I kiss her again. I can't help it.

"I love you."

She pushes my chest hard. "W—what did you say?" I laugh, kissing her neck and making her shiver. "No, Teddy. Stop. Look at me." I pull back and smile, reveling in the look in her eyes. "What did you just say?"

"I love you, Ana." Her mouth parts, stunned. "I think I have for a while. I know you said that wasn't what you wanted, but I didn't listen. I love you."

She blinks. And blinks some more.

"Say something." I laugh, itching the back of my neck in response to her reaction. I've obviously shocked her to silence.

"I... I love you too." She smiles, blushing so damn prettily. "I don't want there to be an expiration date with us anymore, Teddy."

Wrapping her legs around my hips, I lift her from the car. My lips never leave her skin as I walk to the car door, slapping my hand around, looking for the handle before Ana angles her body and tugs it open.

"Maybe if you put me down, Teddy..." She laughs breathily, "It'll be easier."

"Fuck no," I say, kicking the door wide with my foot and bending slightly to maneuver the seat forward, and carefully thread her through to the back seat. "I'm never letting you go, Ana. Never."

She lies on her back, those golden curls framing her beautiful face and cascading down the refurbished leather. My cock hardens in my pants, and I slowly climb my way on top of her.

"Say it again."

She smiles, her eyes twinkling from the streetlamps surrounding the parking lot.

"I love you."

I grin. "Fuck yeah, you do."

Our lips meet in a frenzy. I never knew it could be like this—frantic, all-consuming, needy—but Ana brings those things out with an intensity I know nothing in life will ever match. She's it. She's the one I'll never let get away. What's that saying? When you know, you know? Well, I fucking *know* Morgana Adler was made for me. The other half of my soul, and then I hear the snapping of pieces clicking together.

I need her. All of her.

"I want to fuck you so bad," I murmur against her lips, rolling my hips against her so she can feel just how bad that want is.

"What? Here? Now?" she squeals, wriggling beneath me and pushing at my shoulders.

"Nah, baby," I say, soothingly running my hand through her hair. She's not ready for that yet. She might have hinted numerous times before, but when things progress a little too close to her comfort line, she does things like locking her arms, and her voice becomes higher. She puts on a faux confidence I don't want her to do around me. I will wait as long as she needs to make her first time memorable.

"I'm not going to fuck you in the back of my car, where anyone could walk past and see you." She exhales, the tightness in her body evaporating. "I don't want anyone hearing you moan my name for the first time when I'm inside you. That is all mine. Every breath, every shudder, everything is mine, Ana."

Her eyes flutter shut, and her hips buck upward. She likes the sound of that.

"Tonight, I'll settle for third base." I pump my eyebrows a couple of times, making her laugh. Slowly, I guide my hand up the side of her body and cup her over her shirt. Kneading her skin, I feel her nipple harden beneath my palm. Suddenly, I'm moving, dragging Ana upward as I settle on the seat and drag her onto my lap, my hand dipping beneath her skirt. She gasps when my fingers skim the outside of her panties.

"Teddy, what are you doing?" she asks, looking out the back window as her irises quickly turn that beautiful shade of green when she's aroused.

I grin. "There are other ways I can make you come, Ana."

She sinks down against my hand, trapping it between her and my hard dick as she worries her bottom lip. "Here? Now?"

My grin intensifies. "Let's see how quickly I can make you come before we get caught."

I shift my hips slightly, tilting her enough that I can slip inside her. She draws in a shaky breath as I slowly curl my finger against her walls and her eyes flutter shut. Her hips roll against my palm, and I take the chance to slip in another digit, increasing my pace as she grips the back of the seats with her head hanging between her shoulders. She's fucking beautiful riding my hand with complete abandon, and for once, I don't care about finding my own release. My dick is achingly hard behind my zipper, but watching my girl, eyes shut, mouth parted, golden curls catching the dying sunlight, is everything and more. And when she pants, moaning my name as she squeezes my fingers through her orgasm, I can't believe this girl is all mine.

Bringing my mouth to hers, I say, "Watching you come apart with just my hand has to be my favorite view, Ana."

Withdrawing from her body, I bring my fingers up to look at them coated with her release. Keeping my eyes on her, I suck on my middle one. "And this is my favorite flavor."

Ana takes hold of my wrist and slips the other finger I had inside her moments ago between her lips with a soft moan. *Jesus,* what is this girl doing to me? She grins in response to my wide eyes and gaping mouth.

"Okay, I was wrong. *That* is my favorite view. Fucking hell, Ana. You're going to kill me."

Chapter Seventeen

Morgana

June

High school graduate.

Birthday girl.

Girlfriend.

I might hate that today went by in some disappointing blur, but those three titles—just for today, at least—make enduring my parents' hard stares, passive-aggressive comments to one another, and not being able to see Teddy until he sneaks into my room tonight worth it.

I look at the glossy black folder with my name inside, running my fingers along the gold embossed logo of my school and once my diploma is mailed out, the A4 piece of paper will symbolize the end of that chapter in my life, and the acceptance letter to Arizona, the next.

My phone buzzes on the mattress beside me, and I smile, hoping to see Teddy's name on the notification. My cheeks hurt as my brother's name appears on the screen, my heart warming at the sight.

Skip: HBD, little sis.

Morgana: So you remembered who I am?

Skip: Of course. You're the pain in my ass I can't get rid of *laughing emoji*

Morgana: Ha-ha.

Skip: Can't wait to see you. I miss you.

Morgana: Whatever. Miss me enough not to text me back.

Skip: Sorry, sis. Life's been crazy, y'know. Everything okay? I've got five mins before I need to start work.

Morgana: It's okay. Nothing I can't handle.

Skip: You know I'm here if you need to talk.

Morgana: ...when you're not busy.

Skip: Ouch, that hurt. I've been a shit brother recently Morgs and I'm sorry. But hopefully I'll get to see you soon, okay?

Morgana: You mean that?

Skip: Yeah. Listen I've gotta go, just starting work. Speak soon, kiddo. Love you x

"Love you too," I mutter to the phone, letting it drop from my hand to the bed. Rolling onto my side, I tuck my hands under my face and watch the sunset through the bedroom window. I should be getting ready for this gala I'm being forced to attend instead of celebrating the day the way I want to— with Teddy and Shay while my mom and dad forget I exist. Just how I like it. But I'm certain the only reason I've been invited tonight is so Mom can keep an eye on me.

Misery loves company and all that.

She might be watching me, but I've been doing the same. I used to think the amount of alcohol she consumes was because of Skip, but now I'm not so sure. I see the way my parents act around each other. I see the glazed expression on Mom's face when he starts talking about his campaign. She's a husk of the woman I assume she must have been before she met Dad. Stuck in a loveless marriage, with children I'm starting to think she might not have wanted—not like she brought us up, since our numerous nannies did—and there's nothing she can do to help herself get out. She's every bit as trapped in a life she claims I'm destined for, rather than the one I want. I want to feel sorry for her, and on some level, maybe I do, but she chose this. And now she wants me to do the same.

Well, no. That won't be me. I've seen how happy relationships can be, and I won't stay in line and live like some good little homemaker, whose only there to be seen and not heard. As soon as this gala is over, I'm going to tell them. Tell them I'm not going to Harvard. Tell them about Teddy and that he loves me. That we're going to Phoenix together. Even though we're young, this is serious, and we're going to be together regardless of what mom says.

Leaning over, I turn on the lamp and reach down to pull open the drawer on my bedside table. Rummaging around, I pull out a banged-up metallic box with a padlock attached and swivel the numbers until it clicks open. Four of the acceptance letters sit inside what was once my money box, and I add in the letter from Arizona, safely tucking it away with the others after showing Teddy. My heart flutters like mad with excitement as my fingers linger on the envelopes, but suddenly the box topples to the floor as three loud rasps at my bedroom door make me jump. My hands fumble to catch everything, missing most of the contents as the letters and other precious items spill onto the floor.

Scrambling from the bed, I drop to my knees and frantically shove everything back inside the box, relock the padlock, and quickly slip it back into the drawer. Mom's head pops around the door a second later, her face perfectly contoured and highlighted, her updo done meticulously, not a single hair out of place.

"Why aren't you ready?" She frowns, her lips pulling into a pout as she glares at me sitting on the floor. "What on earth are you doing?"

"My phone fell. I was picking it up," I lie, getting to my feet and straightening my bathrobe.

Her nostrils flare as she glares. "Hurry up and get changed, Morgana. Your dress is hanging in your closet, and Evan will be in shortly to do your makeup."

I bite my cheek, hiding the disappointment that *he* is doing my makeup. He always makes everything so thick and dark and not at all the colors that match my complexion. He makes Mom look radiant and me a little clown.

"Sure," I say through a tight-lipped smile.

Mom's eyes dart around the room like she's looking for something, or some*one*, but when they land back on me, she sighs. "You let your hair air dry."

It's said with disdain. She hates when I do that because then my blonde curls become wild ringlets that will not be tamed no matter how much tugging and pulling and hairspray you use. I smile, unable to stop the muscles tugging my lips upward at the annoyance written across my mom's face— little victories.

"I wish you'd listen to me get them chemically straightened. You're eighteen now, Morgana, not a little girl. It's time to stop looking like one."

My smile drops at the same time my stomach does. I reach up and hold a chunk of my hair like each individual curl could hear her and are personally offended by her comment. Why can't she love me for me? No *happy birthday, honey*, no big celebration for this milestone, simply a teeth whitening kit, a designer handbag, and a pat on the shoulder from Dad.

Happy birthday to you, Morgana.

"I need to get dressed," I say, hating how meek my voice sounds. Mom nods and disappears from the doorway, the soft snick of her closing it behind her, ricocheting like a deadlock bolt through the room.

Turning to my closet, I inhale.

Just a few more hours and everything changes, Morgana.

"My, what a beautiful young lady you've grown into." An older lady with an even older gentleman says as Mom introduces me to yet another one of her *friends*. I plaster on my camera-ready smile and offer a polite nod before looking around the room and counting the number of exits. A fire escape to the left of the bar. A cloakroom by the main doorway to the hall. A staff-only sign, which I think is for the kitchen, by the far end of the room.

"...And you remember Richard, Morgana darling?" Mom asks, her fingers digging into my arm as she forces my attention to a man a few years older than Teddy standing by a lady I'm guessing has to be his mother, going off the similarities between the pair.

"Oh, yes, Richard. Hi. It's nice to see you again." *Even though I haven't seen you since I was maybe ten years old.*

"Morgana," he says, clasping my hand in his and kissing it. "Happy birthday."

"Th—thanks," I stutter, unaware he even remembered who I was, let alone that today is my birthday. He was always the weird, shy boy who didn't want to play with Skip and me when his parents came to our house.

"Richard is graduating from Yale this year, Morgana," Mom beams at

Richard, her grip tightening slightly as she edges me closer to him.

"That's impressive," I deadpan, and while my mom doesn't notice, Richard does, dropping his head and smirking.

"It really is," she continues while Richard's mother looks bored listening to mine gush about her son. "And your father has already headhunted him to work at his firm."

"It's an entry-level position," Richard interjects. "Nothing fancy."

"Oh, nonsense, Richard. I'm sure you'll climb the ranks faster than anyone ever could."

I fight an eyeroll and quickly run my eyes across Richard's perfectly tailored suit, slicked-back blond hair, and classically handsome face. He is the epitome of a *nice-lawyer-boy* Mom has spoken about recently. Every time she sees Teddy outside, she happens to mention how Harvard is full of them, and one day soon, I'll find myself one—a good one—I can make the perfect wife to. Richard's good-looking, I guess, and he seems lovely enough, but he isn't Teddy.

"It was great to see you again, Mrs. Adler," Richard says. "Please let your husband know I would love to speak to him before the evening is over." He turns to me, leaning down to kiss my cheek, lingering for a beat as he says, "You look beautiful, Morgana. I'm glad I got to see you tonight."

His eyes flicker down my long pink dress, and it feels suffocating. Like the material is too tight, and I can't breathe.

As Richard walks away, Mom's fingers claw into my skin. "What is *he* doing here?"

My head swivels to where she is glowering. My heart leaps, and my face breaks into the first genuine smile I've had all day.

Teddy. He's here, completely underdressed in faded dark jeans and an open flannel shirt with a dark gray Henley underneath. He looks like sin, standing there with his hands in his pockets as he looks around, until he notices me and casually walks across the room like he owns the place.

"Ana," he practically purrs, and my body leans into him. "Happy birthday, baby."

Without thinking, I throw my arms around his neck and press my lips to his. Mom gasps in horror, and Teddy hums against my mouth, circling his arms around my waist and hauling me close to his chest.

"You look fucking gorgeous," he mutters against me.

"Morgana Adler, let go of that boy now," Mom hisses, but I hold on tighter. "What do you think you are playing at, Theodore? This is a private function. You do not belong here."

"Teddy," he clips, and I bury my head into his neck to stop from laughing.

"You need to leave. Now."

"That's a great idea, Mom," I say, spinning and smiling at her. She is going to kill me, so I might as well enjoy this. "We're both going to leave."

"Morgana," she warns.

"You're right. We don't belong here." I turn to Teddy and lace my fingers with his. "Let's go."

"Morgana, if you leave with that... that..."

"Boyfriend," I say, straightening my spine and locking eyes with hers. My heart hammers under my ribs, and my free hand begins to shake, so I hide it behind my back.

So this is what standing up for what I want feels like.

Like a heart attack, and I could faint at any moment.

Oh God, this is horrible.

Keep it together, Morgana. The quicker you break the ties she holds around you, the easier it will be.

"Boyfriend?" Mom asks, her lip curling in disgust.

I nod.

"We'll be having words when you get home tonight."

"Sunday night," Teddy corrects, his hand slipping to my waist to hold my hip possessively. "I'm taking her away for the weekend for her birthday."

"You will not. I won't allow it. This is kidnap. Morgana, step away from that boy." A vein in her forehead pops as her face turns a shade of purple, but with Teddy's thumb rubbing against my hip, I feel stronger than ever.

"No, Mom," I say, and then I do the ballsiest thing I've ever done. "And unless you want me to cause a scene in front of all these people"—I wave my arm around the room. Mom's eyes widen in horror—"you'll let me leave with Teddy tonight and won't try to call me until I get home on Sunday." I glance at Teddy, and he nods, brushing a kiss to my temple.

"You'll regret this, Morgana," she says and turns her back, storming off in the direction of the bar.

I sag against Teddy's hold.

"I'm so proud of you, baby," he says, ushering me toward the exit. "For just now, for graduating... but did you really have to try to dive off the stage once you got your diploma?"

My legs stop moving. "What?"

His smile is magnificent when he turns, pulling me into his chest. "What? Like I was going to miss my girlfriend's graduation? I was in the back—didn't want your parents having a meltdown if they saw me there—but I wasn't going to miss it."

"You were there?" Shock doesn't come close to how I feel, knowing he came to see me.

He kisses my forehead. "I'll always be there, Ana."

Oh, my heart.

"Now come on. Let's get you to New York."

Chapter Eighteen

Teddy

"Teddy, please slow down." Ana giggles as I tug her the couple of blocks to the restaurant I booked. Glancing at my watch, I don't slow down. Fuck Juliette Adler for making us miss the train by seconds with her *"you shall not pass"* bullshit. Ana is an eighteen-year-old woman now. She can make up her own goddamn mind about who she will and will not spend her time with. Not to mention, she's my *fucking* girlfriend. Plus, we had to drive across town to get home so she could pack a bag and change her clothes, which didn't help.

Ana grabs my wrist with her other hand, her shoes slapping along the sidewalk.

"Teddy, I can't keep up with you. Please say we're almost there." I come to an abrupt stop, and she slams into my back. "What the—"

She peers up at the sign to Alimento and then down to the large front window. The place looks packed; every table, as far as you can see, is filled with couples or families enjoying their Friday night dinner.

"Sorry, baby. Our table is booked for eight, and we're cutting it close."

She gapes. "Teddy, isn't this really expensive?"

I wink and place my hand on the small of her back, gently nudging her to the door. "Nah, don't worry about it. I know someone who works here."

The hostess shows us to our table and hands us our menus. Another waiter appears, taking our food and drink orders, and then we're left alone.

"How bad do you think your mom's going to flip when you get home?"

Ana shrugs, taking a sip of water. "I don't care. I was going to tell her about Arizona, Phoenix, you... tonight anyway, so I guess you coming to the gala means there's one less thing I need to tell her."

"And what if she cuts you off or whatever rich folk do whenever someone angers them?"

She laughs. "Rich folk?"

"Yeah, I watch movies. The rich characters always hold their vast fortunes over one another to get them to do what they want."

"You're an idiot," she says, eyes widening as her starter is placed in front of her.

"See, you're basically proving my point." I jab my spoon at her plate before dipping it back into my cauliflower soup—not something I'd usually order, but it's tasty as fuck. "Who orders smoked eel and enjoys it?"

She lifts a forkful into her mouth and hums around it. I shift in my seat, my spoon forgotten, halfway to my mouth as her eyes flutter shut and she licks her lips painfully slowly. I'm getting hard just watching her. I want to tell her to get under this table and lick up my cock with that dirty little tongue of hers and make me come before the main course is served.

"Ana," I growl, my eyes narrowed on her mouth.

She opens her eyes and smirks, sucking her plump lips between her teeth. Oh, she knows what she's doing, the little tease. I love how relaxed and confident she's gotten since being with me. I've coaxed out a naughty vixen, and she is all mine.

Thankfully, the rest of the meal isn't as uncomfortable for me as trying to make eating burgers look sexy doesn't work. Getting up from the table, I stop by her side and press a kiss on her cheek.

"I'll be right back, okay? I've got a surprise for you."

She groans. "Please don't say it's a cake, and all the waiters come out and sing '*Happy Birthday.*' I really hate that."

I smirk and walk toward the restroom, tugging my phone from my pocket.

No, Ana Banana, it's so much better than that.

When I get back to the table, our empty plates have been cleared, and our glasses are topped up with fresh water. Ana smiles warmly as I sit down, and I slide my chair closer to hers, resting my hand on her thigh. She swivels on her chair and kisses me.

"Thank you for tonight," she whispers, her eyes hooded as she flicks her gaze down to my mouth. "For everything, really. You've made today better than I could have imagined, Teddy."

She presses forward again, nipping at my bottom lip as I let her control the kiss. Her tongue swipes over mine, just as a throat clears.

"Gross, dude. That's my sister."

Ana's back snaps ramrod straight as she blinks at her brother.

"Skip?"

"Hey, kiddo."

She leaps out of her chair so quickly that the thing topples back, crashing on the ground. Her head is buried in Skip's chest, her arms clinging to him so tight it must hurt. He rests his cheek on the top of Ana's head, his hand patting her back soothingly as her shoulders bounce. Shit, is she... crying? Fuck, did I do the wrong thing?

"Ana?" I say, slowly standing and edging closer to the siblings. "Are you okay?"

Ana spins and engulfs me, her wet face brushing against my neck as she sobs into me.

"Thank you, Teddy. Thank you so much."

I thread my fingers into Ana's hair and hold her until she stops crying. She peels herself away, swiping under her eyes.

"I'll be right back. I need to sort myself out. I bet I look an absolute wreck."

Skip scrunches up his nose. "I didn't want to say anything 'cause it's your birthday and all, but you're a fucking ugly crier, sis."

She playfully punches his arm as she walks past him, making her way to the restrooms.

Skip steps forward, his hand stretched out. "Nice to finally put a face to the name."

"Likewise," I say, shaking his hand and gesturing for him to join us at our table. "I didn't know she'd burst into tears at the sight of you, though."

Skip laughs and flags down our waiter. "Yeah, she keeps her emotions hidden most of the time. But when she's overwhelmed like that, they come out in waves." The waiter stops by the table, and Skip picks up the drink menu. "Dale, can I get a latte, please? Want anything?" he asks me, showing me the drinks list. I shake my head, and Dale pops off to get his order.

Ana squeezes her brother's shoulder, like she needs to touch him to know he's real, as she returns to her seat. "How is this possible? How are you here right now?"

Skip waves down at his chef's uniform. "I work here, dummy. This was all lover boy's idea."

Ana's head whips to me, and I toss a shoulder upward.

"No big deal. I thought this would make your birthday special."

She launches herself at me again, and Skip groans. "Morgana, I'm sitting right here."

"Sorry." She blushes. Settling back into her own seat, she links our fingers together, asking, "How did you know where he worked?"

"I found his Instagram page and sent him a message telling him who I was and what I had planned for your birthday."

"And I jumped at the chance to see you, kiddo. It's been far too long." Skip's eyes sadden as Ana reaches for his hand across the table.

They catch up for a while, asking what's been happening over the last four years and reminiscing about their childhood while I sit and listen, soaking up the stories of young Ana, and enjoying the light that shines out of her eyes whenever she faces me to add in something extra to a story. Eventually, Skip's attention lands on me.

"So, how much does our mommy dearest hate you?"

"Skip!" Ana chastises.

"What? I'm only asking. And don't say Mom doesn't hate him. He's everything she despises in life, the stupid bitch."

Okay, I think I might be in love with Ana's brother.

"Yeah, she's not my biggest fan," I admit.

"I'll say. I had to look through your IG account. You're a mechanic, right?" I nod. "That's so cool, dude. Where do you work?"

"In Stamford right now with my dad, but we're"—I bring our joined hands to the top of the table—"going to head to Phoenix soon. Ana got into the University of Arizona, and I've always wanted to open my own auto shop back where I grew up."

Skip's eyes grow wide. "Arizona? Wow, congrats, Morgana. What did Mom do when you told her you're not following their path to Harvard Law?"

Ana winces. "I haven't told them yet."

"Shit." Skip whistles, then takes a deep breath. "Good luck with that, sis. Just stay strong. Don't let her manipulate you into something you don't want to do, okay?"

Ana's brows furrow, and I can tell she desperately wants to ask what he means. "Skip..."

Skip lifts his wrist and pushes up from his chair. "Shoot, guys, I gotta run. I'm on clean-up duty tonight since I asked for a longer break to see my baby sister." He grabs Ana around the neck and playfully ruffles her hair.

We both stand, and Ana holds on to her brother like this will be the last time she will ever see him again, and I bump his fist with mine.

"Listen, don't worry about the check. I've got it covered," he says, and I hold up my arm, about to protest, when his hand clamps on my shoulder. "I said I've got it, okay?" Lowering his voice, he steps closer. "I feel like, as Morgana's big brother, I should warn you not to be a dick, or you'll answer to me or whatever, but that's a given. Instead, I'm going to say, watch out for my mom. She's got a mean streak a mile long, and for some reason, Morgana feels like she owes her something. But Morgana's changed; she's happier and seems stronger, which I guess is down to you. Just make sure she stands her ground when it comes to our parents, okay?"

I nod, and he releases me.

"Love you, sis."

"Love you too, Skippy." Ana laughs, her shoulders sagging a little as she watches her brother disappear back into the kitchen. She leans against me and looks up. "I can't believe you did this for me."

"I'd give you the world, Ana, if you wanted it."

She chews her lip, shaking her head. "When did you get so cheesy?"

Chapter Nineteen

Teddy

New York at night is amazing. The buildings. The lights. The atmosphere. No wonder people all over the world come here to experience it all. I glance at Ana, admiring everything as we walk toward the hotel. Since dinner, she's had this massive smile that's never once faltered, and I've decided I'll do everything I can to keep it on her face.

Pushing the button to the elevator, she leans against the mirrored wall and crooks her finger. I eat up the short distance, pressing my hips into hers.

"I'm ready."

My eyebrows knit together. "Ready?"

She nods and tucks a curly tendril behind her ear.

"Yeah. I'm... erm... I'm ready to have sex." She blushes so fucking prettily, and it's hard not to drop my pants and fuck her right here. I've been waiting for those magic words for so damn long. Quickly, she tacks on, "With you, I mean. I'm ready to have sex with you."

I laugh, unable to help myself. "Well, thank fuck it's with me and not the random busboy back at the restaurant. He was checking you out all night."

"He was not," she scoffs, lightly hitting my chest with the back of her hand.

I sober and crowd into her space. "Are you sure, Ana? You don't have to do this because you think you owe me for tonight."

"It's not that," she says and immediately grabs my shirt. "I think I've been ready for a while. I was just waiting for..."

"Something special?"

She drops her head, her cheeks flaming. "It's stupid."

"It's not." I put two fingers under her chin, tilting her head upward. "I wanted to make sure it was special too. I want to take care of you, baby. Make sure you enjoy it as much as I know I will."

She exhales quickly through her nose, her eyes more blue than green as she stares up at me. "How can you be so sure you'll enjoy it? I could suck at this."

I press my hard cock against her thigh, letting her feel how much I know this will be off-the-charts good.

"Because you've made me come harder than anyone else with just your hand and your mouth. I know your pussy will be the same."

"Teddy." The way she says my name in a breathy moan has me forgetting we are in an elevator climbing floors by the second, and it can stop at any time, letting strangers join us in the small car and get a show, but I don't care as my mouth crashes onto hers, nipping and biting and sucking. I force my tongue past her lips and tangle it with hers, and she grasps and clutches at my shirt, pulling it like she's trying to tear it from my back.

The elevator dings, and she pushes me back as the door opens to our floor. Grabbing her hand, I practically run down the hallway, fumbling with my wallet to pull the key card from the little slot and slam it into the reader. The door is barely unlocked before I push Ana through it, grabbing the hem of her little black dress and yanking it over her head.

I have never seen anything sexier than Morgana Adler in a matching set of a white bra and panties, her tanned skin making the lace even more virginal now that the seriousness of what we are about to do bares heavy. I stalk toward her, aware that I'm fully dressed, as I stare at her unbelievable body. My thumb brushes over the waistline of her panties, her skin pebbling under my touch. By her sides, her hands shake, and she balls them into fists, thinking I've not noticed.

I take them in mine and hold them between us.

"Ana," I whisper, and her eyes close. "Ana, look at me. Are you sure?"

"Yes." It's so quiet that I need her to repeat it.

"Ana, I need you to say it louder. Are you sure?"

"Yes, Teddy," she says, her chin jutting out as she holds eye contact. "I want you to fuck me."

Yup, that will do it.

Dropping to my knees, I take her panties with me, hooking my fingers around the lace and tugging them to the floor. She steps out of them, and I toss them somewhere behind me as my hands come to each round globe of her ass and bring her to my face. Her hands grip my hair hard at the first swipe of my tongue up her pussy, and I groan, lapping up her taste, relishing in how her body responds to me. Fucking soaking every damn time.

"Fuck, this is the best thing I've tasted all night," I moan, circling her clit before diving back inside. I could do this all day, every day. Just eat her out, listen to her whimper and moan, and whisper my name.

"No, Teddy, stop," she breathes, pulling my hair to get my attention. I swear I could get lost in her pussy, and I'd never want to be found. She taps my shoulder, wriggling her butt out of my hold. "I want you inside me, please. I won't last much longer."

I stand and pull her in for a kiss. She moans, clinging to me harder as she tastes herself on my lips. She's a fucking slut for it, loves to lap at my mouth just as I love to lap at her pussy. Her hands are shaking again as she goes for the buttons on my shirt, clumsily missing some in her haste to rid me of it. I halt her hands with mine and pull back to look at her. Her cheeks are flushed, and her eyes are blown to massive proportions with a mixture of arousal and fear.

I touch my lips gently to hers and whisper, "Don't be nervous, baby. I've got you."

Bending, I lift her and guide her legs around my waist and walk her to the king-size bed. When I say I went all out for my girl's birthday, I went all-fucking-out and booked the best room in the whole hotel. Gently, I lay her down and gesture for her to scoot up to the headboard. She complies, scrambling to reach the top as her breathing comes in ragged pants. Reaching behind her, she unclasps her bra and lets it fall down her arms and onto the floor.

My fingers are still on my pants button as I take in the sight of my girl buck-naked and waiting for me. She bites her lip, and I'm like Pavlov's dog salivating at the sight of her white teeth digging into the plump flesh of her mouth. I tug at the button, then tear off the ones Ana hadn't undone on my shirt, the white cotton fluttering to the carpet as I kick off my shoes and socks. Her eyes roam across my bare chest, and she starts to rub her thighs together to release some tension. I raise a brow, and she stops.

All in good time, birthday girl.

Taking my wallet from my back pocket, I throw it onto the bed and push my pants and boxers down my legs, my erection pointing upward in salute to the insanely beautiful girl fucking gagging for me. Slowly, I creep onto the bed, my knees on either side of her legs, my stomach muscles flexing as I crawl above her. My skin ignites everywhere that I brush against her. Soft legs like silk against my thighs as I move one knee between them and push them open. She gasps as I slide my thigh higher, grinding it on her wet pussy, and she arches her back, her hips rotating against me as her eyes slam shut. With one hand, I grip her hip, pushing her back into the mattress and pinning her there. With my other hand, I reach behind and swat the bed for my wallet.

Her eyes are glued to my hands as I pull out a silver pack and tear it open, rolling the condom down my cock. Looking up at me, our eyes connect, and her legs fall open to let me in. I lean down on one arm, positioning my dick at her entrance, feeling her wetness over my tip.

"This might hurt a little, but I promise it will get better."

She nods, her eyes dropping to where we're about to join, and I edge forward. Her arms fly to my shoulders, and she digs her nails in as the crown disappears inside her. She takes a sharp breath and slams her eyes shut.

"Baby, look at me," I grit out, trying my fucking hardest to go slow as I stretch her open inch by inch until she gradually accepts all of me. "Relax, Ana. Good girl, that's it."

When I bottom out, my eyes roll. She's so tight and warm, and her pussy is gripping me like it never wants to let go. I swear this is how I will die, just cut off the blood circulation to my dick. But what a fucking way to go. Buried deep inside Ana. I swivel my hips, and she shudders around me. I can feel every spasm, every ripple around my cock, and she's worried she wouldn't last long?

"Oh God," she moans, her head digging into the pillow as I pull out a little and gently push back in.

"This okay?"

"Mmhmm." She sucks her lips between her teeth, a slight frown tugging at her brows. "Teddy, this feels..."

"Good?" I joke, but the question still holds a note of seriousness. If she's not okay, I'll stop.

Her eyes open, and every speck of blue is gone. She smiles and brushes her fingers through my hair. "Amazing. Please... don't hold back."

I begin thrusting gently at first, and then I can't stop myself from picking up speed. She's buried her head in my neck, her nails digging into my back, and I can feel the shuddering of her body under mine. She feels so good—too good—writhing and panting, but then she stills, inhaling deeply, her breath shaky, and there's a warm wetness on my shoulder.

I freeze.

"Baby?" Worry creases my brows. Did I hurt her? Did she not enjoy it? "Baby, what's wrong?"

Ana's shuddering breath ghosts my skin as she gulps in air.

"*Icametoofast,*" she says into my skin, the words muffled and incoherent as she speaks. I move away from her to see her face. Her cheeks are flushed and wet, tears clinging to her lashes.

"What was that?"

She slams her hands over her face and groans.

"I came too fast," she repeats, and this time, I made out every single word.

"You came?" I ask, pulling her hands from her face to see her cheeks colored in splotchy pink. She nods, her eyes dropping away from mine. "As in, you had an orgasm?" I question again, needing to be one hundred percent clear with what she was telling me.

She nods again. The smile that bursts across my lips is uncontrolled, and I swear it might make me look like a madman. I made my girlfriend orgasm...

with my dick... during her first time. I bark a laugh, and she scowls.

"Why are you laughing at me?" she demands, fresh tears lining her eyes.

"Baby, I'm not laughing at you," I say, gently sliding out of her and rolling to the side, cradling her naked body onto my chest. "You have massively inflated my ego, giving me bragging rights for years to come."

She looks up at me, her deep sea-green eyes shining with such vulnerability that I want to protect.

"Baby, most girls don't even come during their first time. But you did. Do you know what that means?" She shakes her head. "I am the King of Sex."

She laughs, the sound watery and slightly relieved as she buries her head into my shoulder.

"But you didn't finish."

I tilt back so she can see me. "Ana, we have all night for me to come. I can come in your hand, down your throat, or if you think you could go for round two, I can come inside you." I kiss her, soft and gentle. "We aren't even close to being finished. I'm going to fuck you as many times as you'll let me. Now that I've been inside you, I'm never going to leave."

Chapter Twenty

Morgana

"Did we have to come home?" I ask, wrapping my arms around Teddy's neck from the first stair to my porch as his hands slide into the back pocket of my jeans.

"Yeah, baby. Some of us have to work tomorrow." I pout, and he laughs. "Enjoy it while it lasts. This summer is your last before all the shitty adult responsibilities start."

"I guess," I sigh. "See you tomorrow?"

"As soon as I've finished work."

We kiss, and even though we spent the entire weekend together, I don't want to say goodbye—which is ridiculous since we live next door to each other. But I miss him already.

"Are you sure you don't want to come over and meet Bowie?" Teddy asks, giving my ass a quick squeeze. "He can only Skype for fifteen minutes, most of which is usually him showing us pictures."

I sigh and detangle myself from him. Thumbing over my shoulder, I step backward up the stairs, wincing a little. Teddy's grin is salacious as his eyes drop to my hips.

"Still sore, huh?"

"A little," I whisper, looking behind me, making sure Mom isn't around, listening.

"I'm sorry."

"No, you're not." I laugh, pointing at his smile. "Maybe you should tell that to your face?"

"Can't help it that my baby is insatiable for my dick. Who'd have known you'd become a sex fiend as soon as I popped your cherry?"

I lunge forward and cover his mouth with my hand. "Shh, what if someone heard?"

He shakes his head, breaking my hold. "Heard what? That I fucked my girlfriend good and hard in the bed, the shower, against the wall, and she came more times than anyone ever has in the history of sexathons?"

"You're an idiot."

"But you love me."

I sigh. "I do. Now go home and speak to your brother."

Opening the door to the house, I tiptoe up the stairs to my room. I cannot deal with my mom right now. Sightseeing with Teddy around New York, meeting Skip for coffee again before we had to catch our train, the way he made love to me in the morning—I mean, I'm not exactly a pro when it comes to *that*, but it felt like more than just sex. There was emotion and an intimacy I didn't think would be there so soon, but with my heart so full, I'm not ready for anything to bring me down.

But, stepping into my bedroom, I could scream. The place looks like it's been ransacked; clothes scattered on the floor, my bedsheets in a pile on top of the bed, and my bedside table lying on its side, the drawer flung across the room, the contents spilt everywhere. My limbs and head feel light as I clutch the doorjamb, staring at the padlock to the black box wrenched open, a pair of bolt cutters sitting beside it. My eyes take in the mess before reaching my mom, standing by the window, papers I know to be my acceptance letters clutched tightly in her hand, her face thunderous as she breathes deceptively calmly.

"What the fuck are these?"

"Mom," I say, holding my hands up like I'd expect you'd do to a wild animal. "I can explain."

"What are you doing applying to different colleges?"

"I wanted to know what my options we—"

"You have no options, Morgana. It's Harvard or nothing."

My overnight bag thuds to the floor. "I don't want to go to Harvard, Mom. I don't want to be a lawyer."

"Since when?" she seethes, the crinkling of the paper in her hand the only sound other than our breathing filling the room.

"Since always. But you and Daddy didn't want to ask me what I wanted."

"This is because of *him,* isn't it?"

I blanch. "No, Mom, it's not. This is about me."

She scoffs. "I think it is, Morgana. I think that boy has filled your little head with fantasies and dreams. He has been slowly bringing you down to his level because he knows he can't keep up with you. He's not good enough for you, so he has to make sure he can keep the playing field even. Was it his idea for you to go on these?" She reaches behind her and throws a pink packet at me. I catch them and recoil.

"You've been going through my things again."

"Did he ask you to go on the pill, Morgana?" She clicks her tongue disapprovingly. "Once he gets what he wants from you, he'll be done with you."

"No," I yell. "That was my idea. Teddy doesn't even know I'm on it."

She stares at me and then down at the letters in her hand, sifting through them. My heart's beating painfully hard against my ribs, my stomach is roiling, and my jaw is aching as I fight against the wobble of my lip. Why is she doing this?

She hums thoughtfully. "Stanford University. The University of Connecticut. The University of Virginia. Yale University. The University of Vermont. All these schools want you?" I nod. She pauses when she gets to the last one. "You want to attend business school?"

"Yes," I whisper.

She folds the letters and taps them against her palm.

"Very well. If business school is what you want, I have..."

"It is," I interrupt, rushing forward and holding her hands. "It is, Mom. I want to go into finance or something. I know I'll be good at it—"

She raises her hand, cutting me off. "I have conditions, Morgana." I swallow hard and press my lips together, fighting the swell of hope that skirts along the edges of my heart. "First, you will attend a school your father and I deem suitable. There are some prestigious schools here you've already applied to."

She eyes me with something I wish was pride, but I know it's not. I nod.

"It will not be Arizona, Morgana."

"Mom..."

"You think I'm stupid? I know Teddy's family comes from Phoenix."

I drop her hands.

"You will come off that birth control."

I step back. It's becoming harder to breathe.

"You will break up with that boy."

"No…" I whisper.

"You will stay away from him, Morgana."

"No…"

"That means you are not to speak to him, see him, or contact him again."

"No, Mom…"

"Do I make myself clear?"

"Mom, please, don't do this. I love him."

Her lip curls, and for the first time, I don't recognize my own mother.

"I will let you live your life in whatever field *business* will allow. But I will not have my daughter tied to that trash."

"Then I refuse. I'll go to Harvard. I'll become a lawyer. But I choose Teddy. Please, Mom, don't make me do this."

She slinks toward me, brushing my hair away from my face with force.

"Morgana, I know how much this hurts. My mother did the same when I was your age."

"What?" I ask as a tear lands on my bottom lash. I swipe at it angrily.

"I was in love with my family gardener. I know, the cliché." She rolls her eyes. "But I know my place and sense of duty, Morgana, and so should you. We are there to make sure our men succeed. Your grandfather was the CEO of a bank. Great grandfather, the chairman of Yale New Haven Hospital, Great-great grandfather, worked in the White House. Do you see where I am going with this? All successful, top-of-their-field men, and all because of their wives."

"Why are you doing this?"

"Because a mechanic is an embarrassment to our family, Morgana."

"Then I'll do what Skip did. I'll leave. I'll never speak to you again if you make me do this."

Mom's eyes harden. "You will, Morgana. You forget what your father does for a living. One word from me and your father will file paperwork to the right person, and Teddy's father's shop in Stamford will be shut down. He will go to prison for tax evasion or something equally disgraceful, and I won't stop there. His pilot brother? Wyatt? He will have his pilot license revoked, blacklisted from both private and commercial airlines. Bowie, the one who takes pictures? Well, I'm sure inappropriate images of children could be found in his *personal* collection. And Teddy, I'm sure a boy who's been saving every penny he earns just to open his own shop would never overcharge his customers and skim off the excess."

Each disgusting scenario is like a slash wound across my heart, and my mom blurs as my eyes grow wetter and wetter with every word. How could she be so cruel? Time seems to have slowed, the feeling of happiness and promise replaced by an overwhelming feeling of powerlessness. She's won. There's no way I can stop this. My body gives up, dropping me to my knees.

"Do you get the picture, Morgana? If you don't comply, your little *boyfriend* is the one who ends up hurting. You're eighteen—a child—you don't know what love is. I might break your heart for a day or two, but you'll realize that you made a mistake by being with that boy in the first place."

"You can't do this," I cry, tears spilling down my cheeks as my hands dig into the carpet.

"You underestimate how much power your father has. And you underestimate me. Now, stop with the theatrics, Morgana, and go wash your face. Richard will be here in ten minutes to take you out for lunch."

I choke on a sob. "What?"

She holds the folded letters in the air. "You think I've just found these?

When I saw Yale had offered you a place, I called Richard and arranged a little get-together for you two. As he went there, he is the best person to tell you all about the school, the campus and, if I'm perfectly honest, sweetheart, he is of a caliber I'd expect for you."

"I love Teddy."

She tuts. "Don't be so naïve, Morgana. You don't love him, and if you think you do, you will fall out of it as quickly as you fell into it. Get off the damn floor, wash your face, and make yourself presentable."

She walks over to my discarded bag and digs around for my phone.

"What are you doing?"

"I'm going to message that boy and tell him it's over."

"No, Mom, please…" I sob, scrambling forward on my knees, my face soaked with tears that won't stop coming as I clutch at her pants leg, begging her to give me my cell. "Let me do it. Please. He won't believe it if it comes from you."

She thrusts the phone in my direction, and it feels like a lead brick. "Fine. But you will let me read what you are going to send first. Then you will prove to me you've blocked and deleted him on everything, Morgana. That includes social media. And if I find out you've so much as sniffed in his direction, I will ruin him and his family. Do I make myself clear?"

My head drops forward as my whole world crashes around me. I can barely see as it takes me several attempts to key in my passcode, and I can feel my heart physically breaking inside my chest as I slowly type out the hardest message I've ever had to send. Mom stands behind me, looking down at my shaking fingers moving sluggishly across the screen, detailing lie after lie about how he never meant as much as he did to me. The swooping noise of the text being sent is loud and echoes on repeat in my brain as I become numb, sitting in the middle of my room, cold and alone. Once I've shown he has been removed from everything, she runs her hand down my hair.

"You might hate me now, darling. But it's what's best."

I will never forgive you for this.

Chapter Twenty-One

Teddy

Ana: Teddy, I've been thinking long and hard about my future, and I've decided I need to do what's best for my family and me. And that is attending a school that's well-suited to my needs. I'm sorry, but I can't go to Arizona. In the fall, I'll be going to Yale. We've not spoken about distance, but this thing between us is too new and casual to commit to something like that. I'm still young. I've got to live my life without being tied down to someone I will never see.

I know this isn't easy, and you'll no doubt hate me right now, but you'll move on and find someone else, someone who will love you as much as I wish I could. If we're honest, we both know this was just some fun, a nice distraction, but I've got to think about my future, one that doesn't and will never include you.

Please don't contact me again, Teddy. I hope you get everything you've ever wanted.

Teddy: The fuck?
Teddy: Ana? What the hell? You're breaking up with me over TEXT???
Teddy: What has your mom said to you? Fucking ignore the bitch. She's manipulating you.
Teddy: Answer your fucking phone.
Teddy: Please, baby. Call me back.
Teddy: What changed, Ana? You were the one who said you were all in, you were the one who applied to Arizona, you were the one who said you'd come with me to Phoenix. Not me. I couldn't ask you to uproot your life for me but YOU wanted to.

"Dude, you look like you're gonna puke. You okay?"

My fingers ache as I strangle the phone, reading her message over and over, my mind spinning. It doesn't make sense. I've left her for an hour, and then I get this? No. I'm not accepting that.

"Teddy? Speak to me."

My head snaps to the computer screen, concern etched across Bowie's face.

"I gotta go."

Jumping up from the sofa, I run to the front door, not bothering to disconnect from Skype as Bowie's voice calls out for our parents. I barely feel my feet as I race across to her house, thundering my fist on her door until her bitch of a mother answers.

"Where is she?"

"Nice to see you too," she glowers with an unmistakable tilt to her lips that she's not managing to hide. This is everything to do with her and not Ana's choice.

"What did you do?" I growl, and Juliette actually looks startled. Good, bitch. I'm not playing.

"I did nothing. I only helped Morgana see the truth before it was too late. You and I both know your little tryst with my daughter won't last. She deserves someone a hell of a lot better than you," she snarls, wrapping her hand around the edge of the door. "Why prolong the inevitable and break her heart worse later? Because that's all you're good for; hurting her. And deep down, she knows that too. Why else would she choose to end it now? Leave my daughter alone. Go back to the hole you came from and let Morgana be happy."

"She's happy with me."

"Maybe right now. But can you honestly say you could make her happy in the long run? That one day, she won't wake up and resent you for not giving her the life she deserves? Stay in your lane, Teddy. You will never be good enough for someone like her."

Edging forward, I grit my teeth. "Where the fuck is she?"

"Out."

"Out where?"

She huffs like I'm getting on her last nerve. Well, so are you, lady. Tell me what I fucking want to know.

"On a date."

She could have stabbed me in the stomach, and it would have hurt less.

"A date?"

The edges of Juliette's lip twist as her eyes gleam, like she knows all she has to do is turn the knife a little more.

"Yes, with a lovely young man who's taken her to Doux Désir, the quaint little French place, you know, the one you must be a member of?"

I know which place she's talking about. The pretentious as fuck place A-list celebs can be spotted at.

Spinning on my heel, I dig my car keys out of my pocket and fling the door open. Tearing out of the driveway, I glance in the rearview mirror at Ana's mom, a wicked grin on her face and her arms folded across her chest. I have never hated a person more than I do that woman.

I drive on autopilot, barely remembering how I got from my house to outside the restaurant, but the valet guy is yelling at me to come back and move my car. He can go to hell. The whole world can go to hell until I speak to Ana and figure out what the fuck is going on. She doesn't want this. I know she doesn't.

"Sir? Sir?" A tall skinny guy in a black suit and tie rounds his Maître D stand and blocks my path to the restaurant. "You cannot go in there dressed like *that*."

I look down at my green Henley, torn jeans, and unlaced combat boots.

"I need to speak to one of your customers," I practically growl, but the man doesn't shift. "Please."

"I'm sorry, Sir, but we have standards we need to maintain, and unfortunately, you do not meet them."

Fuck's sake, what is with everyone and their fucking standards?

"Listen, dickhead. My girlfriend is in there with some other dude. Either you let me pass, or I will make you."

The host flicks his eyes behind me and clicks his fingers, but over his shoulder, I see her. Sitting across the table from her *date*, the same guy I had seen kiss her cheek at that fucking gala. And then the douche slides his hand into hers on top of the table.

No.

No.

She squeezes his back just as two security guards grip my shoulders like a vice. Anger flares in my chest, my eyesight narrows on their joined hands, and I thrash in the guard's hold.

"Right, Son, time to leave."

"Get the fuck off me," I snarl, thrashing harder to no avail as their grip tightens, digging deeper into my muscles and sending blinding white pain down my arms.

"Alright, alright, I'm leaving," I yell loudly, and several diners gaze in my direction. Lips tight and jaw clenched, my whole body winds tight as I stare into the wide sea-green eyes of Ana. Her mouth parts and she guiltily drops the hand of her date and gets to her feet. But she doesn't move toward me. I'm not even sure what I'd do if she did. And what's worse is I still see her love for me shining from her eyes. Or is that just wishful thinking on my part? Is this how she always looked at me and I mistook it for more than it was? Let myself be caught up in the forbidden aspect of it all that I was a dumbass to ever think the way she gazed at me, with warmth and sunshine and with something *more*, that meant she truly loved me? Was she slumming it with me until someone better came along? I saw the way she looked at him. Saw the smile that I thought was only for me. Fucking bitch.

This should never have happened. If I stayed away from her as I told myself to, I wouldn't be here like a fucking moron being manhandled by some goons while my girlfriend's date stares.

Fuck this.

Roughly, I shrug out of the bouncer's hold. No way I'm giving any of the posh pricks the satisfaction of watching someone they deem less worthy getting kicked out. Undoubtedly, it would be the highlight of their pathetic lives witnessing that show.

"Please never return to Doux Désir, sir," the scrawny host calls after me as I thunder to my car and wheel spin onto the street. My pulse is thrashing in my ears, every muscle in my body spasming with a rage so nuclear it wouldn't take much to detonate.

I don't close the car door when I get home, leaving the engine running as I dart to my room, grab a duffle bag and start shoving things inside.

"Son? What's happened?" Dad asks from the doorway.

Ignoring him, I storm to the bathroom, sweeping a bunch of toiletries off a shelf and into the bag. The coconut shower gel sits on top, the bottle taunting me of the first time she came here, smelt like me, clung to me as we kissed... lifting the bottle, I throw it at the wall with a thunk. The cap flies off, and the creamy white liquid sprays across the blue tiles like blood spatter.

"Teddy, baby? Please speak to us," Mom implores, her soft touch landing on my back.

I spin, and she steps back like I'd hit her.

"I'm leaving Mom," I say, marching past her and picking up the car parts on the shelves, deciding which to take now and what to get shipped over later.

"What? Why? You can't go now..."

"Son, what happened?" Dad asks again, and I slam the carburetor down harder than I should.

"You were wrong." I jab my finger at him. "Morgana is not a *nice girl*. She's just as cunning and manipulative as the rest of them here."

"That can't be right..."

"She fucking dumped me, Dad. I took her away for her birthday, arranged for her to see her brother after fucking years apart, and then she dropped me on my ass as soon as we got home."

"Baby, can't you…"

"No, Mom, I can't do anything." Mom winces as I yell at her. "She's on a fucking date as we speak."

I go back to ramming stuff back into my bag. Tugging at the zip, it catches and snaps off.

"Fucking piece of shit," I snarl, grabbing the handles and throwing it onto my back. Something falls onto the ground, but I'm too pissed to get it. It can live there for all I care. I just need to leave.

"Teddy, you can't drive like this," Mom cries, trying to clutch at my arm, but I brush her off and race down the stairs. "Please? Teddy, stay and talk to us. Leave when you've calmed down."

Throwing open the trunk, I toss my bag inside. "I can't stay, Mom. I need to leave now. The drive will be good for me, the car can handle it. I promise I'll be safe."

I shove my hands into my pockets, hiding the tremor in them as she crosses the yard, throwing her arms around me and holding tight. Her tears soak into my t-shirt, and I look up to find disappointment and sadness written all over my dad's face. I untangle Mom from me and slide behind the wheel.

"I'll call you when I get to Phoenix."

Chapter Twenty-Two

Morgana

Seven years later

"**D**on't panic, but..."

Don't panic.

God, it's crazy how two little words have my heart rate skyrocketing in seconds. Why is it that when someone tells you not to panic, you immediately panic? Those words are the equivalent of telling someone apoplectic to *calm down*. Everyone knows you just avoid saying that.

My eyes flick up to meet Lainey, my assistant, as she skirts around my office door, closing it silently behind her and pressing her skinny body to the wood like she's hiding from something. Or someone.

Don't panic.

"Please don't shoot the messenger," she begins, a grimace making her petite features bunch, and that doesn't exactly help with the heart palpitations currently threatening a full-on heart attack.

"Okay, so you know how everyone can't stop talking about the Bank of America portfolio, making them the '*biggest client of Clifton & Azora Finances?*'" She air quotes, and I nod. The signing of Bank of America was huge. Bigger than huge. Monumental for C&A, bumping us from a top fifty financial company to one of the top ten.

She glances over her shoulder, checking that the door's still closed, and I can't help the tiny eyeroll. I love Lainey—she's intelligent, efficient, and always goes above and beyond, way more than an assistant should. But her love for theatrics is a tad tedious, especially when I am already behind on what I have to do for the day.

"Lainey," I plead. The suspense of whatever MI6's newest recruit has to say is killing me.

"They're sending you to Phoenix," she blurts on an exhale.

I laugh. "Good joke."

The corners of her mouth drop as she shakes her head. I stare.

"What? No." The breath leaves me, and I fall against the back of my chair, rubbing the place where my heart is trying to tear out my chest. Lainey slowly walks toward me and perches at the end of my desk.

"Silver lining?"

I raise my gaze to meet her sympathetic one. "Is there one?"

"At least it's not permanent."

"How do you know for sure it's me?" The shake in my voice is damn near embarrassing. Anyone else would be honored to be considered for going to Phoenix. Anyone else, that is, who didn't have my history with a certain resident in that town.

Oh God, I'm going to be sick.

You don't know for sure he is there, Morgana. You're getting ahead of yourself.

Lainey scrunches her nose. "I heard it from Howard, who heard it from Lynsey, who heard it from Steph. It's you, hon."

I sigh, dragging a hand through my hair. Steph is our CEO's PA, and the others; assistants to those just under Victoria Wright. And with all the assistants in the audit department being thick as thieves, if Lainey heard it from them... it looks like I'm going to Phoenix.

"For how long?"

"Three months, I think."

I pinch the bridge of my nose. Okay, three months isn't bad. Three months is doable.

A light knock sounds from my door, and then Victoria appears on the threshold, all tall and *boss-ass-bitch* looking in a black pantsuit that I know costs nearly as much as one month's paycheck. Her smile is bright—probably because she's not the one who's being uprooted—as she walks into my office like her arrival didn't bring in a dark cloud with her. Lainey jumps to her feet, nearly toppling on her heels as she does, wobbling slightly as she gives our boss a little curtsey. Embarrassment coats the tips of her ears, I rub my temples, and Victoria chuckles as Lainey speeds away.

"I'll be at my desk if you need me," she calls back, turning her head just as she pulls the door closed and mouths, *"Why did I do that?"* behind Victoria's back.

I smile, feeling marginally better since Lainey dropped that Phoenix bomb. That is, until Ms. Wright lowers herself into a chair opposite my desk. Her platinum blonde hair is pulled neatly into a bun at her nape, her sharp but elegant features only emphasized by her long slender neck and the suit she's wearing hugs her sculpted body like it's been painted on. She is the ultimate cover girl for women in finance. How she manages to be the CEO of a multibillion-dollar company, have three children under fifteen, a doting husband, *and* still finds the time to fit in a workout is beyond me.

"Morgana," she sing-songs my name. "I must say, I have been impressed with your work recently. Very impressed, actually."

An unsteady smile tugs at my lips, unsure of the correct response to such an unfamiliar concept.

Compliments are for the weak and those who need validation. Adlers do not need such a thing. And yet, it's funny how my dad's career in the public eye requires him to have their approval. Almost like he *craves* it. With his second term as State Attorney General ending, it wasn't a surprise when he announced he was running for Governor.

Victoria cocks her head, looking at me funny.

"Oh, thank you," I say when I realize I lost focus... in front of my *big* boss—good one, Morgana.

She smiles, clasping her hands on her knees. "And all this work has made the partners take notice too." Sitting a little straighter, I brace for impact. "Signing Bank of America was great for business. Because of the implications of dealing with such a big client, we would rather send you to their headquarters for the external audit instead of doing it remotely."

"Wow," I whisper.

"Wow, indeed," she beams, mistaking my disappointment for delight. "Phoenix is beautiful, and I'm sure after four months, you'll never want to leave."

This is happening. Phoenix for...

"Sorry, Victoria." My hands fidget on my desk. "Did you say *four* months?"

She smiles, the little crow's feet deepening at the edges of her eyes. Nausea grips the muscles in my stomach, making me go from queasy to downright nauseous, heading for a total vomit fest any second.

Four months in Phoenix.

Four months away from my friends, my apartment, my bed.

Four months stuck in a city, peering over my shoulder, constantly looking for that one person who broke my heart—*more like shattered*—into a million teeny tiny pieces.

Did he really break your heart, though?

Okay, fine, it wasn't *his* fault. But still, my heart broke that day too. Misplaced panic joins my unsettled stomach. Deep breaths, Morgana, he might not even be there. It's not like you asked his mom to find out.

He moved back, you dumbass. His parents might not have come right out and said it, but he's there.

Okay, but still, even if he was, Phoenix is a big place with a population of over 1.5 million last time I checked. So if he had moved back, the likelihood I'd accidentally bump into him would be slim.

"I can't go to Phoenix."

My eyes widen as the words blurt from my mouth. I can't go. Something deep down is telling me this is a bad idea, the feeling getting stronger and stronger with every second that ticks by. Victoria purses her lips, a frown lining her forehead.

"And why not?" Her voice is steely, and I instantly regret speaking out. She glances down at my hands, absentmindedly toying with my ring, and then her gaze softens as recognition dawns on her face. "When is the big day?"

I drop my hand to my lap, hiding the beautiful pear-cut diamond ring Richard proposed with nearly eight months ago. Everything had been perfect. Candles, moonlight, a bottle of my favorite champagne on ice...

"Seven months."

"Perfect. The trip will be for four months. Five tops," Victoria says with a clap. "I can guarantee you'll be home in time for your wedding."

Guilt joins the cocktail of emotions partying in my stomach at my first thought, immediately going to my ex—someone I've had no ties to after seven years—instead of the man I'd promised the rest of my life to. Hell, Richard didn't even factor into my next thought as I panicked with the possibility of accidentally running into Teddy at the mere mention of a city he may or may not be in.

I glance up, lost in my thoughts again, with a look that makes Victoria stiffen. I have no idea what I look like, but I force myself to smile, for my shoulders to relax from where they've migrated around my ears, and I look back at the twinkling diamond on my left hand.

"There's still so much to do... with the wedding. We don't have a band or a color scheme yet. We haven't even chosen our menus."

"The joys of everyone having to find a way to work remotely due to COVID," she states, pulling her phone from her pants pocket and beginning to scroll. "Pinterest has great ideas for décor, all based on different color palettes. And there's a great little website for easy access to the best bands around the metropolitan area... Ralph and I used it when we got married... Oh, shoot, I can't seem to find it." She looks up and smiles, her posture easing as she waves her hand in the air, like remotely planning a wedding is easy and isn't a good enough reason to stop me from going. "But not to worry, I will email it to you as soon as I remember. Everything else your fiancé can sort out, can he not? Food is the way to a man's heart and all. Surely, he'd love a day gorging out on gourmet samples?"

I guess. Except Richard isn't exactly the hands-on kind of fiancé. *I'm* not exactly the hands-on kind of bride either, leaving most, if not all, of the planning to both our mothers. My wedding to Richard Atkinson is fast approaching, and it's a day I'd rather not happen at all. Not that I don't love Richard or want to be his wife. I did... do. But this wedding... it's more of a show, a spectacle where I'm the prized pig brought to market for everyone to see.

"Great. I will have my assistant book your accommodation, travel..."

"I'll drive," I interrupt, and Victoria looks stunned for a second. Sheepishly, I say, "I know it's a long drive, but I'd rather have my car if I'm going to be stu—living in Phoenix for a few months."

Victoria smiles, getting to her feet. "Of course, very well. You'll need to be there Monday."

Monday? That was less than a week away.

"Take the rest of the day off to get organized," she suggests, like there wasn't an hour left of the workday. "The partners and I have agreed you should pass all your ongoing work to Brian. He'll finish anything outstanding. Just send him an email outlining where you have gotten up to." Before leaving my office, she turns back to me. "Oh, Morgana, I forgot to mention, there will be a twelve percent bonus for you taking this assignment. I trust that will compensate for not being here to finish your wedding plans?"

I nod.

Twelve percent bonus—Twelve thousand dollars to move states for a few months is more than enough compensation... it just might not be enough for the constant turmoil of knowing I *could* see Teddy again.

After all this time.

After all the heartache, tears, and frustration at wanting to reach out, but knowing I couldn't.

"Have a safe drive, Morgana. I am sure Phoenix will be great."

Chapter
Twenty-Three

Teddy

"**Y**es," I groan, my head falling back and hitting the back of my chair. "That's it. Take it as far as you can."

The hand I have gripped in her black hair tightens, and my hips buck upward into her mouth as I push farther down her throat, chasing the release that seems to be evading me tonight. I should slow down and take it easy as I feel her constricting around me, spluttering and gagging as spit pools at the corner of her mouth, dripping down her chin and onto my leg, but I can't. I'm too fired up, too restless. Her nails dig into my thighs, the bite of pain the thing I need to finish me off. Thick ropes of cum shoot straight down the back of her throat as I grunt out a curse, holding her head down so her nose nearly touches my pubes. Not that she cares. She loves rough and dirty and brutal. She looks up, eyes wide and filled with unshed tears, as she swallows everything I give her like the good little whore she is. Pride is evident in her smile as she runs her thumb over her swollen lips, gathering what slipped out and sucking it greedily into her mouth.

"Did you like that?" she whispers, her voice hoarse after the punishment from my cock, leaning back on her knees the same as last week. And the week before that, and the week before that too. The same question falls from her plump lips every damn time. She leans forward to lick the crown of my cock again. I hum in approval as she gazes back at me, all starry-eyed and big smiles. My ass sticks to the leather of the refurbished set of old Corvette seats, resembling lounge furniture. I push to my feet and stand, tugging up my boxers and coveralls to stuff myself away before pulling the zipper high enough to keep them on my hips.

Towering over Sophia, I reach out and run my thumb along her jawline. I make her wait for what I know she wants—what I know she *needs* to hear from me—like the asshole I am. She shifts, practically begging like a dog for a bone, reaching up to trace the contours of my abs.

I grin and grip her chin hard between my thumb and finger. "You're such a good little slut for me."

She shudders at the words. I'm not into degrading women, but the endearment she likes to hear comes easy and weightless, and she laps it up every time. I flick my thumb over her cheek, and she nuzzles into my hand, chasing after the contact as I squeeze past her. Grabbing an open bottle of water from my desk, I pop the cap and finish it in one breath, waiting for Sophia to button her two-sizes-too-small pink blouse over her perky tits—the ones her husband bought her for their anniversary last year. Slipping her heels back onto her feet, she leans forward, tits pressed together suggestively as she twirls a strand of that dark hair around her finger. I know what she wants. She got me off. Now it's her turn.

Not tonight, sweetheart.

She pulls her ring from where she'd tucked it in her bra just before she had dropped to her knees and took me in her mouth. Slipping the gold wedding band back on her ring finger, she sucks her bottom lip between her teeth, and her eyes light up with a fire I can feel from across the room.

"I can't tonight, Sophia," I say, shaking my head as she pouts.

"That's not fair, Theo," she says, and my teeth grate at her little nickname. My fucking name isn't even Theodore. "I never thought you'd be a selfish lover."

Getting to her feet, she sways over to stand in front of me, dragging her nails down my bare chest, brushing that line of hair trailing from my belly button and disappearing into the overalls. I wrap my hand around her wrist, halting her movements.

"I didn't ask you to come and suck my cock," I say, cold and distant as I look into her eyes. "You did that all on your own. So don't pretend this is some tit-for-tat. You don't like that you came here and gave me what you thought I wanted. You didn't get to come? That's not my problem."

I drop her arm and walk toward my office door, unlocking it and holding it open. Sophia huffs and storms back over to the chair, grabbing her purse from where it landed when she first arrived.

"You're a jerk, Theo," she scoffs, narrowing her eyes as she tries to pass me. I reach out, grabbing the door frame and blocking her exit.

"And yet you'll be here next Thursday, on your knees, like always. Won't you?" I slip two fingers under her chin and tilt her head up, using my free hand to ghost my thumb over her lips. She sucks her lower one between her teeth, trying and failing to look annoyed. We both know the truth. I use her just as much as she uses me.

I purposely drop my eyes to her mouth, holding my gaze for a beat, then lean in, aiming for her red lips, but veering off last second, catching her cheek.

She sighs, the sound a breathy moan full of desperation and aching for me as she's denied again for another thing she always wants and will never get. I can't stand to taste myself on her lips—any woman's lips—after I've been sucked off, or in general, really.

Not anymore.

"I don't know why I put up with you," she tries to joke, looking to the floor. I grip her chin, squeezing a little, and her eyes dart to mine, big and round and still blown with arousal. She'll need to take care of that herself.

"You do it because while your husband is off fucking the secretary he doesn't think you know about, you get your revenge by sucking the dick of someone *much* younger and *much* more attractive than him."

She chuckles, her hand landing on my chest as her eyes bounce between mine and my mouth, and I bet if I shoved her to her knees again, she'd happily swallow me whole. Instead, I release her face and place my hand on her shoulder to usher her out. She's overstayed her welcome, and her desperation is unattractive.

Slapping her on her surprisingly pert ass for a forty-eight-year-old, she gasps with a giggle and stumbles forward, looking over her shoulder as she walks through my auto shop.

"See you next week," she purrs, checking me out. I flex my stomach—an apology for sending her away unsatisfied—as we both know she goes wild for my chest, the needy slut. Approaching the side door, she does a small finger wave and slips out into the night.

I stare at the closed door, my jaw clenching under the strain of my grinding teeth.

"Fuck," I growl, turning away and slamming my office door behind me. The metal blinds bang against the dirt-stricken window in the middle of the door, and I drop into my chair, closing my eyes. Monotonous is not a word I would usually associate with sex. But every Thursday, like clockwork, Sophia Phillips and her mediocre mouth turn up, eager and willing to help me find release, and it's losing its appeal. She is just another woman whose husband didn't love her enough to stay faithful but is too dependent on his gold card to have any self-respect to leave.

Not that I particularly care. To each their own. I get to come, and she leaves with a smile and a full belly.

I'm a pig—I know I am. A self-loathing, self-sabotaging pig, and I can honestly say I do not concern myself with a consenting woman's marital status. Single, engaged, married, or divorced, I never discriminate. It doesn't matter if they want to keep their two-carat diamond rings on their fingers when they wrap their hand around my cock.

My hollowed black heart doesn't care.

It's all the same: No strings attached sex and a sated dick.

Some might drive Bentleys, while others drive Jeeps, but at least the women here aren't more stuck up than those back in Connecticut, and they understand the *no-strings-attached* part of the arrangement to the T.

I pinch the bridge of my nose. When did it get so bad? I never used to be this way. Even as a teenager, I was never this much of a dickhead with a fuck-ton of cynicism about the opposite sex and relationships, to boot.

Oh, right. Her.

"Please tell me that wasn't Mrs. Phillips I saw sashaying out of here?"

The office door bangs open with a crash, and Ozzy barrels inside like an excited puppy. I crack one eye open, watching my best friend pick up my discarded t-shirt, toss it, and it lands, covering my face. "You lucky bastard. What I wouldn't give to be on the receiving end of that, Teddy Bear."

"Fuck off," I snarl at his nickname, immediately reminded of a time I wish I could permanently forget. Two people to give me that stupid nickname. The same two people more similar than I would have ever thought, and I wish now I never made that connection. Fucking Connecticut.

Yanking my shirt from my face, I sit up to pull it over my head. "She's all yours, man."

Flopping into the chair next to me, Ozzy reaches forward and opens the mini-fridge door built into a coffee table made from an old engine. I'm a total mechanics cliché. Anything car related, it's mine.

"Nah, I don't need your sloppy seconds." He laughs, handing me a beer and settling back in his seat. "Besides, when this comes to bite you in the ass, I want front-row seats with popcorn. Since you came back, the scandal in this town is off the charts."

"Her limp-dick husband wouldn't do anything. Not when he's screwing some twenty-something intern at his office."

Ozzy whistles, cracking into his can with a hiss and taking a sip. My eyes narrow as he laughs through a burp and stretches to punch my shoulder.

"What's up with you?" I frown and wait for him to elaborate. "You're more of an asshat tonight than your usual delightfully prickish self. Mrs. Phillips not live up to expectations?" He pauses, then jumps forward in his chair, joy spreading across his clean-shaven face. "Oh, oh, I know. Did little Teddy not live up to expectations? Mrs. P's face wasn't all blissed out like she'd had fun playing with her favorite toy when I met her as I was coming in."

I take my shoe off and throw it at him, knocking the beer can from his hand. "Hey!"

"First off, there's nothing *little* about me, Oscar. Secondly, why do you always need to make me sound like some perverted child's toy?"

He shrugs. "Not my fault that's the name your parents gave you."

Reaching forward, he reopens the fridge for another can, the lazy bastard unwilling to get off his fat ass and get the one that rolled away. Instead, he lets beer spill across the floor. I sigh, leaning my head on the back of my seat and looking at the ceiling tiles dotted with damp patches.

I need to get that fixed.

"Dude," Ozzy says, and I lift my head a little to look at him. Leaning his elbow on his knee, his face turns all serious and shit. I fucking hate it when he does that. Nudging my knee, he asks, "What's up? C'mon tell me, I am *the* best secret keeper."

I arch a brow. "Says who?"

"Sierra, that's who," he says, his proud uncle smile lighting up his entire face. And I must admit, his niece is the cutest damn thing ever to be born. "Went to my sister's last night, and she sat telling me everything. And I mean *everything,* bro. Which of the girls in her class were the meanies, boys she had crushes on, and there wasn't just the one kid either. And all because Uncle Oscar is the bestest secret keeper."

I chuckle, swallowing the lump that always seems to form whenever I think of that kid. If I were ever to have a kid—*fucking unlikely*—I hope she's like Sierra. "Your sister will have a little hell-raiser when she grows up."

"Doesn't she know it." He laughs. Sobering, he knocks my knee again. "C'mon, dude, spill. What's up your ass tonight?"

His eyes twinkle as I side-eye him, far too eager for me to share, and all I know is that this will be a bad idea. He might be a good secret keeper to a six-year-old, but that doesn't mean he won't use whatever I tell him to wind me up later. But does that stop me from opening my mouth anyway?

"It's just something my mom used to say. That our gut knows things before our heads do."

He hums thoughtfully, brows pinched together like a shrink listening to all my problems. I roll my eyes and continue.

"It just feels like—" I scrub a hand down my face, resigned to the fact that no matter how fucking dumb I feel right now, I've started, and Ozzy won't let me stop until he gets it all out of me. "I dunno, like a bad omen or something."

He's silent for a while, his chin in his hand, fingers strumming against his cheek.

"It could be. I mean, you have been making waves with *married* women and all. Or..." He holds his hands out. "Hear me out. Maybe, just maybe, you're about to get your period."

I laugh. Typical fucking Oz. "Fuck you. This is why I don't tell you shit. What happened to guys being more open about their mental health and shit?"

"Okay, sorry. If you need real talk, I'm here. Tell Uncle Oscar what's wrong, and I won't judge." Ozzy smiles, bringing his drink to his lips, but I quickly swipe it from his hand. "I was drinking that!"

"It's your night to be on call, asshole," I say, sinking back and kicking my feet up on the coffee table, conversation forgotten. "And you can't exactly do that if you've been drinking."

Making a show of the whole thing, I swallow some of his beer and then gulp down mine, sighing obnoxiously loud with a smack of my lips for good measure.

Ozzy scowls. "It's one beer."

I shrug. "No drinking when on call. You know the score. Don't make me fire your ass."

"We're *partners*," he reminds me, "you can't fire my ass without my approval. Besides, you'd be lost without me. This gorgeous mug brings in all the ladies I so graciously pass to you."

He circles his finger around his face. Poor bastard is delusional. We look at each other, expressions solemn for a beat, before we both erupt into laughter. God, I needed that. Oscar Ford has been my best friend since kindergarten and was just as devastated about the move to Old Greenwich as I'd been seven years ago. But the day I called him and said I needed a place to crash, he was there with open arms and his mom's sofa. Then, after one too many beers and drunken scribblings on the back of a napkin, we had Grease Monkey Auto Shop mapped out. And the rest was history.

Slamming his boots to the ground, he stands, stretching his arms above his head with a yawn. Walking to his locker, he grabs his hoodie, an oversized gray thing with the shop's logo on the back—a cheeky little monkey with a wrench in his hand—and pulls it on.

"I'm gonna head out," he says, swiping the keys to the tow truck from my desk. "I need some seriously strong coffee if I'm going to last the night."

I tilt my head back, seeing his upside-down profile checking himself out in a mirror.

"You know you don't have to stay up the whole night? Only need to move your butt outta bed if you get called."

"Yeah, I know." He smirks, winking at me from the mirror. "But Roseann is working tonight. It's her night to do the night shift, and Thursdays are usually dead. Soo..." He wiggles his eyebrows. "You might not be the only one whose eyes roll back into their head tonight."

Coming over, he leans down, going in for a kiss like that scene in Spiderman when he's hanging upside down, and Mary Jane pulls down his mask before they make-the-fuck-out in the rain. Tilting my head, I roll out from the seat, managing to save the beers as Ozzy clicks his fingers in mock disappointment.

"Damn, so close," he says. "I'll kiss you on the lips one day, Vivienne."

"Who?"

"The prostitute from *Pretty Woman*." I stare blankly. Ozzy groans. "You're so uncultured! Julia Roberts's character never kisses the *Johns* until rich and handsome Richard Gere comes along. Then *bang*, they kiss, fall in love, and live happily ever after."

"Sounds like a load of shit to me."

That and the fact that I've already made the mistake of doing that once before. Never again.

Chapter Twenty-Four

Morgana

"Tell me why I didn't push harder not to go?" I whine into the empty car, rubbing at my tired eyes. *'Push harder'*... yeah, right, when I didn't put up any fight to begin with.

But maybe doing the whole two thousand, four hundred odd mile drive alone wasn't the most brilliant idea I could have had. My back aches, my butt is numb, and the lights in the middle of the interstate are starting to blur.

"From what you said, I don't think you had a choice." Richard's voice fills the car from the speaker, and I relax into my seat. He's right, I didn't, but that doesn't mean I needed to roll over with my belly up. "Besides, by the time you get home, it will be less than two months until you become Mrs. Morgana Atkinson."

Mrs.

Why does that thought make my stomach clench?

"Are you sure we can't elope? Run away and get married, just the two of us?" I joke, my already too-tight fingers gripping the wheel harder, slick with sweat as I think of my upcoming nuptials.

He chuckles, unaware that his future wife is panicking with every waking minute that the clock ticks. "Your mother would have a heart attack if we had a Vegas wedding. Could you imagine? She'd think you were pregnant out of wedlock, or something equally scandalous." He gasps, and I can picture him signing the cross as he mimics my mother while my hand subconsciously flies to my empty belly, and I shudder at the thought of having his baby... right now. "And let's not even mention my mom. One can only hope she'd have a heart attack if we eloped."

"Richard!" I cry, biting my cheek to stop laughing, my mood lightening a fraction.

Richard's mom is a witch. A mean, bad-tempered old witch who thinks the sun shines out of her other son's butt. It's no wonder she and my mom are friends. But when it comes to this wedding, the mothers are like *wedding-zillas, mom-zillas*? Either way, neither can be outdone by the other.

My mom wants roses for centerpieces. Daphne wants ice sculptures.

My mom wants a string quartet. Daphne wants a children's choir.

When Mom suggested a champagne reception, Daphne insisted on Oscietra caviar canapés, imported from London, made with a bubble gold roesti that made the extremely overpriced appetizer look like a ring. Seriously, out of all those words, does anyone know what that food is?

Skip would. Too bad he RSVP'd no to the invite. Not that I could blame him. After that fantastic night in New York, when I saw him after years, our relationship became even more strained.

"I'm joking, sweetheart," Richard sighs wistfully. "But she wouldn't be acting this way if it were George and Penelope's wedding she was planning…"

And I'd probably be more invested if it wasn't my wedding too.

I clutch at my chest at the painful, solid lump rising in my throat. Did it suddenly get hard to breathe? Gasping, I press the button on the door panel, gulping in the cool night air as the window slowly slides down and out of sight. My pulse beats like a drum, echoing in my ears as my neck grows clammy. I slide my arm under my hair, holding it up and letting the breeze filter around my body.

"Morgana? Sweetheart? Are you still there?"

I nod in answer, even though he can't see me. But mentally, I'm miles away in this sea of fear as I imagine my life as Mrs. Atkinson: cocktail parties, expensive luncheons with other dutiful wives from our social circle, talking about the best schools to send their unborn children for Pre-K.

"It's just cold feet," Shay had said when I told her how I felt.

Cold feet.

Freezing blocks of ice weigh me down, dragging me deeper and deeper into a darkness where I can't—

"Morgana!"

I jump, tugging on the wheel, swerving a little out of my lane.

"Shit," I puff as a car flashes its high beams from behind.

"Morgana? Are you okay? Stop ignoring me and tell me what is going on."

"Yeah, yes. Sorry," I reply, lifting a trembling hand to my throat. "A cat ran across the road."

"A cat?" He laughs skeptically, and I can picture the pull of his brow and the twist of his lips in my head. "On the highway?"

Right.

"Uh-huh," I lie, my voice an octave higher than before. "That's why I got so scared."

"Maybe you should pull over and have a break. You've been driving for hours."

No sooner has he suggested that, does an illuminated sign for Phoenix in fifteen miles give me a second wind. I am so close, I can almost taste it. Fresh nerves roil in my stomach. Tiny baby butterflies that only hatched a day ago are a thriving colony, as I'm finally nearing the Airbnb I'll call home.

"Good idea, honey," I agree, knowing I'll continue driving until I'm there. With renewed energy, I glance at the time on the dash and say, "Richard, I've got to go. I promised Shay I'd call her every night when I was on the road, and it's already after eleven. She'll be home from work."

"Work," I hear him scoff, even though it's not directly spoken into the phone. My eyebrows dip, and I feel that prickle line my arms in a way that happens every time before he's even said his following sentence. "I wouldn't exactly call what she does *work*."

Maybe not up to your standards.

"Why not?" I ask, defensive of my best friend. For some reason, Richard and Shay have never gotten along. Not when they first met and not now that I'm engaged. It isn't that Shay dislikes him; it's Richard who despises Shay. She hasn't done anything to warrant such a reaction, but Richard always says she is a bad influence. No wonder my mom loves him. At times, I wonder if she's more suited to him than me.

"She goes around eating free food, Morgana. Like a poor person."

"In return for a review on her *three*-hundred-thousand follower Instagram page," I reply. "She's a blogger, Richard, a food critic."

"Hmm," he mutters, the noise bouncing from the speakers like bad static.

"Besides," I cut in before he can bash her job some more, "she has been asked by the New York Times, on several occasions, might I add, to write reviews for their column."

"Okay, okay." He chuckles, yet I don't see anything funny. "No need to get defensive. I just meant she could be doing that on the side. Being *an influencer* isn't exactly a long-term job. Especially with the connections her parents have. Such a waste."

My finger hovers over the phone icon on my steering wheel, itching to hang up on him. Very rarely does Richard aggravate me to the point of wanting to disconnect our calls, but when he starts talking down about Shay... Maybe four months apart would do us some good.

"I'll call you when I get to the apartment if it's not too late."

"Okay, honey. Drive safe. I love you."

"I know. I love you too."

The words barely leave my lips before I slam my thumb down on the button, ending the call.

"I think this could be good for my career," I said, adding an extra pair of socks to my suitcase.

"I understand that, but do you think that's what's best right now?" Richard asked, unbuttoning his shirt and tossing it in the laundry basket. "Surely, there are more qualified people they could send? Someone more senior with more experience."

My fingers dug into the sides of the case. "What is that supposed to mean? They wouldn't have chosen me if they didn't think I could handle it."

"Of course, sweetheart. You're being too sensitive. All I meant was I thought we'd decided you'd cut your hours closer to the wedding. You know, get prepared for when we have children."

You decided, you mean.

My back instantly tensed. I might have been apprehensive, annoyed even, that this new portfolio blindsided me, but once the initial shock had disappeared, a sense of excitement—and dread—flurried. I would have been a fool to try to get out of it. Not to mention, I am the youngest auditor at C&A to take the lead on such a high-profile client.

It's a big deal.

"We did." *A ghost of a smile was all I could manage as I flipped the suitcase lid and slowly pulled on the zip. Each click of the teeth joining together sounds heavy in his large bedroom. A room that will be ours after we say our I dos.* "But I thought that wasn't happening for at least a few years. I'm only twenty-five, Richard. Plenty of time before we need to start trying for children."

His arms snaked around my middle, cupping my flat, empty stomach. Kissing my shoulder, he said, "It is. But why wait? We love each other. So why wait to start the inevitable?"

The inevitable.

He kissed my shoulder again and left to brush his teeth while I put the suitcase by the door, ready for the morning.

That night, while Richard and I made love, I fought back the tears that pricked my eyes, telling myself I was just upset that I was leaving the man I cared for deeply... The man I loved.

Then I did something I'd never done before.

I faked it.

Breathing heavily and clenching my legs around his waist, I scrunched my eyes, feeling the unmistakable twitch as he filled the condom, and I pretended to enjoy our last time having sex for four months. Rolling off me, he kissed my lips, turned his back, and fell asleep—no cuddling, no intimacy as always once it's over.

And I stared at the ceiling as silent tears slid into my hair.

"This can't possibly be my *ex*-best friend, back from the dead, can it?" Shay booms through the hands-free. "Nearly three days, and *poof*, I'm already forgotten. Left behind like last season's Vera Wang."

I laugh, even though mentioning my wedding dress designer threatens another panic attack. Taking a steading breath, I say, "I told you I'd call tonight, and it's tonight, isn't it?"

"*Tonight* meant three hours ago, not when I just got into bed."

I wince, checking the time and realizing it's almost two a.m. on the East Coast. Stupid Mountain Standard Time. "Sorry, I'll let you go."

"No, no," she says, and I can see her waving her hand in dismissal in my mind. "I'd rather talk to you than binge reruns of *Married at First Sight* anyway."

"Thank you for putting me first," I drawl. "Wait, why do you sound sober? I thought you had that new opening tonight?"

"Urgh," she groans dramatically. "Don't even go there. The thought alone is enough to make me want to hurl."

"That bad, huh?"

"Bad?" she scoffs, her loud voice bouncing around the car again, causing the speakers to shudder violently, telling me that I need to turn down the volume. "Bad doesn't begin to describe that place. How can someone get Italian so wrong?"

"At least it was a free meal," I say, trying to find the silver lining and hating that I said the one thing Richard was berating.

"I guess. I'm glad I never took Lenox. He'd have walked out, it was that bad." She laughs. "Did I mention it was *bad?*"

"I think you did." I chuckle as a calmness like no other washes over me, all from hearing my best friend speak. "*Soo,* how are things with Lenox?"

"Good. Things are good."

"Will he be the one to take Shay off the market, you think?"

She hums. "We've been on three dates, Morgs. It's not exactly exclusive. He's a nice guy, but mega busy, y'know. He's at a medical conference in Chicago right now."

"I knew it wasn't me you missed," I joke. "You're just bored because your man is away, and you have no one to annoy now."

"Not my man, just a bed warmer." She laughs, and I smile. The sound of rustling sheets fills the car as she shifts in bed. "Four months is the longest we've ever been apart, babe. I don't know if I can handle it."

"I know, me neither."

"Oh, oh," she squeals through the sound of things dropping to her floor as if she jumped up in excitement. "I can come to visit. Check out the hot Phoenix boys... what the bars and restaurants have to offer... My followers would fucking love it."

She speaks loud and fast, planning a trip to a state I've not yet set foot in, when a loud pop echoes through the car, then a quiet *tick-tick-tick,* then a *hiss* as it begins to slow down.

Shit.

Chapter
Twenty-Five

Morgana

"What was that?"

Shay's voice barely registers as my eyes dart up to the inside mirror, checking around the darkened road, then out the front again.

Please say I didn't hit anything.

Please say I didn't hit anything.

Please say I didn't hit anything.

There's nothing. Just quietness, desolate and eerie.

"Shit, Shay, I need to go," I say, tugging hard on the wheel. The loss of assisted steering makes it nearly impossible to veer off onto the shoulder, out of the way of anyone driving this late. And when smoke starts to billow from under the hood, terror quickly spears its claws deep into me as I hang up, cutting off Shay shouting my name. Unbuckling my belt, I grab my phone from the center console and dash from the car. My hands shake, my cell in a vice grip as I back away on unsteady legs from the white plumes rising from the vehicle.

Oh God, what if it catches fire?

Fumbling, I unlock the phone and google the nearest 24-hour mechanic, clicking on the first one that appears without even reading the name. I wait, biting my thumbnail, urging whoever is on the other end to answer their goddamned phone. Finally, a gruff voice of an older man answers, barely managing to say hello as I barrel ahead.

"Is this the on-call mechanic?" I blurt, my tongue feeling so thick that I stumble over my words. "I need your help, please. Something is wrong with my car."

"Okay, ma'am, I'm gonna need you to slow down and take a breath." I do as he says. "Okay, good. Now tell me, what's up with your car?"

"I think it's about to catch on fire. There was a bang, the car slowed, smoke and—" I rush again, barely pausing for air.

"Ma'am? Ma'am?" His voice is loud and steely as he demands my attention. I squeeze my eyes tightly together and force another calming breath while my racing heart gallops ahead. "Tell me where you are."

Shoot. I have no idea.

Opening my eyes, I glance around, seeing a neon sign above some trees flashing bright blue off in the distance. The relief is palpable as my legs begin to wobble.

"I'm not sure, exactly. I passed a sign not far back for Phoenix, and I can see a sign for Buddy's Diner."

"Buddy's? Oh, what are the chances? That's where I am right now." I hear the jingle of keys and a muffled *"thanks, Roseann,"* and then he's back on the line. "Stay where you are. I'll be there in five. Can you put your hazards on so I can see you?"

I take a hesitant step toward my car. "The car isn't going to go up in flames or anything, right?"

He chuckles. "No, ma'am. Sounds to me like a blown cylinder head. The coolant leaked, seized up your engine, and created steam. It's safe to go back into the car and collect your stuff."

"Are you sure?"

"Can't be sure without looking under the hood, but it's safe enough for you to go inside."

"Thank you," I breathe, my shoulders sagging a little.

"No problem." The slam of a truck door and the rumble of an engine fill my ears. "If it makes you feel safer, you can stand away from the car. But stay in the headlights, don't want to be running you over. I'll be there soon."

He disconnects our call, and I quickly return to the car, leaning over the driver's side and tapping on the hazard lights. Pulling the phone charger lead from the USB port, I stuff it into my purse, swiftly ducking around to the trunk to start removing my suitcases. As I set the last one on the dirt, a white and blue tow truck pulls up alongside me. The man I assume I spoke to on the phone hops out of the cab, and I feel foolish for thinking he would have been old. Flipping down the hood to his sweater, the man—only slightly older than me—walks toward my car, eyeing me and then my luggage.

"I meant you could grab your purse or whatever. Not everything you own." He laughs, itching the thin layer of hair on his jaw. Thank goodness for the night sky masking my embarrassment as I, too, look at my four large suitcases standing side by side. "Moving or visiting?"

"Visiting?" I murmur, heat climbing my neck as the man whistles low and starts to repack my trunk.

"Are you asking or telling?" he asks, putting the first case back into the trunk.

"Telling. Here for a few months for work."

"City girl, huh?"

I laugh quietly, rubbing the tips of my fingers along my forehead. "That obvious?"

"Uh-huh," he huffs, straining to get the last and heaviest case into the tiny trunk of my Chevrolet Volt. "Plus, no girl I know around here has Louis Vuitton luggage."

Great. Barely entered the town, and the first person I meet already thinks I don't belong here. I pull at the edges of my denim jacket, tightening it around my body.

"Thank you for coming to help me," I say, watching him close the trunk and smile. It's broad and cheeky, and for a complete stranger, it suits him.

"It's my job, ma'am." He stretches out his hand. "I'm Oscar, but you can call me Ozzy. Everyone else does."

I slide my hand into his. "Ana."

"Lovely to meet you, Ana, and welcome to Phoenix."

Shay: Are you dead? Please say you're not dead.

Shay: Morgana Fuckface Adler, answer your phone this goddamn minute.

Morgana: Did you just middle name me "fuckface"?

Shay: SHE'S ALIVE. And yes, I middle-named you fuckface. That's what you are, you dickhead. How could you leave me like that? I thought I'd have to come identify you at the morgue or something.

Morgana: Why would you have done that and not my mom? Or Richard?

Shay: Yeah, Richard probably wouldn't let me anywhere near your dead body.

Shay: Anyway, what happened? Are you alright?

Morgana: Yeah, just a little issue with my car. Had to get it towed away.

Shay: Aw that sucks. Hope everything's okay. And with that, I'm going back to sleep. Night night, babe.

I glance at the time in the corner of the phone. 6:00 a.m. and back to sleep. Oh, the life of an influencer.

I stare at the popcorn ceiling of the bedroom, twisting my engagement ring around my finger and thinking about calling Richard. By the time I got settled in the small apartment, it completely slipped my mind that I told him I'd call as soon as I got in, and instead, I fell asleep as soon as my head hit the pillow. I could call him now, though. He'd be at the office sitting behind his polished desk, working on whatever submission my father had given him. He wouldn't be surprised if I called and told him about the car. He hated it. He has repeatedly told me how unsafe it was, how unreliable it would be, and that I should trade it in for something a little more *fitting*.

Well, I'm not going to let him know any of it. I'll pay cash and avoid the '*I told you, Morgana, you should have listened*' speech he is so good at giving me.

Slipping from the bed, I walk into the bathroom, turning on the shower before grabbing my toiletries from my suitcase. Tension, fatigue, and long days of travel wash from my limbs as I rub my body wash across my arms, the stress from driving across state and car issues dissipating with every splash of the cascading water.

"Today will be a good day," I mutter, giving myself a much-needed pep talk. "You are a badass boss bitch. Blown cylinders or whatever won't stop you from killing it today and proving to Richard why they were right to send you here."

Finishing my shower, I dress in a white blouse and black pencil skirt, taking one last look in the bathroom mirror before grabbing my bag and heading outside. It is beautiful. The quaint little Main Street, the community gardens near the Airbnb, everything is just picturesque. No wonder Teddy always wanted to move back.

Teddy.

"Phoenix is a big place, you moron. Get a grip on yourself," I chastise, earning a worried glance from a man as I approach the door to a café, and he holds it open. I smile, embarrassed. "Sorry."

He arches a brow and grumbles under his breath.

Officially the weird city chick now.

The strong aroma of coffee, coupled with the unmistakable scent of cinnamon, fills the air, and my stomach instantly grumbles as I wait in the long line to the counter. Smacking a palm over my belly, I rub it as I glance up at the chalk menu board on the wall. Approaching the counter, I eye the various cakes and pastries filling the glass display case and my mouth waters.

Cinnamon roll, oh, how you taunt me.

"Hi, what can I get you?"

"Could I please ha—"

"Hope you don't mind. I'm running late, and I need my fixing of coffee before my meeting."

I blink, standing with my mouth parted as a tall, skinny woman in a white knee-length skirt turns back to the counter and orders two tall Americanos with creamer, pulling a twenty-dollar bill from her purse and sliding it over the counter. The barista stares at her, her jaw flexing before plastering on the fakest smile I've ever seen and wordlessly filling two paper cups from a coffee urn, setting them to the side.

Turning back to me, she's all *genuine* smiles and cheer, as she says, "Sorry about her. Let's try again. Welcome to Grounded. What can I get you?"

"Um, excuse me?" The woman butts in *again*, holding the paper cup in front of the barista. "I asked for creamer?"

"It's on the side, as always. Help yourself."

"Is it always like this?" I ask, voice low.

She side-eyes the woman and shrugs her shoulder. "Nope, just her. But we all know she'll be much more tolerable when she comes in tomorrow." I quirk my brows, and the barista winks. "Not from around here, I take it? Well, it's a small town. I'm sure you'll bump into Prince Charming sometime soon."

Why do I feel like I've already met him?

Chapter
Twenty-Six

Teddy

"**D**ude. Am I glad to see you."

Ozzy's large palm smacks my ass so hard I can feel the vibration in my teeth. God help any poor woman who lets him spank her.

"Jesus, fuck, Oz," I grumble, rubbing my stinging ass cheek. That's going to leave an Ozzy-shaped handprint.

"Sorry." The fucker laughs, joining in to massage my butt with his indelicate sausage fingers. "Better now, baby?"

Batting his hand away, I push at his chest. "What are you doing here? Aren't you meant to be asleep?"

"Nah, man," he says through a stifled yawn. I drop my head in a *really?* look, which he shakes off with a sleepy smile. "I needed to come in this morning. Helped the *hottest* damsel in distress last night."

He tilts his head back, biting on his bottom lip with a groan, which is Ozzy speak for just how hot he thought this girl was. Also, for Ozzy to be here at the ass crack of dawn, she must be something spectacular. My best friend and business partner wouldn't be caught dead before noon on the days he works nights. And by the scruffy way-past-five o'clock fuzz on his jaw and the dark rings starting to line his tired eyes, I'd say she must be someone worth staying up for.

"And you wanted to be here when she comes by?" I hedge.

"Hell yes, I did. I needed to get here and call dibs before you see her." He wiggles his brows. "Honestly, Teddy, tight little ass, tits that just begged to be held. There's no way I'm letting you fuck her, then toss her to the side and ruin any chance I have with her."

I huff. "Pfft, how do you know I would have done that?"

He stares incredulously.

"Seriously? Do I need to remind the manwhore himself just how many women he's been with since moving back to Phoenix? You've got yourself a reputation, my man."

"I'm not that bad," I try to protest. I mean, I'm red-blooded, *single*, twenty-seven, and I'm a guy. My sexual appetite is perfectly normal—albeit slightly indulgent—but if the girls are interested, who am I to say no? But I know what the locals call me, and even if it bothers me a little, I try to ignore town gossip.

"Yes, you are, my friend. That girl of yours back in good Ol' Greenwich must have really done—"

"What have I told you about mentioning that bitch?" I snap, and he winces, holding his hands up apologetically. He knows better than to mention *her* in this garage. In fact, anywhere in my vicinity. The one name that has my skin prickling in pain and makes the blackened stone *she* created squeeze from deep inside the cavern of my ribs. He knows a little of my life in Old Greenwich, of the girl who was once mine. But she was never fucking truly mine, was she? Not in the way she always whispered—*promised*—she was.

My teeth grind hard against each other, the scrape of enamel loud enough I'd bet Ozzy could hear.

Happy fucking Monday to me.

"Okay, wow, dude." Ozzy rubs the back of his neck, glancing at the floor. "I was only joking."

I sigh.

Shit. Why am I such a dick?

"Yeah, I know," I say, pulling my baseball hat off and dragging a hand through my hair, not giving a shit that it's covered in grease. "Speak of the Devil, and he doth appear, y'know?"

"Doth?" His nose furrows in confusion. And just like that, my mood lightens.

Shoving my cap on backward, I roll my eyes and get back to the 1965 Austin Mini Cooper. Our garage doesn't specialize in old motors like when I was working with my dad, but on the odd occasion they come in, these beauties are my favorite to work on.

Some things never change.

The old engines, the mechanics, the chassis—a mechanic's wet dream.

As he walks past, Ozzy smacks my ass again, leaving me to tinker with my new toy.

"Just do me a favor and let me know when she comes in?"

"And how would I know who she is, dumbass?" My voice is muffled from under the hood.

"Believe me, you'll know," he whispers right next to my ear, making me jump. Sneaky little fucker he is this morning. "But her name is Ana."

Ana.

My fingers freeze around a loose bolt, the tiny piece of metal slipping somewhere inside the car, the little *tink, tink, tink,* sound of metal hitting metal deafening with each drop.

"What was that?"

"Ana?" he repeats slowly. I swallow hard, and Ozzy's head drops back as he groans. "Shit. You know her, don't you? Please say you don't know her."

I straighten, peering over at him from across the car roof, hoping to fuck that my voice sounds normal. I can't stand another *Uncle Oscar* talk so soon after the last one. "Nah, dude. Don't know an Ana from here."

He shrugs, the boyish smile that gets him into more trouble than it should spreading across his face. "Phew, that was close. Good thing she's not from here then, right? You'd have probably got to her first if she was."

Not from here.

There's no way.

My head repeatedly nods like one of those bobbleheads, just bouncing over and over as something unsettling coats my skin like tar.

"Teddy, you alright? You're acting weird. Nearly tearing my head off before, and now, you look like I've just kicked your puppy."

"Yeah—" I clear my throat, trying to deflect from a sudden panic I have no right to feel. "Yeah, all good. Enjoy your nap."

He looks at me for a second longer before dragging his tired ass to the annex above the office, where there's a hideaway bed and a shower. I watch him go without actually *watching* him.

Ana.

It can't be.

No, Ana is a popular name. It isn't her. It couldn't be her. I have more luck saying *Bloody Mary* three times in a mirror for that scary bitch to appear than summoning Morgana Adler.

"I am in desperate need of a mechanic, and I was wondering if you could help me." A stiletto-clad foot runs up my calf, the voice dripping with seduction as she purrs, "Please. I'll do *anything*."

I smirk, glancing down at the pair of long legs standing at the foot of the car. Mrs. Claudia Beckman. Soon-to-be Ms. Claudia Smith; once her poor old husband signs the divorce papers, she gets half of everything.

Slowly, I dig the heels of my boots into the ground, sliding the mechanic's creeper out from underneath the car until she's standing over me, her tight skirt straining against her thighs, her bare pussy in my eye-line. There's no playing about. She knows what she wants and how to get it. And she is *definitely* going to get it.

"How can I help you, miss?" I ask, gripping her ankles in each hand, keeping her still as I admire her spread above me, my cock thickening under my coveralls. I'm not a roleplaying kind of guy—cosplay, sexual fantasy... it's not really for me—but Claudia loves this little game. Loves to pretend she's the naughty little housewife who can only pay for services rendered with her body. A sexy as all hell body that I fucking love to sink into. And what's even better is she knows exactly what this *thing* between us is—a quick fuck where we both get off, and she will be on her merry way to her divorce proceedings, with an ache between her legs and a relaxed high from her orgasm.

I lean up, sliding back a little as the wheels from the board shift from the weight change. Kissing the inside of her thigh, she shivers, biting on that red-painted lip.

"I think I need a full service, Mr. Mechanic."

I laugh. I can't help it. The whole charade is fucking insane.

"Claud, seriously?" I say, dropping character as I get to my feet. She stomps a heel, pinning her hands to her hips with a huff.

"Teddy." My name is a whine, a warning not to ruin this for her. "We've only got twenty minutes before I need to leave. You're killing my buzz."

My eyes dart to the clock pinned to the wall. She is right; the shop opens at eight, so if we are doing this, we have to be quick, even though my first drop-off of the day isn't due until at least nine-thirty, and Ozzy would be dead to the world in the back office, snoozing away until his dream girl comes by. He doesn't know about this arrangement Claudia and I have every Friday at seven a.m., and hopefully, never will.

"Well, maybe you should have been on time," I say, stifling a laugh as she glares at me. I roll my lips between my teeth, taking a deep breath. "Right, right. Sorry. Where was I?"

I step closer, but she puts a hand on my chest. Arching a brow, she glances down at my grease-slicked hands. Shit. I smirk, gripping her hips. The oil and grime have already dried into my skin, so there is no way it will stain her perfectly white skirt. Walking her back, I kiss down her neck—neck, thighs, pussy... the only places I'll ever kiss a woman—tasting the bitter flavor of her perfume on my tongue, a scent so different from the floral tones Ana used to wear.

Fucking hell, Teddy.

One mention of a girl who's not even here, and she's all you can think about. Get the fuck out of your head.

But even still, my dick twitches, the treacherous bastard enjoying the short trip down memory lane. One memory—any memory of her—and my dick and heart harden instantly.

Claudia's ass hits the sink, a breathy moan drawing from her lips when I lick along her collarbone to the soft skin of her shoulder. The silky smoothness of her chest peeks out from the top of her shirt, the buttons undone a lot lower than would be appropriate for her upcoming meeting at her lawyer's office. I cage her in, gripping the sink on either side of her hips.

She licks the shell of my ear. "Maybe you could show me how to use the stick shift?"

Fuck me. Did she google mechanic innuendos on her way over here or something?

Shrugging out of the top half of my navy boiler suit, I let it pool around my waist. Claudia's eyes widen, her slender fingers finding the hem of my shirt, slipping under to skim up my abs.

"I can certainly do that, miss," I say, dragging the bottom of her skirt up just enough to reach between her legs and slide my index finger along her pussy. She's soaked as I push inside her, my thumb strumming lightly against her clit. Her knees wobble, and she sighs like there's a coil, slowly releasing the tension that's built up since her last divorce proceeding.

"Teddy," she moans, her hips rolling to meet my finger's slow and unrushed ministrations.

"Unbutton the rest of your shirt," I demand, and she quickly flicks at them, tugging the hem out from the waistband of her skirt. Pebbled nipples strain against the fabric of her lacy pink bra, and my head drops, my mouth suctioning against the silk, tongue lapping, taunting and teasing until it soaks the material. Just another reminder that *Teddy was here* while she sits across from her husband at the conference table.

"Let's take a look under the hood, shall we?"

With both hands, I grip the bottom of her skirt, shimmying it over her ass, bunching above her hips as I pick her up and sit her on the edge of the sink. My lips meet the hot flesh of her thighs, goosebumps chasing my trail as

I kiss up to her pussy.

Claudia grips my shoulders, pushing me away on a plea. "No, Teddy, no. Just fuck me. We don't have time."

A woman after my dead heart. Straight to the point.

"Okay, doll." I wink. Standing, I dig around the pocket of my sweats, already prepared for her arrival, as she shoves at the waistband of my coveralls, my pants and underwear, desperate to rid me of them. They drop to my feet as she wraps her hand around me, stroking and coaxing my dick to full mast as I rip open the top of the foil packet of the condom with my teeth. Taking it from me, she sheathes me in latex, widening her legs, her chest spilling in heavy breaths, and I slide my finger through her middle again, circling her clit with the slightest bit of pressure as she writhes under my hold.

"Please, Teddy. I'm ready."

I smirk, gripping the base of my cock and pressing it to her entrance. Blood pounds in my ears, every sense focusing on the need to fuck away the emptiness that permanently lives in my veins with this woman who's desperate for me right now. Open. Ready. Willing.

I am not focusing on the light wrap of knuckles on the garage door.

Or the soft voice calling inside.

Or the sound of heels clicking on the cement.

Not even focusing on a gasp—one I know too well—the breathy whisper that's engrained in my brain. One I wish I could forget.

Her throaty "Oh my God" has my already hard dick turning to steel. Throbbing, practically weeping for someone it shouldn't, just as I'm about to sink inside someone who isn't her.

Fuck my fucking life.

Speak of the Devil, and she doth appear.

Chapter Twenty-Seven

Morgana

A bare ass.

A muscly bare ass with slender feminine legs wrapped around their hips.

This can't be right. I cannot be in the correct place. Except my poor, broken-down car sitting in the middle of the forecourt, the hood still half open, looking all sorry for itself, says I am indeed in the right place. Oh, shit. Have I walked in on Ozzy and his girlfriend about to have sex? I check my watch. It's ten to eight in the morning. Surely, he wouldn't be so reckless as to do something like that when he *knew* I was coming by.

A giggle snaps me out of my stupor, and my eyes refocus on the well-defined muscles of Ozzy's butt, his tanned, thick thighs which make his white peachy cheeks stand out in the florescent lighting, and the slender feet with red painted toenails hooking around his waist to drag him closer.

Stop staring, Morgana!

"Oh my God," I gasp, whirling around, my hands flying to cover my face.

"Oh my God," the woman echoes in a screech, and I swear I can feel her embarrassment just as thickly as I can mine.

What a way to start my first day in a new city.

Hushed whispers, ruffling of clothes, and the distinct clipping of heels on concrete fill my ears as I keep my hand plastered across my eyes.

"I am so sorry," I murmur, standing still with my back to them, unable to give my brain the signals needed for my legs to move far, far away from here. I don't really need a car, right? Uber can be expensed to the company. "I didn't mean to just walk in. I—I called out, but no one..."

"Fuck." The word, gravelly and harsh, is choked out in a voice I'd recognize anywhere. One I know doesn't belong to Ozzy. One I can still hear in my dreams.

Dizziness is hard and fast and so insanely numbing that I'd half expect to look down and see someone reaching inside my chest and wrapping their ice-cold hands around my heart. The pain that lances through me shouldn't be as intense as it is and so it the jealousy of this gorgeous woman getting to call Teddy hers. They don't deserve a place to exist at seeing him with someone else. I've moved on, and so should he. He deserves to be happy. But now I'm back to being seventeen, lost in a boy I know I could never have when I watched him with Brittany. Except this time, I've had the chance to know how gentle his touches are, how beautiful the sound of his laugh is, and how cherished I felt when I was with him. And now that's all hers.

God, why is it with over 1.5 million people in Phoenix, the second person I have to meet is *him?*

And when did breathing become so hard?

Please, world, please open up.

"Shit, Teddy, I'm going to be late." The words kick-start my brain as

Teddy's girlfriend speaks in the same impatient, clipped voice from the café earlier. "Your coffee's on the side. I'll drop by later or..."

Finally, my legs move, shaking and unsteady, as I make my way back to the door and out into the street. I'm still sleeping. This has to be my subconscious playing games. Ready to push the door open, my heel snags on something, and my hand darts out, flailing around for something to grab onto to stop me from falling, but lands on a stack of tires. A tin can balancing precariously close to the edge knocks over, spilling everywhere. Nuts, bolts, and other bits slide across the stone floor, each rattle startling, and with my foot stuck, the only direction I can go is down, which is what I do, bringing the entire pile of tires down with me.

"What the fuck is going on?" Ozzy flies through a doorway, leaning over a set of metal stairs to see what made the noise, his hair disheveled and a thunderous look on his face as he looks around.

I sag farther into the ground, sucking my lips between my teeth, begging myself not to cry as the unmistakable telltale wobble of my chin starts. How embarrassing.

Not here. Not now. Please.

Coming here was a bad idea. Phoenix was a bad idea. But glancing back over to the boy whose heart I broke is the worst idea.

Hatred, as I've never seen before, stares straight back as he tugs at his overall zipper—seven years of resentment and betrayal lasered in my direction and the mess I'm currently surrounded in. I look away quickly, unable to keep eye contact, and as short as it might have been, I didn't miss a thing. The dark beard cut close to his jaw, the cords of veins rippling up his forearms and diving under the sleeves of his white Henley, the same baseball hat slung on backward as he did all those years ago. He's changed so much, yet not at all. No longer the boy who lived next door, but the man he always wanted to be.

Ozzy appears by my side, pushing a tire off my leg, gently grabbing my forearms, and helping me to my feet.

"Fuck, Teddy, you were meant to fill that," he admonishes, kicking at the small indent that caught my heel and created this disaster. He smooths his hand down my arm, squeezing my hand lightly. "I am so sorry, Ana. Are you okay?"

"She's fine," Teddy clips, guiding the tall and beautiful lady from the coffee shop around the spillage and out the door without so much as a second glance.

"Fucking asshole," Ozzy mutters, staring at where Teddy disappeared. "Can't believe he did that."

It wouldn't be my first time catching him in a compromised position.

My stomach lurches at the memory as bile rises.

"It was my fault. I should have waited until the shop opened."

Ozzy frowns, his lips pursing in annoyance. "No, we always have customers drop cars off before opening hours, so he should have known better. It's not professional. I can only apologize that you had to see that." He huffs a laugh, combing his hand through his short blond hair. "I'd like to say he doesn't normally do that, but he's been getting worse recently." He winces. "Shit, now I sound like the unprofessional one, airing out my boy's dirty laundry."

I force a smile, trying to look unaffected, even though I want to be sick. "It's okay. I guess he and his girlfriend can't get enough of each other. My fiancé and I are the same way."

Why did I have to say that? Richard and I have never been the can't-keep-our-hands-to-ourselves kind of couple.

Ozzy almost chokes as he inhales. Coughing and spluttering, he laughs as if I had just told the world's funniest joke. "Girlfriend? Teddy doesn't have a girlfriend."

I gape, unable to form words. This is like history repeating itself.

Thankfully, Ozzy doesn't notice my impersonation of a fish as he lifts my left wrist, holds my hand out, and whistles.

"Damn, Ana, just break my heart, why don't you."

Oh God, he really is Teddy's friend.

He jiggles my hand, making the light bounce off the diamond that suddenly feels too big to be worn in public. "I thought for a second you were only saying you're engaged so I wouldn't ask you out. But damn, this is some rock. He's a lucky guy."

As I bend, I mutter a quiet thanks, gathering everything back into the tin can—anything to avoid having to answer questions about Richard.

Between Ozzy and I, we tidy everything quickly before he walks to the shutters, clicks a button, and the loud buzz of a motor and metal rolling up on itself comes to life. I'm speechless as warmth and sunlight filter into the garage, touching everything with its rays, showcasing Teddy's dream come true. Four cars are suspended mid-air, another two are in various states of repair, and the whole shop floor is covered in car parts, oil, and machinery that I have no clue what they even do. It's magnificent.

"So," Ozzy says with his wide smile firmly back in place, stretching his arms, "Welcome to Grease Monkey, home of your *almost always* professional mechanics here in Phoenix. Now, let's talk about your car, yeah?"

I nod, dusting off my hands on my skirt as Ozzy begins to explain the issue with my car when all I want to do is explore, look at everything, touch everything, bask in how much of himself Teddy has poured into this place by the bucketload. My heart twinges, an ache I have no right to feel. It's a sort of loss and regret that I wasn't by his side to do this with him.

"Earth to Ana?" I blink, my eyes snapping to Ozzy, confusion etched on his face. "Are you sure you're okay?"

I nod, glancing under the hood with fake interest as if I know what I'm looking at while Ozzy points at different things. I keep nodding, adding in a few "*oh, I see*," or "*that's a good idea*," anything to hurry this up so I can disappear from here.

I can find another mechanic to fix my car. Grease Monkey surely isn't the only garage in this town. Then I won't need to face Teddy or his perfect girlfriend again, and I can try to forget I'd ever seen him.

Chapter
Twenty-Eight

Teddy

Storming, I circle the block a few times, waiting enough time for her to get the fuck out of my garage.

Ana. Fucking Ana.

Morgana Adler was Ozzy's damsel in distress. My gut fucking knew it, a sixth sense in the pit of my stomach warning me something terrible was going to happen. What did I do in a past life to deserve this? Fine, I wasn't perfect, but I never hurt anyone. To send her to my fucking doorstep has to be some sick joke from the universe. And for her to walk in while my ass was out, cock so fucking close to pushing inside Claudia, my fingers still slick with her arousal... that had to be the universe's way of saying my way of living as a fuckboy needs re-evaluating. Well, fuck you, karma. The only thing I'll be doing is making sure Morgana's life is fucking miserable now that she's here.

Mess with the bull? Get the horns, bitch.

I fumble, trying to pull my cell from my pocket and stabbing the *Call* button hard enough that my finger buckles under the weight. The dial tone pierces my head as it rings, each double drill sound only serving to piss me off more.

"Hey, man. I'm just about to head into work, can I—"

"Did you know she was coming?"

"Who?"

"Your fucking sister. Couldn't have picked up the phone to say, *'Hey, man, my bitch of a sister is heading to your neck of the woods. Be on the lookout?'"* I spit, and I know it's a dick move blaming Skip for Morgana's appearance, but rationale doesn't have a meaning with how I'm feeling right now.

"Wow, Teddy. Say that again. Morgana's in Phoenix? Why?"

"How the fuck should I know?" Scrubbing a hand down my face, I try to breathe. "Her car broke down, and it's sitting in my lot right now, waiting to be fixed."

Skip exhales loudly down the phone. "Shit, man. I'm sorry. I would have called to give you the heads-up if I had known. But you know I've not spoken to her for as long as you have. Unless I really needed to."

I nod, even though he can't see me, and stop my thundering march a couple of shops down from the auto shop to lean against the brick wall. Skip and I are an unlikely friendship after the shit with Morgana went down. One day, he called saying he'd heard of this new restaurant he'd wanted to try, and asked if we'd like to join him and, well, a rant and a few choice words about his family, and we bonded. I told him all about being blindsided by Morgana's text, and he told me why he no longer talks to his parents. To say the Adlers are fucked up is an understatement.

"Yeah, I know," I sigh. "Listen, I'm sorry. Seeing her... it was unexpected and messed with my head."

"What did she say when she realized it was you?"

I laugh humorlessly and rub at the back of my neck. "She knocked over a stack of tires."

He barks a laugh. "She always was clumsy."

"Yeah, probably didn't help that I was almost balls-deep in some girl."

"Dude. Epic man points there," he sniggers, and I hear a bell ringing through the phone. "She would not have liked that. But they say payback's a bitch."

Yeah, too bad as soon as I saw her and the sadness in her eyes, the gratification of her seeing me with another woman, basking in the hurt I always hoped she'd feel, didn't come like I always thought it would. Instead, it stirred old memories of her catching me with my pants around my ankles and my dick down *what's-her-name's* throat and suddenly I had the same feeling of wishing it was Morgana's lips around me as I had felt back then; I wanted Claudia to be her too.

For fuck's sake.

I quickly say goodbye to Skip, letting him know I'll keep him posted.

She's still inside when I get back, her soft and sweet laughter echoing around the forecourt as I storm past them and into the back office, slamming the door behind me. My sad and pathetic dick perks up as the smell of citrus twinges at my nose, the condom still clinging to it for dear life, hoping it will still see some action.

Did Ozzy bring her in here too? Or is this some sort of torment now she's slow close and I can't touch her. *Can't* touch her? Not can't. *More like will never, ever, ever touch her again, you fucking idiot.*

My dick doesn't agree as it swells in my pants.

"Don't fucking think about it," I mutter, pointing to the treacherous thing like it has ears, but does my warning stop it from thickening up faster than it ever has with any other woman? No, the fucker is harder than granite, and I know the only way it'll calm the fuck down is to jerk it.

Well, over my dead body will I come thinking about her. No fucking way.

I reach into my pants and roughly tug the condom off, the latex snapping the tip of my dick, and I hiss, hating and loving the little sting of punishment at my reaction to Morgana. Balling it up in a tissue, I chuck it in the trash before pacing my office, cracking my knuckles as the walls draw closer and closer with each pound of my boots. Knowing she's out there, close enough that I could touch her, has my racing pulse spiking higher, the muscles in my legs tightening and quivering with pent-up energy, and my chest heaving uncontrollably.

How the fuck can she still affect me like this?

The office door opens, and Ozzy saunters in with a stupid shit-eating grin on his face. It drops when his eyes meet mine, replaced by something I've never seen him wear before.

"What the fuck is wrong with you?" he growls, stalking toward me, arms held wide. "Getting sucked off in the office after hours is one thing, Teddy. But *fucking* some girl just before we open isn't okay. We could get shut down for that shit."

My eyes snap to his, rage bleeding from every cell in my body. "What about you, huh?" His lip lifts in confusion. "Flirting with the customers?"

It is not the same as getting caught with my pants around my ankles by the bitch who ruined me. But it's the hill I'm prepared to die on.

"Are you for real? I didn't have Ana's skirt around her waist about to sink my cock—"

My arm bands across his chest in a heartbeat, pushing him back and slamming him against the wall. Our noses nearly touch as I pant in his face like some deranged psychopath, jealousy and possessiveness and hatred fighting for dominance deep inside my veins.

"Watch your fucking mouth," I sneer. Ozzy's eyes widen, shock palpable at the way I've never spoken to him before. As quickly as I take him off guard, he's back in control, shoving at my chest and breaking my hold, and I stumble backward.

"What the hell has gotten into you?"

"Fuck," I roar, balling my fist up and punching metal drawers. The pain is welcomed, a distraction from whatever the fuck is warring inside me right now. I drop my head, unable to look at Ozzy as I say, "She's Morgana."

"Who?"

"Ana. Connecticut."

"The girl who was just here?" I nod, and he inhales sharply. "Oh, shit."

He sighs, and I hear him drop into one of the chairs.

"You okay?" he asks, and I begin pacing again, rubbing my palm over my red, angry knuckles. "Well, I'll order the part I need to fix her car, get it sent on fast delivery, and I'll have it—"

"No."

"Teddy..."

"No, Oscar, you'll have nothing to do with her. I'll order the part. I'll fix her car. You're fucking done with her. Do you hear me?"

"Dude, you need to calm down."

"Why is she here?" I roar, asking yet another person the question that won't stop nagging at me as I round on my best friend for the second time. Ozzy doesn't skip a beat as he jumps up and kicks his foot behind my ankle, making me topple into his vacated chair. He spins and plants his ass on my lap, making himself a dead weight as I thrash under him.

"Get the fuck off me."

"No."

"Oscar, fucking move."

"No. You're in a time out," he says, fastening his hands to the armrests and baring down. I relent, huffing and puffing as I pretend to let the fight in me die for his benefit, but inside, I'm still apoplectic.

"Alright, I'm calm. You can get off me now." He wiggles his hips and then gets up. "I do need her contact details, though."

"Dude, seriously?" he groans, turning to drop his ass back onto my lap.

I push at his lower back, stopping him in mid-air. "I need it to log her into our system. That's all."

Not completely a lie.

He huffs and straightens, grabbing a clipboard from the coffee table and tapping it on my knee. I review the address, noting that she's staying not that far from here, and her number has changed.

Right. Cool. Good. That'll make avoiding her that much easier.

Fix her car, send her on her way, and then forget all about her.

Easy.

It isn't easy. Not by a long shot when I'm constantly reminded of her as I work on her car.

Open the door to release the handbrake—her unique scent barrels out.

Turn on the ignition—the stereo flares to life with Planet Rock radio blasting seventies rock.

The anger at her being in Phoenix rears its ugly head again as a text from Claudia pops up in the afternoon, calling our arrangement off. Apparently, getting caught about to screw someone else while fighting for an unfair share of her husband's wealth is enough to have her rethink everything. Money comes first and all that. Not that I care. She was a fuck, nothing more, but it's Morgana *still* causing issues in my life less than twenty-four hours after arriving back in it.

I'm a live wire, bursting and buzzing with energy, and I need an outlet.

"You okay to close up?"

Ozzy turns off the engine of the white Hyundai Sante Fe and jumps out. "Yeah, where you going?"

"Out."

"Teddy..." he warns. "Dude, I can read you like a book. You're going to see Ana, aren't you?"

"Fuck no," I say a bit too firmly.

"Whatever," he scoffs. "No good can come of this, but there's no point trying to stop you. Just don't be a dick."

I shrug out of my coveralls and grab my car keys, driving the short distance to her rental place. It's funny how quickly hatred and betrayal can stir the beast inside. My hands vibrate around the wheel as I pull into the parking lot, taking up two spaces like a douche and killing the engine. I look up at the building, to the window on the second floor, where I know she's staying.

So sue me. In my anger, I might have googled the address. I might have also looked at the rental advert on Airbnb too.

I sprint to the front door just as an older man is leaving, and my first issue of how the fuck I'm meant to get into the building disappears. I thunder up the stairs and right to her door. My thudding bangs ripple on the wood and through the hallway, one after the other, banging, pounding, and thumping until, eventually, the lock unlatches, and the door opens.

"Teddy..."

Chapter
Twenty-Nine

Morgana

Barreling through the door, Teddy doesn't give me any time to move out of his way as he bulldozes into the rented apartment, crowding my space and sending me backward. The thin tights covering my feet slip and slide as I struggle to find purchase on the wooden floor, and my hand flies up, gripping Teddy's arms to keep balance.

Wrong move. Major wrong move as sparks of electricity jump from his body to mine. Heat pools, my mouth dries, and my lips part. Even after seven years, he affects me. How is that possible?

"Teddy, please..." I try, needing him to stop forcing me back and give me a second to catch my breath. His nostrils flare as he glances at where I'm touching him, and I snatch my hand away as I bump against the small island in the kitchen and curl my fingers around the edge instead of his bicep like I'm almost dying to do. I want to feel his warm skin under my palm again, even if it's only for a second. I need to feel the muscle that's grown so much since I last saw him, need to know if the shock of me touching him was something else or he felt it too. Maybe it's all in my head. Maybe the friction from my feet and the wooden floor created static. That must be it, because the dark glow of his pupils isn't from any lingering lust or feelings he harbors for me.

"What are you doing?" he snarls, his hands splayed out on either side of mine, caging me in with his arms. He's so close I can feel the warmth of his breath against my skin.

"I... I..."

I can't speak.

"Why are you here, Morgana?"

Ouch, no longer Ana. I guess I deserve that.

"For work. I..."

"Bullshit," he spits, and I flinch against the counter. "After all this time, you happen to get sent to Phoenix? Just happen to step into *my* auto shop the day after you arrive?"

"How did you..."

"Ozzy." He's breathing hard, each inhalation filling his broad chest, and we'd touch if he were an inch closer. Even so, that doesn't stop him from being any less imposing as he towers over me, and my eyes nervously roam his face, comparing everything I remember to the new things. Like the dusting of freckles on his nose that only appear in the sun. Or how the lines around his eyes have become more profound, making him look older. Or his pink lips surrounded by the hair covering his jaw that once used to smile at me are now pulled into a tight line. Or his dark soulful eyes that used to be filled with mischief, are now cold and hard, and I hate the way they look at me. I want to fix them, take away the pain I *know* is because of me.

My lips part, but no words come out. What would I even say? Sorry isn't enough. Sorry is too late now. Sorry is... His gaze drops to my lips, and I wet them without thinking. It's a reflex, it seems.

"Teddy," I whisper, glancing at the thick veins beating furiously against his neck. "Teddy, I'm—"

His head snaps down to where my fingers lightly rest against his chest, and I look at them too, completely unaware that I moved them, let alone that they are now touching him. I curl them back as Teddy pushes away from the counter, flexing his hands by his sides. Clenching them over and over as his jaw works, grinding his molars together, and he stares at me with such blinding hatred it makes me shrink.

I hate this.

He reaches up to where my fingers were, the vein in his neck relaxing for the briefest of seconds that I think maybe he was just shocked to see me after all this time, but then his face hardens again, and he jabs a finger in my direction.

"Don't say another word, Morgana. Whatever bullshit lies... just don't. I stopped believing a single fucking word you said years ago."

He turns his back to leave.

No, don't go.

My hand darts out before I can stop it, latching onto his wrist and tugging him back. He rounds on me so fast, my chin in his grip, squeezing to the point of pain. My eyes widen, and my breath hitches. *Oh God, this hurts so good.* I watch his Adam's apple bob as he swallows, and I suddenly want to trace my tongue along it.

You're engaged, Morgana.

I swallow, and his fingers move in time with the muscles under my jaw.

"I really am here for work," I say hoarsely, and he drops his hold but not his eyes. They remain focused on where his fingers held me tight, and I wouldn't be surprised if he'd left marks. Teddy always was strong. I itch to step forward. For some reason, I want to make him believe me that I'm not here to cause trouble when I really shouldn't care if he's mad I'm here. It's not like we're together, we're barely even friends. But his glare directed at me is worse than anything I could ever imagine. "I promise I'm not here for anything else. Just auditing a new client for a couple of months, and then I'll be gone."

"Auditing?"

"Yeah, I'm an accountant."

His eyes narrow. "So, no law school?"

I shake my head, fighting a smile as I say, "No, I went to business school after all."

Reaching up, I brush back wayward strands that fell from my ponytail and something glints in Teddy's eyes as they snag on my engagement ring. He half-laughs, half-huffs as he steps back, leaving a chill in its place and shakes his head.

"Well, looks like you got everything you ever wanted, huh, Morgana?"

I want to shout—scream—that I didn't get everything. That the only thing I truly ever wanted is about to walk out my door. But I'm glued, stuck to the floor, only able to watch as he approaches it and throws it open.

He doesn't meet my eyes when he turns over his shoulder and says, "Your car will be ready in a few days. I'll let you know when you can come by and get it."

"I thought Ozzy was working on it?"

"You thought wrong, sweetheart." The endearment isn't nice as his lip curls around the word. "You're dealing with me now."

As the door slams shut, relief so thick it makes my stomach bottom out, and exhaustion hits me hard. Less than twenty-four hours, and Teddy's back in my orbit, flying dangerously close that I'm not sure I can survive his gravitational pull for the second time.

My feet scramble against the floor as I race across the small space, and grab my handbag, digging around in it until I find my cell. My fingers shake as I unlock it and pull up Shay's contact.

"Why, hello there," she sings. "How was the first day of being a boss-ass bitch?"

"Teddy's here."

Silence.

I pull the phone away from my ear and check that we are still connected. "Shay, did you hear me?"

"Um, yeah. When you say *here*, do you mean in your apartment? Phoenix?"

"Phoenix? The apartment? B—Both?"

"Fuck."

"Yeah. Fuck. And he's the one fixing my car."

"Wow. Talk about fate, huh."

"More like bad luck."

"How is he?"

"What do you mean, *how is he?*" I ask, digging my nails into my scalp, my fingers getting caught in the hair tie in frustration. "I don't know. We didn't exactly have a friendly catch-up like *hey, how you doing? What's been going on since I saw you last? You know, in that restaurant where you took off like your ass was on fire, and I never saw you again?*"

"Okay, okay." Shay laughs. "Always so dramatic, Morgs."

"Not in the slightest. He hates me, Shay. Full-on wants-to-see-me-dead-and-buried hates me."

"I highly doubt that, but whatever," she snorts. "What did he look like?"

"Painstakingly beautiful. He looks the exact same, only not."

"You don't..." She clears her throat. "You don't still have feelings for him?"

I splutter out a cough. "What? No. That's absurd. I'm engaged."

Did my body react to him like it never has to Richard? *Yes.*

Did I want to feel the scratch of his beard on my lips while we kissed? *Yes.*

Did I want to cry and beg and come clean about why I broke up with him and pray he forgives me? *Yes.*

But that doesn't mean I have *feelings* for him. It means I'm a deluded moron, and the next four months will kill me. I know it.

Chapter Thirty

Teddy

Ozzy's fingers waggle through the doorway to the office as he waves goodbye on his way out until he spins around, planting his hands on either side of the doorjamb and leaning forward.

"You ordered that part yet?"

I nudge my bottom drawer closed, hiding the new cylinder for Morgana's car inside. "Nah, it's out of stock."

He frowns. "You sure? I've never had an issue with our supplier and their stock before. Maybe try—"

"They're out of stock, Oz. It's fine. It's not like she can't afford the Uber fare for a couple of weeks."

"Uh-huh."

He gives me a knowing stare.

"What?"

"Nothing. You seem chill for someone who could have rampaged like Mad Max a week ago."

I tilt my chair back and link my hands behind my head with a relaxed grin I know is the picture of calm serenity. "Yeah, well, maybe I got some perspective and decided that it's time to let bygones be bygones. Might have also fucked a yoga teacher and *Zenned* my stress away."

He drops his head toward the ground and laughs. "Only you."

Not only me. Because instead of doing just that, I spent the last week thinking of ways to make Morgana suffer while she's here instead of not giving a flying fuck that she's back in my life and carrying on with my playboy ways, because, well... fuck her. Nope, apparently now I'm acting like a teenage girl with a grudge a mile long, and if she thinks we can go on our merry way and try to avoid each other, then she's got another think coming.

When Morgana *dumped* me by text—not that I'm bitter or anything— she destroyed anything good inside. I might be giving her too much credit. Maybe over the years I've been stewing on something that happened a lifetime ago and making it worse than it is. And yes, to some, my hatred toward poor, *innocent* Morgana Adler might seem a tad severe, but as it turns out, I have a bit of a vindictive side.

The first thing I decided was to hit her bank balance. Even though any cabs or Ubers would most likely be expensed, it still produces a devious smirk because submitting expenses can be a bitch. But thinking of ways to hit her where it would really hurt has caused more of a problem. My issues with the bitch aside, Morgana is actually a... nice—*groan*—person. She'd do anything for those she loves. A chronic people pleaser, unlike me, a quality that was one of her best while simultaneously being her worst.

My fingers curl around the bill of my cap, making the headband tighten painfully around my head, squashing down any form of sentiment or this weird *flutter* that hits my gut hard. I must have eaten bad sushi a week ago because my stomach won't fucking settle.

The newly installed bell above the side door jingles—a requirement Ozzy enforced, and I can't say I mind. If it stops me from being caught off guard by the She Devil's arrival, that suits me fine. I kick my feet from under my desk, the wheels of my chair sliding back, and I get up with a long exhale. Let's get this shit done.

"Morgana," I clip, leaning against the open office door, eyeing that tight as fuck pantsuit she's wearing, the material clinging to every curve like it was painted on. Why does she still have to look so damn good after all these years? I shift, standing to my full height with a frown as the rogue thought floats around my head. Then she whirls around, her eyes dropping to my open coveralls and taking in my shirtless chest. It was hot as balls today and wearing a shirt just sucked, and a chest covered in motor oil doesn't bother me. She sucks her bottom lip between her teeth.

Fuuuuck, she still does that.

"I never got to say it before, but this"—she waves her arm out, turning her back to me, and I quickly palm my dick, squashing the fucker down as it also noticed that little lip bite—"is amazing, Teddy. What you've built... I can't believe you did it."

Pride surges through me, but I crush that feeling like a motherfucker. I don't need her empty words of praise.

"Yeah, well, you'll have to admire it another time. I'm closing up." I walk past her and lift a funnel I'd washed earlier, placing it on a shelf.

She gawks. "I thought your text said the car would be ready by the end of today?"

"Did it?" *It did.* I click my tongue. "Well, unfortunately, the part isn't in"—*the car*—"so it's still not fixed."

Because it's in a box, in my desk drawer, and I'll let it collect dust before I fit it.

She huffs, trying not to look agitated by my wasting time. "You couldn't have messaged me that?"

I shrug. "Lost track of time."

She loudly inhales through her nose, and I know she's biting something back. Morgana was never one to let her true emotions slip. Had that beaten out of her from a young age, but I could always see through that.

"Say it," I goad and unable to help myself, my eyes drag down her body again.

"Say what?"

"Whatever you're holding back. You're mad. I never told you it wasn't ready."

Her eyes narrow a fraction, and I'd have missed it if I wasn't looking. Lifting her chin, she smiles weakly.

"It's fine. If I'd known I couldn't collect it, I could have stayed later at work to submit a report. But I can get into the office early tomorrow to do it. No big deal," she says, and I must admit, I'm slightly disappointed she didn't yell at me. Instead, she itches her head, that obnoxiously large rock sparkling in the overhead light, and she turns her back to what I can only assume is to stare at my garage again.

While she's looking at whatever, I take the chance to properly check her out unnoticed instead of trying to be sneaky, starting from her feet, up her long slender legs, round ass, waist, hips and... what the fuck?

"You straightened your hair."

She spins, her eyebrows pinching together. "Yeah? So?"

"I don't like it."

She huffs a laugh, her hand lifting and running down the length of her *straight* blonde hair. "Fortunately, your opinion doesn't matter anymore, Teddy."

I step toward her and pick up a piece of her hair, still as soft and silky as I remember. *Damn it.*

"I still don't like it," I repeat, tugging on a strand, and dropping it with a scowl. *Why the fuck do I care?* I cross my arms over my chest and lean casually against a Jeep Cherokee I plan to finish tomorrow. Smirking, I say, "Must suck for your fiancé. Whatever does he hold on to when he's fucking you from behind?"

She gasps, her eyes flaring with shock and embarrassment? *Oh, this is too fucking good.*

"Jesus." I laugh loudly, loving the way her cheeks pinken. "Don't tell me he's a missionary kind of guy?"

"I'm not discussing my sex life with you."

I howl with laughter again and start to wander around her, raking my eyes up and down her body at every angle. "He is, isn't he? Morgana, did you break up with me for that *loser?*"

"I didn't break up with you for anyone, Teddy. I broke..." she spits, her composure slipping before she breaks off just as it gets to the good bit. She sighs heavily. "Teddy, can you please stop that?"

"Stop what?" I drawl from behind her, and the smell of her shampoo fills my nose. Fuck, if that doesn't go straight to my dick too.

"Stop circling me."

She spins as I continue to round her, like a vulture around its prey, around and around as she turns with me, her movements jerky as if she doesn't want to let me out of her sight. I wouldn't want to do that either if I were her. Vipers are dangerous when you don't have your eyes on them every single second. Blink too long, and you could get bitten.

"You've filled out."

She chokes.

"Excuse me?" Her hands fly to her hips, holding them in a death grip, and I can only imagine it's because she wants to hit me. "Did you just call me fat?"

"Fuck no, Morgana. It's merely an observation. You're not the scrawny little girl I remember."

"I'm not a lot of things you remember."

Kitty can scratch.

I smile.

"I can see that." I do another full circle again, taking in her full hips, her ass and thighs that have a lot more meat on them than before, and if I didn't hate her so much, I'd sink my teeth into them, so she wears my mark. And then there's her tits. The perfect handful she had at eighteen are bigger now, like they grew in time with my hands, *especially* for *my* hands, and I'd love nothing more than to run my thumbs over her pink nipples. Watch them pebble under my touch. Y'know, if she was *anyone* else other than Morgana Adler.

And then, just as I'm about to say something else about how she's changed, I see it. The same reactions—the *ticks*—she gave years ago. Parted lips. Stilted breath. Green irises overtaking the blue flecks. And the thin bra she's wearing... yeah, I don't need to imagine those hard, pretty nipples. If I tugged her shirt, they'd spill out for me to see. Fuck, she wants me. *Still* wants me. I thought I had imagined her blown pupils, her labored breathing, and the look of arousal flooding her eyes when I held her jaw firmly in my hand when I barged into her rental.

This is what I needed. *This* I can fucking work with. And suddenly, charging her unnecessary cab fares is child's play. Not when there is a game only adults can play.

I halt behind her and press into her back. Her shoulder blades constrict, pushing those mouth-watering tits forward.

"I bet there are some things I still remember about you well enough," I say, my voice low and gravelly. I slowly slide my hand onto her hip, my skin tingling with the contact, and feeling her tense under my palm. "Does your fiancé know that if he teases your asshole a little while he finger-fucks your pussy, that you come harder than if he were to fuck you with his cock?"

"How dare—"

I cut her off, splaying my other hands across her stomach, tugging her into my chest, and for the first time since I've been around her, I don't hate that my cock is throbbing as it presses into her ass. Not when she lightly pushes back against me, relieving the pressure a little, and I would bet she isn't aware she did that.

"Does he know what your pretty little face looks like with mascara streaks, tears and saliva running down your chin as you choke on his dick? Or is he too uptight to give his dirty girl what she really wants?"

My hand slips down to her pants, my fingers deftly undoing the top button and dragging down the zipper, the click of teeth snapping out of place louder than any engine I've worked on. Her hand snares my wrist, stopping me from dipping my fingers inside.

"Teddy," she breathes, her head knocking back against my shoulder. "What are you doing?"

I edge forward, the tips of my fingers skimming through her open pants and brushing along her silk panties.

"You can't do this," she breathes, the refusal so weak it's almost laughable. I'm glad her back is to me so she can't see my smile that is far too cunning for someone wrapped around his ex, fingers so dangerously close to the one pussy that set the bar so high, no one else compares.

"Tell me this..." I say into her ear, her hair fluttering against my breath. "Does your fiancé know he willingly sent his future wife to the city where the guy who got all her firsts lives?"

The shake of her head is so tiny that I almost miss it. My grin expands.

"Her first proper kiss?"

My head dips forward, and when I run the tip of my tongue up her ear, I'm rewarded with a shiver.

"Her first orgasm?"

Her hold on my wrist loosens.

"Her virginity?"

Her eyes flutter shut.

"Everything belongs to me. I knew how your body felt convulsing around me first. I knew how your body tasted first. I knew..."

Her eyes snap open. "We were kids. You were just a boy when we did all those things."

I laugh sadistically and slide my hand under the waistband of her panties. Short, neat hair meets the tips of my fingers, and the overwhelming need to drop to my knees, strip off her bottom half, press my nose to her and inhale her scent is strong.

Dig deep, man. She needs to pay.

"And yet the thought of everything we did all those years ago still makes you wet. Isn't that right, Ana?"

She inhales a sharp breath, her fingers grasping my wrist again, but I don't think it's to stop me. It's because I slipped up and used my name for her out loud.

Ana.

Fuck.

I grit my teeth and drop my hand lower. "Let me show you what this *man* can do."

I don't give her a choice as one thick finger delves inside her tight pussy.

This is bad, so very bad. Her vice-like grip around my digit is enough to make me want to lose all resolve and feel her squeeze other parts of me. My dick is throbbing behind my zipper as I press my hips into her ass. When I momentarily didn't care that she knew she still affected me before... well, right now, with my finger buried inside her, it's pretty fucking stupid, and I wish I could separate this from what this really is. Opportunistic revenge. But she feels so good, I *almost* wish I was doing it for me.

She shudders, her arm coming up behind my head and knocking my hat to the ground. Her fingers dig into the hair at the base of my neck, pulling hard as I curl my finger deep inside where I know that spot will make her see stars. Ana's body is one I could draw a map to on the back of my hand. I know the right flicks, the right strokes, the perfect amount of pressure... every-fucking-thing that can make her detonate.

She widens her legs—if by accident or on purpose, I don't care—as I harshly thrust a second finger in with the first. She cries out, her head tipping backward, exposing that beautiful slender neck I want to suck, bite, kiss, claim as mine once again. I bite the inside of my cheek, drawing blood as I pump my fingers in and out of her, her arousal coating my palm.

"Teddy. No, you... you need to stop," she pants, each breathy moan of my name bringing me dangerously close to coming in my pants.

No. You will not come to the sound of her crying out your name. Fuck her and fuck her fiancé.

My little pep talk spurs me on, wanting to make her come and revel in the guilt I know she will feel when her high fades. Because I live with it too. It's the same fucking emptiness that fills me.

"That's it, baby, say my name. Remember who owned you first."

She grips my forearm, her nails digging into my skin as her pussy clamps around my fingers, spasming and clenching as she rises to her tiptoes.

"Te—*urgh.*" She bites her lower lip hard, fighting all instincts to call out *my* name again and again as I bring her closer to her undoing.

"Say it, Ana," I growl, sucking her earlobe between my teeth and biting down.

"No... *Ohhh,* God..."

"Wrong. Try again."

"Fuck you," she grits out, her grip on my hair tugging hard, like she's trying to pull it out. But a smarting scalp is nothing compared to the joy of provoking sweet, *innocent* Ana.

My husky chuckle sounds foreign as I dig my hard cock into her ass again. "Don't tempt me, but if you beg nicely, I suppose I could bend you over that car over there and fuck you hard enough that you forget about all the shit sex you've had to put up with since me." With the hand not down her panties, I wrap it around her throat, using my forefinger to turn her head to the left. "Or maybe that car?" I sharply push it to the right while pressing my thumb to her clit. She moans, then clamps her mouth shut. "Or what about that one? It's a small town, Ana. You'd see any one of these cars every time you go out for a walk, go to grab a coffee, before work, after... one of these drives by, and you'd remember my cock buried inside your tight little pussy, fucking you hard against the hood until you came."

"Shit, Teddy..." Her whole body tightens in my hold as her orgasm smashes into her like a ton of bricks. It's haunting. Hearing the sound that only exists in my nightmares.

When she's stopped convulsing around me, I slide my hand out of her panties and press my forefinger to her lips.

"Open. Remember what you taste like when a real man makes you come."

She lets me push my finger inside her mouth, and I swear all it will take is one stroke when she's gone, and I'll come quicker than ever before. Because apparently, I'm a masochist. I watch her suck her arousal from my finger before sliding my middle one inside my own mouth. Everything that is uniquely Ana bursts on my tongue, and I barely notice her scrambling to fasten her pants and run for the door.

I wanted her regret. I wanted her guilt... so why does it taste so sour now that I have it?

Chapter Thirty-One

Morgana

W hat have I done?

Horrified at myself, I sag against the brick wall outside and close my eyes, forcing steadying breaths through my nose. This isn't me. I'm not some kind of adulterer but as my heart pounds, my legs feel weak, and my clit is still purring from the best orgasm I've had in years, I can't help but feel like this is most alive I've ever felt in well, seven years. Never has Richard turned me on like that, never has he played with my body like a well-oiled machine, and never has he made me come with blinding white lights behind my eyes that at one point I could have sworn I had an out-of-body experience.

I knew it was wrong, knew I should have made him stop. But with every weak whisper, my protesting against what he was doing changed to something I *didn't* want him to stop.

I groan, covering my face with my shaking hands. I'm a terrible person. Richard doesn't deserve that. Infidelity. Deceit. Lies. Something about Teddy makes all the wires in my head cross, and I can't think when I'm around him. There's still a strong attraction to him, and as much as I don't want there to be. I can't deny the pull I still feel and damn it, he might play hot and cold, but I know he feels it too. Why else would he have touched me?

My phone buzzes in my handbag, and I startle, almost dropping the damn thing as I pull the device out.

"H—Hello?"

"Honey? Are you okay?"

My chest tightens, and I rub over the sharp pain with my knuckles at the sound of Richard's voice. How do I look my fiancé in the eye and know he wasn't the last man to touch me?

"Yeah, yes, I'm fine. Long day at work."

"I can imagine," he hums, and even down the line, I know condescension when I hear it. "It was a good thing you decided not to become a lawyer if you think nine to five is a long day in the office."

I grit my teeth, biting back words I know will only end in an argument. Technically, my day started at eight today and didn't finish until seven thirty, but it's not like Richard's *"full-time"* job where he works fifteen hours a day.

"No one works harder than you, honey."

He laughs. "Got to, sweetheart. If I'm to help your dad get into congress, got to put in the time."

Urgh, campaigning. I swear that's all my dad's life is; campaign after campaign after campaign. At least he's got Richard by his side—the ever-dutiful future son-in-law... the son I bet he always wished he had instead of Skip.

"Dad's lucky to have you," I say, tipping my head back to rest against the brick wall, still supporting my weight. At least my legs don't feel like they'll give out anymore. "I think you see him more than I ever have."

"Morgana, he is a very busy man. What do you expect?" he says sharply, and I picture his brows knitted, and his lips pulled into a straight line. "How can he expect his career to be where it is now without dedicating all his time to work? That's why I wish you'd reconsider working when we have children. I need you there, Morgana. *They'll* need you there."

I need you to look pretty and take care of the home. Nothing else.

I pinch the bridge of my nose. "Can we not discuss this right now?"

He sighs. "Fine. Well, why don't you tell me about your day now that you got the first week jitters out of the way. Settled in better?"

An overwhelming sensation of dread fills my veins as my body lights up, my mind going straight to Teddy. I need to tell him. This is the part where I say it, like word vomit, get it all out in the open, apologize profusely and hope he can forgive me. But over the phone?

Don't tell him anything, Morgana. He'll go straight to your mom, and you know what happens next.

The tips of my fingers feel numb as they tighten around my phone. Pushing as much excitement into my voice that doesn't come across as fake, I tell him about the office, the people, and how pretty this town is. I know he's not listening, his *"interesting," "that's good,"* and *"uh-huhs"* are all lackluster at best, and I swear I can hear the clacking of his keyboard while I talk, then a faint murmuring.

He's talking to someone instead of listening to me.

"And they want to buy me a puppy for doing such a good job on the first day."

"That's great, honey," he says, and my arm bands around my stomach as an odd sensation of neglect rears its ugly head. Why do I care if he's listening to me or not? "Listen, Tom's just popped in, and we're going to head out for a few drinks. You know I hate to cut this short..."

Sure.

"Oh, right. Of course. Where you going?" I ask, hating that I'm almost sad that he's barely paying me any attention. It's not like this is new to me. I can hear his desk drawers opening and closing, the jingle of his keys, and the chuckle of a male voice I can only assume is Tom. I've never liked that man.

"The Gentleman's Club."

I pull the phone from my ear and check the time. "Isn't it like ten o'clock?"

"Yes, what does that matter?"

"I just mean..."

"I did say I've had a long day, Morgana. I need to relax with the boys."

I startle as the side door to the alleyway opens, and Teddy steps through, shutting the light off behind him.

"I'll call you in a few days, okay?"

"Sure."

"Love you, sweetheart."

Teddy locks up and leans against the door, his dark eyes raking down my body as he plays with his lower lip with the fingers he had inside me. He smirks, inclining his head slightly as he looks at my phone, and I immediately look to the ground.

"Morgana?" Richard asks.

"Oh, sorry, love you too," I stutter out as quickly as possible, hanging up as soon as I've said goodbye.

Teddy shoves from the wall, stiff and tight, as he walks toward me, the smell of motor oil and gasoline becoming stronger with each step. The smirk that tugged at his lips has slipped, and his intense stare isn't like the way he looked at me in the shop. It's cold and unyielding, and I can see it... the torment that lives there when he looks at me. He wants to hate me, wants to make me suffer, and maybe, that's what he's done. Guilt is an unbearable thing to live with—I would know. It's been embedded in me from the moment I pressed *Send*. But to be with one man while bound to another... He wouldn't have done it as some game. Would he?

"Teddy...?" I whisper, needing to know why he touched me, when right now, he looks like he wouldn't go near me if I were the last woman on earth. "Why..."

"Go home, Morgana," he says scathingly, and I hate how much I hate how my name sounds on his lips. "I'll let you know when your car's ready."

Two weeks pass, and my car's still not fixed.

Chapter
Thirty-Two

Morgana

"Here are the files from 2013 you wanted, Ms. Adler." An assistant puts five thick blue notebooks on my desk in the little office that's been mine since I arrived, smiling politely. "Do you need anything else before I head for lunch?"

I shake my head. Taking my pen out of my mouth, I say, "That should be good for today. Thanks again..." I'm about to say his name when I realize I cannot remember it. Bobby? Joshua? No idea, so I suck my lips between my teeth and awkwardly wait for him to leave me to my work. I've reviewed three years' worth of documents—completely old school, no digital files or anything—and everything seems to be in order so far.

Closing the final page for 2012, I pull one of the 2013 binder closer and run my hand over the cover. The blue fabric texture is rough under my fingers, and it smells musty, not quite like the old historical books with yellowing paper that have that distinct earth smell, but you can tell they have been kept in a dark room and forgotten about until now.

Opening a new tab on my spreadsheet, I open the cover and flick a couple of pages in as my phone skitters across the table, dancing in time with the vibrations of an incoming call.

I grin and slide my thumb across the screen. "Hello, my lovely."

"I think I've got food poisoning."

I sit up straight and lean on the table. "Oh no, are you okay?"

"Yeah, I'm fine and don't have food poisoning." Shay huffs. "But I wish I did. If I have to go to another new Italian restaurant opening, I might throw up at the sight of pizza or pasta."

"Such a drama queen."

"I know, which is exactly why I'm calling. You on your lunch break?" I check the time on the bottom right of my laptop screen, holding in a sigh as I already know what's coming next. "Morgs, you better be taking breaks. I know you and your bad habit of working straight through."

I laugh and push my chair away from my desk, hoping it will force me to take a break.

"Want to FaceTime, and we can have a pretend lunch date?" she asks, and I hear the beep in my ear, indicating she's switched to a video call. "There's my gorgeous best friend. I've missed you, babe."

And like that, my guilt, anxiety, fear, dread—at this point, it would be quicker to name the emotions I'm not feeling—disappear into the backdrop of my mind as Shay's blue eyes and a wide smile fill my display. Propping my phone against my laptop, I angle it so she can see me, and I take out the food I brought on the off chance I got too hungry and needed to eat.

"I've missed you too. It's been so lonely without you."

"Good. Remember that if you ever think of leaving me again," she says, pointing her finger at the camera. "Catch me up. What's been happening? It's been nearly a month since you arrived. How are things?"

I take a deep breath and nod my head in that way that's not quite a nod but not exactly a shake either. "Things have been good. Work has been busy but manageable, which is great. There's not been anything untoward I've found so far, and my bosses seem to be..."

"Okay, sorry, Morgs, but I don't care about your work. It's boring and dull, and I need to get ready for this stupid opening, not falling asleep because of your poor choice in career."

"Ouch, Shay. Tell me how you really feel." I smile because, even though she does think those things, she doesn't mean it maliciously. I like math and business, while she likes frog legs and escargot. We can't all be the same.

"Sorry, but I am dying to know..." She looks around—from what I can see through the tiny screen—her empty kitchen, and leans in conspiratorially. "How are things with Teddy? Still being an asshole, or is he a nice Teddy Bear right now?"

I run a finger under my eye, avoiding the screen while I get myself under control. The mere mention of his name and I'm all flustered, getting unbearably hot in the over-airconditioned room, and I know my neck is flushing right up to my chin.

"He's fine," I say, my voice croaking. "He's still got my car. No surprise there. And our texts are short and not very often."

"Ooh, texts. Tell me more."

I pull my long, straight hair over one shoulder and twirl a chunk around my finger. Shay doesn't know about *the incident*. The less I think about it, the fewer people who know, I can forget it ever happened, right?

I huff a noise and roll my eyes. "It's not like *texting*-texting. I message asking if there's an update, and he replies hours, if not days, later, saying no."

"No. Like one word?" I nod, and she scowls. "What a dick. Want me to come to Phoenix and kick his ass?"

My whole body flies forward as I grab my phone and hold it close to my face.

"No," I shout and close my eyes. "No, Shay, it's okay."

We're silent for several seconds, and I know I've messed up.

"Morgana?" My eyes snap open, and Shay's worried face stares through the phone. "Is everything alright?"

"Yes, why wouldn't it be?" I ask the question, nothing more than a squeak.

"You can talk to me. You know that."

I smile warmly. "I know. I promise I'm fine. I guess I'm a little homesick. And I miss Richard." Even to myself, I can hear how fake that sounds, and the lie doesn't taste that much better either. Richard has never been further from my mind.

She chews on her bottom lip as she watches me. Eventually, she sighs, and I'm unsure if it's a placated or disappointed sound.

"Okay, but you know where I am if you need me."

"I know. I love you."

"I love you too. Listen, I've got to run and start getting all dolled up. Call me soon?"

"I will."

She blows me kisses through the phone and then hangs up. The disconnecting beeps are heavy in the empty room filled with paperwork and self-loathing.

I itch my eyes as the words on the screen dance. I've been staring at this for too long. If it's not making sense at seven-fifteen at night, it won't make sense at all. This can wait until morning.

Just as I'm packing my laptop into its case, Richard calls.

"Hey, you," I say, balancing the phone between my shoulder and ear as I finish gathering my things for the evening. The office is always locked, but I don't risk it. Besides, I don't want the employees at Bank of America thinking I'm messy, leaving files strewn all over the desks and floor.

"Have I got some great news for you," he says, and I can hear his excitement. I smile as I pile a stack of dossiers I've finished with on one side of the desk, then move the ones I'm working on next to it, followed by documents I still have to review.

"Tell me."

"Tom's sister's friend is a realtor, and I asked her if she could get an evaluation sorted for your little apartment..."

I stand, the loose documents in my hand fluttering to the ground. Realtor. Evaluation. Apartment.

"Reckons we'll get at least two hundred thousand over the asking price, and it can be on the market by Friday."

"Friday?" I mutter, dropping to my seat.

"Yes. Isn't that great? She also thinks it won't take that long until it sells. One week, tops."

"But I don't want to sell my apartment."

"Morgana," he sighs, and I know he's pinching the bridge of his nose. "You're moving into my place the day after the wedding. You're there all the time as it is. The fact you still own that place is... well, I don't understand why you haven't put it on the market already?"

I wasn't sure either. All I know is that every time Richard brought up selling it, I'd laugh and change the subject, and it would be forgotten.

"I love that apartment, Richard," I say softly, not wanting to argue with him. It is slowly becoming painfully obvious that's all I ever do—avoid arguments. "I was thinking of putting it up for rent, actually. Making some money off of it?"

"Renting is a fool's game, Morgana. Do you know how much money you'd waste rather than earn? The stove breaks, *you* need to pay for a new one. The boilers on the fritz, *you're* the one calling an out-of-hours plumber. And believe me, they aren't cheap. Morgana, you wouldn't believe the number of claims the domestic lawyers I used to work with were inundated with for petty tenants. It's a waste of time renting."

"I don't mind. I'm sure I could find a nice couple or someone from my office to take it."

He scoffs, and the hairs on my arms rise. "Unless you put a lot of work into refurbishing that place, you can't ask someone to pay you to stay there, Morgana."

"What is that supposed to mean?"

There is nothing wrong with my apartment. Maybe because it's *smaller* than he'd have wanted when I bought the place, but what am I going to do with anything bigger than a two-bed?

"Well, the kitchen needs replacing, the stairwell is poorly maintained, and your neighbors are..."

"Lovely. Mr. Hollie might be an eccentric old man, but he's harmless."

"Eccentric. Ha. He tried to have his pet cat bite me, Morgana."

I bite down hard on my bottom lip. Any other time, I wouldn't be trying to stop myself from laughing at the memory of my eighty-year-old neighbor setting his fourteen-year-old tabby on Richard, but not now.

"Morgana." Richard's voice softens, and I lower my defenses. "I did you a favor by sorting this out. I thought you'd be happy."

My hand clenches my thigh as I count to three, my hackles going straight back up. This is everyone's problem. Richard. My mom. My dad—when he's present enough to care. Everyone *thinks* they know what's best for me.

"Richard, you went behind my back, didn't discuss it with me first, and ultimately decided what would make you happy. I know you don't like my apartment, but it's *mine*."

"Listen to yourself right now, Morgana. You're acting like a child," he says, and I swear if I had something I could throw at the wall, I would. "What is your obsession with holding on to it?"

"Richard." I suck in a deep breath. "Please do not put my apartment up for sale. I know you are only looking out for me, but you didn't have to do that."

He growls, and not that romance-book-make-your-panties-wet kind of growl either.

"Morgana, this happens all the time. I suggest something and you drag your heels or decide something different to what I said, and it ends up being the wrong choice," he says, and I'm glad I decided to not tell him about my car now. He sighs, and I know he's grinding his teeth. "Fine. I'll tell Saskia to *hold off*... For a few days. When you've calmed down tomorrow, you will see it's the best option to get rid of it, and you'll be glad I did this for you."

He hangs up without another word, and my body aches with how tightly my muscles are coiled up. Who does he think he is? I would never dream of arranging for his house to go on the market without consulting him, so what gives him the right?

Is this what it's going to be like? My life? Constantly being told what's happening without being consulted?

The pain in my chest is back, and I massage my fingers into my skin. My phone vibrates again in my hand, and I really want to let it go to voicemail. But if it's Shay, she'd calm me down. But then again, if it's my mother, I don't think I could handle it. Turning the device over, Teddy's name lights up my screen and, well, now I don't know how to feel.

"Hello?"

"Hi, Morgana, it's erm, Teddy." He exhales like it's painful to even speak to me. If I wasn't close to tears with rage and resignation, I think I'd cry at how much I wish it were the old Teddy on the other end of that phone—the one who made me feel like I could do anything and he would never dictate my life.

"Hi, Teddy," I whisper, feeling deflated.

"The car's ready. Sorry it took so long, but if you can pick it up in the next half hour, I can keep the shop open." He pauses, and when I don't answer, he says, "Or if tomorrow's better?"

"No, it's fine. I'm finishing up here now if you're okay with waiting."

"Sure. Fine. No problem at all."

"Thanks, Teddy." My voice wobbles, and I pinch my arm hard, fighting the lump in my throat to disappear.

Stop being so pathetic. You're a twenty-five-year-old strong-ass woman. No man should make you cry.

"Is everything okay?"

I wish people would stop asking me that.

"Mhmm," I hum, afraid that if I open my mouth to speak, I really will cry.

He's quiet, and I can hear him breathing down the phone. "Okay, then. I'll see you soon."

Chapter
Thirty-Three

Teddy

"Finally, my baby remembers me," Mom coos, and I cringe.

"Mom, I'm twenty-seven. Hardly a baby."

"Oh, hush, you'll always be my baby," she says, her voice full of love and adoration I can feel through the phone. "So, tell me, what's new? How's the garage? How's Oscar? Did he get the care package I sent?"

"Yeah, he loved it. Thanks for mine too, Mom," I say sarcastically as she did not, in fact, send me a box full of instant mash, sunscreen, a five-pack of socks and other crap like she did for Ozzy.

"Well, it made you call me, didn't it?"

I itch the back of my neck, feeling guilty that I haven't called my parents in a couple of weeks. "Sorry, Mom, I've been... busy."

"Busy, huh?" she asks, thick with innuendo.

"Not like that, Mom."

"Then like what?" I'm silent for a beat too long, because she says, "Teddy? Tell me what's happened."

"What makes you think somethings happened?"

"Mother's intuition. Now spill."

Inhaling, I turn and lean against my workbench, pushing a hand into my overall pockets. "Morgana's in Phoenix."

Now it's her turn to be quiet.

"Oh."

"Yeah..." I say, looking at my work boots.

"How is she doing?"

"She's engaged."

Mom sighs. "Yeah, sweetie, I heard. How are you doing?"

"I'm okay."

"Bullshit, Son. Don't think we've forgotten that day when she ripped your heart in two and made you leave," says Dad, and I roll my eyes as I realize Mom must have the call on speaker.

"Miles," she chastises.

"What? It's true," Dad replies. "Always knew that girl was trouble."

"No, you didn't. You thought she was just as sweet as I did. If I recall correctly, *you* were the one who thought it would be a good idea to try to push them together."

"I think you'll find that was your idea, Sadie."

"No, Miles..."

"Hey, hey!" I shout, stopping them mid-argument. "If you two are just going to talk between yourselves, I'm gonna go. Morgana's going to be here any minute to get her car, and I—"

"You're fixing her car?" Dad asks, and I can practically see his eyes bugging out of his head.

"Yeah, Dad."

"That's nice of you, honey," Mom says as Dad mutters something in the background. "I bet she really appreciates it."

"It's not like that, Mom. She's here for work, her car broke down, and we're the only mechanic open around here."

"But still..."

"I'm just doing my job," I say, pulling my hand from my pocket and reaching up to play with my hat.

"Teddy, I hope you know what you're doing."

"Of course he does," Dad's voice booms down the phone, and I need to hold it away from my ear. "He's a professional, like his dad. Works on a car without complaint, regardless of who the client is."

Except my dad would have fitted the part and sent her on her way, unlike me, who had the new cylinder in my desk drawer for nearly a month.

"Make sure you charge that girl extra for labor, Son. I don't care how unethical it is. She broke your heart, it's the least she can do."

"Miles, will you go away?" Mom berates. "I want to talk to our son without your hot head getting in the way."

There's a scuffle, and then a door closes before Mom's voice sounds through the speaker. "Sweetie, you're not doing anything stupid, right?"

Define stupid.

"Not sure what you mean."

"I know you, Teddy. You're just as hot headed as your father, and I know seeing her again after all this time can't be easy."

"It's fine."

"You can't lie to me. Remember, I can see through your bullshit just as easily as I can with your dad. Why do you think I never bug you to come visit? I know you can't stand being somewhere that reminds you of Morgana."

How does the woman do it? See straight to the bottom of everything without ever having to be told.

"All I'm saying is, don't be mean to her because of the past."

"Be mean? What is this? Sixth grade?"

"Teddy," Mom warns. "Don't hold what happened between you two over her forever, baby. You never saw her after you left. She was just as heartbroken, if not *more* than you. Whatever reason she had for ending things... it took some of her sparkle from her. Don't take any more because you're still angry at her."

There's nothing worse than a mother's guilt is there?

"I won't, Mom." *Well, not any more than I already have.*

"Good. I love you, Teddy."

"Love you too."

"So, Dad doesn't like her much, huh?"

Mom tuts. "You're dad's a big drama queen. I think he feels somewhat responsible for everything that happened. If you two never got together, you wouldn't have left, and I wouldn't have cried myself to sleep for a month..."

"Mom," I whine, feeling like a little boy.

She laughs. "Have I made you feel bad enough now that you'll call me more often?"

I smile, feeling a little lighter. "Yeah, Mom. I'll call you more."

We hang up after a couple more minutes of catching up and several more tellings-off about not being in contact with my brothers as much as I should be, and I vow to call them later in the week. I check the time on my phone and notice Morgana is running late. Shit. I should have fixed her car when it first came into the garage instead of being a major douchebag and making her wait. I really need to grow the fuck up, stop holding my grudge, and move the fuck on.

But then why does that sound like the hardest thing I'm ever going to have to do?

Chapter
Thirty-Four

Teddy

I'm cleaning up my workbench when the bell above the door dings and Morgana walks in, looking flustered.

"Sorry I kept you," she says, flicking her wet hair over her shoulder and shaking out her arms. "I couldn't get an Uber, and when I did, I had put in the wrong address, and he wouldn't let me change it, and when I got dropped off at the wrong location, it started to rain, and well, let's say it's the perfect end to a perfectly shitty evening." She takes a huge breath and shakes her head, looking to the ground. "But why am I telling you this? It's not like you care." She sniffs and gestures toward her car, her head hung. "So, you ready?"

I nod, scooping the loose nuts from the bench and putting them inside an old soup can I'd cleaned. I need to sort this shit out. Get nice boxes with homes for everything that all slot away instead of the current system. It's organized chaos at its finest.

I dust my hands down my legs and eye Morgana's wet clothes. *Yeah, I'm a fucking asshole.* Taking the three steps needed to stand in front of her, I notice her hair has a soft wave now that it's wet as I tower over her. My fingers itch to brush the flyaway strands already dry from her face, which is not okay. Fuck's sake, one thought about being nice to the girl and I'm slowly drifting back to my old ways with her. She's engaged. To another douchebag. He is the one who gets to brush her hair back from her face.

I'm just not going to be as big of a dickhead around her now. But I don't like feeling something's up with her, and not just from the tone of her voice when I called earlier, but she won't stop staring at the ground. Her shoulders are slumped, and she looks small, like someone crushed her spirit.

"It took some of her sparkle from her. Don't take any more."

"Yeah, it's ready," I say hoarsely and then clear my throat. Side-stepping her, I shake myself out of whatever gross emotion seeps into my consciousness as I open her car door and slide inside. Pressing my foot to the break and holding down the *On* button, the engine roars to life just as Morgana lifts her head, her lips tilting upward a little, but not enough for someone who should be pleased their car is fixed.

Happy I proved the thing works, I step out, leaning on the door and watching as she slowly walks over, her arms hanging loosely by her sides. She stretches her hand out for the keys and sighs.

"Thank you," she whispers, looking into my eyes. Long gone are the bright two-toned irises I could have stared at all day when we were younger, trying to work out whether, depending on her mood, the blue hue ever managed to dominate the green. Instead, they're dull, almost tinged red like she's been crying.

I lift the keys from her grasp and wrap them in my fingers. "What happened?"

She huffs and rolls her eyes, the first flicker of emotion sparking in her gaze. "Nothing."

I half-snort, half-laugh at her trying to bullshit me. "Really? Going to try to pull that with me?"

"It's fine, Teddy. It's nothing you'd want to hear."

"Try me."

"Believe me when I say you don't want me speaking to you about my jerk of a fiancé."

"Why not?" I ask, although I'm not sure I do want to know. But I'm trying to be *nice,* and for some unknown reason, I'm not ready for her to leave yet. Because once she does, there won't be any reason for us to see each other again. And if I'm being honest with myself, the idea of that sits worse than when I first seen her in my garage. My head is so messed up when I'm around her.

So, crossing an ankle over the other, I lean against her car, my arm resting on the open doorframe, trying to look casual, instead of like I'm ignoring the incessant buzzing of my mom's words in my head or how her looking upset stirs something deep inside me making me want to end the fucker for making her feel like that.

"It's weird," she whines, and my stomach does this weird *whoosh* at the sound. She was never one of those girls whose whines would make my teeth ache. Hers was always soft and had a throaty quality I fucking loved. And hearing it now, knowing that asshole who gets to call her his hears it any damn time he wants and probably doesn't appreciate it like he should... Fuck, it makes me feel a possessiveness toward her. Something I long thought was dead and buried in the graveyard of memories surrounding my heart.

I should just ask her to leave. Talking to her about her love life is a mistake, but I stand up and close her car door, pocketing her keys, which ultimately forces her to stay.

Teddy... This is wrong.

She lifts her eyebrows in surprise, a silent question crossing her beautiful features. But I'm lost; I've no fucking clue why I did that, either.

I scrub a hand across the scruff on my face.

"I've got vodka in the office if you think it would make it less weird?" I ask, shrugging a shoulder as I take off for the office and hope she follows. "Let's make a drinking game out of it. Every time it feels like it's getting weird, we'll take a shot."

Her laugh is loud enough that I don't have to turn to know she's behind me. She takes her jacket off, hanging it on the hook reserved for my overalls, and places her handbag and laptop case by the door.

"If I were a betting girl, I'd put down money that you're happier when you know I'm upset, Teddy Grant." Her tone is teasing, but hearing her say that is almost like a kick to the gut. Does she honestly believe that? I mean, I guess my track record recently with her could argue that, yes, I do enjoy it, and that makes my chest tighten uncomfortably.

Swallowing thickly, I walk to my desk and open the bottom drawer, taking out an almost full bottle of vodka and two glasses. Gesturing with my head, I motion for her to sit as I place the glasses on the engine coffee table and pour a sizeable amount inside. Handing one glass to her, I take the other and hold it out. She clinks hers to mine, and I sink the contents in one go, reveling in the burn. Morgana, however, takes one sip and grimaces, her face cutely scrunching up. Her nose wrinkles, her eyes tightly shut as she shakes her head, trying to work through the afterburn of this cheap as-shit liquor.

I chuckle, flopping into the seat beside her and refill my glass. "Ready to talk yet?"

"Nu-huh," she mumbles, bringing the glass back to her lips and whispering, *"one, two, three,"* before taking a deep breath and swallowing the rest of the drink. She exhales, and I swear you can see heat waves coming from her breath as she sticks out her tongue and palms her chest.

"How can you drink this without wanting to vomit?" she asks, tilting her empty glass toward herself and peering inside.

I smirk and angle the neck of the bottle her way. "More?"

She bites her bottom lip, holding her glass out.

That lip bite will be the death of me.

Pouring her another, I set the bottle down and lean back in my seat. It's awkward, and we do more shots than I anticipated when I first suggested as we try to navigate through the conversation.

"So..." I glance at the clock on the wall and note we've been sitting here for ten minutes. I could have sworn it's been hours. Morgana shifts in her seat, her eyes darting around my office.

"So...?"

"Still friends with Shay?"

Her shoulders release their tension, and she sucks her bottom lip between her teeth and laughs. "I couldn't get rid of her if I tried."

And that does the trick. The conversation flows as she tells me about college, and the summer her and Shay went to Europe with Shay's parents. That surprises me that Morgana's mom would let her out of her sight for a whole month, but then again, Shay was always pushy. I swear, if we decided we wanted a third in our relationship back then, Shay would have been up for it faster than we could have asked. Thank fuck I don't share, but Shay and Ana together... damn, that would have been hot.

Aaaand the vodka's clearly working as my dick perks up, and a sensation extremely close to *happiness* settles in my stomach. Yup, the vodka is definitely working.

"So..." I drawl, kicking my feet onto the coffee table. "What did fuck face do to make you cry earlier?"

She pulls a face, one I remember her making when she wanted to downplay something important.

"I didn't cry."

"Ana, cut the crap."

Her lips part, and it's hard to tell if that one word made her eyes blow or if it's the alcohol. Either way, her shortened name is familiar and rolls off my tongue before I can stop it.

She gulps her drink before saying, "He spoke to a realtor about selling my apartment."

"You don't live together?"

She flushes, glancing away as she itches her cheek. "No. I didn't want to officially move in until we were married."

"But you guys fuck, though? You're not like *saving yourself for marriage?*"

"Drink," she says, nodding to my glass and thank fuck she said it 'cause as soon as I asked that question, I instantly regretted it. No one likes to know who their ex is sleeping with. We both drink, Morgana appearing to handle the burn better the more she has.

"Of course, we have..." Her voice drops to a whisper as she says, "*sex.*" Her cheeks flush brighter as she takes another gulp. I join her, then top our glasses back up, the pleasant warmth from the neat vodka blanketing me as I watch her mouth, the perfect bow, move as she talks without hearing the sound.

"So if you were going to move in together eventually, what's the big deal about him talking to a realtor?" I hear myself ask, the other side effect brought along by vodka of loose lips.

Her brows dip, and she grips her glass tight. "He went behind my back, Teddy. That's the big deal. He just decided for me without discussing it to see how I felt. And I get it. I do. Sometimes renting can be a pain in the ass, especially if you get awful tenants. But I would get references and background checks and try renting it to someone I know." She sags in her chair, looking into her glass like it holds all the answers. "I guess giving up my last piece of freedom terrifies me. Knowing it's there... it's like a safety net. Stops the constricting feeling in my throat. But it's not like I have a choice. He'll get what he wants, so fighting is not worth it."

"You seem to do that a lot."

"What?"

Shit.

Oh well, in for a penny, in for a pound or whatever that saying is.

"You clearly love that apartment. Want to keep it." She nods. "But you're a people pleaser, Morgana. If something you're doing makes someone unhappy, you'll stop it. You've done it for so long that I don't even know if you realize you're doing it." Then I ask something that's been on my mind since I first noticed it. "Whose idea was it to get rid of your curls, Morgana?"

She looks down, and we both know the decision wasn't hers. It's quiet, so quiet that we can hear the ticking of the clock on the wall and the cars driving outside on the road, and I wish I had kept my big mouth shut. But didn't I say vodka and loose lips go hand in hand?

"You're miserable, but you're too afraid to stand up for what would make you truly happy." Her eyes jump to mine, and I can see how right I am. I'd guess I always knew she wasn't happy. I could tell the moment I stepped up close to her in her apartment, the way she reacted to my touch, and I used it against her. Used her desperation to be happy to take what I wanted. Just like everyone else in her life. My hand curls around my glass, my knuckles turning white as the heaviness of that sinks into my stomach. But rather than admit that I fucked up, I focus on *him*. "No wonder your parents think your fiancé is the right guy for you. You're just as much a *yes* person to him as you were to them, Morgana."

"Why do you do that?" she asks, her voice quiet.

I lean forward, topping up my glass with the remainder of the vodka.

"Do what?"

"Call me Morgana? Not Ana like you used to. Well, except that one time."

That's... not what I thought she was going to ask me. If I'm being honest, I was waiting on her calling me out for being a dickhead, ask how I am any different to her fiancé. But how do I tell her it's too hard to say that three-letter word without my pulse beating too quickly? That the way her lips parted the last time I accidentally let it slip when I took something from her I shouldn't have was the best sight I've seen in seven years? I drum my fingers against the empty bottle, unable to look at her as I tell her the truth.

"Because you're not my Ana anymore. You're someone else's."

From the corner of my eye, I see her nod and gently place her empty tumbler on the table before pushing to her feet. I do the same, shoving my hands in my coverall pockets and watching as she collects her jacket and bags, surprisingly sober for how much we drank. Pausing by the door, she drops her head, looking across her shoulder to the floor so I can only see her profile.

"Thanks for fixing my car, Teddy."

Digging in my pockets, I pull out her keys. "Here."

She takes them with a tight smile.

"I can call you a cab if you like?"

She shakes her head. "I'll walk. Goodnight, Teddy."

Slipping out the office door, it quietly closes behind her, and I stare until my eyes burn with the sight of her walking away from me again.

Chapter
Thirty-Five

Morgana

I press myself against the wall outside his office, clasping the hand holding my keys to my chest as my heart beats the unusual rhythm it always does when things with Teddy grow tense. Not like when he asked if Richard and I had slept together. No, this intense presence is different, like chemistry or a force between us that screams to make itself known when we're together, wanting to see if we'll collide under an invisible pull I now know Teddy *has* to feel too. Why else would he have let me talk out my issues? The seams around my carefully constructed life are fraying, coming apart the more time I'm around him.

I can hear him shuffling around his office, and I want to go back inside. Tell him that he's right. I never do what makes me happy, so for once, I want to do something that will.

Because you're not my Ana anymore. You're someone else's.

I know I shouldn't. I know it's wrong, and if there is a Hell, there's a section reserved for me, but as I raise my hand to knock on the glass window, I don't care. I want this. Just this once.

My fist doesn't connect as the door swings open, and I stumble forward, my bag, laptop, and keys dropping to the ground. Teddy's hands wrap around my arms as he stops me from face-planting into his chest.

"What the—"

I reach up and wind my arms around his neck, tugging him down wordlessly until our mouths collide with years of regret, what-ifs, and unadulterated lust. He groans, and I swallow the sound greedily as he bends, his hands running under my thighs to my ass as he lifts me, and I wrap my legs around his waist. His tongue pushes past my lips, and I moan as his taste fills my mouth. One so familiar, yet so different at the same time, all with a hint of vodka. Knocking off that damn baseball cap, I thread my fingers in his thick, dark hair, whimpering when he breaks the kiss to run his lips along my jaw and down my neck.

This is what I've been missing since the day I let him go. The piece of me I lost finally found in his kisses.

"Morgana...?"

Please don't stop, Teddy. Don't take this away from me.

He pulls back, his eyes darting between mine, a small furrow between his brows.

I shake my head. "Please, Teddy. Let me be your Ana again. Just for tonight. Let me be her."

He stares, gripping the back of my neck like he's contemplating his next move. Perhaps he knows what we're doing is dangerous and is giving me a chance to back out. But I won't. I'm all in. I want his lips on mine, his body weighted down against me as he lets me forget. It gives us both the closure we so desperately need.

"Please." It's said in such a whisper that I wonder if I even said it. But Teddy's fingers squeeze around my neck and nudge me forward, his lips taking mine in a demanding kiss.

The office door ricochets against the wall as we move through the shop and toward the stairs that Ozzy appeared from when I first came here, but we veer off and take a different route, down a hallway and up a different set of stairs. He doesn't stop kissing me the entire time he walks us out of his garage, doesn't for one second let us part as his tongue tangles with mine, cruelly reminding me that *this* is what I could have had for all these years. One arm tightens under my legs as he opens a door and walks us inside a dark room. My thighs are protesting with the strain of holding myself around his waist, but I'm scared that if I break contact, rational thoughts will fill us both, and we will stop this before we even start it. And I know in my gut that the regret over not being with Teddy again will always outweigh the guilt I'll face tomorrow.

He sets me down on a bed gently, and I lean on my elbows, panting with swollen and tingling lips as I look around the converted space. It's small, not even big enough to be classed as a one-bed apartment, and in the dim light from the streetlights outside, I can't see anything except a kitchenette and another door that I assume is to a bathroom.

Did he bring me to his apartment?

Teddy stands at the foot of the bed, his large presence formidable in the dark.

"So this is my home," he says, flicking his hand out.

"It's nice."

He laughs, shrugging a little, and I swear it's like he's embarrassed or something. "It does the job."

I extend my hand, and his gaze drops to my fingers. "Come here."

He pauses, chewing on the edge of his lip. "How drunk are you?"

I huff a laugh. "I'm not."

"We just drank an almost full bottle of vodka together, and you're not drunk?"

I crawl to my knees to be in front of him and rest my fingers on his chest, feeling his heartbeat under them.

"You shouldn't feel guilty about taking advantage, if that's what you're worried about." I pause, and Teddy's gaze drops to my mouth.

"If we start this, I don't think I will be able to stop," he says, his voice low and gravelly, sending chills down my spine.

"Good thing I won't tell you to stop."

My tongue darts out and swipes along my lower lip as I grip the zipper of his overalls and slowly pull it down, never taking my eyes from his. Energy crackles around us, and it's taking all my power not to rush undressing him. The muscles in my arms strain, the butterflies in my stomach electric with anticipation. And it finally hits me how right this feels. Nothing has ever quite felt the way it does right now. Not with Teddy when I was eighteen. Not with Richard when we first started dating, first slept together, or when he proposed.

Fuck all the consequences.

Fuck all the fear of what could happen if my mom finds out what I've done.

Fuck everything.

I need Teddy more than I need my next breath.

"You've changed, Ana," he says, his fingers grazing down the side of my face. "What happened between now and earlier?"

"You said I should do what would make me happy." My fingers trail up the inside of his overalls, the soft cotton of his Henley bunching as I move up his chest.

"And that would be me, huh?" He's trying to be funny, trying to lighten the mood and thank God, because, Jesus, it's almost suffocating.

"You take what you want when you want it. No questions asked. So why can't I do the same?"

I slide my hands up and over his shoulders, dragging his sleeves down his arms. He helps me by shaking his hands free, and grips the back of his shirt at the neck, tugging it over his head. The tips of my fingers ghost down his chest, over each bump and ridge of his abs and skimming through the trail of hair that runs beneath his boxers.

Everything heightens as he reaches forward and undresses me with the same speed I did him. It's like we are both savoring this, slow and steady, taking our time, mapping, memorizing, making each other remember how it used to be with the tips of our fingers. My shirt flutters to the bed, and one large hand cups my breast, thumbing my nipple over my silk bra. It's like I've been hit with a thousand volts as I arch into him and close my eyes.

"Fuck, Ana," he says hoarsely, and I swear his voice is my new favorite sound. Knowing that's what he sounds like now when he's aroused. I don't want him ever to stop.

Teddy

"Now is the last time to tell me to stop, Ana. Tell me right now, because as soon as I'm inside you, I won't ever let you go."

Her eyes are wide, and I wish I had more light than the pathetic dribble from outside so I could see the dark green of her arousal in them. Her eyes were always my favorite thing about her.

"I won't say stop," she promises. "I didn't before, and I won't now."

I pause. I should ask her again, maybe mention her fiancé back home, make sure she understands the severity of what we are about to do. Because once we do this, things will never be the same. But I'm a weak, selfish man and this is more than revenge or a quick fuck. This is *my* Ana, back in *my* arms, and I will make sure she knows this is where she belongs.

"Kiss me, Teddy."

I groan, dropping my head to her perfect tits and biting down on the soft, plump skin. She hisses, her hand flying to my head and threading into my hair, pushing and tugging simultaneously. Soothingly, I run my tongue along my mark, loving the ridges of my teeth on her pale skin. I reach behind her, unclipping her bra and letting it pool on the bed, taking her nipple into my mouth and sucking.

Fuck, I've missed these.

My fingers dip to the waistband of her pants, expertly flicking the button and shoving my hand inside. She's soaked. Fucking ready and so damn wet, I know if I don't get inside her soon, I'll die. Seven fucking years I went without her, trying to replace her with meaningless sex after meaningless sex. Every woman who came after her was an empty reminder that *no one* could ever replace her. But she's here now and I don't care the reasons why she's ended up in my bed. She was never meant to have left it and she never will again.

Tearing my hand from her panties, I grab the backs of her thighs and knock her onto her back, her beautiful tits bouncing as she lands. When I told her before she'd filled out, I meant it. Her tits, her thighs, her ass... every part of her I want to touch, kiss, bite. She was gorgeous back then, but now... she's fucking magnificent.

I shrug out of the rest of my coverall, grabbing my wallet from my jeans before they hit the ground, and pulling out a condom I always keep there.

"You're prepared." She laughs as she watches with that bottom lip rolled between her teeth as I tug down my boxers, my cock springing free, hard and painfully excited as it salutes her. I tear off the top of the wrapper with my teeth and cover myself up before tugging off her pants by the ankle. She lifts her ass and hooks her thumbs into her panties, wiggling them down her legs like she can't wait for me to fully undress her.

"Gotta be, baby. Burning when you pee isn't something I want to experience again," I say. "Even if you know you can trust the other person's sexual history."

"Nice save," she deadpans, tossing her panties at me.

I catch them and bring them to my nose. "Nice smell."

"You're vulgar." She laughs, and I smile as I'm smacked in the stomach by a memory.

I join her on the bed, crawling up her body until we're face to face, and my cock is lined up perfectly with her pussy.

"I can vaguely remember you calling me that before and I'm pretty sure after you said it, I made you come hard with my tongue." She inhales, and I push the tip of my dick inside her. "So stay quiet and let this *vulgar* man fuck you better than anyone else ever has."

I thrust inside her in one fluid motion as she cries out, her nails biting into my back as her pussy strangles my cock. Something snaps, clicking into place like it had been misaligned for too long the moment I bottom out. I'm home. She's fucking *home*. I rest my forehead to hers, scrunching my eyes shut, needing a second to stop the pounding in my head or the tightening in my chest before I voice something I really shouldn't.

"Teddy...?"

I pull back to see her face marred with concern. I force a smirk I don't feel and say, "Just giving you time to adjust, baby."

"I don't need time. I need you to fuck me."

"I love it when you talk dirty."

I cage either side of her head with my elbows and pull out of her, slowly pistoning my hips forward until her feet dig into my back, just above my ass.

"*Teddy,*" she whines, canting her hips upward, trying to increase the lazy tempo I'm toying her with.

"And I love that. How fucking desperate you are for me. Say it. Tell me how desperate you are for my cock, Ana."

"I want it, please." She tilts her head backward, her teeth biting hard on the corner of her lip as she writhes beneath me. I slam down, hips meeting hips as she whimpers and moans and rakes her nails up and down my back, carving grooves into my skin as I thrust faster and faster, our breaths mingling as I fuck away the years of resentment and hurt. She is mine. She was always mine, and now, she's choosing me.

I lean down and kiss along her neck, reaching her collarbone and sucking hard until she's bruised. Her jaw drops as she wordlessly screams, her chest convulsing, her thighs quivering around my waist, and I rock my hips harder, gripping her ass with one hand, making her back bow off the bed.

"I'm so close," she moans, her eyes rolling closed as I speed up. Sliding a hand between us, I circle her clit in time with my thrusts, feeling every ripple of pleasure around my dick as she gets closer to her orgasm. The tingling sensation at the base of my spine urges me on, pushing deeper inside her as she moans my name in an endless loop, and where I thought she was tight before, it's nothing like the death grip her cunt has me in now.

"Teddy," she whispers, and our eyes lock as I roll my hips once more. Her legs tighten around my waist while she comes with wide eyes and parted lips, looking so fucking good beneath me, my heart skips a beat. I come with a guttural roar, sharply tugging her onto my cock as my cum fills the condom instead of deep inside her like I want. My rhythm slows as we continue to stare deep into each other's eyes, breathing each other in, bolted together forever. Arms shaking, I can't hold myself up any longer, and I flop on top of her, our sweaty bodies pressing together as we catch our breath. Ana's fingers trail up and down my spine, and my eyes roll closed. Her warmth, the sound of her breathing, her smell. Everything I hated and missed all at the same, here with me now. And I'm never letting her go again.

Chapter
Thirty-Six

Morgana

It's still dark when I wake up wrapped in Teddy's arms, his breath puffing against the back of my neck each time he softly snores. I stare across the darkened room, allowing myself five more minutes surrounded by him, by his warmth, by what could have been. As much as I wish it did, this changes nothing. Instead of closure, the small hole I'd managed to live with since breaking our hearts has become a chasm. A vast empty space that I will never be able to fill. But his life, his family's lives, mean too much for me to risk it all.

Carefully, I slip out of his hold, searching blindly for my clothes, sliding my legs into my pants and buttoning up my shirt. Gathering my underwear in my arms, I pause, watching Teddy sleeping. He looks so beautiful that it hurts, even with the oil stain I can now see splattered across his forearm.

My Grease Monkey.

I turn and tiptoe toward the door, trying not to wake him.

"I didn't think you were a *walk-of-shame* kind of girl." His voice is groggy but tinted with amusement. "Come back to bed."

"I can't," I say, turning to face him and instantly wishing I hadn't. His hair has that just-fucked dishevelment, and his eyes look unfocused as the edges of his lips tilt upward.

He pats the space I vacated not that long ago. "C'mon, Ana. It's too early to be up."

I thumb toward the door. "I need to go back to my apartment. I've got work in the morning."

"So? You've got your car back now," he says and, shit, I dropped my keys in his office. "You can shower here while I make you breakfast, and then you can go home to get changed before heading to the office."

I open and close my mouth, wincing as I say, "I can't. I'm sorry."

He sighs, dramatically dropping his head to his pillow, the sheet bunched around his hips, making it ridiculously hard to remember that I need to put his safety first.

"Fine," he drawls, turning onto his side and propping his head against his hand, his impressive muscles taunting me. He grins, knowing exactly what he's doing as he rubs a hand up and down his chest. "Will I see you after work?"

I frown. "Why?"

His frown matches mine. "Because I'd like to?"

"I thought you were a once-and-done kind of guy?"

He chuckles. "You are not someone I'd ever be *done* with after one time."

"Shame you'll have to make do with the memories, then," I say, trying to be funny, but when his soft smile falls and he sits up in bed, I'm suddenly hit with the thought that we hadn't been on the same page last night. My palms sweat as I watch every painful emotion cross his face, his dark orbs freezing me in place as he slashes me open, leaving me to bleed out.

But it's not my blood I'm covered in. It's his, because my words are like knives, cutting and cutting agonizingly slowly as he realizes what last night meant to me. Bile rises in my throat, but I have to know. "Teddy, you know this was a one-time thing?"

He cocks his head, his brows furrowing, causing deep lines to appear on his forehead. "No. I didn't."

He shoves out of bed, and I can't help looking at his naked body as he grabs his boxers and roughly shoves them up his legs. Even limp, his dick is still the most impressive one I've ever seen.

"So what the fuck was that?" he asks, throwing his arms wide. "A revenge fuck because the princess is being forced to sell her apartment to move into a mansion?"

"Teddy..."

"No. What now? Huh? You gonna go run back home and play happy families with a guy you don't love? Go home and live your mundane life with your mundane husband and have mundane children?" My stomach clenches like it's actively protesting the idea of carrying Richard's child, and my brain stupidly pictures a little boy and girl with *Teddy* as their father instead. My throat tightens and my lungs burn as it feels like I'm being starved of breath. The image suddenly disappears as Teddy thrusts his hand into his hair and tugs on the ends, pacing with such anger, the floorboards vibrate. I clutch my neck, trying to breathe, as he growls to himself, and then he's on me again, spitting fire in my direction. "Fuck. I'm such a fucking idiot. All of you people from Greenwich are the fucking same. Rich assholes who don't care who they use as long as it makes them happy. Did he even upset you? Or was that all an act to make me feel sorry for you?"

My hand drops to my stomach as if he struck me. Every part of me aching as I watch my horrible mistake of giving in to last night tear him apart. This is why my happiness isn't worth more than someone else's. This right here. Watching the man I love—loved—torment himself because of me.

"That's not fair, Teddy," I say, my voice shaking.

"What's not fair, *Morgana*"—I cringe at the sound of my name—"is you coming here after all these years and fucking with my head. I was fine without you. Fine living my life trying to forget you, and then you show up just as I was so *close* to doing that."

I step forward, but he raises his hand.

"Get out."

"Please, Teddy..." I beg.

"Save it. Do you know I canceled a *date* last night all because I heard the crack in your voice when I called to tell you about your car, and I felt *bad* for you? Worried something happened, and against all better thoughts, I wanted to check you were okay."

"You shouldn't have—"

"Too fucking right, I shouldn't have." He picks up his Henley and tugs it over his head, his eyes like ice as they stare at me. "But once again, I'm that fucking idiot who believed every word that came out of your mouth. *I want to be your Ana again...*" He scoffs, shaking his head angrily. "Do you know how many women I've fucked because they wanted revenge on their partners?" I flinch because I don't want to hear about the others he's been with and to know that he does this regularly... it makes my insides pinch with regret and sorrow for him. Did he never want to find someone he could settle down with?

"Don't give me that pitying look, Morgana. If they didn't care, why should I? It's not like *I* sought them out. They came to me, begged me to fuck them like their husbands couldn't." His laugh is cold as he takes measured steps toward me. "I never would have thought you'd have done that too."

"It's not the same thing," I yell, the pressure pounding against my skull at the mere idea that he could add me to a group of women who'd only use him for sex.

"Isn't it? Let's see, shall we?" He lifts his hand and starts checking off his fingers. "You're engaged to a man who controls you. You are so painfully unhappy with your life that *you* came on to *me*. Made the first move. Begged me..."

My hand cracks across his cheek so hard my palm stings. Dragons breathe less fire than Teddy right now. The sun has started to rise, casting a warm orange glow through the curtainless window as Teddy towers above me. The vein in his neck throbbing in time with his deep breathing.

"It's not the same because we mean something to each other, Teddy. As much as you hate to admit it, you know you still care about me. Unlike anyone else you've slept with. I'm different because I was always yours first."

He sneers. "*Meant*, Morgana. We *meant* something to each other." His voice lowers, his face softening ever so slightly as his gaze drops to the ground. "Or at least I used to think we did back when we were kids." His eyes snap back to mine like he's realized he said that out loud. His eyes turn to steel again as he shouts, "What are you still doing here? I said, get out."

I swallow the thick lump lodged in my throat and scramble for the door, running down the metal stairs. Running past his office, I grab my handbag and laptop case, forgetting all about my keys and car, and I frantically rush out into the cool morning air that hits me almost as hard as Teddy's words. My lungs burn from lack of oxygen, each lash of his tongue slicing through skin and right to the bone. I grab my cell from my bag and hit the one person I know I can depend on.

"Babe, isn't it like 4 a.m.? Is everything okay?"

"I can't do this anymore, Shay. I can't be the person they think I should be."

"Okay, deep breath. What are you talking about?" She sounds more awake now, and I should feel guilty that I called at six her time, but I feel like I'm suffocating.

"I fucked up. I've messed everything up so badly, Shay. I don't know who I am anymore. I'm so lost, so tired of it all."

"Morgs, what happened?"

"I slept with Teddy."

She's silent.

"Oh, shit," She breathes.

Yup. *Oh, shit* is right.

Chapter
Thirty-Seven

Morgana

"Ms. Adler?"

I lift my head and blink at Garret, the assistant whose name I could never remember, as he steps inside my little office.

"Hey," I say, lifting my lips into a smile? A grimace? Just simply baring my teeth at the poor boy? Who knows at this point. "Didn't I say you could call me Morgana?"

His cheeks turn pink.

"Oh, right. Sorry." He stares at my face for a second too long before he frowns. "Is everything okay?"

And isn't that the loaded question of the day?

Two days since I slept with Teddy and he tossed me out of his apartment.

Two days since I cheated on my fiancé.

Two days since Ozzy dropped off my car keys.

Two days since I've barely slept or eaten. The mess I made for myself consuming me that I've forgotten how to function as an adult. Which is clear since the young assistant is looking at me like I'm grotesque or something. Okay, so I didn't put makeup on today, or wash my hair, so I scraped it back into a ponytail... or wear proper work attire, but I didn't think I looked *that* bad.

"Yeah," I sigh, leaning back in my seat and scrubbing at my over-tired eyes.

"Are you sick?" he asks, taking a small but noticeable step back.

I open my mouth, about to tell him I'm fine, but then I close it again and nod. "Yeah, my stomach's not great, actually."

Garret glances behind him before leaning down conspiratorially. "Well, it's Friday, and you worked your lunch. Why don't you just play hooky and take the last couple of hours off?"

I laugh for real for the first time in what feels like a lifetime and glance at the clock.

"You're a bad influence," I say, pointing my finger at him as he grins.

"Well, you work too hard. You deserve it."

"Thanks, Garret. Want to give me a hand to pack these binders up so I can go home?"

He nods and we quickly clean up the office, ready for the weekend.

"Have you been out much since you got here?" he asks, closing the lid to one of the boxes he was filling.

I shake my head.

"What have you been doing with all your time?" He laughs. "You've been here for a month and all you've done is work?"

And mess around with my ex.

"You need to have a night out. Go drinking, go dancing, have fun that's not looking at numbers."

"I think I'm a little old to be going out dancing with you," I say, and then burst out laughing when I see his face. "I'm kidding, Garret. It was a joke."

He nods, itching the back of his neck. Oh, shoot, I made the kid uncomfortable.

"How old are you, if you don't mind me asking?"

"Twenty-five. You?"

"Nineteen."

"See? Too old," I say with a smirk, but freeze when Garret steps a little closer.

"I actually like older women," he says, running his gaze up the length of my body.

I shift on the spot. "Oh... um, Garret..."

"I'm kidding," he beams, holding his hands up with a laugh. "You are so not my type. Plus, I have a girlfriend."

"Oh my God," I huff, shaking my head in disbelief. "You had me going there."

His grin widens. "I know, right. But I took your mind off whatever was making you sad."

I place some loose paper in a pile and turn to look at him. "What makes you think I'm sad?"

He wrinkles his nose, but is kind enough to not look me over again like some wounded animal.

"I'm training to be a psychologist." He waves his arm around the office. "I'm just a temp here during the holidays."

"Wow, smart kid."

He beams and lifts a box, taking it to the office door. Looking back over his shoulder, he offers a small smile.

"If you're ever lonely, a bunch of us have lunch in the cafeteria every afternoon at one if you want to join us. It must be isolating up here on your own every day."

"Thanks, Garret."

He nods again and disappears out of the office door, leaving me feeling extremely alone for the first time in my life.

"Shay?" I open the door, late the following afternoon, slack-jawed and eyes instantly brimming with tears as I grab my best friend and haul her against me for a hug.

"I knew you missed me." She laughs, awkwardly patting my lower back as my arms trap hers to her sides. I grip her tighter, my hold almost punishing, as the irrational fear of waking up to find I'm dreaming makes me want to never let go.

Burying my head in her shoulder, I inhale her expensive perfume as she giggles. "Okay, Morgs, let me breathe."

I slacken my arms, and she wraps hers fully around me.

"What are you doing here?" My voice is muffled in her brown hair, and her palms slide up and down my back soothingly.

"Do I need an excuse?" she asks, and I finally dislodge myself from her and wipe my eyes. "I'm here because I am the bestest friend ever, and when your girl calls you having a mid-life crisis, you drop everything and make sure she's okay. Plus, I'm going to make sure you don't make any more mistakes with that man. I'm worried about you, babe." She pulls away from me completely, holding me at arm's length, her face hard. "One month. You're here for one month, and you've made multiple poor life choices. Not that Richard is an amazing one..."

"I'm so fucked, Shay. I'm the worst person in the world," I whisper, my bottom lip quivering, and in an instant, her stern look melts into sympathy. "I'm horrible and deserve to be alone."

"Hey. Hey now. Stop that..." she says, running her thumb under my eye and catching a wayward tear. "I will not have this self-deprecating bullshit. You're confused. Hurt. Terrified of marrying the wrong guy."

"Richard is nice, Shay. He's intelligent, strong-minded, nice."

"That's nice twice, Morgs."

I grimace. "But he's not Teddy."

Shay clicks her tongue, kicks her suitcase through the door, and closes it behind her. I'm so much up my own butt that I forgot to invite her in. She links her arm in mine and tugs me toward the couch, dropping to one side and pulling me after her. She shifts, moving toward the edge and narrows her gaze.

"What am I going to do?"

"Morgana, I'm not going to sugarcoat it. Cheating is fucking awful. Like the worst thing anyone could ever do to someone that they are meant to love. What were you thinking? What the hell was *Teddy* thinking? He knows about Richard, right?" I nod and sag into the sofa, hating every word she says because it's exactly how I feel. She sighs, sounding exasperated. "Well, how could he not? That thing on your finger is fucking huge." She cuts her hand through the air. "Not the point. Teddy is just as bad as you are. So, what now? Break up with Richard and get back with Teddy?"

"He hates me."

She laughs. "Girl, that boy has been head over heels in love with you for years. There is no way he hates you."

"You didn't see him the other week, Shay."

"Well, apologize. Tell him you've ended it with fuck-face and want him back."

"It's not that simple. I made a promise to Richard."

"Pretty sure that promise wasn't to go screw your ex the first chance you get," she chastises.

I drop my eyes to my hands, picking at the edge of my nail until it bleeds.

"I can't be with Teddy."

"What?" she shrieks, throwing her hands up, and I wince. "Why the fuck not? Morgana, what was the point of all of this? Fuck Teddy until it was time to head home and live the rest of your life feeling guilty and miserable that went behind your husband's back for months or because you're not with the guy you're meant to be with?" She grips my hands, pulling them onto her lap. I lift my gaze to look into her soft blue eyes. "Honey, any idiot can see you two are soulmates. Even back then. Richard is an asshole who is not good enough for you."

"You can't say that, Shay."

I should be mad she said that, but somehow her admission makes me feel... free?

"I said I wasn't going to sugarcoat it. Morgana, since Teddy left, you've been a shell of yourself. You *loved* him. You were so madly in love with him, and it sorta made me want to settle down." I raise my eyebrows, and she laughs. "Yeah, for like two seconds until I remembered I'm a total hoebag for the D."

"Aren't you seeing someone?"

"It's not exclusive, so we can do whatever we want." She shrugs. "Stop trying to change the subject. My point is that one day you were happy, and the next, you weren't. And now you're both in the same city, clearly just as dumb as you were years ago. You've been given a second chance and you're doing nothing about it."

"I'm engaged."

"And yet you conveniently forgot about that fact while bouncing on someone who *isn't* your fiancé's dick." She levels me with a stare. "Do you love him?"

"Of course, I agreed to marry him, didn't I?"

"Not Richard, you moron. Honestly, do I need to spell everything out to you? Teddy. Do you love Teddy?"

I swallow roughly as every part of me wants to scream *I never stopped.* But she doesn't know the truth. She doesn't know why I ended it seven years ago, and she doesn't know that if I break up with Richard and get back with Teddy, his life is over.

When an awkward amount of time passes, she sags in defeat. "I need a drink. You got any alcohol?"

"Only white wine, and I know you hate that."

She blanches. "Looks like we're getting drunk at a bar, then."

The Dirty Duck isn't the usual place I would go to for a drink. It's small and dark and has a vintage quality that I instantly adore. None of the uptight, everything-made-of-glass, and overpriced drinks I'm used to back home.

"Oh my God, this is amazing," Shay drawls, pulling her phone out of her pocket and snapping pictures for her Instagram feed. "I love how retro it is."

"I'm not sure *retro* is the feel they were going for," I laugh, dragging her to the bar as her thumb pulses on the button on her screen, taking picture after picture of the bar. Picking up the menu, I study the list, running my finger along their logo of a duck in a muddy puddle with a weird—and not at all creepy—salacious grin on its face.

"What can I get you?" the bartender asks, and Shay immediately props her elbow on the bar top.

"You?" Shay beams as the guy sends her a wink.

"Starting early, aren't we? What about Lenox?" I ask, nudging her hip with mine.

Shay's back stiffens as she pointedly ignores my question. "Hey, I didn't judge you for being a cheat... much... so you can't judge me for being forward." Suddenly, the good mood I managed to somehow put myself in disappears. Shay notices. "Shit, Morgs, I was only joking. Too soon, huh?"

"A smidge."

"Fuck. Okay, we'll have two shots of Patron... each." She shoots me a wink. "A large-as-you-can-make-it white wine and..." She wiggles her hips as she thinks, tapping her long finger to her lips. "A beer. Whatever's good around here works."

"You got it."

No sooner has she ordered, the four shots slide in front of us. Shay pumps her brows as she pours salt on my hand and shoves the small plate of lime wedges in front of me. Clinking our glasses together, we throw back the first shot, followed by the second, the burn of the tequila making my insides all warm.

"*Wooo-eeeee*, fucking hate tequila."

"Then why do you always do it?" I laugh, sucking on a lime.

She shrugs. "Gets you drunk. Remember when we turned twenty-one and drank cheap rosé because it got you hammered fast? Well, this is the adult version of that."

The bartender sets our other drinks on the bar, and Shay hands him her card. "Keep them comin', handsome. For every round, bring a shot of tequila too, and"—she thumbs over to me—"if you manage to get this one nice and drunk, there's a hundred in it for you, as well as my phone number."

My cheeks flame as, according to his name tag, Beau shamelessly runs his eyes over the tight dress Shay *made* me wear.

"Come on," I say, picking up my wine. "Let's go find a table."

The bar isn't busy, but the music's already loud enough that we need to lean in close to hear each other speak. And considering it's a Friday night, finding a table isn't hard, but since this is the only local place in town, give it a few hours, and it will be packed.

"We need to eat, or I'll be in trouble," I say, sliding over the food menu to the food connoisseur, and Shay picks a couple of appetizers before returning to the bar to order, coming back with yet another round of shots. This time something red and tastes a little like chili.

The constant gnawing in my gut—guilt for Richard and an endless hunger for Teddy—slowly ebbs to a manageable level as Shay fills me in on the last month while I've been away. Even though I so kindly asking Shay to keep an eye on her, my mom's still being a huge bridezilla for a wedding that's not even hers, Dad's frequently in the news—not that I pay attention—and her parents are trying to convince Shay to come with them on a month-long cruise to Europe again.

"So nothing out of the ordinary," she says, taking a sip of her beer and casually looking around the bar. She splutters, her eyes bulging as she sets her glass down and thumps against her chest. "Oh, shit."

"What?"

"You said Teddy hadn't changed much from when we were younger, right?"

"Yeah...?" I draw out the word, skeptically looking at her as I slowly twist my head to see what she's looking at. Grabbing my chin roughly, she snaps it back to face her.

"Okay, I might have been a bit hasty in my lecture earlier, 'cause damn, Morgs. That boy's glow up is..." She shakes her head with a low whistle. "I get why you couldn't stay away."

I try to shrug out of her hold, but her fingers bite into my skin. "Ouch, Shay, what are you doing?"

"Believe me, you don't want to see what I see."

"I'm a big girl. I'm sure I can keep it in my pants." *I think.*

But it's not my pants that are the issue. Standing at the bar is Teddy and the most beautiful woman I've ever seen. Tall, curves in all the right places, long, flowing auburn hair that cascades down her back and brushes along his arm where he's curled it around her waist. My chest twinges, and my stomach bottoms out. I have no right to feel like this; I told him nothing was going to happen between us, and even though rationally I know that I can't, the sense of betrayal barrels into me hard as I struggle to peel my eyes from them.

His date says something, all smiles and wide eyes as she tilts up toward him. The mix of tequila, wine, and the other spirits that kept coming all night sours in my stomach, leaving a sickly taste in the back of my throat. Teddy grins and ducks down, brushing her hair away from her neck and leaning into it as the woman's eyes flutter closed.

I slam mine shut, blocking the view of Teddy, and steeling myself for a second before turning back to Shay.

"We need more drinks."

Chapter
Thirty-Eight

Teddy

She's drunk.

Like messy, no inhibitions, can't string a sentence together drunk, and if it were anyone else, I would find it amusing. Not only is she distracting me from my *date* with Savanna, but she and Shay are also putting themselves in a situation neither girl should be in, in a town they don't know. I'm not saying people around here are sleazy, but the number of guys who've approached their table with that gleam in their eyes we all get when we're out on the prowl, does not sit right with me.

"You're not listening to me. Are you?"

"Huh?"

Savanna huffs, but she gives me a knowing smile and places her elbow on the table, resting her chin on the back of her hand. "I know I'm a sure thing but a girl still likes some effort, Teddy. You've been staring at those two drunk girls the whole time I was speaking." She purses her lips and swivels on her seat, glancing over to watch Shay howling with laughter and Morgana's face turning the prettiest shade of red.

No. Not pretty. Just red.

"Do you know them or something?"

I scrub a hand over my jaw. "Nah."

"But you did? I can tell," she probes, pumping her eyebrows and leaning closer. "So, who is she? Client? Fuck buddy? The one that got away?"

Her eyes narrow in on the last one like she's hoping she hit the jackpot, which she obviously has, but I'm not admitting that to anyone.

"She's no one important," I say, reaching over and running my hand up her bare arm to her neck, wrapping my fingers around her nape and bringing her closer to whisper in her ear. "She's not the one I'm going home with and fucking to within an inch of her life."

She pushes my chest and laughs. "Oh no, Prince Charming." *I detest that name.* "We aren't having sex tonight."

"You just said you're a sure thing," I tease.

"Nu-huh. Not when you have this kicked puppy look going on each time you look over at her." Savanna's finger waves around my face. I drop my hold from her neck and lean back.

"I don't have..."

"Yes, you do," she says, sipping her red wine. "Besides, Ozzy warned me you might be *absent* tonight."

"You talk to Ozzy?"

"Yes, Teddy," she says pointedly. "We're friends too, and sometimes we even talk." She gasps like it's a huge shock.

"And the topic of conversation is me?"

She pats my hand. "Oh, sweetie, don't be so full of yourself. We talk about a lot of things, but you happened to be mentioned, and he told me you might not be the best company since you've been acting all sourly for the past week."

Her brows tug together, giving her this look that can't be... pity?

"Don't look at me like that, Savanna. Oscar should keep his big mouth shut. I've been acting like normal."

She scrunches her nose like she can see right through my lie because, deep down, I know I've been an unbearable asshole to everyone who's crossed my path.

Ozzy not putting a tool back where I left it last? I kept everything we use daily in a bag by my side the whole day, and he had to ask for permission to use any of it.

The barista at Grounded messed up my order? I asked to speak to the manager.

A client wanted to book her car for a service? As soon as she said her name was Annabelle, I informed her we don't accept any variation of that name and to try somewhere else.

Petty and pathetic, but apparently, that's who I am now.

Great, I've only just realized... Savanna—Ana. I'm a mess.

Savanna's eyes widen as she suddenly becomes still, her mouth dropping slowly.

"Oh my God. She's the reason you're the way you are, isn't she?"

"I don't know what you're talking about," I say with gritted teeth, roughly gripping my beer bottle and gulping half the liquid in one go.

This night is not going the way I planned at all. All I wanted was to get under someone else to get over *her*. Sav was the girl I had told Morgana I had bailed on when Richard had upset her. It wasn't a date, I *never* date, but the opportunity to get a painful punch to the kidneys presented itself, and I took it. And even though at the time it was a lie, now that I'm here with Sav for real and Morgana's shit-faced across the room, I feel like the biggest asshole.

"Savanna, I don't need you psychoanalyzing me as you do with your patients. You're not Dr. Caplin right now."

Great. Instead of guaranteed sex, I'm now getting a free therapy session.

"Hey, I know that. I'm talking to you as a *friend,* not a therapist." She quirks a brow and jerks her head backward toward Morgana's table. "So, which one is she?"

"I'm not telling you."

She hums. "Guess I'll just have to find out myself."

"What...?" She doesn't let me finish and, instead, seductively slides from her stool, wraps her arms around my neck and touches her lips to mine. I freeze, my back going rigid as she kisses me, the warmth of her toned body pressing against me, sending chills down my spine. It's unwelcome. Cold, hard, and completely unfamiliar, and it's taking everything I have not to push her away and wipe her taste from me. Not that she's tried to stick her tongue in my mouth or anything, but this kiss—the type that's awkward and weird, like when your grandma manages to get you right on the mouth—it's wrong.

She pulls back and scrunches her nose. "Thank God you don't fuck as bad as you kiss."

"What did you expect? You took me off guard."

She laughs. "Teddy, it's like you've never kissed someone..." Her smile drops, and she's back to looking pitying again. "Oh. Honey. Is that why you've never kissed me before? Or anyone, for that matter?" My brows lower, and Savanna props her hip against the table, cocking her head like she can't believe why I'm confused. "People talk in this town, Teddy."

"I know. Fucking *Prince Charming.*"

She huffs a laugh. "Yeah, gotta love that nickname. But that's not what I mean. Everyone knows you're the guy to show a girl a good time, but never expect to get a goodnight kiss."

"And? Maybe I don't like kissing. Maybe I'm just about the sex. What's wrong with that?"

"Nothing at all." She holds her hands up placatingly. "There is nothing wrong with a healthy sexual appetite. Your morals might be a tad loose, but you control your body. No one should decide the appropriate number of sexual partners another person has. You sleep with one or one hundred people, and no one should care. But, sweetie, I think the real reason you don't kiss any of the women you're with or the fact that when it comes to fuck-buddies, you're not picky, is because of her." She discreetly points at Morgana.

"That's fucking bullshit."

"You're not over her, Teddy. And with the way the petite little blonde keeps checking you out with the same kicked-puppy expression but also with this feisty *wants-to-cut-a-bitch* look, and said bitch being me... I don't think she's over you either." Savanna plants a kiss on my cheek and returns to her seat. "And that was from Dr. Caplin, free of charge."

"Thanks," I deadpan, playing with the label peeling away from the beer bottle. Movement snags my attention as Morgana pushes to her feet, swaying as she tries to stand. I grip the edge of the table, my knuckles turning white as she stumbles down the hallway leading to the restrooms.

Fuck me, I must be a glutton for punishment. Not long ago I shouted in her face and chucked her out and now I'm thinking about playing rescue...

"Teddy? What are you—"

I shove back my stool, the sound of metal scraping on wood barely registering against my heartbeat pounding in my ears. The bar is gone. The patrons are gone. My *date* is gone. It's just Ana, drunk, vulnerable, and alone.

Savanna grabs my arm. "Some free advice, Teddy? Don't be a dick to her like you are with everyone else." I go to argue, but she holds up a hand. "Hey, we all know what to expect when we get with you. Emotionless, hot-as-fuck sex with one fine-ass man and nothing more. Whatever happened between you two, let it go, okay?"

First my mom, now her?

I press a kiss to her cheek. "I'm sorry about tonight."

"It's okay. I'd say you owe me, but I have a feeling there's a chance this town will be losing its highly sought-after bachelor."

I half-laugh, half-snort. "You going to be okay?"

"Hell yes. Tonight's not a total bust. A certain bartender is just as slutty as you, and has been watching me all night. I bet he'd be willing to take me home." She winks and angles her body toward the bar, crossing her legs and letting her creamy thighs show. "I'll be fine. Go get your girl."

I squeeze her shoulder quickly, then take off toward the restrooms. The nearly pitch-black hallway is empty as I walk down it, and I worry for a second that I missed her leaving. Approaching the ladies' room, I lean my hands on either side of the door, straining to listen over the echo of the music from the bar for someone inside. I knock and push it open, calling out before stepping fully inside.

It's empty.

Shit. Maybe I did miss her? Or maybe she didn't come down here?

"Oops." A tiny giggle, then a watery sigh, comes from one of the closed stalls, followed by a loud *bang*. "Oh, man."

"Ana?"

A gasp. "Shay?"

I suck in a laugh and lean against the row of sinks on the far wall, watching her shadow dance under the door as she takes an insane amount of time to finish what she's doing.

"Unless Shay has a man's voice now, it's not her. Come out here, Ana."

"Ana's not here."

I stalk toward the closed door, noticing it's not locked, and push it open with one finger. Ana looks up at me, mascara coating her cheeks, her long straight hair a mess on the top of her head like she fisted it in her hands, and there's a long line of tissue, still attached to the roll on the wall, in her hand.

She blinks and blinks again before swaying, her shoulder landing on the side of the stall.

"Hi," she hiccups.

"Hey. Are you okay?"

"Yup. Just a bit tippy," she slurs, running her nose along her arm, completely bypassing the tissue. "Tipsy."

"I think you've passed tipsy, Ana."

Her eyes flutter shut, and she rests her head against the wall, humming softly as the edges of her lips tilt upward.

"Ana," she whispers. "I like it when you call me that."

Then she's quiet, her mouth lilting downward, and she sucks in a shaky breath. I step closer and drop to my haunches. "Ana?"

Her eyes snap open.

"You're so pretty." She weakly lifts her hand in the air, the tips of her fingers brushing against the scruff on my jaw. "I hate that you're so pretty. You're not allowed to be pretty when you said such ugly things to me." She sniffs. "And you're on a date. With this beautiful woman. After being with me."

I swear it's a kick in the gut.

Is she this drunk because of me?

She closes her eyes again, and a single tear drops down her face. I sigh, dropping my head before running my thumb across her cheek, the warm salty drop of water coating it. I place my hand on her knee and shake her leg.

"Ana? Can you stand up?" She shakes her head no. "Want to try?"

"Sleepy."

"I know, so why don't we get you home?"

She opens one eye and peers at me, the most adorable little scrunch to her nose, making her look confused.

"Okay." Leaning forward, she pushes to her feet, her hand flattening against the wall as she steadies herself. Suddenly, she jolts forward. "Oh God."

She pushes me out of the way, reaching a sink and hurling herself over it, barely managing to position herself above it before throwing up. The sound of water hitting porcelain, the smell of fruity drinks, and Ana's body racked with sobs as she vomits up her entire stomach, fills the bathroom. Gathering her hair from her face, I hesitate before gently rubbing small circles on her back as she breathes deeply between bouts of vomit.

"I just want to feel better," she cries, her fingers tightly curled around the sink as her arms shake from the shock of throwing up.

"Tylenol, water, and a good night's sleep. You'll feel better in the morning."

"No. I want to stop hurting." Her shoulders slump, and some of her hair lands in the bowl. I swallow hard, trying not to gag as I reach around her and turn on the tap, dipping the puke-covered strands under the water, and then tucking them over her shoulder.

"I don't think you'll be sick again. It will stop hurting soon."

"No. You don't get it," she whines, and I can see her bottom lip lower in the mirror. "He hates me. He treats me like shit, but he doesn't get how much I miss him. I don't want to hurt anymore."

Her voice cracks, and it takes me a second to realize she's talking about me. Shit, how drunk is she that she doesn't realize she's talking about me *to* me? I squeeze my eyes shut, unable to watch her as her sobs carry over the sound of the tap.

"Why did you do it?" I hear myself asking. The one question that I've never had the chance to get the answer to. Maybe this is what I need to let her go and move on for good because Savanna was wrong when she called her *my girl*, but completely right that I need to let it—*her*—go.

"I can't say. If I say, Mom will ruin his family."

I freeze, my blood turning to ice. "What?"

"I want to go home," she says, lifting her head and grabbing paper towels.

I spin her and lean her against the sink. "Ana. What did you mean your mom will ruin my family?"

Her red-rimmed eyes meet mine, and she tries to focus. "I..."

"Morgs! Where are you?" Shay bursts through the bathroom door, her wide grin dropping as she takes in Ana's tear-stricken face and my arms around her biceps. "What the fuck did you do?"

She pushes in between us and holds Ana's face in her hands. "Babe? What happened? Are you okay?"

"She's fine. She's just drunk."

Shay glowers at me from the mirror, and I swear I shrink in size. Shay is one scary bitch when she wants to be. "Did I ask you, asshole?"

"Shay..."

"No, Teddy. I don't want to hear it. Just..." Ana groans, her head flopping to Shay's shoulder, and her fight ebbs slightly. "Just leave so I can get her home."

She wraps her arm around Ana's waist, trying—and failing—to lead her to the bathroom door.

"Shay..." I start and rub the back of my neck. Without another word, I lift Ana from her, threading my arms under her legs and behind her back and carrying her bridal style out of the restroom. Bringing her to my car, Shay jogs in front and opens the door, popping the driver's seat forward to let me lay Ana across the backseats, resting her head on a balled-up sweatshirt as Shay settles up front.

"How come you're not as drunk as she is?" I ask, taking one last look at a passed-out Ana.

Clicking on her seatbelt, Shay glances over her shoulder at her best friend and sighs. "I forgot Morgs could never handle mixing her liquor."

I want to tear her a new one. Berate her for letting Ana drink so much if she *knew* she couldn't handle her liquor. But I'm too tired and drained from seeing her—not just tonight, but since the first day she arrived in town. But more so, her drunken admission in the bathroom won't leave room for much else.

Pulling up to Ana's rental, Shay unlocks the front door as I carry Ana to her bed.

"Water and pain pills, Shay. She's gonna be sore tomorrow."

Shay nods, carefully pulling off Ana's shirt and pants, leaving her in her underwear as she lifts the comforter over her body and tucks her hair away from her face. I stand watching, knowing I should go, but the overwhelming need to ensure she's okay, when I know Shay is more than capable of looking after her, keeps my feet rooted to the spot.

Ana sighs in her sleep, and Shay grabs a pack of wet wipes and starts to clean her face. The floorboards must creak or something because Shay glances over her shoulder, clearly surprised I'm still here.

"I've got this, Teddy. You can go. She'll be fine."

I nod and brush my hand through my hair, awkwardly leaving the girls alone.

"Teddy?"

I turn back, and Shay looks between Ana and me. "Thanks."

I nod again like one of those bobbleheads, with a voice echoing inside my head repeatedly saying, "*Mom will ruin his family.*"

Chapter
Thirty-Nine

Morgana

Why does it feel like someone's bashing my head with a hammer? Groaning, I roll over and squint through the bright light streaming through the open curtains. Why did no one close the damn things when we got home?

Wait. How did we get home?

"Good morning, buttercup."

Slowly, I turn my head to the other side of my bed. Shay's leaning against her elbow, wearing the smuggest grin I've ever seen and looking far too fresh for how much we drank last night.

"Why do I feel like death and you don't?"

"Water, babe," she says, like it's the most obvious explanation. "Water in between each round."

"Why didn't you give me any?"

"I tried. A whole pitcher was on the table, and you didn't have any of it."

I groan, planting my face into my pillow. "How did we get home last night?"

"What was the last thing you remember?" she asks, and my hangover kicks up a notch. No one asks what the last thing you remember is unless you have done something really bad.

"Erm, I remember drinking that green shot and you getting some guy's number, but that's about it."

"Oh boy."

"Oh boy? Why 'oh boy'?" I sit up too fast, the room spinning around me.

"You disappeared for like ten minutes to go to the bathroom, so I went to find you."

"Did I fall asleep again?" I ask, knowing too well that during college, drinking with Shay usually meant a catnap in the bathroom stall for me.

"Not exactly," she grimaces. "When I came in, Teddy was there, and it looked like you'd been crying, and I think you threw up."

I cover my face with my hands. "He was in the bathroom with me? Did he see that?"

She makes a non-committal noise like it's highly likely he did. "Then you sort of passed out, and Teddy brought us home."

That's when I realize I'm sitting in my bra and panties. "Shay, who undressed me?"

She stretches through a yawn. "Don't worry, that was me."

My anxiety lessens, and I rearrange the pillows, lying back against the headboard and dragging the covers up to my chin, trying to tell myself that's not too bad in the grand scale of how badly I've messed up recently. But fear and flashbacks of the night before are funny things, especially when your brain decides randomly to kick you when you're down.

"Oh, shit," I groan, bringing my knees up and burying my head in them as fragments of the night slowly make their way through the drunken fog.

Me sitting on the toilet.

Teddy helping me to my feet.

Him holding back my hair. Oh God, he saw me throwing up and *helped* me.

"Do you know if I said anything to him?"

Shay shrugs, slipping out of bed and going to the adjoining bathroom. Leaving the door slightly open, she pees. Honestly, the girl has no boundaries. "Not sure. What would you have said?"

She flushes the toilet, and the sound of running water and Shay's electric toothbrush is like a jackhammer buzzing about my brain. She appears in the doorway, dabbing her mouth with a towel.

"Why do you look like that?"

"I feel like I maybe said something I shouldn't have last night, but I can't remember," I say, rubbing my aching forehead as everything in my body protests at being awake and having to function as an adult. "I think I told him I missed him."

Shay laughs, quickly getting dressed in yoga pants and a tee before brushing her hair into a high ponytail. "Not exactly the worst thing you've done with him recently, Morgs."

I grab a pillow from behind me and throw it at her. "When will you stop bringing that up? I feel guilty enough without you piling it on."

She picks up the pillow that landed nowhere near her and tosses it onto the bed.

"Okay, I'm sorry. I can't believe out of everyone, sweet, innocent Morgana would do that." I drop my head, hating how she always speaks the truth, even when I don't want to hear it. She claps her hands together and rummages around my closet. "Right. No more wallowing. Let's go out and do something.

Take your mind off Richard, Teddy, your hangy. So get your ass out of bed and shower because, my God, Morgana, you fucking stink."

She chucks clothes onto the bed, practically drags my sorry ass into the bathroom, and turns on the shower. I strip from my underwear as she leaves me alone, telling me she will make us coffee.

"Morgana, do you have any creamer?" Shay shouts from the other room. I hear a small knock and ignore it, assuming she is searching my near-empty shelves as I open the shower door.

"There should be a new one on the top shelf in the fridge," I yell, dipping a toe into the water and testing the temperature.

"Actually, Morgana, can you come out here?"

I groan, suddenly desperate to hop in the shower and let the warm water do its magic. Showers when you're hungover are the ultimate cure. Grabbing a towel, I wrap it around my body, tucking the edge into the top as I join her in the kitchen.

"Why can you never find anything unless it jumps out and smacks you in the face, Shay?" I look up, and my feet almost trip over themselves. "Teddy."

He looks at Shay, who's pivoting from foot to foot, and I can tell she wishes she was anywhere but here. Or maybe she wishes she had popcorn. She does like drama.

"I brought you coffee," he says, extending the cup holder to Shay, and she greedily grabs one of the three white paper cups and brings it to her lips. He reaches behind and pulls out a yellow drink he must have had in his back pocket. "And also, a Gatorade for, you know, electrolytes and shit after last night. Lemon lime still your favorite?"

I nod, hesitantly accepting the bottle, my eyes unblinking as I watch him set the other two coffees on the counter and shift his weight awkwardly.

"Can we talk?" He glances at Shay, and then back to me. "Alone?"

"Oh, right, yeah, I, um, was going to go for a walk anyway," Shay says, pointing to the front door. "Such a nice day and all. I might as well go see the sights."

"Shay, we have plans," I say, my voice a little croaky as I stare in horror as she backs down the hall. She can't leave me here with him, not after last night. Not after the past few times we've been together and ended up... doing stuff. And this whole "nice Teddy" is throwing me off. It's like he's had a personality transplant. Not too long ago, he was throwing me out of that little apartment in his garage and now coming over here with coffee and my favorite sports drink. I can't handle it.

"We never made plans," she says, and I swear to God, I want to dump her as my best friend.

"Shay," I growl, taking a step forward.

"*Byeee*," she sings, ducking out the door in a blur and leaving Teddy and me alone while I'm dressed in a towel.

"I'm going to shower," I say, tugging the soft yellow cotton tighter around my body like a shield. "I'll be five minutes."

Every minute I'm in the shower is torture. Every possible scenario floods my brain as to why he's here and makes my stomach churn so viciously that I have to jump out of the shower to vomit again. My head swims, dizziness starts, and all I want is to curl up in a ball and hide from the world.

I stare through the crack in the bedroom door, watching as he sits on the sofa and looks around. I quickly shove a shirt and sweats on, rolling the waistband up a few times around my hips. I don't understand why he's here.

What does he need to talk about? Pretty sure we both made ourselves clear the last time we spoke.

He's flicking through his phone when I walk into the living room, my coffee and Gatorade set on the small wooden table at the edge of the couch. Sitting on the far end, as far away from Teddy as possible, I take a sip of the coffee, the instant taste of vanilla dulling my hangover.

"I'm sorry about last night," I say, deciding it's best to rip the Band-Aid off and get that out there while being completely unable to look anywhere else but at my cup. "Shay said I was in some state, so I can only apologize that you had to take care of me."

He's quiet, so I force myself to look up at him. His eyes are stuck on my chest, but he quickly averts his gaze and clears his throat.

"It's fine." His tone isn't exactly emotionless, but it doesn't have the kind, soft pitch he had years ago or the hard-edged gruffness he usually adopts when he's with me now. I don't know how to decipher it.

"But still, it was nice, and you didn't have to do it, so thank you."

"You've still got it."

"Got what?" I ask, confused.

His eyes flick back to my chest, and I look down. My mouth dries as I see what I'm wearing, what Shay chose for me, and I didn't pay attention. I pull at the hem of the shirt, the Pink Floyd logo stretching out flat in front of me.

"Oh, yeah," I say, lifting my legs and tucking them up to my chest, hiding the shirt from view. "I couldn't bring myself to bin it."

He nods, his eyes glued to the shirt he can no longer see.

"And the sweats? Couldn't throw them out either?"

"Oh shoot, these are yours too?" He nods. "I thought they were an old pair of Skip's. God, I've been wearing these almost every weekend for years thinking they were my brother's. They've even got a hole in the crotch."

I go to move to show him, but stop as soon as one leg drops, remembering where I am and who I'm with. I smile awkwardly and Teddy shifts in his seat. We're silent for what could be minutes, but it feels like hours. Teddy flicks his phone in his hand again, and I slowly finish my coffee.

"Teddy..." "Ana..." we both say simultaneously, and I nervously smile, waving my hand in the air. "Sorry. You go."

He puts his phone face down on the sofa, moves to the edge, and takes a deep breath before saying, "Last night, you said something about your mom."

A cold sweat prickles my spine, and I can almost feel the blood draining from my face.

"Yeah? What about her?" I ask, tremors lacing my voice.

He turns, pinning me with his dark eyes. "What did you mean, your mom would ruin my family?"

The hairs on my arms rise, and the dizziness I felt earlier is more debilitating now as my legs weaken and my brain screams for me to run.

If I find out you've so much as sniffed in his direction, I will ruin him and his family.

"I..."

"What did you mean?"

I push off the sofa, trying to distance us, but Teddy doesn't let me. He follows, matching me step for step as he rounds on me.

"She's the reason you broke up with me. I've always known it. What did she say?"

"Teddy, please don't do this."

"Tell me, Ana." His eyes beg for me to let me in. "Whatever happened, we can fix it."

"Stop, Teddy."

He eats up the remaining distance, taking one step toward me and wrapping his large hands around my arms. Even though he isn't working today, the smell of oil swamps my nose, like it's permanently part of his scent now.

"Tell me, or I'll fucking ask her myself."

"No. You can't," I cry out.

I need out. I need to leave. Go back to Connecticut, leave here, and jeopardize my job to keep him safe.

"Tell me!" he roars, tightening his hold, and I flinch. Long gone is the Teddy who brought coffee this morning and was shocked to see I still had the shirt he bought me at the planetarium, replaced by this enraged beast with wide eyes, flared nostrils, and veins pulsing profusely in his forearms, neck, and temples. He breathes like he's in pain, swallowing down a fit of anger so deep you could almost touch it. Suddenly, he lets me go, and I stumble forward, gasping for air as he finds my phone on the kitchen counter and unlocks it with the same passcode I've always had.

"Teddy, no, what are you doing?"

Holding the phone to his ear, he snarls, "Calling your fucking mother and finding out what the fuck is going on."

I scramble toward him, tugging at his wrist and trying to pry the phone from his grip. "No, stop Teddy; she will destroy you. And not just you. Everyone. Your dad, your mom... your brothers. Please hang up the phone." My nails dig into his skin as I try to force him to listen, my breaths coming hard and fast as I fight him for my phone.

He lets me take the device, and I smack the end call button and power it down, air finally filling my lungs. My hands shake as I clutch the phone to my chest while Teddy's are in tight fists, his lips pulled back, baring his teeth.

"What?" The word sends chills down my spine. I run my hand through my hair over and over, trying to swallow the lump in my throat as I start to pace. Teddy steps in front of me, the thick veins in his neck bulging as he grits out, "Speak, Ana. Now"

I press a hand to my stomach, wishing it would stop roiling. My eyes dart around the small space, bouncing from wall to wall as I try and fail to come up with a way out of this. I can't tell him, I can't risk him, but as he towers above me, shrouding me in a cold shadow, I know I've lost.

"She found out about the college acceptance letters. She saw the one from Arizona, found this shirt..." I tug at the tee. "The clothes I borrowed that day in the rain, the birth control..."

"Birth control?"

"I never got the chance to tell you I went on it. But it doesn't matter anyway. She found all of it and was mad. My room was a mess when I got back from New York. She'd ransacked everything, trying to find..." I shrug. "Who knows what, but then she told me to end it. Told me we would never last, so why wait for the inevitable?"

"So you did as you were told, like a good little girl." His voice is cold, and I rub my arms as goosebumps scatter over my skin.

"I didn't want to, Teddy. When I said I wanted *us*, I meant it. I was going to tell her about Phoenix as soon as I got home, but she beat me to it. I told her I chose you, that I'd do whatever she wanted—Harvard, law school, anything, as long as I still had you. I loved you, Teddy. More than I've ever loved anyone in my life, but it wasn't enough." I risk a glance at him and immediately drop my gaze as I'm met with blackened eyes. "I promise I never wanted to not be with you. She said if I didn't, she would make sure your father's business went under, that he'd get convicted for tax evasion or something. Bowie would be found with child pornography, and Wyatt would lose his license. I couldn't let that happen, Teddy. I couldn't let my happiness ruin your family."

"How. How could she possibly do that?"

I scoff, and Teddy growls.

"My dad knows people in high-up places. He's not a good man. He gets the worst kind of criminals off for a living. Getting someone to plant photos, falsifying documents... that's child's play to him." I step forward, and Teddy steps away. I want to touch him so bad, it hurts. I want to force him to see that what I did was necessary. That my actions hurt us both. "It was better for me to break your heart than be selfish and break your family, Teddy. You have to see that?"

Teddy's silent, staring at the ground as he processes my story. That has to be a good sign, right? He's taking his time. Thinking it over... But slowly, his head rises, and I'm floored by the look of disdain he throws my way. "All I see is a coward. A pathetic little puppet who followed Mommy's orders and didn't try to fight for what she wanted. Fight for us."

"That's not fair, Teddy." I say, my throat burning, my eyes aching with the pressure of tears fighting to break free.

"Fair?" he snarls. "Fair? What's not fair is being told by the girl you love that it's not working *by text*. What's not fair is going to her house, only to have her mother tell you that you are not and will never be good enough for her. What's not fucking fair is going to the restaurant that her mom told you she was at on a fucking date, only to have it confirmed that your girlfriend couldn't even wait five minutes before moving on with someone else."

Date? I wasn't on a date. Oh God. He thought Richard and I were on a *date*.

"Teddy, I..."

"She told me you were on a date. That day you broke up with me, she said you were on a fucking date, and when I turned up there, you were with some *guy*, smiling as he held your hand."

No. no. no.

"I can explain..."

I don't get to finish. He turns and storms to the door, slamming it so hard behind him that the walls shake, taking the little piece of my heart that still beats for him along with him.

Chapter Forty

Teddy

I'm shaking. I'm so fucking angry. While I get it—believe me—I really fucking do, I don't get why she didn't fight. I would have gone round for round with my folks if they *ever* dared to do what her mom did. Not that they ever would. *Jesus*, even after everything, Mom *still* has a soft spot for her old neighbor.

Threatening my family to stop us from being together? That's fucking low. The thing is, if Mrs. Adler had waited, we probably wouldn't have worked out anyway. I'm a realist. Most high school romances don't last, especially whirlwind ones like what Ana and I had...

But who am I kidding? Every fiber of my being *knew* that she was it for me. It might have only been six months we were together, but I know people who've met, got married, and are now expecting their first kid in less time. I don't care what anyone else might have to say, Ana and I would have still been together now if her meddling bitch of a mom hadn't gotten in the way.

I feel like I've been driving aimlessly for hours. She's been calling, texting, trying hard to get me to talk to her. But I can't. I just... can't. My phone flashes again, and this time it's a different Adler calling.

"Dude, what the fuck happened? Your message made no sense. My mom did what?"

"Ruined my life." I quickly fill him in with what Ana had told me, and by the time I'm done, my fingers ache with how tightly they strangle the steering wheel.

"Fuck. I always knew she was a heartless bitch, but..." He releases a long breath and is then quiet as I continue driving. "Listen, I'm pissed at her just as much as you are, but... I've got to ask. Is my sister okay?"

My jaw clenches at the same time my heart does. "I don't know. I can't talk to her. Fuck, I can't stand to *look* at her right now. I just stormed out of her place."

He hums. "I've got a few days off coming up. Want me to fly out?"

"Nah, man. I'll handle it. Thanks, though."

"You sure? You'll need backup if you're considering going up against my mom." He chuckles humorlessly before continuing, "What's done is done, Teddy. Now you know the real reason behind why she did what she did, but there isn't anything you can do about it. So you either cut ties completely with Morgana, let her move on with her fiancé, or you take my bitch of a mom down."

Cut ties. I scrub a hand down my face. *Yeah, I don't think I can do that.*

"I can't let her move on, man. I can't stop thinking about her, and I know she wants to be with me. She's just scared."

"Did she say she wanted to be with you and not Richard?" he asks, and I instantly wish I hadn't said anything.

"We, um, had sex."

"Well, shit."

"That's all you've got to say?"

"What else can I say? Do I think her cheating on someone she made a commitment to is okay? No. Morgana's a big girl, she can do what she wants."

I turn onto the main street in silence.

Skip eventually clears his throat. "Teddy, you can't let the bitch win. You love my sister, right?" I don't answer. I can't answer. "Of course you do, or else you wouldn't be this hard up on some high school fling from seven years ago. Let me check flights, okay? Maybe Morgana needs some brotherly advice to kick her ass into gear. That was always my sister's problem. Always had to be the people pleaser. Doing what she thought made others happy."

My knuckles turn white as I listen to him speak about her. I can't take it anymore, so I say, "Skip. I've got to go." And hang up before he can reply.

An ache behind my eyes pulses as I approach a red light, and I lean against the headrest, letting my eyes close as I take calculated breaths in for two, out for two. *What's done is done, Teddy. There isn't anything you can do about it.* That makes my jaw clench. I hate being told that I can't do something. You're the maker of your own happiness, blah, blah, blah, and Juliette Adler being the thing stopping that is not okay. But what do I do? She can still ruin everything for me and my family. Not to mention, Ana is terrified she will actually go through with her threats. This is a fucking mess.

A horn blares behind me, ringing in my ears as the car behind me pulls out and overtakes me, glowering through their window as they pass.

"Fuck you, asshole," I yell after him, flipping the bird with both hands. Other cars follow suit and slowly make their way around me as I keep my car in neutral, ignoring the blinding green light up ahead. Grinding my teeth, I watch the traffic lights flicker to orange, then red, and then green again, throwing rude arm gestures to every fucking driver who slows down enough to stare me out through the window.

What, motherfuckers? Never had a public meltdown?

Suddenly, my passenger door swings open, and Ozzy ducks inside.

"Come on, dude, I know your car's not dead, so why don't you drive her home, stop causing a traffic jam, and we can talk?"

"Get out of my car, Oz. I don't want to talk."

He reaches around and pulls the seatbelt over his chest, and even the soft click of the buckle has me on edge. Everything is just fucking grating.

"No, Teddy. We're going to talk whether you like it or not."

Great. Someone else who wants to talk. I huff and slowly move the car away from the stoplight and toward home.

"How did you know it was me?" I look up in the rearview mirror, picturing my red Mustang holding everyone up. "Back there, how did you know?"

Ozzy chuckles, fiddling with the radio. "You know this town is small. Everyone is all up in everyone else's shit. You were parked outside *As Good As It Tastes*, so Mina called."

I grunt a response, and we silently drive to my apartment. I'm not nearly as mad when we reach my little place over the auto shop. Yes, rage still beats through my chest like a drum, but at least I no longer want to end the world. Ozzy helps himself to a beer in the fridge, grabbing one for me too, and we settle outside on the makeshift veranda—basically the rooftop of the auto shop.

"I'm ready when you are," Ozzy says, sinking into the deck chair next to mine and not allowing me time to wallow. I prop my elbows on my knees, the beer bottle dangling from my fingers between my legs as I listen to the hustle and bustle of a sunny Sunday afternoon.

"Her mom broke us up."

Ozzy doesn't need to ask who, so I tell him about the best six months of my life, followed by the most lonely ones. Even as I repeat it, I can barely believe that I was so hard up for her in just six months, always wanting to be around her, never not thinking about her laugh, her pouty pink lips, or her unique sea-glass eyes. I always knew the chemistry between us was intense, but looking back, nothing's changed. I still feel the same ferocity for her now as I did then.

"That's some romance novel shit right there, isn't it?" Ozzy asks right after I tell him about returning home from New York.

I swallow down a gulp of cold beer and laugh. "You read that?"

Ozzy lifts a shoulder, nonchalant. "I've read some of my sister's books when I babysit Sierra sometimes. Don't knock 'em till you've tried them."

"Isn't it just porn?"

Ozzy's eyes widen, his mouth dropping. He points his bottle at me firmly, "Okay, firstly, don't think I don't know what you're trying to do, Teddy. And secondly, there's nothing wrong with women enjoying books that describe relationships and include sex. Men don't get shamed for watching porn, so why should romance readers be?"

My brows fly up my forehead at his passionate outburst. His cheeks flame, and he tugs on his ear.

"I might have got told off by Tasha when I claimed she read porn." We both wince because Ozzy's sister is scary as fuck. "Anyway. Please continue. Your pathetic ass turned up to the restaurant, and then what?"

I kick his foot with mine and fill him in on Ana's revelation. Each word brings a fresh round of fury, and by the end, I'm on my feet, pacing along the small balcony, itching for a fight.

"Well, that's a scandal and a half. Like daytime soap opera shit," he says, a cross between surprise and complete disbelief marring his face. "How could someone be so controlling like that? To her own daughter. It's twisted, man."

I grunt a non-response.

"So what you going to do?"

"What do you mean? There is nothing I can do. She's engaged..."

"To a guy she clearly doesn't want to be with." He stands, his hands coming down on my shoulders, and he spins me to face him. "You love her, Teddy. You can't let her get married to that dude."

"I loved her back then too, and what good did that do? Her mom can still bury my family."

"Surely, she can't touch you here in Phoenix?"

"Fuck knows, but I wouldn't put it past her to try."

We're silent as the whole fucked-up conversation weighs heavily.

"Didn't you say Ana's dad is running for office?" I nod. Ozzy's face breaks out into a slow, mischievous grin. He taps his finger on his chin and hums. "As I said, this is a scandal and a half."

"Oscar, I'm not in the mood for riddles."

"She blackmailed her daughter to break up with you, yes?"

I nod. I guess that's technically right.

"And her husband is running for Governor after serving two terms as State Attorney General, correct?"

"Thanks for the fucking history lesson."

"Honestly, Teddy, stop letting rage fuel you and think for a second. If it was to come out that Ana's parents threatened the livelihood of their daughter's working-class boyfriend, a class which the majority of his voters happen to fall into, do you think he would win the election? Play her at her own game, Teddy. Say you'll sell your story if she wants to get between you two. Pretty sure Ana's dad's opponent will spin the shit out of that."

I grip either side of Ozzy's face and smack my lips against his. He shoves me off, dramatically wiping at his mouth.

"I don't know where that mouth has been, you dirty fucker."

"That wasn't what you were saying each time you tried to kiss me before." I grin because, damn it, my best friend is a genius, and for the first time, I let a tiny seed of hope bury in my stomach. "Honestly, Ozzy, when the hell did you become so smart?"

He pushes my shoulder. "I have my moments when my boy needs me. Now, what are you still doing standing here with me? Go get your girl."

Chapter
Forty-one

Morgana

Morgana: Teddy, please talk to me. I need to know you're okay.
     Morgana: I get it. I fucked up. I should never have listened to her, but the thought of her doing something to your family, to you... If I could go back and do it differently, I still wouldn't. I won't apologize for keeping you safe.

     Morgana: For fuck's sake, Teddy, please just let me know you're okay. I'm worried.

With my hangover well and truly gone, the dread filling my stomach is for Teddy. He stormed out in such a fury, driving anywhere in his mental state is not safe. As fifteen-minute intervals pass one after the other, and my texts go unanswered, my worry goes into overdrive. It's dark now, and he could be anywhere. Got himself into an accident. Or lying somewhere in a ditch, unconscious, bleeding out, lungs punctured, and all because he found out the truth.

He's fine, Morgana. If something happened, you'd know by now.

But would I? The only other person I know is Ozzy, and it's not like now after we slept together, I'd suddenly be on his emergency contact list. I need to calm down. My overactive imagination is *not* doing me any good right now.

My phone buzzes on the table, and I snatch it up in a panic, almost dropping it in my haste but groan when it's not him.

Shay: Hope you guys aren't killing each other over there. I managed to talk myself into a new wine bar soft launch. Won't be back till later. Don't do anything I wouldn't do *wink emoji*

I send a quick reply and hide my phone between the couch cushions, anything to stop me from constantly checking for a reply or turning into a stage-five clinger who won't leave him alone. Switching on the TV, I choose something I don't end up watching, the actors' faces are a blur, the storyline a dull din as my head replays the morning. Since arriving in Phoenix, I couldn't have told you Teddy's true feelings toward me; his hot and cold treatment was so hard to judge until I was standing right in front of him, and even then I'd have to wait to see what version I'd get when he spoke to me. But now... the hurt in his dark eyes, the hardness of his jaw, his knuckles slowly whitening as I kept talking. I've never seen so many emotions, all dancing the gray line of hatred, written on one person's face.

Three heavy knocks on my door have me jumping up from the sofa and rushing to answer it. He's come back. Those knocks were too light to be Shay's.

"Oh, thank God," I say, throwing open the door. I thought he'd come back; we still have so much left unsaid, but my head and heart are as irrational as each other because the person standing in the hallway isn't the person I want to see most. "Richard? Hi?"

"Expecting someone else?" He chuckles, walking over the threshold and kissing my mouth hard and fast. He wraps an arm behind me and pulls me into his chest. "Surprised, sweetheart? Oh, this is cozy."

I'm speechless as he drops his hold and strolls around the apartment in about three strides, his face composed so as not to give away anything, but as Teddy can read me, I can read Richard. He disapproves.

"For how much profit your company made last year, you'd think they could have got slightly better accommodations for you."

Shutting the door, I regard the rental in the same way he had, trying to find the faults apparent to him the second he walked through the door. But I don't see any. All I see is a quaint open-plan, one-bed, with minimalistic décor and enough natural light that you feel like you are outside. "I like it. It's homely."

His arm circles my waist, tugging me into his side, completely unaware of how tense my muscles are under his touch.

"Homely is the nice six-bedroom house you will move into once we're married, sweetheart. This... this barely qualifies as student accommodation."

I shrug out of his hold and step into the kitchen, busying myself by opening a cupboard and pulling out a glass. "Do you want a drink? Something to eat? You must be exhausted after traveling." I peer into my empty fridge. "Sorry, I don't have much. I didn't know you were coming. If I did, I would have gone out to the grocery store. Made sure I had your favorites or *anything* for you to eat..."

I'm rambling, and Richard knows it as he looks at me in amusement and comes to join me, wrapping his arms around me once more and bringing me into his chest. Was he always this touchy-feely? His hold feels wrong, and I want him to let me go, to give me space, but he dips his head and presses his lips to mine. I close my eyes, blocking out the immense shame that slams into me as I wish it were Teddy's lips on me more than anything.

"Is it too much for your fiancé to come all this way because he missed you?" he asks, breaking the kiss and brushing the flyaway strands of hair from my ponytail away from my face. "Why do you insist on wearing your hair like this, darling? It doesn't suit your face."

Why don't you wear your hair off your face, sweetheart?

Why do you insist on wearing your hair like this, darling?

Why are the two people who are meant to love me unconditionally, always wanting to change me?

Smiling weakly, I step away from him, pulling out the band keeping my hair up.

"Much better, sweetheart," he coos. "Why don't we go out for dinner? Surely, this dingy town has somewhere half decent."

"No," I blurt, and Richard's eyebrows raise at my sudden outburst. But I can't help it. I don't want to go out *anywhere* with Richard with the chances of bumping into Teddy after everything we've done, everything he just found out about, being so high. It would be a disaster in the making. "Why don't we order in? I don't feel that great and a night in, snuggled up with a film, could be nice?"

He hums, his fingers itching his clean-shaven chin. "I guess we could do that. I do have some work I could get on with while you watch your chick flick."

"Sounds good," I say, pulling out the drawer I'd tossed all the takeout menus that had been posted through the door, and grab a selection. It won't matter what I suggest. Richard will always disagree with my choice and decide on somewhere else. It's best to avoid the whole thing and let him choose. He decides on Italian, and I quickly call the restaurant and place our orders.

"Why don't you find a movie, and I'll get set up with my laptop?" he asks, kissing the top of my head as he walks to his briefcase, just as there's a knock at the door. "That was quick. That doesn't bode well for the food if it took less than twenty minutes to arrive after ordering."

"I can get it."

"No, it's fine. I want to inspect it before the delivery boy leaves, and we're left with yesterday's reheats." Richard opens the door, and I hear him talking to whoever's outside. "You're not the delivery boy."

"No, I'm not." Shit. *No, no, no.* "Is Ana here? I need to talk to her."

"And you are?"

"He's the mechanic," I splutter, rushing to Richard's side, trying to take over for him. "My car broke down when I arrived, and he's been fixing it."

"Your car?" Richard eyes Teddy up and down, lingering on the backward baseball cap, and sighs, shaking his head in disapproval. Looking down at me, he says, "I told you that car was an unreliable waste of money. Maybe this will prove that you should listen to what I tell you and follow my advice, Morgana." His eyes flick to Teddy as he possessively palms my hip. "So, you do house calls? A bit unorthodox, is it not?"

"Unfortunately, an unresolved issue needed a good pounding to fix. And then, when it was ready for collection, Ana was tangled up in something else, and we forgot to get the paperwork signed."

My eyes bulge, imploring Teddy to stop whatever he thinks he's doing by goading Richard. Surely, he wouldn't tell him anything about what happened between us. He wouldn't be so cruel.

"And it couldn't wait?" He exhales impatiently. "Well, I'm here now. I'll deal with whatever you need doing. Especially since Morgana has clearly demonstrated her lack of understanding about cars by buying one that broke down less than three years after she test-drove it."

Teddy's jaw muscles flex as his gaze bounces between Richard's hand on my body and me. "I think Ana is capable of making her own decisions."

"Yes, well." Richard clears his throat. "As her fiancé, I feel better suited to speak on her behalf."

"And as *my* customer, and since I've been handling her since she got into town, I will discuss it with Ana, and *only* Ana." They both stare at each other defiantly, neither wanting to back down.

"It's okay, Richard," I say, pushing at his chest. "I'll be five minutes, okay?"

Richard's eyes, still trained on Teddy, narrow, and he grunts before storming off down the short hall and out of sight. Teddy grips my forearm and tugs me into the hallway and down the stairs until we reach the ground floor and barrel out onto the street.

"Does he always try to control you like that?" Teddy snarls, his body coiled tight as he drops my arm and walks the short distance to the parking lot out the front of the apartment building. He laughs, taking his cap off and roughly shoving his hand into his hair. "I fucking hate him. Hate him for speaking to you like you're an idiot, speaking to me like I'm nothing better than the dirt on his shoe. No wonder your mom thinks he's a great fit for you. But what do I know? I'm *just the mechanic.*"

I rub my hands up and down my arms, the cool breeze nipping at my skin. "What was I supposed to say, Teddy? *Don't mind him, he's my ex?*"

"I was thinking more, don't mind him, but we had mind-blowing sex last week and I came harder with him than I ever have with you."

My eyes narrow. "Oh, really? And then, should I also add that he threw me out like day-old trash as soon as the sun was up?"

"Hey, not my fault you were only after one thing from me," he growls, spinning to face me. I can't have this argument with him again. The streetlights above hit all the sharp features of his face, his jaw, his nose, his chin making him look devastatingly handsome. It almost steals my breath.

"Teddy..."

"Why is he here, Ana?" he asks, his face pinching and his nostrils flaring, and while he doesn't look happy when he reaches up and runs his hand through my hair, his touch is gentle, and I know he's still thinking about my missing curls. He drops my hair and gently runs the backs of his fingers down my cheek.

My eyes flutter shut, leaning into his touch. "I don't know. He just showed up and..."

"Are you leaving with him?"

My eyes snap open. "Now? No." I lower my head. "But... eventually? Yes. When my time's up on this contract here."

"Then why tell me about your mom? Was it to torment me?" He steps closer, our chests almost touching as shadows blanket his features, and I suppress a shudder, the air thickening as his scent invades my nose. "If you were always going back to him, what was the point in telling me? Have you had fun? Playing your little games? Coming here and fucking up my life?"

I shove his chest, pushing him away, allowing me space to breathe. "What is wrong with you? Why do you do this?" He looks affronted, like I've no right to be annoyed with him. But no, I'm done. He can't keep blaming me like this, his mood changing on the turn of a dime at every encounter. I did what I had to. I hurt just as badly as he did, but he doesn't want to look beyond *his* pain to accept this was how it had to be. "I can't keep up with you—the constant hot and cold. One minute, you're caring; the next, you're this spiteful man I don't recognize. We were kids, Teddy. We never stood a chance against my parents."

"And what about now?"

"Nothing has changed..."

"You've sure made it feel like something changed when you fucked me."

"That was closure, Teddy. What part of not wanting you or your family to suffer because of me don't you understand? If I could change it, make it work between us, don't you think I could have been here before now? Seeing you last night with that woman killed me. Do you think I like being reminded that you've been happily moving on for the last seven years while I'm stuck playing the dutiful daughter and fiancée? Too terrified to go after what I want. Too terrified to call you and beg you to forgive me. I was barely eighteen, Teddy. I did what I thought was right."

"Happy? You think I'm happy?" In a blink of an eye, he's pressed against me, both hands threaded in my hair, holding either side of my head as his eyes and body root me to the ground. "I'm fucking miserable without you, Ana. Every girl was compared to you. Every. Damn. Time. None of them ever came close. And they still fucking don't." My breath gets lodged in my throat as my lips part. "That night wasn't fucking closure, Ana. It was the start of us again if we want it."

"We can't. My mom..." My head pounds, my eyes burning with unshed tears.

"We'll handle her," he says, his dark orbs filled with as much anguish as I feel. "I wish you had told me back then what she made you do. We should have gone through that together. We were young and stupid and maybe fell in love too fast, but we had each other. Even when I was twenty, Ana, you were always mine to protect. Let me do it now." I try to drop my head, but his hold in my hair won't let me. "Seeing you again has been fucking torture. I hated you, so fucking much, but when I saw you, I realized I hated myself for not fighting to keep you. So I'm doing it now. Stay with me. Once your time in Phoenix is up, don't go back to him. Stay with me. Stay because it's me you love, Ana Banana. Come back to me."

Tears splash down my cheeks, and Teddy's head dips down and kisses them from my skin. "Please, baby. Come back."

His lips meet mine, and he gently kisses every inch, over my top lip, each corner, my bottom one, touching his mouth to mine as he begs me to stay. My hands circle his wrists as I release his hold from my head and step back.

"You need to go," I whisper as my lip trembles. "Please."

He's blurry as I stare at him. He doesn't move for what feels like an eternity, then finally, "This isn't over, Ana. I'm going to fight for you 'cause I'm not losing you again. But at some point, you need to start fighting for me too."

I watch as he turns and jogs to his car, pausing briefly as we stare at each other before he ducks inside and drives off. I suck in a shaky breath and swipe at my wet cheeks before heading back to the complex door. But as I look up to the window to my apartment, I see the curtains flutter back into place.

Chapter Forty-Two

Morgana

Richard's arms are folded across his chest when I walk through the door. His lips are pulled into a tight line, giving nothing away as he watches me shrewdly.

"He's not really a mechanic, is he?"

"He is," I say with a croak. "And my car really did break down."

"And he's also your ex-boyfriend," he says, an ugly twist tugging at his mouth. "The boy who caused a scene at Doux Désir when we met for dinner to discuss Yale several years ago."

My mouth falls open. "How do you remember?"

"I'm a lawyer. It's my job to remember details, Morgana. And remembering security having to escort someone who couldn't afford the membership, let alone one drink in that restaurant, is something I'd be unlikely to forget."

"He thought we were on a date. My mom told him that's why I was there, and when he turned up, he thought it was true."

"He didn't recognize me, though?" I shake my head. He hums, the sound barely moving a muscle in his face. I swallow, waiting for the calm before the storm. "Did you know he was here before you accepted to head up this audit?"

I want to lie and tell him I had no idea, but I can't. "I wasn't sure, but I suspected he could be. He always wanted to move back to Phoenix to open his own garage."

He's silent, and I want to go to him. Apologize, tell him I made a mistake, beg him not to tell anyone. But every time I try to speak, my voice dies, and I freeze.

"Did you fuck him?" I flinch at the harshness of his tone and lower my head. His exhale is long and heavy, and I hear rustling like he's playing with his tie or something. "Did you at least wear protection?"

My head snaps up in disbelief. Did he really ask me that? Instead of yelling, shouting, or cursing me, he asked if I was *safe*?

"Of course."

"Good. We will still schedule you to see our doctor for a full blood panel to be safe. But I think it's best that you come home with me now. We'll leave first thing in the morning. I can drive your..."

Spots dance before my eyes, and my hand flies out to the wall as dizzying waves crash over me. Suddenly, I understand why Richard thinks this apartment is too small because the walls are closing in, the air is being sucked out, and I feel like I'm drowning.

"You want me to get checked for STDs?"

Richard pauses from gathering his things from the coffee table and levels me with a stare that my mom would be proud of.

"Why wouldn't I? I can't exactly sleep with my wife, not knowing if she's clean or not."

I shiver, suddenly feeling exposed and dirty. "You still want to get married?"

Richard huffs, roughly buckling his briefcase, and throws it on the sofa. "Why would I call off the wedding? Would I prefer it if my fiancée hadn't been unfaithful? Of course, I would have. But we both know this is a marriage of convenience, Morgana. And I won't let one little hiccup stop this from working out."

Marriage of convenience?

I snap out of my stupor and rush to his side, gripping his arm and forcing him to look at me instead of the paperwork he's neatly collecting into a pile.

"I slept with someone else, and your response is, *I'd rather my fiancée wasn't unfaithful.* Why aren't you threatening to tell my mom about this? Why aren't you yelling? Throwing things? Reacting the way anyone else would if it were them?" My voice quakes as I wait for the other shoe to drop. This isn't normal.

Richard straightens, his lips sneering, and releases a bark of laughter as he focuses his gaze on me. I used to think Richard's blue eyes were warm, filled with kindness whenever he looked at me, and I hated that I couldn't fully love him the way he deserved. But the eyes trained on me now aren't those belonging to the man I promised to spend the rest of my life with. They are hard, the blue like soulless shards of ice, and I recoil, dropping to the sofa in a bid to create space.

"People like us don't get the luxury to fall in love with whomever we choose. We marry for status and power to improve our social standing. A hand-selected partnership, if you will. My mother and father were set up long before they even met. As were my grandparents. Morgana, even your parents met at a function that I can only describe as a *bride-finding-ball*. I don't understand why you look like this is brand new information. Your mother said she explained all this to you?"

"She..."

But then it hits me. What she said the day she threatened Teddy. *But I know my place and sense of duty, Morgana, and so should you. We are there to make sure our men succeed.* How did I not see this relationship for what it is? I had been so consumed with grief and guilt over the way I ended things with Teddy, that instead of seeing the red flags, I thought Richard being there for me was out of friendship and then it evolved into something romantic. I am so pathetically dumb.

"God, my mom always did think I was a naïve little girl," I mutter, clutching my stomach as I feel like the rug's been pulled out from under me. Which is stupid, since she told me what was expected of me, but I didn't listen.

"What was that?" he huffs.

"I can't do this," I murmur before lifting my chin high and feigning a confidence I do not feel in the slightest. Louder, I repeat, "I can't do this, Richard. Teddy's right, I need to start standing up for myself. I don't want to be a *'yes girl'* for the rest of my life. I *cheated* and you find that to be nothing but a "blip" in your life plan, one you can hide under the rug and forget. If you loved me, you would never be able to forgive me. Instead, you want to make sure I'm not carrying any diseases."

He frowns. "I'm not exactly thrilled..."

"And you're not exactly upset about it either. God, I've been feeling so guilty over what I did, so scared I was breaking your heart..." I pause. "Why do you want to still be with me? You're already working closely with my dad. You're well-respected in our community. I add nothing extra."

"You're the future Governor's daughter. You're smart, you're nice company to be around, attractive..."

"But they aren't qualities to base a marriage on," I say, jumping to my feet and tugging at my hair as years of pent-up frustration roils and bubbles, and I can't stop. "The moment I said yes to your proposal, you've been nothing but demanding. First, it was your idea for me to stop working as soon as we were married so we can start having a family..."

"Because you always said you wanted kids?"

"Did I? We never had that conversation. I don't even know if I *want* kids," I say, my mouth ridiculously dry as I let everything that's been festering come to the surface. "Then when this opportunity to lead an audit for a huge client came up, instead of supporting me, you asked if I was really the best candidate for the job."

"I don't think I said that, Morgana."

I scoff, starting to pace as restlessness fills my veins, begging me to move. Standing still is too hard.

"You did. And then my apartment. Not once did you ask if I wanted to sell it. *You* decided I would. Like *you* decided I'll be a stay-at-home mom. Like *you* decided we'd get married in the country club. I hate the country club. Every single member is a snobby asshole who used to look down at my brother because he said he hated golf. He was *ten*, Richard."

"Okay, so we don't have to get married at the country club."

"That's not the point. For years, I've been saying yes to everyone when I know how unhappy it makes me. All I wanted when I was eighteen was to move to Phoenix with Teddy and go to business school. My mom let me have that one thing, in return for giving up Teddy, and every day since then, I've continued to let people take little bits of me to make themselves happy. Are you happy, Richard? Because I'm not. I was just too much of a coward to admit it."

I blink and realize that Richard is staring at me, a pained expression on his face, and that's when I see his eyes aren't soulless. They are empty, tired, resigned. He drops to the couch and holds his head in his hands.

"You don't want this," I say, coming to the sofa and gently lowering myself next to him. He glances at me from the corner of his eye, and I reach over and take his hand in mine. "You don't want me. Not really. We don't have to do this. We don't have to get married."

He looks at me with so much regret I almost feel bad.

"Don't we? Morgana, all my life, I've grown up following a rule book. Attending all the same schools—including pre-school—as my father, being friends with the children of my *parents'* friends, public speaking lessons at thirteen, tailored suits at fourteen." He chuckles hollowly, running a hand through his hair, and the ends stick up in different directions, making him look so different from his usual kept-together state. "While boys my age were playing soccer, I was learning about foreign politics and shadowing my dad while he was at work. By the time I was heading off to college, they told me I had four years of freedom. Four years to meet new people, date girls *I* wanted to. Basically, get it out of my system before coming home and expecting to marry someone proper. I hated them, Morgana. Four years felt like more than enough time to satisfy the longing to do what I wanted whenever and with whoever I chose, but that only made it worse.

"This is how our families have worked for generations, an archaic patriarchy that keeps repeating itself through each new family line. I was doing what was expected of me, Morgana. I thought you knew."

"I didn't," I admit.

"Seeing you again at the gala on your birthday, I thought maybe it would be okay. I always remembered you were sweet, and I was certainly attracted to you, so over time, we would make each other happy, right? I didn't want to fail. I *couldn't* fail. My brother and his wife seem happy, my parents seem happy, so why wasn't I?" He tugs at his hair. "Fuck, I know you're not happy.

I could see it every day, but I didn't realize how much of a fucking asshole I was being to you. I never meant to undermine you. I guess I was projecting my frustrations onto you, which is not an excuse. I am sorry I didn't see it until now. What is it they say, *misery loves company?*" He reaches out as if to touch my face, but stops, dropping his hand, thinking better about it. "Jesus, I could even tell you didn't enjoy it whenever I touched you too. That should have been a huge red flag for both of us, right?"

"It's not that I didn't enjoy it," I say, my cheeks burning. "It's just..."

"You weren't in love with me."

"Like you aren't with me."

"But you love this Teddy guy?"

I nod, sucking my lower lip between my teeth because if I don't, I know I'll cry. The stupid overwhelming emotion of being able to admit that is crushing.

"He's a lucky guy." We stare at each other for a second and then Richard picks up a strand of my hair, twirling it loosely around his finger. "Do you know I always preferred your curls?"

A weak smile manages its way onto my face, and I reach to touch my head. "You never said."

"Yeah, well..." He shrugs, an embarrassed smile pulling at his lips that reminds me of the old Richard—the one before we got engaged. "I always thought they made you look innocent and sweet. Guess I got that wrong, huh?"

My lip trembles as shame fills my veins. "I'm so sorry, Richard."

"I know," he whispers, tucking the strand behind my ear.

We both lean back into the sofa and stare at the blank television.

"So, Teddy..."

I angle my head, resting it on the back of the sofa as I ask, "What about him?"

"Is he the reason you've lit a fire under your butt and finally stood up for yourself?" The corner of my lips tug. He nods, humming to himself as he thinks. "He could have done it sooner. We'd have all saved ourselves a lot of time."

We're quiet and I let my eyes flutter closed as exhaustion sets in. "What do we do?"

Richard links my hand with his and squeezes, and I feel a closeness settle between us for the first time.

"I don't know, Morgana. But we'll figure it out." The buzzer from the front door screeches in the quiet. "That will be the food."

Richard goes to pay as I grab plates and a couple of sodas hidden in the back of the fridge, setting them on the coffee table and wait for him to return. He places my pizza box in the middle, while pouring his linguini into a bowl and we sit, facing each other, eating it like I'm back in college and he used to come to keep me company. It's awkward and sometimes uneasy, but with the weight of everyone's expectations no longer on my shoulders and I feel... *free.*

"There's a flight back to Connecticut first thing in the morning I'll get," Richard says, scrolling through his phone hours after eating.

I check the time on my cell and gasp. "Oh God, it's nearly three a.m. You'll be so tired."

He shrugs. "It's okay. I actually feel the best I have in a long time."

I nibble the bottom of my lip and wrangle my hands in my lap. "Me too."

When the Uber arrives outside, Richard's things are by the door. The only luggage needing repacking was his laptop bag. We shuffle beside each other, unsure of what to do now.

"I'll let our parents know what's happened as soon as I land."

I nod shakily. "Am I being a total wimp by making you do this alone?"

He laughs.

"Maybe. But we both know our moms are scary as fuck, and I can handle them better." He wraps his arm around my shoulder and pulls me in for a hug. Kissing the crown of my head, he says, "I won't tell them about Teddy either."

I wrap my arms around him, pressing my cheek to his chest. "Thank you."

He drops his arm and goes to open the door.

"Oh, wait," I say, slowly sliding my engagement ring from my finger. He holds out his palm, and I place it in the middle. He curls his fingers around it, trapping it inside.

"It's funny. I thought it would have hurt to be given my ring back. But it feels like I've just been given the keys to my prison cell."

A watery burst of laughter bubbles from my throat. "I'll try not to take offence to that."

His smile drops, and his eyes go wide. "Oh shit, Morgana... I..."

I wave my hand. "It's fine. I have the same feeling." I reach onto my tiptoes and kiss his cheek. "Have a safe flight home."

His hand lands in mine and he squeezes. "Thank you." I frown. "For helping me pull my head out of my ass and for being the stronger one out of us two to actually end it."

I watch as he disappears down the hallway and out into the street. Closing the door, I sag against it and close my eyes, breathing lightly for the first time in years. Quickly, I dart to the kitchen, grab my keys and purse, and run to my car.

There is only one person I need to see right now.

Chapter
Forty-Three

Teddy

Excessive pounding hammers on the front door as I tug on a pair of sweats on my way to answer it.

"Calm the fuck down, would you?" I yell, flicking the deadbolt while the knocking *still* thumps against it. "Jesus Christ, could you just—*oomph...*"

Ana throws herself into my arms, and mine instantly wind around her back, holding her close to my chest. Her feet dangle mid-air as she crashes her lips to mine, softly moaning as she demands entry with her tongue. My hand fists her hair as her lips inside, lapping and exploring like she's never kissed me before.

Before I sink into the kiss, I yank myself away, confused and so fucking excited that this means what I think it does.

"I ended it," she says through open-mouthed kisses to my throat. My hands grip her hips so tight I'm sure to be leaving bruises, but she just said... "It's over. I couldn't do it anymore. It's you, Teddy. It's always been you."

The world ceases to exist as our mouths clash together, teeth, tongue, noses—a mess of carnal desire at her admission. I lift her higher as I kick the door closed. Her legs tangle around my hips and as she clings to me, I walk us blindly to my bedroom.

"I'm so sorry," she murmurs against my skin as she kisses along my jaw, my neck and back to my lips again. "I'm so fucking sorry, Teddy."

"Better late than never, baby," I say, sitting her on my bed. She doesn't let go, her hands grasping my wrists and tugging me on top of her. I laugh as she claws at my skin like a woman possessed, so I take both her hands in one of mine and pin them to the bed above her head.

"Take a breath, woman," I say, a ridiculously huge grin splitting my face in two.

"No, please, I need you," she pants, the soft light of dawn flittering through my window, her long blonde hair like a halo on my pillow, and her beautiful green eyes sparkling like emeralds. She pulls her arms, trying to break out my hold, and when they don't budge, she resorts to using her feet, lifting them on either side of my hips and trying to hook the waistband with her toes. She manages to get purchase, and my sweats are clumsily shimmied down my legs.

"Damn, I forgot about your disgusting finger-feet," I snigger, looking from the concentration line across her forehead to where the waistband is almost halfway down my thighs. My cock springs free, brushing against her thigh, then hitting off my stomach, and she falls still.

"You sleep naked?"

"Uh-huh." I lean down and lick a stripe up her neck to her ear. She arches her back off the bed as I suck her earlobe between my teeth, nipping at her flesh before whispering low. "And you will be too from now on."

"Is that so?" she rasps, her fingers curling over my hands.

"It's a rule of mine. Instated just now, in fact."

"Then why am I still dressed?"

I groan into the side of her neck and inhale her scent—citrus and Ana. Fucking mouth-watering.

Shifting off her, I release her hands and quickly strip her out of *my fucking sweats* she's kept after all this time as she yanks her shirt over her head and throws it to the ground. I'm about to help her with her bra when she pulls the middle section where the cups meet, and they come apart. I bring a fisted hand to my mouth and bite down hard. A fucking front clasp. Is she trying to kill me?

Her eyes never leave me as she painfully slowly pulls the two red lacey cups apart until her full tits are freed, her rosy nipples pebbling in the cool air. My thumb brushes over one before rolling it between two fingers as she hisses, her eyes fluttering shut. I do the same to the other one, relishing in every gasp, every moan, and then when she bites her fucking lip, I'm done for. My tongue flicks out, tasting, savoring, loving the feel of her warm skin as I close my lips over her nipple and suck hard. Her hands fly to my head, yanking my hair so hard that it stings my scalp. But for once, when I welcome the pain, it's not to get me off. It's a reminder that she's here, mine, and I am never letting her go again.

I bite her nipple lightly between my teeth, testing her pain threshold as I look up into her face. Her lips are parted, her eyes narrowed in on my mouth, and when I cup a hand over her panties, she's soaked. I kiss down her body, pressing my lips against every freckle, and as I reach her hips, I place a kiss on them too. I slide my thumbs under her panties, pulling them down her legs as she lifts her ass a little.

"Fuck, I've missed this pussy," I say, leaning down to trail my tongue along the groove between her thigh and her hip. She wriggles, so I do the other side too. She's panting, her hands fisting my sheets as I glance up to look at her face before thrusting my tongue inside her without any preamble.

She cries out, her feet digging into the mattress, her hips pivoting upward as she grinds into my face. Fuck, this feels better than I remember. Her taste, her noises, her responses. I rut my hard cock against the bed, needing to release some tension or else this is going to be over before I get a chance to be inside her again. I wasn't kidding when I said the last time we fucked wasn't closure. I was addicted at twenty, forced to quit cold turkey, and then one little taste and I relapsed. Now? I'm never quitting again. What doesn't kill you makes you stronger.

I grip her hips, the tips of my fingers biting into her ass cheeks as I push my tongue in deeper, letting my teeth lightly scrape against her pussy. She moans a beautiful sound, her legs trying to close, pinning my head in place. I move my hand, running my fingers through her folds while I circle her clit, then ease my finger in where my tongue was and crook it forward.

"Oh God, Teddy. I'm not going to last."

"Good. Come on my face, so I can then fuck your pretty little mouth before I fuck your pretty little cunt, and make you come again."

She screams, her orgasm detonating before I am ready, and I revel in the fact that my girl gets turned on by dirty talk. Her hips push into my face as I lap and suck at her clit until she's oversensitive and shaking and begging for me to stop.

"On your knees," I say, wiping my mouth with the back of my hand as I stare down at Ana, her body like Jell-O as she pants on the bed.

"I need a second."

"No, now, Ana." Her eyes flare with something, a cross between defiance and arousal. I wrap my hand around the back of her neck and squeeze. "Get on your knees and let me use you while you look so fucking beautifully wrecked."

She sucks her bottom lip between her teeth and sleepily slips from the bed and onto her knees on the floor. I stand and gather her hair in my hand, holding it like a ponytail at the back of her head. Her lips part, eyes blown wide as they gaze up at me. She looks like a fucking dream, all wrapped up in a delicious bow.

She licks her lips and places her hands on her lap. "Use me."

Fuck yes.

I grip my cock at the base and run the tip along the seam of her lips. She opens, then sticks out her tongue, and I have to squeeze my dick to calm down. I've got a short refractory period, but coming all over Ana's face at the sight of her parted lips before she's even touched me is not something I'd be proud of. She sways forward, eager for my cock, but I back away.

"Please, Teddy," she whimpers, licking her lips again. I hold myself still, allowing her to edge closer and run her tongue along the slit. I inhale sharply. Already, that's the best head I've ever had.

I massage my fingers into her jaw and say, "Open wide, baby."

She does, and I feed her my cock, watching as she swallows the damn thing whole, gagging when I reach the back of her throat. I try to pull back, but she sucks me down, moaning as her eyes close. I let her set the pace, back and forth, back and forth, until her hand cups my balls, rolling them in her palm as her other hand grips the base of my dick. She pops off, her fucking sexy eyes glued to mine as she licks the tip again, and then presses gentle kisses to the tops of my thighs.

"Fuck my mouth like you promised, Teddy," she says, kissing my dick before taking me between her hot, wet lips again. I tighten my grip on her hair and tentatively thrust forward. She gags again, but wraps a hand around my leg and grips my ass, urging me to do what I want with her. I move harder this time, pumping in and out of her as she moans, saliva running down her chin and tears pooling at the corner of her eyes. But she doesn't let me stop, keeping the grip on my ass tight as I fuck her face with abandon, and then she does something that makes me see stars. Still cupping my balls, her other hand moves farther back between my legs, and then she rubs a finger along my taint.

The hand I had dangling by my side joins the one holding her hair as I thrust faster, matching the stroking she's doing until I roar my release, cum leaking from her mouth as she swallows what she can while milking me until I'm a trembling mess above her.

"Fucking hell, Ana," I pant, pulling out from her between her lips and hauling her off the floor. She runs a finger up her chin, gathering my spilt cum before sucking it into her mouth. "Fuck, I love you."

Her finger drops from her mouth. "You do?"

I brush her hair from her face and nod. "I never stopped."

She smiles, sated and filthy, and drops her forehead to rest against my shoulder as her fingers ghost over my abs. "I love you too."

She looks up and presses a kiss to my jaw. Yawning, she says, "I believe you promised to fuck me now."

I laugh, lifting her into my arms and pulling back the comforter to settle her into my bed. Sliding in beside her, I pull her against my side, her head resting over my heart as I play with her hair. "I can promise you that we're not done, but you need to rest for a bit, and then I'll fuck you." She hums, snuggling closer. My fingers brush the length of her spine when I have the sudden urge to know, "That thing you did with your finger?"

She breathes a tired laugh. "Yeah?"

"Where did you learn that?"

"I read a lot of romance books." She shrugs. "I thought I'd try it out. Did you like it?"

Did I like it? Fucking hell, maybe Ozzy was onto something. "That was the best blowjob I've ever had. I fucking loved it."

She smiles into my chest, and it doesn't take long for her breathing to even out, each small puff of air over my skin tickling as she breathes. I shift slightly, tightening my arms and holding her while she sleeps, wondering how long we've got until shit fucks this up again. Because if there's one thing about Ana, I know her family is going to be pissed.

Chapter Forty-Four

Morgana

Teddy stirs, his body slowly waking up as I kiss along his jaw and down his neck.

"*Mmm*, if this is how I'm going to be woken up every morning from here on out, I'll always wake up a happy man."

I giggle, the sound muffled against his skin as his hands skim down my back and land on my ass, hauling me up to straddle him. "It's not morning yet."

He stretches his head back to check the time on his alarm clock. "We've only been sleeping for an hour."

Wiggling my hips, I grind down on his growing erection. "Well, someone promised..."

I let out a yelp of surprise as Teddy flips me so I'm lying under him, rolling his hips against me. His lips crash down on mine, and he devours me, licking and sucking and biting as I return the kiss just as eagerly. I wrap my arms around his shoulders, pinning our chests together as I hold him to me, and the little nugget of residual guilt—that less than twenty-four hours ago, I was engaged to another man—tries to grow bigger. But with Teddy's weight pressing me down, it doesn't get a chance to.

Something this right could never be wrong.

Wrong was agreeing to break Teddy's heart in the first place.

Wrong was agreeing to marry a man I didn't love.

Wrong was missing all this time with the person who was made for me.

Teddy nips my bottom lip, and I whimper, hating the loss of heat from his skin touching mine as he leans across to his bedside table to take out a condom from his drawer. Getting to his knees, he tears at the foil packet and slowly rolls the latex down his dick. I lick my suddenly dry lips as I watch him, desperate to taste him again. Him using me the way he did when I sucked him in my mouth was single-handedly the hottest thing I'd ever experienced. His roughness, the way he let go...

Teddy smirks as he notices me rubbing my thighs together, trying to relieve some of the tension radiating from me.

He leans down, lining himself up and pushing in ever-so slightly, that I whine. It's not enough.

"So needy for me." He chuckles, pushing in inch by excruciatingly slow inch, purposely stopping each time I lift my hips, urging him to go faster.

"*Teddy...*"

He pauses for a beat before slamming home, and I feel like I can breathe, which is ironic because the air whooshes from my lungs as he rests against my hips. His head dips as he looks into my eyes, and then his lips are on mine again. Still, instead of the harsh, desperate, virile way he kissed me before, he's gentle, exploring my mouth with his tongue with long, languid strokes that match the roll of his hips as he starts to fuck me... no, not *fuck*, something a lot more emotional, and with every thrust inside me, it's like we're slowly being put back together. I thread my fingers into his hair and deepen the kiss, pouring every raw and vulnerable emotion into it as he rocks back and forth, our bodies sliding together, our hands intertwined as he makes *love* to me.

He breaks the kiss, pressing our foreheads together as his pace quickens. The sound of the headboard lightly banging against his bedroom wall joins our panting, and he thrusts harder, losing himself in my body as I wind my legs around his waist and dig my nails into the back of his head.

"Fuck, Ana, I've fucking missed you," he murmurs, his eyes squeezed shut as he pistons his hips and grinds against my clit. I moan, my back arching off the bed, my breasts brushing against his chest, and my nipples painfully hard and desperate for attention.

"You've got me," I breathe, angling my head to kiss his jaw, his chin, his cheeks. "You've got me, and I'm never leaving."

"I wouldn't let you if you tried," he growls, his dark eyes opening and pinning me with the undeniable truth that he would never let anyone get between us again. "Mine then. Mine now. Mine always."

Like he's in sync with my every need, his head dips to my chest, sucking a nipple between his lips and lavishing it with his tongue. My pussy clenches around his cock, and he moans, the vibrations sending goosebumps across my skin. My body is practically glowing as he continues to suck and pump and ravish me. Every sense is heightened, every color brighter, every sound happier, as Teddy pushes me closer and closer to my release.

His lips leave my breast, the cold air hitting my wet nipple, making it impossibly harder, as Teddy looks between us, watching for a beat at where we're joined. He brings his thumb to his mouth, sucking it inside before dropping it to my pussy, sliding it lightly over my clit. His eyes snap to my face, and he blinks, then pushes down harder as I cry out. His lips are right there again, swallowing my moans as he fucks me thoroughly, his thumb working faster, and his kisses becoming more frenzied as I soar off the edge and unravel. My whole body tenses as his hips stutter, my pussy rippling around him, triggering his own release.

He sags on top of me, his sweat-soaked hair brushing against my neck and the smell of oil and grease stronger somehow.

"I love your smell," I whisper, and his body shakes above me as he laughs.

"I smell like sweat, sex, and cum. You like that?"

I smack his ass. "No, smart-ass. You smell like cars." He dislodges himself to lean on his elbow, his softening dick still inside me as he brushes the hair from my face with a smile. "It reminds me of back then. You were always happiest surrounded by cars, tinkering with them, breaking them up to put them back together..."

"I was always happiest being with you." He presses a light kiss to my lips and slowly slides out of me. Hopping from the bed, he ducks into the bathroom to dispose of the condom and returns with a warm washcloth. Softly, he brushes the cotton across my skin, following the path with his lips until he is finished, then drops the cloth by the side of the bed. He brings the duvet over us, drawing me into his chest and holding me tight.

"I want us to get checked."

I tilt my head up to look at him. The early morning sun hits off his disheveled hair, making the strands seem lighter.

"You're on birth control, right?" I nod, and his hand flutters against my stomach. "Not that I don't want to see you carrying my child... if you even want that..." My heart skips at the thought of having his kids. I wasn't sure if I wanted Richard's... but Teddy's... "But right now, I just want you to myself.

And next time we fuck, I want to fuck you bare."

Teddy and I fall asleep for a couple of hours until I wake up to him sliding back in beside me with a to-go cup and a breakfast bagel. He kisses my temple as I clutch the cup in both hands and sigh as the warm liquid fires up my tastebuds with vanilla and coffee.

"What you got planned for today?" he asks, sinking his teeth into his bagel, and the yolk leaks out the side and down his chin. I laugh, reaching into the bag for a couple of napkins and passing them over.

"I need to go back to the apartment and check that Shay's okay."

"She's got a key, though?" he asks with his mouth full, and I nod. "Then I'm sure she's fine. Stay here, in bed with me. I want you here all day."

I laugh, taking a small bite and not making a mess like he had. "That sounds amazing, but I should still go home and shower. Plus, I need to fill her in on last night."

When I give him a pointed look, he grins, scrunching up the napkin and empty bagel wrapper and tossing it inside the paper bag.

"When do you need to go?" he asks, and I shrug. "Fine. I'll give you some time with your best friend. Is two hours enough? Any longer, and I'm coming to get you."

I roll my eyes as he gives me a wolfish grin, taking my cup from me and setting it on the bedside table. I bring my bagel to my lips, but his large hand wraps around it, plucking it from my grasp, and my mouth follows.

"Hey! I was eating that."

He chuckles, blanketing my body with his, and starts to pepper my throat with open-mouthed kisses. My man is so insatiable.

My man.

My heart flutters in my chest, feeling so full it could explode as he touches my naked skin anywhere he can with his mouth or his fingers, and I wriggle as he brushes over my hips at the sensitive skin there.

"How about we go for a shower, and I'll eat you instead?"

Heat blooms low in my stomach, but I don't get the chance to answer as Teddy hauls my ass out of bed and throws me over his shoulder, carrying me to the bathroom and turning on the shower. He turns his head and sinks his teeth into the flesh at the top of my thigh, and I yelp, squirming against him as he laps over his mark with a dark chuckle.

"You're such a barbarian, Teddy Grant."

"You bring it out in me, baby. Make me feel possessive. Like I need to claim you as mine." He bites me again, but this time not enough to make it sting. He sticks his hand under the water and then smacks my ass. "Think you could straddle my shoulders while I eat your pretty little cunt?"

I gasp when he trails two wet fingers between my ass cheeks to my pussy and teases me by circling my entrance but never dipping inside. His fingers pull back, circling the tight little ring of muscle and pushing down.

"Teddy…" I moan, writhing on this shoulder, desperate and needy for him again, as he teases my ass while leaning back into the shower and assessing the height of the ceiling.

"Fuck. That would have been hot as hell."

I whine when he suddenly removes his hands and I'm on my feet. Teddy's grin is pure evil as he quickly removes his shirt and sweats, dropping them to the ground, his hard cock proudly pointing to the ceiling as he gathers me in his arms again and carries me into the shower.

"Was someone enjoying her ass getting teased?" He asks, backing me against the cold tiled wall and I gasp.

"Yes," I pant. "It's been too long."

"Well then. I better make up for lost time." He sinks to his knees, guiding my legs over his shoulders and licks one hot stripe up my center. I cry out, the steam from the shower and the feeling of his tongue heating my skin to such epic proportions I could combust. My body hums at a frequency I've never felt before. Vibrating and convulsing as Teddy works my pussy with his tongue like a pro, edging his fingers back between my ass cheeks and probing my hole with a finger. I've never done this before. Sure, when we were younger, he'd tease me while he fingered me, but he's never *breached* there before. I push my ass back against his finger, and he looks up from between my legs. I nod with a pant, and he slowly pushes inside, the tight ring of muscle protesting at the intrusion with a stinging pain that I almost ask him to stop. But suddenly, the pain makes way for a delicious pleasure as he slowly moves it inside me. It's strange and foreign and my hand grips his hair hard, my other hand slapping at the wall, trying to find purchase, as he leads me to orgasm faster than I ever have before. I cry out his name, over and over, until I'm too sensitive and need him to stop. He lifts my legs from his shoulders, and I immediately drop to my knees as he stands.

"Oh, shit, Ana, are you..." He stutters to a stop as I swallow him down without warning. Hissing, he gathers my wet hair in his hand, angling his back to the spray, so the water doesn't soak my face. Drowning with a dick in my mouth might not be the best way to die. His free hand clasps my cheek, and this time his thrusts are gentle, never too hard or too deep, until he unloads down my throat, and I greedily swallow everything.

"That was better than the bagel."

Chapter Forty-Five

Morgana

"Where the hell have you been?" Shay crosses her arms over her chest. Her brows are pinched down so low on her face that I can't help but grin as I throw my arms around her neck and hug her hard.

"Someone's happy," she says, returning the hug, then swiftly pushing me away and gasping. "You didn't. Please tell me you didn't. Not again."

I roll my lower lip between my teeth, biting down to rein in my laughter. She looks so mad right now that it's comical. She throws her hands up and spins on her heel, her feet pounding the hardwood as she paces the kitchen to the living room and back again.

"Honestly, Morgana, how could you be so stupid? I left you for a few hours, and you run off with *him?*"

"It wasn't a couple of hours, Shay. You were gone for almost a whole day," I say, walking to the fridge and pulling out a bottle of water. "You missed a lot."

She taps her foot, her lips pulled into a tight pout. "Well, are you going to stand there or tell me?"

I drop onto the sofa and grip her hand, tugging her down hard to sit beside me. She shifts, so she's facing me, and I smile as she appears to be getting madder and madder with every second I don't talk.

"Richard came by after you texted about the new bar opening."

Her jaw drops so low I can practically see her tonsils. "Shut the fuck up."

"And Teddy came up."

She sits up straight. "And I *missed* that? What happened? Did Richard find out? Did Teddy out you guys? Fuck, Morgana, where are they now?"

I take a deep breath and answer her questions in order. "You were drinking free wine. *I* told Richard all about us. Teddy didn't say anything. He made up some story about needing to speak to me about my car. Richard is back in Connecticut with the engagement ring, probably telling my parents that the wedding is off as we speak."

I think I've broken Shay. She's sitting unblinking, slack-jawed, and I'm not convinced she's still breathing. I lean back against the armrest and wait. Eventually, she closes her mouth and swallows hard.

"Okay."

"Okay? That's all you have to say?"

She nods. "Uh-huh. I guess I'm trying to channel whatever energy you've got going on right now because you do *not* look broken up about ending your seven-year relationship." My smile drops as Shay looks genuinely worried.

"Shay, I don't look broken up about it because I'm not. Richard and I spoke. A lot. We both weren't happy. I didn't realize our whole relationship was arranged, and I lost it. I told him everything: how unhappy he'd made me, about Teddy, about not wanting to get married, and we agreed it wasn't what we wanted. It was actually a very boring break-up."

"And what about your mom?"

"Richard promised not to tell her."

"And we believe him?"

I shrug. "I don't have a reason not to believe him."

She huffs and rubs at her temples. "Okay, so what about Teddy? I assume he knows the wedding is off?" I nod. "And he knows the reason you broke up with him all those years ago?" I nod again. "And are you going to fill me in?"

"Mom threatened his family."

Shay's face grows redder and redder the deeper into the story I go. "Why aren't you more mad, Morgs? Your mom is the devil incarnate."

I shrug. Maybe I'm just desensitized by it all, but after rehashing it several times for different people, I don't want to think about it for a long while.

"And you're not scared about the fallout when your mom comes here next and demands you go home? 'Cause you know she will."

"Oh, I have no doubt she will." And that thought alone is enough to make my stomach curdle. "And as for the fallout—I'm fucking terrified, Shay. But I didn't trust Teddy enough to tell him the truth the last time, so when she tries it again, we'll be together."

"Together as in..."

"Together-together." I look away, embarrassed, as heat spills onto my cheeks. "He was always it for me, Shay. It just took me too long to stand up for what I wanted..."

My door bangs, and we both jump, our panicked faces turning toward the noise.

"You don't think she's here already?" Shay whispers, clutching my arm. "Like by speaking about her, we've summoned her?"

I side-eye my best friend like she's crazy, but honestly, who knows with that woman?

The knocking sounds again, and I wearily drag myself to answer. My hand trembles as I unlock the door and slowly open it. My shoulders sag as Teddy pushes through, ducking down slightly and slinging me over his shoulder, swatting at my ass as I giggle.

"Put me down." I laugh, kicking my legs until he bands an arm across them, rendering me helpless in his hold.

"Nope, sorry, couldn't stay away. I tried, Ana, but I'm addicted."

"It has been like an hour, you big dummy."

Teddy swats my ass again as he kicks the door closed and walks into the living room. He tilts his chin up when he notices Shay.

"Cockblocker."

"Teddy Bear."

"Nice to see you without a hangover," he says, keeping me over his shoulder.

"Nice to see you finally got your head out of your ass," Shay counters.

"Nice if I could be put on my feet, so the blood stops pooling in my head," I say, stretching down to tap Teddy's butt.

"Sorry, baby," he says, gently letting me to my feet, but wrapping his arm around my waist and drawing me in for a kiss.

Shay groans behind me. "*Urgh,* you guys are disgustingly sweet. Why am I suddenly getting flashbacks of being in high school again, like some bad acid reflux looking at you two?"

Teddy's hand palms my ass as he presses my thigh against him. My eyes widen, and I inhale sharply as I feel the outline of his hard cock. When my eyes snap to his, his face morphs into a cocky grin as he subtly grinds his dick on my leg.

"Told you I was ad-*dick*-ted," he whispers, then flicks his eyes toward

Shay. "Can you get rid of her?"

"I can hear you, asshole," Shay clips, pushing to her feet and stopping by our side. "Good thing this town has so many places to eat and drink, or I'd get bored. So what do you need? Fifteen? Twenty minutes?"

Teddy narrows his eyes playfully at Shay, and she grins devilishly back, holding her hand out. Teddy's brows raise in question.

"Give me the keys to your place," she says, shaking her hand impatiently. "I wanted to binge a series with *my best friend* today, but since you get to monopolize her time, I'll go do it on my own."

"Are you sure?" I ask, suddenly feeling a little bad that we've barely seen each other since she arrived, thanks to my drama.

Teddy pulls his keys from his back pocket and hands them to Shay. She tosses them in the air and catches them. "Yeah, babe, I'm sure. If I got back with my hottie of an ex after seven years, I'd want to be banging his brains out all day long too."

She pumps her fingers at Teddy again, and he stares at her empty hand. "What?"

"I need snacks," she says, her face pulled into a *Duh!* expression. He tugs a fifty from his wallet, never releasing his hold on me, and hands her the bill. Shay does a little happy dance and finally heads for the door, yelling over her shoulder, "No glove, no love, you two."

"She's still a pain in my ass." He laughs. "Now... where were we?"

His kiss is consuming as he walks us backward, tripping over the side table by the sofa, knocking a glass to the floor and making the TV shake, until he breathlessly asks, "Where's the bedroom?"

I gesture somewhere over my shoulder, and his lips are on me again, kissing me like he has no intention of stopping. Like he's making up for lost time, and I am so here for it. Every time our mouths collide, I can feel it all;

the love he has for me, the terrified idea that I might leave him again, and the sliver of anger he's trying to let go of. But I pour everything right back, imploring him to know I'm here and not going anywhere.

He strips my shirt up my body, breaking the kiss to tear it over my head, then does quick work to my pants. I laugh against his lips as he struggles to undress, tripping on his sweats as they refuse to leave his feet.

"Slow down. There's no rush." I chuckle, standing on his pants to pin them to the floor, so they slip from his feet.

"There is definitely a rush," he says, unclipping my bra and then yanking my panties down my legs. He tugs at his underwear before bending over, bare ass in my face, to get his wallet out of his pocket. I sink onto the bed and lean forward, nipping his ass with my teeth, and he spins, eyes wide and his hand pressed to where I bit him.

"Do you have this much finesse with all your conquests?" I tease, hating the flood of jealousy that fills my stomach, but I can't help asking because he looks like an excited puppy. It's damn near adorable.

Teddy growls, tearing into the packet and covering himself before nudging my knees apart to stand between my legs. He strokes his dick in his hand, and I lick my lips expectantly.

"I have never needed to be inside someone to the point I thought I could die like I do with you. I told you before that no one ever compared, and that was the truth. I've missed out on seven long years being with you, and every second I've got you back fucking counts. I'm not wasting them."

I reach up and cup his cheek. "Then don't."

"Wasn't planning on it," he says, running the thick head of his cock through my pussy, then pushing inside in one swift thrust. I gasp as he stretches me, making me feel so unbelievably full at this angle. Wrapping my legs around his waist, he stands, lifting me from the bed and slamming my back into the wall with a hard *oomph* as he starts to pump his hips up. I dig my nails into his shoulders, my back rutting against the wall as he pounds hard and deep, each upward thrust hitting all the right spots. My head knocks back, and he sucks the skin between my shoulder and neck, marking me for everyone to see. His hips punch upwards, reaching that place that always made me see stars.

My eyes roll back as I pant, "Yes, Teddy. Fuck, right there."

He turns abruptly, lifting me off his dick and setting me on the floor as my pussy clenches around nothing, suddenly feeling empty. Wordlessly, he grips my shoulder and turns me, pushing between my shoulder blades to bend me over the bed with my ass in the air. His hands tap my thighs apart, and then he's right there, pushing back inside me until his hips touch my ass. Teddy runs his hand up and down my spine soothingly as his other hand grips my hip, his thrusts forceful as he grunts and moans behind me, my name like a prayer from his lips.

"You're so fucking perfect, Ana," he pants, pressing his chest to my back and kissing along my shoulder blades. "Fucking perfect. Made just for me."

And he for me too. He feels so damn good, pounding into me with a perfect rhythm that my back arches. The sound of skin slapping skin joins the beat of my heart in my ears, his soft groans and words of adoration making my entire body quiver. His hand slips between the bed and my chest, sliding down to find my clit, his fingers circling it fast, and the orgasm that was rising in the distance, the one staying far enough back as to not end this faster than I wanted, barrels down to the finish line. There's nothing I can do to stop it as I scream, my legs losing all hope of standing as I fall to the bed, my face buried in the comforter, knees pressed into the edge of the mattress. Teddy's firm hold keeps my hips high as he rides me through each contraction, each spasm, each flutter of my pussy around his dick, until he's pulsing inside me, filling the condom with his cum and cursing my name.

"That was..." he pants, slipping out of me as I crawl sluggishly up the bed and collapse on the pillow.

"Amazing," I breathe, my eyes shutting as I give him a sated smile. I can hear him remove the condom and disappear into the bathroom. He returns, tucking me into his side, and kissing my forehead.

"Give me half an hour and we'll go again."

I huff a laugh. "Haven't you had enough yet?"

"I will never get enough of you, baby," he says. "It's about time you know that by now."

Chapter Forty-Six

Morgana

"When are you going back?" Teddy asks Shay as he joins Ozzy and us at his kitchen table for dinner. I hide a smile behind my fork and quickly shove some salad leaves in my mouth.

"Why are you always asking me that?" she replies, sipping her wine. "I swear it's like you want to get rid of me. Is he always this rude to his dinner guests?"

She looks at Ozzy, and he cocks his head toward Teddy. "I think this is the first time he's ever had dinner guests."

"That's not surprising. He's a terrible host."

"Least he's not a terrible cook."

"Morgs made that. I've still not had the pleasure of trying his food."

"Thank fuck for that. I thought he had been feeding me his burned leftovers on purpose for a second."

"Stop talking about me like I'm not here, dickheads." Teddy growls, dragging the bowl of salad toward him. "And I didn't feed you any leftovers. You *stole* them from the fridge and continued to complain even though it's *my* lunch."

Ozzy points his fork at him. "There he is. I was also worried you had a personality transplant too."

"What is that supposed to mean?"

"Your ass hasn't been as grumpy this week." He points to the food, then smiles warmly at me. "I assume that's because of you too? Good food, less grumpy best friend... If I'd known all it took was for you to get his sorry ass out of his funk, I'd have got you to Phoenix sooner."

I laugh and place my hand on Teddy's over the table. "Thanks, but I think Teddy's ass will always be grumpy."

"I agree," Shay says.

"That's because all you fuckers are not Ana, so I'm allowed to be grumpy with you." He slyly winks as he digs into his carbonara.

The chat around the table moves on from teasing Teddy as Ozzy tells us about a new restaurant Shay dragged him to. They are becoming fast friends, and I can't stop my smile as I look at our unlikely group sitting around the small table. Teddy and I have been in our own little bubble for days now, rediscovering each other before work, after work, in the middle of the night... and I couldn't be happier. That was, until Shay and Ozzy barged into Teddy's apartment tonight and demanded we spend time with them too. Hence the dinner party.

Richard had also texted me the day after he left, telling me he had spoken to our parents, and while I thought Mom wouldn't be happy, I had expected to hear from her by now. The fact that it's been five days and there's been nothing but radio silence, I'm on edge, jumping every time my phone rings in case it's her.

"Are we still on for going to The Dirty Duck tonight?" Shay asks, pushing her empty bowl away and tapping her stomach.

"Nah, not me. I've got plans," Ozzy says.

"Hot date?" Teddy asks, and Ozzy shakes his head.

"Uncle duties."

I've not met little Sierra yet, but from what Teddy's said, she's the cutest little hellion he's ever known.

"Ana? Teddy?" Shay asks hopefully.

Teddy looks to me, and I nod. "Yeah, sounds good. I have to run back to the apartment and get changed. I need to get out of these office clothes."

"I can help you out of your office clothes," Teddy says suggestively, leaning over and kissing me long and hard. I inhale, the smell of engines permeating my lungs.

"Nope, no, c'mon, Morgs. Let's go before you two end up fucking on the table or something and never leave."

"That's not a half-bad idea." Teddy pumps his brows.

Shay scowls and points her finger at him. "Down, boy!"

Teddy's phone chimes in his pocket, and he reads the text with a frown, then immediately smiles.

"I've gotta do something real quick before going to the bar. I'll meet you two at your apartment?" he asks, and I tilt my head in question. "It's a surprise, baby. But I know you'll like it."

He stands and gives me a quick kiss as he and Ozzy start cleaning the table. I hug Ozzy goodbye, and then Shay and I drive over to the rental apartment so I can get changed.

"You know I do not want you to leave, right? But Teddy did have a point. How long are you staying for?" I ask Shay as we step into the apartment.

"Not sure yet," she hums thoughtfully as she lifts her shirt over her head and walks away in just her bra.

"What are you doing?"

"Getting changed. I can't go out looking like this if I'm going to score tonight." She rummages in her suitcase splayed out in the corner of the bedroom, and pulls out something silky.

"What about Lenox?" I ask again, remembering she didn't answer my question that night in the bar when she was flirting with the bartender.

She sighs and throws over a top that I can only assume she wants me to wear. "That sort of fizzled out."

"What? When?"

"A few days before you called to tell me about you and Teddy." She shoves her top over her head and pulls it down to cover her stomach, which is about all it covers. The low V-neck showcases her cleavage, and she shoves her hands into her bra, rearranging her boobs to make them sit even higher. "And before you say anything, I didn't tell you because you had all that shit going on with Richard, and then I forgot. But I'm fine. It wasn't serious anyway, so I'm moving on."

I watch her apply lipstick in the mirror and decide she's telling the truth. She really doesn't care that they didn't work out.

"Anyway, what about you?" she asks, pouting at herself in the mirror.

"What about me?"

"You've only got just over two months left of being here. What you going to do when the times up and you need to head back to Connecticut?"

I nibble on my bottom lip. "If Teddy asks me to stay, I'll stay."

"Really?" she gasps. "Oh shit."

I grimace. "I know, but I can't leave him, Shay. I love him."

She nods thoughtfully, then smirks, her eyes sparkling with trouble. "Think Teddy would let me be your roommate if you move in with him?"

I laugh and push her out of the bedroom so I can quickly swap my blouse for a top she'd given me for tonight. Ducking into the bathroom to brush the taste of carbonara from my mouth, I'm just wiping my lips with a towel as a knock sounds from the door, and I shout, "That's probably Teddy. Can you get that?"

Shay's footsteps echo in the small apartment as she walks toward the door. Swapping my purse and phone from my laptop case to my handbag, my hand freezes mid-air as she shouts, "Oh, hell no."

I dart out of the bedroom, and nearly trip as my mom glares at me from the doorway.

"Mom? Wh-what are you doing here?"

Mom's glower flicks to Shay, who's standing like a bouncer at the door of a club, not letting her inside the apartment.

"Ms. Sylvester, do not test me. Please move so I can speak to my daughter."

Shay shrinks as her false bravado slips. She might like to think she could stand up against my mom, but we both know whenever she looks like she could kill you with her eyes alone, none of us stands a chance. We are back to being teenagers all over again, being told we aren't allowed to be friends.

Mom steps forward, her handbag clutched against her stomach and her arms squeezed tight against her body like she's afraid to touch the walls or something. Her eyes scathingly search the space, her top lip twitching as her gaze runs the length of my body.

"Alone, Ms. Sylvester." My voice cracks through the silence like a whip, and Shay and I both jump.

"Erm, Juliette..."

"Mrs. Adler."

Shay's face pales. "Sorry, Mrs. Adler. I want to stay if it's alright with Morgana."

"Well, it is not alright with me. Need I remind you that this is a family matter, and you are not family, Ms. Slyvester. When I arrived, I should have known I'd find you here too. Was this your doing? Filling my daughter's head with ridiculous ideas?"

"I..." Shay's wide blue eyes blink frantically, like she's trying not to cry; that's just how powerful my mom's icy tone can be.

"Shay's got nothing to do with this, Mom. This was all me."

Mom's head whirls around to me. "Oh right, I see. And this has got also nothing to do with Teddy?"

My heart stops. "Wh-what?"

Mom levels me with a stare, and then aims it straight at Shay. Shay backs toward the door, sending me a look of apology before slipping out and closing it behind her. Mom looks around the small kitchen before placing her handbag as close to the edge of the counter as possible without it falling off.

"I know you don't take me for a fool, Morgana. An assignment to Phoenix? To the place that *boy* wanted you to run off to, and just over a month later, your engagement is broken off? I don't think so. Pack your things. We're leaving."

"No. Richard doesn't want to marry me. And I don't want to marry him. We don't love each other."

"What is with your obsession with love, Morgana? It's a pointless, meaningless emotion that makes people make irrational decisions." She steps past me and walks into the bedroom, going to the closet and pulling out my cases. "Lucky for you, Richard has agreed to forget all about your *indiscretions* and take you back as his wife."

Indiscretions? He wouldn't have told her about Teddy and me, would he?

"He'd never agree to that. He doesn't want this," I growl, but as soon as the words leave me, I'm suddenly unsure. He told me he was groomed to follow a specific path his whole life, and maybe a quick five-minute conversation with me wasn't enough to make him change his mind. But my gloves are tied and ready and I won't give up without a fight.

"No?" Mom laughs in surprise. "Richard is smart and knows what is best for him."

My breathing falls short as my shoulder smacks against the bedroom doorjamb, watching my mom pile my clothes into cases. "What did you do?"

Calmly folding a pair of pants, she sets them inside the case and runs her hand over the top. "What needed to be done."

My heart lurches in my chest. "How can you be so cruel?"

She smiles, vindictive and vicious, as she takes calculated steps toward me. I flinch as her hand tucks my hair behind my ears. "When you have children of your own, you will realize you will do whatever it takes for them to succeed. Now hurry up and pack."

Chapter Forty-Seven

"**H**ey, thanks for picking me up, man."

Skip tosses his bag in the back of my Mustang, and we do one of those *bro hugs*. "No problem. Ana is going to be so happy to see you."

"Yeah. I can't wait to see her and tell her what a fucking moron she was."

I punch his arm as he laughs, dropping into the passenger side while I round the car to get behind the wheel. "Hey, don't be too hard on her. Your mom was a bitch, and she was young and scared. You'd have done the same thing."

"I *didn't* do the same thing."

I roll my eyes and make the short drive from the airport to the garage to drop off the car before we walk to Ana's to meet the girls.

"If I can forgive her, you should too."

He hums, his eyes roaming over the big Grease Monkey sign outside the auto shop. I'm about to open the trunk to get Skip's bag when he places his hand on my arm. "Leave it. I'll get it later. Let's go see my sister."

We catch up on the walk over to Ana's, Skip telling me about his new job in a Michelin-star restaurant and me filling him in on the whole Richard/Ana shit. We round the corner before the apartment building as Shay bursts out of the front door like her ass is on fire. Her eyes widen as she spots us, doing a double take at Skip with a slight frown and then completely disregarding him.

"Oh, thank fuck you're here," she says, anxiously looking back to where she came from.

"What's wrong?"

"Her mom's here."

I glance at Skip and take off running for the door, pausing briefly to yell out for Shay. "Are you coming?"

She shakes her head, looking visibly scared. "Fuck no. That woman is terrifying. I'll catch you at the bar with a fuck-ton of drinks waiting."

The doors thankfully not locked as I let myself inside. I hear Ana's voice rise and jut my chin in that direction for Skip to follow.

"I'm not going with you, Mom," she says, stuffing clothes back into a drawer as Juliette removes more clothes from hangers, folding them neatly before adding them to cases scattered across Ana's bed.

I hold Skip back as we watch from the doorway, the two women unaware of our presence.

"Stop packing my things and listen to me!" Ana yells, and her mom startles at the disrespect I know for a fact Ana has never shown her before.

"Who do you—"

"I'm not some little puppet! You can't tug on my strings and make me dance to your tune. I'm my own person, Mom, and I am not going back with you. I'm happy here, finally free of the unrealistic expectations you set."

Juliette scoffs. "Unrealistic? I'm walking proof that they are manageable."

"And you're a sad old woman, desperate to take me down with you." Ana gasps as her hands fly to her mouth. "Mom..."

"And you're an ungrateful little girl who will never amount to anything. Why did you think I chose Richard for you? He was everything. Great bloodline, intelligent, excellent career prospects, and you've thrown that all away for what? Some scrap-yard junkie who is not welcome in our family?"

"What the fuck is going on?" I boom, and Juliette tenses as Ana flies into my arms, but she doesn't press her head into my chest to hide like I half expect. She grips my neck and tugs me down hard to kiss me in front of her mom.

"Of course, all this would be because of *you*," Juliette sneers, jabbing her finger in my direction. "Morgana, get away from him. Need I remind you of our conversation about consequences?"

Ana twists in my hold, pressing her back against my chest, and I possessively splay my hand across her stomach. "Oh, I know all about your *consequences*, Juliette."

"What do yo—" Her nostrils flare as Skip walks into Ana's room. "Brody?"

"Hi, Mom."

"What are you doing here?" she asks, for once looking unsettled, like she's losing the upper hand I'm starting to believe she didn't have in the first place.

"I'm here to make sure Morgana doesn't let you manipulate her like you always do." He links their hands together and winks. "Hey, kiddo."

She sucks her lips between her teeth, stopping the quiver to her chin. I kiss the back of her head, and she shifts, her stance widening, her spine straightening, and she suddenly looks ten feet tall.

"I'm done bending over backward to keep you happy while I slowly die inside. I'm done being controlled by your threats and my fear. I'm just done, Mom." Her fingers link through my hand still on her stomach, like I'm her anchor. "You're a user and a liar."

"I have never lied to you."

"Maybe not to me, but you did to Teddy."

"I have no idea what you're talking about," her mom says, folding her arms across her chest.

"I know you told Teddy I was on a date that day you made me break up with him. You knew he'd fight for me. You knew he'd turn up and find me there with Richard"—my hand flexes in hers at the mention of that bastard—"and think it was more than a lunch to discuss Yale as a potential school. I cried for most of that meal while Richard tried to comfort me. That was the worst day of my life, and finding out when I got home that he'd left, and I never got to say goodbye... You stole seven years from us, and you're not stealing any more."

"Think about what you're doing," Juliette spits, her hands balling into fists. Her eyes flick to me, then to the son she hasn't seen in years. "Do you want to end up like your brother? Cut off? No longer part of this family? Living paycheck to paycheck, barely scraping by. Because that is exactly what will happen if you stay with *him*."

"I think, if you remember, *I* didn't have a choice in that, Mom," Skip says with a growl. "But hey, you did me a favor. I might not have the money I would have had if I had followed in Dad's footsteps, but I don't live paycheck to paycheck either. I'm a *successful* chef—no thanks to you—cooking for celebrities and even royalty."

"You do?" Ana beams at her older brother, pride and love radiating from her.

"Yeah, but I'll tell you about it later," he says with a fondness for his sibling before narrowing his eyes and glaring at their mom. "Believe me when

I say, Morgana would be better off without this family."

"Morgana," her mom growls.

Ana tilts her head back to look at me, and I press a gentle kiss to her lips, giving her the strength I know she already has to do what's needed.

"Leave, Mom. Get out of my apartment and go home."

"I'm not going anywhere without you. Your father won't allow it."

"My father won't care," she says, agitation coating her words. "He's never cared. I'm not fully convinced he even knows he has a daughter."

"Mor—"

"You had no problem letting go of one kid. You should have no problem letting go of the other," Skip interrupts, and Juliette's face finally shows something as the vein in her forehead pops out, and her cheeks flush pink.

"I will not forget about this, Morgana," she spits.

"Yes, you will, Juliette," I say, tightening my hold around Ana's stomach. "You will forget about Ana. You will leave us alone, and you will not try to get between us again because, believe me when I say, my threats are much worse than any you could dole out."

"What is that supposed to mean?" she seethes.

I drop my hold on Ana and take one step toward Juliette. "Your husband's opposition might find it interesting to hear that his wife forced her daughter to break up with her boyfriend because he doesn't come from money. Over eighty percent of your husband's demographics are working-class, *Mrs. Adler,* and who knows how many would change their minds on who to vote for as their next Governor if they found out his wife thinks she's better than them?"

"No one would believe you."

"Maybe not him," Skip says, coming to my side. "But as their only son, who was cut off at eighteen, they might just believe me."

Juliette's jaw clenches as she stares between her son and me.

"Who do you think you are?" she says through gritted teeth, and I grin back at her.

"Your future son-in-law." Ana inhales sharply, and I'm dying to go to her. Sure, we haven't spoken about it, and she was engaged to someone else a week ago, but I will marry her one day. "Now get the fuck out."

Chapter Forty-Eight

Morgana

A silence settles over us as we watch my mom leave. I bite down hard on my bottom lip as it quivers again because, as much as I know I'm doing the right thing—she was controlling and manipulative and toxic—she's still my mom, and I worry this will be the last time I see her.

"I'm so proud of you, baby," Teddy says, taking me into his arms, just as my legs want to give out. I sag into him and bury my face in his shirt, trying so damn hard not to cry.

"Morgana, I know it sucks now, but it's for the best." Skip places his hand on my back, and I swap one embrace for another, wrapping my arms tightly around my brother's back, and then the sobbing starts. Years of frustration, hurt, anger, and sadness flow through my tears that I can't seem to stop. My body shakes against Skip's, and he lets me cry. "It's okay. I've got you."

"Where were you?" I sob, pulling back to look at him with wet eyes and an even wetter face. "Why haven't you been in contact for the last seven years? Why are you here now?"

Skip grimaces, and I see him look at Teddy silently, asking for help. He sighs and itches the side of his face. "I was mad at you."

"Why? What did I do?" He looks at Teddy *again*. "Will you stop looking at him, please?"

"Well, I feel like a dickhead now, but at the time, it made sense," he says, trying, *and failing*, to keep his eyes off Teddy.

"Skip!"

"Okay, okay. After you broke things off with Teddy, he called me to see if I knew anything—which I didn't—but when he told me what had happened, I got mad and sided with him."

I wince. "But you're my brother. I needed you," I croak, my heart splintering in two.

"I know, okay, I am a dickhead. But it brought up all these old feelings from when Mom kicked me out and knowing you went along with what she wanted you to do without a fight... Fuck, Morgana, you were always the one who followed her blindly. Always doing what she expected from you and I just thought she had finally managed to turn you into her *mini-me* or something."

"I was scared Skip."

"I know that *now*. But, Morgs, seeing you both in New York, how happy you were... And then to find out you dumped him by *text*. I hurt for the guy."

"Baby, don't be too upset with him. I think it's fair to say your mom has caused a lot of hurt for a lot of people. And she still wins if we don't move past it."

I stare at Teddy. When did he become levelheaded? But, still, it doesn't stop the pain in my heart that my brother chose Teddy over me.

"Besides," Teddy says, coming behind me and wrapping his arms around my waist. "We bonded over the whole thing and became sorta friends."

I eye Skip skeptically. "Really?"

"Yeah, Morgs. Teddy's good people. I like him." He smirks at Teddy, who flips him the bird. "Plus, I'd rather him for my brother-in-law than some stuffy asshole Mom picked out."

I freeze, remembering what Teddy said to my mom. I twist to face him, my throat thick as I ask, "Did you mean that?"

"What? That I'm going to marry you?" He laughs and kisses my forehead. "Fuck yes, Ana. If you didn't have the faint line where fuckface's ring was on your finger, I'd have done it already."

I lift my hand and notice I do have a mark like a tan line circling my finger. Teddy links his hand in mine and brings it to his lips. Kissing the back of my empty finger, he says, "One day, you'll wear my ring, but not right now. But when it happens, you'll be mine forever."

"You don't need to give me a ring to know I'm yours forever. I already am."

"*Bleeeeh,*" Skip pretends to gag, pulling us out of our moment as he walks into the living room, leaving Teddy and me alone. "You two are disgusting."

I laugh. "That's what Shay says... Oh shit, Shay."

"She went to the bar. Couldn't handle your mom and her rampage," Teddy says.

"I should text her and let her know we're okay," I say, grabbing my phone from my purse and sending her a quick message. "Are we still going to meet her?"

Teddy licks his lips suggestively. "I'd know what I'd rather do..." He stalks forward and trails his hands up the side of my body, his thumbs brushing the side of my breasts, and I have to bite back a moan.

Skips in the next room, Morgana.

Teddy snatches my phone out of my hands and texts Shay.

Morgana: We can't make it. I need to suck Teddy's cock more than I need air. Stay at a hotel, and Teddy will pay you back.
Shay: Okay, I KNOW that wasn't Morgs who texted that. Teddy... you're a pig.
Morgana: Get a hotel room, Shay.
Shay: Fine. But I'm choosing the most expensive one and putting all my drinks on a tab for you to pick up.
Morgana: Fine.

He hands back my phone, grinning like a fool, and when I read their thread, I gasp, slapping the back of my hand to his chest as he laughs.

Morgana: I am so sorry about him, Shay. Are you sure you're okay with staying somewhere else tonight?
Shay: Of course, babe. Hot bartender is working tonight, so I might not need a hotel after all. But don't tell Teddy cause he's still paying.
Morgana: I love you.
Shay: Love you too. Happy sucking.

I pocket my phone, Teddy sticks his head out the bedroom door and asks Skip, "You okay if we catch up tomorrow?"

"Yeah, no trouble. I'm starving anyway." He rubs his stomach. "Going to see what Phoenix has to offer."

Teddy rummages around for his keys and tosses them to Skip. "You okay to get back to my place?"

He nods, pocketing the keys and lifting his phone.

"Google maps are a thing of the future," he teases. "Just text me your address, and I'll be fine."

"You two really are friends, aren't you?" I ask, something warm settling in my stomach as I watch their interaction. I hate that Skip chose sides, especially since it wasn't *mine*. But their bond is sweet, and I like that something good came out of something so horrible.

"Are you okay?" Teddy asks me once Skip leaves. I nod, and he trails his fingers across my cheek and down my neck, his large hand cupping it and tilting my head back for him to kiss me. I welcome it, moaning when his tongue runs across the seam of my lips, teasing me to let him in. Sucking on my tongue, I moan, clutching his shirt in my fists and pulling him hard against me.

He walks me backward until the backs of my knees hit the mattress, and I drop down, taking him with me as I refuse to let go of him. His body blankets me in warmth, and I rake a hand into his hair, my nails scraping at his scalp, while the other slips between us, deftly flicking at the button of his jeans.

His hand captures mine as he breaks the kiss. "Ana, you don't have to..."

"I want to," I say, nipping at his jaw.

"Are you sure?" He holds himself up with one hand on the bed, the other still holding my wrist. "It's been a long, emotional day. We don't have to do anything if you don't feel up to it. I'm happy just to hold you."

I smile and tug my hand free, pushing on his shoulders until he rolls and flops on his back, and I straddle him.

"I believe I said I was going to suck your dick," I tease, unzipping his pants and pushing his shirt up enough to reveal the dark line of hair running from his belly button and under his boxer briefs. "Don't make me out to be a liar."

His eyes flare with desire, and he helps me remove his jeans. Grabbing the back of his shirt, he tugs it over his head until he's fully naked. Beautiful hard lines glint in the evening sun from the window, and I run my finger in the valley between each abdominal, loving the way the muscles contract and flex as I travel down toward his hard cock resting on his belly. I ignore it, running past it to his thighs, the angry-looking tip leaking pre-cum onto his skin as I tease him by doing the same to the other side. It jumps against him, and I grin.

"Fucking tease," he grunts, his hands fisting by his side.

Still fully dressed, I feel an odd satisfaction, like I have him at my mercy, like I've got some kind of power while he's naked and leaking for me. I wonder if this is how he feels when I'm the same for him.

His legs widen as I position myself between them and lean down to glide my tongue up the thick vein running from base to tip. He inhales through his nose, his hand gently resting on my head, and I smile as I take him in my hand and lick along his slit. He's salty and tangy, and I can't get enough of him. I wrap my lips around his tip and suck lightly. His hand grips my hair, knowing I like it rough to the point of pain without ever hurting me and I relish the sharp tug of my strands in his fist. I swallow his cock, taking him to the back of my throat, triggering my gag reflex.

"*Fuuuuck,* Ana," he pants, his hips canting upward. I gag again, spit running down my chin, as I remind myself to breathe through my nose. We find a rhythm. Him fucking my face while I bob up and down his shaft, making all the obscene sounds I know he loves. And when I add my finger, trailing it along his taint, his groan is animalistic until he pulls me off him with a pop, and I moan.

"Wha—"

He flips us, my back bouncing on the mattress as he frantically tugs at my pants, throwing them off my legs and grabbing either side of the low V-neck, yanking hard until there's a loud tearing sound. He keeps tugging at the material, ripping the top down the middle.

"That was Shay's." I giggle as he licks his lips at the sight of my front clasp bra. "She's going to be mad."

"I don't fucking care," he says, freeing my breasts and taking both in each hand. "I'll buy her a new one. Right now, I need to come inside you."

We've both gotten tested, and as soon as we got those negative results... well, I thought Teddy was insatiable before. But now, he's like a man possessed.

I spread my legs, wiggling my hips, and he grins.

"Always my needy Ana Banana." He fists his dick in his hand and drags it through my wet pussy, coating the tip in my arousal as my eyes flutter shut. "My fucking soaking Ana Banana."

He pushes inside me, stretching me so deliciously my back arches. The same feeling floods my cells every time he bottoms out inside me. I'm home and that I was made solely for him.

I wrap my legs around his waist, digging my feet into his ass as he starts to move, thrusting in smooth, gentle motions until he loses control and can't hold back. His fingers are biting into my skin, his hips bruising when they knock against mine, and his cock hits that spot that steals my breath each and every time that I feel faint.

"Yes, Teddy, yes," I pant, sweat pricking at my hairline, my skin overheating as his magical dick leads me straight to my orgasm. I drop my knees wider, his fingers moving to brush against my clit, and I moan his name the way I know he likes as I topple over the edge and into ecstasy.

"Fuck, I love feeling your cunt squeeze my dick when you come. Love the way you gush around me. Your pretty pussy loves my cock inside her, doesn't she?"

I silently scream, my head tilting back, pushing into the pillow as he continues to talk dirty to me.

"Fuck yes," he moans, grunting as he releases inside me, slamming hard against me as he unloads all he has.

He flops to the side, taking me with him, his cock still buried in my pussy. We breathe hard against each other, our sweaty bodies pressed together as he cups the back of my head and kisses my forehead, my eyes, my nose, and then my lips.

"Give me five minutes, and we'll go again."

I giggle, burrowing my head in the crook of his shoulder. "You're insatiable."

"I did say that I will never get enough of you." He kisses the top of my head. "It's about time you know that."

Chapter Forty-Nine

Morgana

Two and a bit months later

"Hey, baby." Teddy jumps onto the bed behind me, kissing the back of my shoulder. "What you doin'?"

I groan and close down yet another job advert that I'm underqualified for.

"Why is looking for jobs so hard?" I whine, fake crying, as I lean back against him and scrub at my eyes. "I knew my family had influence, but when you're trying to do things on your own, it's harder than I expected."

Teddy's fingers dig firmly into my traps, and I sag into him, my aching muscles from being bent over my laptop for hours loving the reprieve.

"How did your work take it when you called?"

I close my eyes. "Victoria was disappointed that I wasn't coming back, but understood. She's only sorry she couldn't keep me on down here permanently since she liked what I'd done on the audit."

My time in Phoenix auditing Bank of America had finished last week and the rent on the Airbnb was up tomorrow. Not that I used it since getting back together with Teddy, as he swiftly moved me into his apartment and told me this was my home now too, but I had to call my boss and tell her I wasn't coming back.

Skip had left to go back to New York two days after arriving for the big blow-up with Mom, and Shay returned not long after, deciding she was going to go on that European cruise with her parents after all. And Teddy and I had been back in our little bubble ever since.

"You know the offer to come and work for me still stands, right?"

"I know, and I appreciate it, I do. But I want something that's my own, not because of my parents' connections or because I'm sleeping with the boss."

Teddy groans, dropping his head and biting in between my neck and shoulder. "But if you did work for me, I could tie you up again with jumper cables and make you scream any time you wanted."

I laugh and squirm against him, remembering the way he bound me naked in his garage and made me come harder and so much more than I've ever come in my life. I was so exhausted, he had to carry me up the stairs to bed.

"It's probably a good idea I don't take you up on your offer, then," I tease. "You'd never get any work done."

"That's true," he says, kissing my shoulder again.

"Besides, I still have the bonus money C&A gave me for having to relocate for the audit in my savings, so it's not as if I need to find a job right now," I say. "But twelve grand won't last forever."

"Still can't believe your mom cut you off."

I snort. "Why? Weren't you the one who said that's what all us "rich folk" do?"

"Yeah, but I didn't actually think she would go through with it."

"Just one less thing to bind me to them, I guess."

Had it hurt when I found out I no longer had access to my trust fund? Yes. But there was also something so unbelievably liberating. I might be poor ass broke with no job prospects, but I couldn't be happier.

Leaning around me, Teddy points to another browser page. "Hey, what's this?"

I drag the laptop closer and scroll down the page. "I, um, wanted to see if there was a way to get my curls back."

Teddy combs his fingers through my hair. "Any luck?"

I shake my head. "No, apparently, once you've chemically straightened the curls out, you've broken the bonds. And because I got it done regularly... unless I cut my hair off and let it grow back, I'm pretty much stuck."

"So why don't you do that?" he asks. "Not that I mind whatever you want to do, but I know you miss the curls."

I reach up and twist a strand around my finger. "I do, but if I cut it short and it grows in with my ringlets, I'll look like a poodle."

"A sexy poodle," Teddy says.

I laugh. "You're an idiot."

"Yeah, but you're the one who agreed to marry me, so who's the *real* idiot?"

I lift my left hand and let the sun glint against the gorgeous cushion-cut with a halo engagement ring Teddy gave me. Sure, it might be fast, but we've missed out on seven years together.

I swivel on the bed and press my lips to his, moaning when his tongue pushes into my mouth and tangles with mine for the quickest of kisses in the history of kisses.

"What the hell, Teddy?" I complain as he shifts from the bed and grabs my hand with a laugh.

"Oh, no, you can't distract me with your tempting mouth, Ana Banana. We've got a family zoom call to join."

I groan. "Do we have to? Your family still hates me after what I done."

He tuts and lifts the laptop from the bed and carries it to the kitchen table. "That's not true. I told you, Mom and Dad get why you did what you felt you had to. I swear Dad had to almost lock Mom in their room, she was so mad. She wanted to go tear your mom a new one." Teddy pulls out a chair for me, and I slump down. "And my brothers are assholes who just like to stir shit. They don't hate you, baby."

Teddy pulls up the call and the faces of the entire Grant family shine back at us.

"Look what the cat dragged in," says Bowie.

"What do you mean "dragged"? You look like you've not seen a shower or a razor in weeks, bro," Teddy snaps back.

"Me? What about our douchebag older brother over there in his designer suit?"

"Now, now, children, maybe if you two were half as good looking as me, you'd pull off a suit too," Wyatt says, making a show of fixing his cuff links.

"Does the stick for your ass come with the suit, or do you order that in special?" Bowie asks.

"Oh, Bowie is on form tonight." Teddy laughs.

"Shocker, considering he's usually the slowest in the family for comebacks." Wyatt grins, and Bowie flips him off.

"Boys, are you done yet?" Mrs. Grant asks, unmuting herself as she and her husband fill the screen. "Teddy's got some news."

"Did his sorry ass get dumped again?" Bowie asks.

"Yeah, did Morgana finally realize she's better off without you?" Wyatt tacks on.

"Oh, fuck you," Teddy says, giving the screen the middle finger.

"See, I told you they don't like me," I mutter, glancing at the ring on my finger.

"Nonsense, sweetheart," Mr. Grant says, leaning extra close to the laptop like he needs to be nearer to be heard over his sons' bickering. "That's how they show they care about the people they love. Shooting the shit and being giant assholes about it."

I smile weakly.

"Yeah, Morgana, we like you. There's nothing to worry about," Wyatt says into the camera.

"Yeah, Morgana, if anything, I'm glad you broke my brother's heart. He was becoming too big headed for his own good." Bowie winks.

"Fuck. You. Asshole," Teddy grates.

"Okay, okay, enough," Mrs. Grant says, clapping her hands, and everyone falls silent. "Now, honey, what did you have to tell us?"

Teddy glances at me, and then lifts my hand to the screen. Sadie screams, the boys yell, and I cover my face as it turns beetroot.

"This is great news," Sadie says.

"Oh shit, she's stuck with your sorry ass now, Tee." Bowie laughs.

"About time one of my boys settles down," Miles says.

"Welcome to the family, Morgana." Wyatt smiles warmly.

Teddy leans forward and kisses me softly.

"I love you," I whisper against his lips.

"I love you too, Ana Banana."

Epilogue

Teddy

1 year later

Pulling up to the top of the long driveway, I shut off the rental car's engine and lace Ana's hand in mine. She tears her gaze from the window and smiles weakly before turning back to stare at the big white house across the lawn.

"I can't believe coming back here makes me feel like a stranger." She sighs, touching her fingertips to the glass. "They're my family, and I can't even knock on the door to tell them I'm here."

I bring my hand to her lips and brush a kiss to the back of it.

"Your other family is right inside there, excited to see you. Don't worry about them, baby."

She nods, unbuckling her seat belt and stepping out of the car. We've barely reached the bottom stair to the porch when Mom flings the door open and screams, "Miles, they're here! Our babies are home."

Ana laughs as she gets pulled into a bone-crushing hug, and my dad clatters down the stairs, tackling me to the ground.

"The prodigal son has returned!" he booms in my ear, knocking my hat off my head and digging his knuckles into my scalp.

"Get off, old man." I laugh, wrestling with him on the grass as Mom examines the engagement and wedding band on Ana's left finger.

"I still can't believe we weren't invited." Mom pouts.

"We told you we wanted it to be just us," I huff, pinning my dad's arm behind his back and waiting for him to tap out.

"Miles Grant, will you stop rough-housing with your son on my front lawn," Mom says sternly. "Whatever will the neighbors think?"

"Is that my pain in the ass, younger brother?"

I jump up, releasing Dad and darting up the porch stairs as Wyatt sweeps Ana into his arms and squeezes her.

"Nice to see you again, Wyatt," Ana says, laughing as he drops her back to her feet.

Wyatt grins when he sees me, and we crash into each other, arms flailing everywhere as we hug. "Little bro."

"What are you doing here? Mom didn't tell me you were coming."

"She called and said you were flying in today, and I was off, so I couldn't resist surprising you."

"Yes, yes, we're all surprised," Mom says, ushering us indoors. "I want to see all the pictures from the wedding. Tell me everything. Miles, get the kids something to drink."

Ana mouths *Help* as Mom drags her into the living room while Wyatt and I help dad with the drinks.

"How is she holding up?" Dad asks, popping the cap off a beer bottle and holding it out.

I take it, nodding while I take a deep pull. The flight and the drive here were long. Especially being hard as fucking nails the whole time while sitting next to my *wife* and unable to do a damn thing about it. Maybe if Wyatt had picked us up in his boss's private plane, we could have joined the mile-high club.

"She's okay," I say on an exhale. "Her parents ignored her invitation to the wedding, so we decided to elope instead. Sorry, we didn't tell you guys."

"Hey, you do what makes you happy, and if that is just the two of you and some fat Elvis impersonator, well, that's fine by me." Dad chuckles, and Wyatt nods in agreement.

After Juliette walked out of Ana's rented apartment, everything was a whirlwind. Ana's placement in Phoenix finished, so she quit. Shay helped organize her apartment back here, so it was ready to be rented—and the couple currently with an eight-month lease absolutely love it. And to top it off, we also had a pregnancy scare. Not that I was scared. I was fucking delighted that my sperm beat her birth control. Still, with everything Ana had gone through emotionally, her body needed some time to heal, making her periods a bit wonky or something sounding a little more biologically technical. But after that, I knew I needed to marry my girl and fill her with as many babies as she'd let me, so we eloped in Vegas, fat Elvis and all.

We join Ana and Mom in the living room, the two of them huddling around her phone as she swipes through the pictures of our wedding. Dad turns on the TV, flicking to the Cardinals game, and Wyatt and I drop down on either side of him on the sectional. Dad starts his commentary as my brother shares silent looks above his head whenever he's clearly talking out his ass. I glance at Ana, smiling when she catches me staring.

"Love you," I mouth.

"Love you too."

"Hey, guys."

Mom squeaks and my dad's explanation of how the Cardinals will make it to the playoffs this season ends abruptly as we all stare at the man coyly smirking in the doorjamb. Like when I arrived, we barrel into Bowie, Wyatt and I crashing on top of him, sending him flying to the ground with a thud. Then my dad's there, his heavy weight crushing down on our human pile-up.

"Can't breathe, can't breathe." Bowie's voice is muffled beneath us, but he's laughing.

"Let my baby up." Mom giggles, slapping each of us on the back of the head until she helps Bowie to his feet. He hauls her against him, and Mom lets out a sob.

"Is she okay?" Ana asks, and I wrap my arm around her waist, bringing her flush against my side.

I kiss her temple and watch as Dad hugs Bowie next. "Yeah, she just gets all emotional when we're all together. It's been..." Fuck, I don't even know. "Years since we've all been in the same room."

She snuggles into my chest, watching as Bowie and Wyatt talk.

"So this must be my gorgeous sister-in-law. It's great to see you in the flesh." Bowie grins. Ana sticks out her hand, but he bats it away, tugging her out of my hold and crushing her to his enormous chest. She groans as he squeezes too tight. "Oh, sorry, did I hurt you?"

"No, no, I'm fine." She chuckles, but I snatch her away from him anyway and press her back to my chest, my hand splaying protectively over her stomach. She dances her fingers up my arm as if sensing my concern. "I'm fine, Teddy. I promise."

I brush my thumb up along the top of her belly and relax.

"How long are you home for?" Mom asks Bowie.

He sits on the arm of the chair, bending down to grab either mine or

Wyatt's beer.

"Undecided." Mom sucks in a giddy breath, but Bowie holds his hand up. "Don't get too excited, Ma. It could be six months or six years. I don't know. All I do know is that after eight years, I missed you guys and needed to come home for a bit."

"You still taking pictures, though?" I ask.

"Hell yeah. I've got a couple of gigs set up for the next few months in New York," he says, but he doesn't look happy about it. I raise my brows expectantly, and he grimaces. "One of them is this up-and-coming new hot-shot billionaire that Forbes want me to photograph."

"That sounds like fun," Ana says.

"Yeah..." he drawls, finishing the beer and putting the empty bottle on the coffee table. "He just looks like your stereotypical douchebag pretty boy with money, and they are always divas to work with."

"I heard *you're* a diva to work with," Wyatt states from the corner of the room.

Bowie holds up his middle finger. "But I'm also the best at what I do, so I'm allowed to be."

Wyatt snorts.

"So what's the problem then, Son?" Dad asks.

"It's nothing, Dad. I'm a professional. I'll snap a few pics, send them to the people at the magazine and never see him again."

Bowie pushes up from the chair and walks away into the kitchen. Mom watches after him with concern.

"I'll go," I say when my mom tries to follow. Bowie's leaning against the counter, gazing out the kitchen window as I sidle up beside him. "What's wrong?"

He looks at me, a muscle in his jaw ticks as he stays silent for a pause, his eyes glazing over before staring back out the window. "Calvin and I broke up."

"Ah, shit. I'm sorry. I thought you guys were hooking up, not together-together."

He lifts one shoulder noncommittally. "It was complicated."

"Is that why you came home?"

He nods. "Part of it. But I did miss you guys." He knocks his shoulder into mine. "It'll be fine. I just need to remind my dick that we don't fuck straight boys anymore, regardless of how good-looking they are."

"That's gotta be tough," I say, squeezing his shoulder. "So what's the problem with your new client? Your face looked like you were chewing on a wasp just there."

"*Urgh,* it's nothing. But apparently, after spending so much of my time out in the wilderness with assholes like Calvin, I suddenly have a type."

I frown. "Are you not allowed to find your clients good-looking?"

"Yeah, but as a self-imposed rule, I shouldn't." He turns and throws his arm over my shoulder. "I'll just need to get laid before his appointment with my camera next month, baby bro. It's all good."

If he says so.

He laughs and leads me back to the living room to join the rest of the family. Tugging Ana to her feet, I steal her spot and pull her onto my lap, my hand instantly going to her stomach again.

"Will you stop? Everyone's going to know."

I kiss the back of her shoulder. "I don't care, Ana Banana. I want everyone to know that you'll be mine now forever."

She twists on my lap, burying her head against my neck. "I always was, Teddy."

The End

Coming Soon

Well you got a little glimpse of Bowie, Teddy's brother, throughout this book and his story is next.

So what happens when a photographer, who has sworn off men, meets his latest client? A young, hot, *straight* millionaire whose made himself known in the crypto world. Gotta be a disaster right?
Bowie's story is a MM, sexual awakening, strangers to lovers with a guaranteed Happily Ever After.

Sign up to my newsletter to keep up to date with Bowie, Wyatt and Skip along with other stories that cause chaos in my brain. PLUS there might just be a little surprise from Teddy and Ana with the QR code below!

More from Vari Scott

Deadly Liars Duet

Together We Lie

Together We Burn

Not Suitable for Work

Grease Monkey

Shutter Bug – coming soon 2023

Fly Boy – coming soon

Chef's Kiss – coming soon

Acknowledgments

Holy sh*t! Whoever said writing a book while starting a new job, moving out of their old house, into their parents and then into their new house was a good idea is an idiot... oh right, that idiot was me!

Well it's done, Teddy and Morgana are live and I am *unbelievably happy!* Teddy and Morgana are far different to Stevie and Jake. I've got to give it to contemporary romance author's, that is hard work! I have a dark heart with a dark sense of humour so to not have Teddy stab someone with a wrench or electrocute someone with jump leads attached to a car battery was hard work – lol jokes!

I always knew I wanted to write Teddy, he had been in my head for a long, long time so while he was a pain in my butt to get onto paper, cause believe me when I say that boy was stubborn, I'm so glad he's free for all to (hopefully) enjoy!

So, who to thank? I think everyone that I speak to on the daily. This book was tough but as per usual, my amazing Alpha, Emily – thank you from my soul for getting me through this! Please don't quit being my alpha after this ⊠

Then we've got my wonderful Betas, Ari, Sarah, Robin, Victoria, and M – your feedback was amazing when all I wanted to do was through the damn book off a bridge.

As always my friends and family – mainly my mum and sister. Moving into mum's house with all my crap, and taking over my sister's spare room as my office was a nightmare, especially when all I did was complain how cold I was. But thank you, and I love you.

To my wonderful, PA, Sara – you know what my brain is like and you managed to keep on track with it. Also how beautiful is the formatting of this book? Whether you're reading it on eBook or paperback, you should see both – I **love** them! So if anyone needs formatting done, she is your girl <3

And finally, this amazing group of women I am so lucky to have met through our love of spicy books, naughty photos and Magic Mike – you know who you are ladies, the amazing RARE London 2023 chat. Biggest group of cheerleaders if you ever needed some! Also to the authors in that group too, both published and so close to being published, I am so grateful for the advice and words of support. I am so glad our love of books and the cost of a RARE ticket brought us together. RARE ladies on tour forever now!

But mostly, thank you to the readers, both new and old. I am so unbelievably thankful for you getting to this part (if you've stuck around to read my ramble). When I started writing I thought one, maybe two people would read it, and they would most likely be my friends I forced to read it, but for you to be here, reading it because you *wanted* to... Well I love you from the bottom of my heart!

About the Author

Okay, I can't write in the third person. It's like being back at school and writing a personal statement to get into uni.

"Vari is this... Vari is that..." Well, Vari can't do it.

When I'm not writing smutty romance, I am monitoring clinical trials from my home office in Scotland, with a pug snoring under my desk and another one taking up most of my chair behind me. And when I'm not working, I'm reading smutty romance of any trope. But enemies-to-lovers or forbidden stepbrother MM are my kryptonite.

Stalk Me on Instagram, Facebook, Tiktok, Goodreads, and don't forget to sign up for my newsletter for a bonus scene featuring more of Teddy.

VARI SCOTT
INDECENTLY DECENT ROMANCE

Made in the USA
Middletown, DE
13 September 2024

60879522R00236